Out on the Panhandle

R. E. BRADSHAW

Titles from R. E. Bradshaw Books

Rainey Bell Thriller Series:
Rainey Nights (2011) (Lambda Literary Award Finalist)
Rainey's Christmas Miracle (2011) (Short Story)
Rainey Days (2010)

The Adventures of Decky and Charlie Series:
Out on the Panhandle (2012)
Out on the Sound (2010)

Molly: House on Fire (2012)

Before It Stains (2011)

Waking Up Gray (2011)

Sweet Carolina Girls (2010)

The Girl Back Home (2010)

Out on the Panhandle

A Decky and Charlie Adventure

R. E. BRADSHAW

Published by
R. E. BRADSHAW BOOKS

USA

•R.E.B.BOOKS•

Out on the Panhandle
By R. E. Bradshaw

Website: http://www.rebradshawbooks.com
Facebook: https://www.facebook.com/rebradshawbooks
Twitter @rebradshawbooks
Blog: http://rebradshawbooks.blogspot.com
For information contact rebradshawbooks@gmail.com

Acknowledgments

I sat down to write this with my list of folks to thank. The usual suspects are on there, beta readers, consultants, my editor, friends, and family. I've tried to write this acknowledgment page for days. It's the very last thing I have to do before publishing. An author friend of mine said the only people that read the acknowledgments page are other authors. If that's true, then I'm speaking to people that have also stared at a blank page, unable to form the words.

Why has this acknowledgment page been so difficult to write? The beta readers helped me clean up the story, encouraged me, and rescued me from the self-doubt one experiences after completing a manuscript. I am indebted to them. Judge Kate once again came through with legal advice, and is someone I've come to depend on. I couldn't write half the books without her guidance. Kaycee edited the book quickly, so I could meet my deadline. I have to thank her for making my novel a priority with all the other demands on her time. My friends lift me up, when I'm feeling overwhelmed. My family loves and supports me daily. Deb is my rock, Jon my pride and joy. So, what's the problem? Just thank them and be done.

My dilemma stems from a nagging main character that insists the people to thank are no longer with us, well, in physical form anyway. The Native Americans and pioneers that I write about in this novel are the people I owe gratitude. I did an immense amount of research for this novel. I spent months buried in the history of the Texas and Oklahoma Panhandles, the Chickasaw and Comanche nations, the tragedies and triumphs of the homesteader and the native. I read the real stories, eyewitness accounts of men and women who were there. Decky is right, I do owe those people the thanks for this book. They were the inspiration, after all.

To everyone that made <u>Out on the Panhandle</u> possible, I say thank you. To the spirits that wandered the land all those years ago, I say thank you for telling your stories. I hope I have done you justice. And to Merdy and Grace, thank you for reassuring me that love never ends.

I believe!

REB

About the book…

Decky and Charlie were the main characters in my first novel, <u>Out on the Sound</u>. They have a special place in my heart. So, when the readers asked for more of them, I was happy to oblige. I decided to send Decky and Charlie to the Panhandle of Oklahoma, where Charlie grew up. I needed a story and one presented itself while doing genealogy research for my wife. I discovered that one of her ancestors was kidnapped by the Comanche and rescued by members of a posse that included more of her ancestors. I was hooked.

I read everything written by actual Comanche captives that I could get my hands on. I was fascinated by the respect and love most of them expressed for their captors. It went beyond Stockholm Syndrome. There was a deep and abiding admiration for their adoptive native families and their culture. Many of the captives returned to the tribe, after being rescued, preferring tribal life to the white man's world. Once a person was adopted into the Comanche tribe, they were one of them, a brother, sister, wife, or husband for life. I came to have the same respect as the captives for these Lords of the Plains.

During my research of tribal culture, I found that many of the tribes had a deep respect for what modern Native

Americans refer to as "two spirits." Homosexuals were not looked upon as abominations, and instead were accepted as one of the Great Spirit's creations. Thought to be gifted with the perspective of both worlds, masculine and feminine, homosexuals were often mediators, healers, and leaders in these cultures. Until white men arrived with their contrasting belief system, homosexuals were not abominations. I found that fascinating as well.

So, the resulting novel combines the issues confronting the modern LGBT community with the challenges faced by a young woman born in 1860, a two spirit with an unforgettable story to tell. In the end, I hope you too will believe.

REB

PLAYLIST

I am often asked about the music I play while writing. The following artists saw me on the journey through this book. I encourage readers to listen to the songs as you read <u>Out on the Panhandle</u>. I think it will add to the experience. I also encourage the purchase and download of the songs legally. As a victim of piracy myself, I understand the financial drain that is the illegal download world. Save an artist, stop piracy!

REB

Name	Album	Artist
Something Good	The Sound of Music (Original)	Various Artists
Pink Cadillac	Natalie Cole: Greatest Hits, Vol. 1	Natalie Cole
Happy Days Theme	As Seen on TV	The Hit Crew
Route 66	For Sentimental Reasons	Patti Page
Oklahoma!	Oklahoma! Royal Nat'l Theatre Co.	London Cast
Famous in a Small Town	Crazy Ex-Girlfriend	Miranda Lambert
The Fishin' Hole	American Originals	Andy Griffith
Rawhide	Television Themes	Frankie Lane
Lizzie and the Rainman	20th Century Masters	Tanya Tucker
Mamas Don't…Grow Up to be Cowboys	Ultimate Waylon Jennings	Waylon Jennings & Willie Nelson
All My Exes Live in Texas	50 Number Ones	George Strait
Sweet Dreams	Reba Live	Reba McEntire
Oh What a Beautiful Morning	Best of Rogers and Hammerstein	Gordon MacRae
Trashy Women	Best of Confederate Railroad	Conf. Railroad
Sea of Cowboy Hats	The Definitive Collection	Chely Wright
San Antonio Rose	Reba Live	Reba McEntire
Mama Tried	40 Greatest Hits	Merle Haggard
Should've Been a Cowboy	Toby Keith	Toby Keith
You're the Reason God Made Oklahoma	Best of David Frizzell & Shelly West	Frizzell & West
Cowboy Take Me Away	The Essential Dixie Chicks	Dixie Chicks
Sin Wagon	The Essential Dixie Chicks	Dixie Chicks
Oklahoma Swing	When I Call Your Name	Vince Gill & Reba
Once Upon a Dream	Sleeping Beauty (Original)	Shirley & Costa

COMANCHE PRONUNCIATION GUIDE

This novel contains Comanche words. Each word is defined within the text, so the reader does not need to know the Comanche language. The following is meant to assist the reader in correctly pronouncing these words. The Comanche did not have a written language, per se. In an effort to preserve Comanche speech, Lila Robinson and James Armagost compiled the <u>Comanche Dictionary and Grammar</u> book, published in 1990. The guide below is from that publication.

The Comanche alphabet, consisting of six vowels and twelve consonants, is as follows with vowels having both voiced and voiceless realizations.

Single vowels are pronounced as follows:
a – as in *a* of *father*
e – as in *ei* of *eight*
i – as in *ee* of *see*
o – as in *o* of *go*
u – as in *oo* of *boot*
u̱ – as u with the lips spread: not found in English. The closest sound in English would be the A in America.

The letters used to represent consonant sounds pretty much follow the standard American English pronunciation. One symbol the reader may find puzzling is the "?" found in some words. It is used to represent a glottal stop as in Uh?oh, where air is cut off in the throat between syllables.

A little perspective...

"The White Man goes into his church and talks about Jesus. The Indian goes into his Tipi and talks with Jesus." ~ Quanah Parker, Principle Chief of the Comanche Nation from 1875 until his death in 1911, founder of the Native American Church.

"During the years 1865 and 1866 the great plains remained almost in a state of nature, being the pasture-fields of about ten million buffalo, deer, elk, and antelope, and were in full possession of... a race of bold Indians, who saw plainly that the construction of two parallel railroads right through their country would prove destructive to the game on which they subsisted, and consequently fatal to themselves... we realize today that the vigorous men who control Kansas, Nebraska, Dakota, Montana, Colorado, etc., etc., were soldiers of the civil war. These men flocked to the plains, and were rather stimulated than retarded by the danger of an Indian war. This was another potent agency in producing the result we enjoy today, in having in so short a time replaced the wild buffaloes by more numerous herds of tame cattle, and by substituting for the **useless Indians*** the intelligent owners of productive farms and cattle-ranches." ~ William T. Sherman from <u>The Memoirs of General W. T. Sherman, Complete</u>, Chapter Twenty-Six, "After the War."
    *R. E. Bradshaw's emphasis.

CHAPTER ONE

She was swimming, which was not unusual. Decky Bradshaw swam whenever she had the opportunity. It was her therapy, her thinking time, and having a lap pool in her house made it convenient to take a dip whenever she wanted. So, finding herself stroking through the water at high speed, leaving a foaming trail in her wake, was not what disturbed Decky. The fact the water was red and she could not see the bottom of the pool, however, gave her pause. She slowed her strokes and coasted to a glide, before lowering her feet in search of the bottom, which she found unexpectedly to be made of sand. Removing her swim goggles, she wiped away the water falling into her eyes, pushing her strawberry-blond bangs off her forehead. When her vision focused on her surroundings, she stumbled backwards, losing her footing. After a moment of frantic splashing to regain her balance, Decky squinted into bright sunlight at a sandy beach and the steeply sloping wall of a red-clay canyon beyond.

"What the hell?"

She turned in a circle and saw a matching bank of sand and clay behind her. Decky was standing in a pool of mud-red water at the center of a shallow sandy-bottomed river carved out of a canyon that curved out of sight in either direction. Insects in the throes of song announced that it was indeed a very hot summer day. The cicadas were especially loud in their mid-day mating calls. The tiny bit of breeze felt as if an oven door had been opened in front of her face, just more baking heat blowing up from the south. The high-pitched call of a hawk, "Kee-eeeee-aar," echoed off the canyon walls. Decky looked up to see the red-tailed predator soaring through a wide lazy circle, in the clear blue sky above her head.

"Where am I?"

A strange sound followed her question. Fffssst!

Decky turned quickly to see an arrow slicing into the water a few inches from her hip. Fffssst! Another one. It happened so fast she did not have time to react. Her eyes jerked up to the wall of the canyon, now rimmed with Native American warriors about to descend upon her. She had not taken even a step when the next arrow found its mark in her heart. It did not hurt, but Decky had to admit the shaft with its colorful feathers protruding from her chest was disconcerting.

"Now, isn't this a hell of a way to go," she said, just before she thought of Charlie. "I sure didn't think I'd end up with an arrow through my heart. I'm sorry, Charlie. Really, I'm so sorry."

Suddenly a hand gripped her shoulder and shook her hard. Too focused on the arrow piercing her chest to notice the warrior's approach, she now grasped the hand clasping her shoulder, trying to pry it loose.

"Decky, Decky, it's me."

It was Charlie's voice. How the hell did Charlie get here? Decky struggled to make sense of her impending doom.

2

"Decky. Rebecca Elizabeth Bradshaw! Wake up!"

In a flash, Decky was back on the airliner, with Charlie shaking her shoulder. She blinked a few times and looked down at her chest to make sure the arrow was not really there.

Charlie gave her another gentle shake. "Are you awake now?"

When her mind cleared Decky answered, "I'm awake. There's no need to resort to calling me Rebecca."

"I tried waking you up the nice way. The situation called for desperate measures. People were beginning to notice your rather loud apologies to me. What did you do in this dream that you were so sorry for?"

"I got shot by Comanches."

Some people might find Decky's answer puzzling. Charlie simply pointed at the Kindle in Decky's lap. "You were reading that book about Indian abductions in Texas, weren't you? Sometimes I think I'd like to see inside that head of yours, but I think it's probably better not to know."

Decky grinned back at the love of her life. "If you could see inside my head, you would never get naked around me again."

Charlie laughed. "You're all talk. You don't scare me."

The flight attendant approached with warm moist towels. "We'll be landing soon. Would you like to freshen up?"

"Thank you," Decky said, reaching for a towel.

"We'll be on the ground in fifteen minutes," the attendant said.

Charlie took a towel and thanked the young man. Decky watched as Charlie dabbed the lemon-scented fabric on her cheeks, once again overwhelmed with the sensation that she had been so very lucky to have found her. Since Charlene Ann Warren came into Decky's life two years ago, it happened several times a day. The soundtrack from "The Sound of

3

Music" would begin to play on her ever-present mental jukebox, "Somewhere in my youth or childhood, I must have done something good." Decky would smile and freeze there in the moment, wanting to hold that contentment for as long as possible.

"You're stunned in my presence again," Charlie said, with a wink.

Decky chuckled, answering, "I'm working on disguising my obsession, but I don't seem to be able to come up with an expression that doesn't look like I'm in pain."

Charlie patted Decky's hand. "You have more of a dumbstruck appearance, at the moment. I think it's cute, but other people may think you've gone catatonic."

The pilot's voice came over the intercom. "Ladies and gentlemen, we'll be arriving at Will Roger's World Airport, Oklahoma City, in about ten minutes. We've turned on the fasten your seat belt sign. Flight attendants, prepare the cabin for arrival. Local time is twelve-fifteen. It's already ninety-three degrees with a dry, hot wind out of the south. Welcome to my home state of Oklahoma in the summer, folks, and thanks for flying with us today." The microphone crackled and the pilot added, "Boomer Sooner!"

He was answered by at least half the plane with a loud, "Boomer Sooner!"

Decky raised her brow in question.

Charlie laughed. "It's the University of Oklahoma cheer. Boomer Sooner! The mascot is the covered wagon, the Sooner Schooner. You've seen it on TV during football games."

Decky stored her Kindle in the laptop bag at her feet and raised her seatback, before being told. She never messed around with airline procedures. "Yeah, I've been meaning to ask you about that. I thought the 'Sooners' were the people

4

who left early before the official start of the land-run. I understand that wasn't very sporting of them."

"I think the OU fans look at it as a representation of the unconquerable pioneer spirit," Charlie said, while pulling her seat belt tight. "My family bleeds Oklahoma State orange, so we think it's more along the lines of what you're talking about."

Decky leaned back against the headrest and yawned. Awake since four a.m., they had driven an hour and a half to the airport in Norfolk, and were seated on the plane by seven. It had already been a long day.

Charlie noticed the yawn. "Perk up there, girl. We still have a ways to go. Four hours driving to God's Country."

The plane began to slow into its final approach. Decky enjoyed flying. It was the taking off and landing that made her nervous. She tightened her seat belt again and braced for the landing, keeping up the conversation with Charlie to distract herself from thinking about all the aviation technology-meets-gravity videos she had watched.

"I thought they called the Panhandle of Oklahoma – No Man's Land."

Charlie instinctively knew when to redirect Decky's attention from one of her many phobias. She employed the technique often, and it was another reason Decky loved her so much. Charlie understood Decky, her whacked out, former drama teacher turned writer and part time genealogist way of absorbing the world. They never had an awkward phase of getting to know each other's habits, fitting together seamlessly like hand and glove from the beginning.

Charlie answered Decky's question. "The entire quote refers to the ownership of the land before it was settled. It was said to be, 'No man's land, but God's land.' No man's land has such a negative connotation. I think God's Country sounds better."

"At home, God's Country means no one but God would have it."

Charlie cautioned, "Why don't you just call it the Panhandle while we're here, okay?"

The wheels of the plane touched the ground and yelped against the pavement. The plane shuddered with the application of the brakes. Decky gripped the armrests and pressed her back into the seat. Her feet dug into the carpet, fighting the momentum that propelled her forward. In those few seconds, the forces of physics displayed their awesome powers, demonstrating how futile Decky's attempts to control them were. Having no control was at the root of her anxiousness, fueled by her inability to do anything other than hold on and hope for the best. Her stress meter was pinging in the red, as it seemed to take forever for Boomer Sooner Pilot Man to get the plane to stop. Charlie patted her hand until the plane slowed to a crawl and began taxiing toward the terminal, restoring Decky's stress level to manageable.

She exhaled the breath she had been holding and turned to Charlie, saying, "Welcome home, honey."

"Home is where you are," Charlie said, flashing Decky with the smile that always received one in return.

Decky replied with enthusiasm, "I'm glad you feel that way, but I can't wait to see where you grew up."

"I hope you're ready to meet the clan. With my nine brothers and sisters and their families, the sheer numbers can be daunting."

The metallic sound of seat belts being released sounded about the cabin, as the aircraft coasted to a stop at the terminal. Decky unbuckled and stood to retrieve the carry-on bags from the overhead bin, while responding, "I already met half of them when they came down last summer. I'm sure the rest of your family will be just as charming."

"My, aren't you shooting for brownie points."

Decky grinned back at her. "I try. I'm also dying to ask your mom about this Meredith Ethridge person in your family tree."

Charlie slid over to Decky's abandoned seat. "I'm sure she can help, if you can get her alone for a few minutes. That may be difficult with this crowd. Our family reunions are like an open range roundup. Not everyone will belong to our herd, but they come along anyway."

Decky looked down at those blue eyes she had come to adore. "Just don't forget about me. Or at least leave me with your sister, Franny. She's a familiar face."

Charlie winked. "You think I'd bring you out to the Panhandle, and just throw you to the wolves?"

Decky lowered one of the carry-ons to the aisle and paused to look at Charlie. "Nobody said anything about wolves. Are there really wolves out there?"

Charlie grinned mischievously. "And coyotes too. You can hear them circling at night." She let Decky panic a second, before adding, "You let me swim naked in water with I don't know what all. Paybacks are hell. Welcome to my world."

Decky handed down the other bag and moved aside, so Charlie could stand in the aisle ahead of her. She leaned down to the much shorter woman's ear. "I assume I'm about to experience a whole other form of wildlife."

Charlie looked up, whispering so only Decky could hear, "Play your cards right and you just might." She winked and then spoke at normal volume. "But you have to promise not to wander off alone into the prairie hunting for buffalo and native tribesmen. I know how you get when you're researching something."

7

They headed down the aisle toward the exit. "I promise not to ride off into the sunset, little lady," Decky drawled, using her best John Wayne impression.

"I'm not kidding, Decky. Don't go off on the ranch without someone with you. It's in the middle of nowhere and everything looks the same if you're not from there. You can get yourself in real trouble."

Decky unconsciously reached for her chest. "Just don't let me swim in any red-river canyons and I think we're safe."

#

They stopped at Ann's Chicken Fry House for some much needed lunch, before setting out on the four-hour drive to Charlie's parents' home. Ann's began as a gas station in 1948, before becoming a famous eatery on historic Route 66. It was a favorite of Charlie's since childhood and had become part of her homecoming ritual.

She explained, "I always wanted to eat here when we came to the 'City.' That's what everyone calls Oklahoma City. I mean, as far as cities from here to the Panhandle, it is *the* city. Now, I come to Ann's when I get off the plane to reconnect. It's the first thing that says home."

Home apparently said eclectic diner, Decky thought, as the sun glinted off the hot pink fins of a vintage 1959 Cadillac. The Natalie Cole version of Springsteen's "Pink Cadillac" erupted in Decky's head. The Caddy was parked next to an antique gas pump in front of the diner. A 1950, black and white, Dodge Coronet police car parked near the front door appeared to await service from a paper-cap-wearing waitress on roller skates. Upon seeing it, the jukebox in Decky's head switched to the "Happy Days" theme. Decky felt as though the clock was rolling back to the glory days of Mother Road, one of the most legendary motorways in American history.

Inside the restaurant, the walls were covered with relics from the historic highway's past, including signed Willie Nelson, Kiss, and Elvis guitars, quite a diverse collection. Every inch of wall space, not covered by autographed pictures, vinyl records, and other memorabilia, contained the signatures of the famous and not so famous, who ventured in from the Mother Road. Charlie pointed out where she had signed the wall back in 1985. Decky added her signature by the kitchen door, in one of the few places not already claimed.

Now, stuffed to the gills with delicious but heavy chicken fried steak and mashed potatoes, both smothered in thick white gravy, Decky was not handling the sweltering heat outside very well. As they approached the car, something about the copious amounts of fat in her stomach made the boiling asphalt under her feet that much hotter.

"Good Lord, it's hot," Decky said, rubbing her overfilled stomach.

Charlie opened the driver's side door of the rental car. "Quit whining. It hasn't even reached triple digits yet."

Decky climbed in the passenger side, while Charlie started the engine and turned the air-conditioning on full blast, leaving the doors open so the trapped heat could escape. They sat there for a minute, with Decky continuing to comment on the weather.

"I mean, I know you told me it was a different kind of heat, but I don't think I ever grasped it until now. It's like walking around in a kiln, like the heat is seeping up out of the ground. Even the wind is hot."

"O ye, who thought being a pioneer would have been 'so cool'. We've only been here an hour and you're already crying for mercy," Charlie teased. "Shut your door and let's get going. Momma will have dinner waiting for us."

Decky moaned and pulled her door shut. Snapping her seat belt in place, she said, "I don't think I'll need any more food for a few days. That was great, but I couldn't eat like that all the time."

Charlie aimed the car back toward the highway. "I told you not to order the large serving. You should have seen your face when the waitress put all those dishes down in front of you."

"I was hungry. We had breakfast at the crack of dawn. How was I to know a large could feed a family of four? I didn't eat a fourth of it. I promise to take your advice next time."

Charlie scoffed at that. "When, in all the time I've known you, have you taken my advice? I bet, when your momma told you the fire was hot, you just had to touch it anyway."

"I knew you were hot and I just had to touch you," Decky said, placing her hand on Charlie's thigh. "Aren't you glad I didn't listen to my momma?"

Charlie grinned over at her. "Yes, very glad. Speaking of your momma, Lizzie said to call her when we landed. If you don't call soon, you know both our phones will ring repeatedly until one of us picks up."

Decky sighed. "I know. That's why I didn't turn my phone back on yet. I was enjoying the peace."

Right on cue, Charlie's cellphone rang in her purse. She looked at Decky. "It's either my mother or yours. I'm betting on Lizzie. Care to take that bet?"

Decky's shoulders slumped. It was a natural reaction to her mother, after years of engrained conditioning. She just never knew which side of her mother's bi-polar personality she was going to have to deal with.

"No bet." Decky sighed and dug in Charlie's purse, coming out with the phone. "I know it's her." She slid her finger on the screen and tapped the speakerphone button. "Hi Mom, you're on speaker."

Lizzie Bradshaw's southern drawl rang through the car. "I thought you were going to call me when you landed. Your daddy says the plane landed over an hour ago. He's looking right at it on the computer screen."

Decky tried misdirection. "We just got back in the car. We had to get something to eat. We're on our way to Charlie's house now."

The distraction tactic did not work. Her mother launched into a minor rant, just a tiny bump on the bi-polar road that was their relationship. "And why am I having to call you on Charlie's phone? Why didn't you answer yours? You're halfway across the country." – Here it comes, Decky thought, the guilt trip. – "What if your son needed you? What if your daddy had a stroke?"

Charlie had to stifle a laugh. Lizzie's desperate attempts to control everyone's lives, using any means necessary, had become comical to Charlie. At least after the first couple of go-rounds with Lizzie, Charlie had learned to find the humor in Decky's dysfunctional relationship with her mother.

Decky rolled her eyes at Lizzie's declaration. "Mom, Zack is almost twenty and has been living on his own at college for two years. I think he can handle a week at home without me." The fifteen hundred miles between Decky and her mother emboldened her. She added, "And why is it Dad that is always going to have a stroke?"

Charlie's hand flew to her mouth to catch the giggle trying to escape.

Lizzie went for the ultimate guilt line. "Well, I could drop dead any minute, but you know that from our family history of heart problems."

The family curse, the bad ticker, Decky had heard it from childhood, how she was going to give her mother a heart attack. She answered, "Yes, the heart problems caused by heavy smoking and a diet with bacon grease as the main component, neither of which applies to you."

At the heart of Lizzie's valiant attempt to make Decky feel guilty was her mother's disappointment at being left behind. She had hinted numerous times at how much she liked Charlie's mother, Louise, and how she would so love to see Oklahoma. Decky thought it best to let the rest of Charlie's family form their opinions about her before she threw her mother into the mix. Lizzie was the perfect hostess when some of Charlie's family came for a visit last summer. Her mother could charm the Queen, if necessary, but Decky was always prepared for the worst. It was not a matter of if, but when, Lizzie was going to plant her foot firmly in her mouth. Thwarted in her endeavor to make Decky feel badly about not taking her on the trip, Lizzie tried another tack.

"I can't believe you turned your house over to a bunch of teenaged boys. I sure hope Zack is looking after Dixie. She could have stayed over here. That dog is just like a grandchild to us, you know that, and I can't believe Charlie thinks those boys can handle Miss Kitty, either. What if she gets loose?"

"I don't know, Mom. Why don't you ask her? She's listening to you. I said you were on speakerphone."

Charlie chimed in, "Hello, Miss Lizzie. I'm sure Zack is doing a great job looking out for the fur babies."

"Oh hello, Charlie. I don't like those speakerphone thingies. I don't know who I'm talking to."

"You're talking to me and Charlie. You called Charlie's phone," Decky reminded her.

Lizzie was not making any headway so she gave up, for the time being anyway. "Well, all right then. Since you're not dead in a plane crash, I guess I'll let you go. Have fun. Tell Louise to come see me."

"Bye Mom, and tell Dad not to have a stroke while I'm gone."

"Your daddy is healthier than most forty-year-olds. It's me you should worry about."

"Love you too, Mom." Decky hung up before Lizzie could get started again.

Charlie finally laughed aloud. "I am always in awe that you turned out as normal as you did."

"I'm amazed at how much she loves you and your family, after her initial reaction," Decky said, putting Charlie's cellphone back in her purse.

Charlie took the ramp to join Interstate 40-West and let out a short laugh. "Defending your family against murder charges has a way of putting things in perspective."

All Decky wanted to remember about the murder charges was that no one had to go to prison. It had been her deepest desire. The lawsuit she and Charlie recently settled, with the people who set in motion events that allowed a maniac to nearly kill them, would keep them comfortable for the rest of their lives. It made the terror of that night and subsequent events easier to come to terms with. Except for that blemish, her relationship with Charlie was all she could have dreamed of, but Lizzie's complete turnaround after her initial reaction left her dumbfounded.

"It still boggles my mind how my mother went from being a crazed lunatic, because I was gay, to the person her friends turn to when they find out their child is too. How in the hell did that happen?"

Charlie kept her eyes on the road and answered flatly, "I think they finally got her meds right, but that's just me."

13

"You know, I really never knew how weird my life was until I went to college. Even then it took a few trips home with friends to figure out my mother's behavior wasn't normal."

"We'll see how normal you think my family is after this week," Charlie said, while peering in the mirror and changing lanes. She continued to talk, as she settled into the fast lane and set the cruise control. "I'm just glad we have Aunt Lena and Uncle Paul's RV to stay in. The house is going to be jammed as it is."

"It sounds like there will be a small RV park, from what you've said."

"There are fifty of us, counting Mom and Dad, my siblings, and the grandkids. That's just the immediate family. Add in the great-grandchildren, uncles, aunts, cousins, friends, and friends of friends, it gets up in the hundreds. Having the reunion on the Fourth of July makes it easier for everyone to come. People bring RVs, campers, tents, and start coming in the day before. It's really quite the party. I hope it doesn't overwhelm you."

"Are you kidding? Family reunions are a genealogist's dream. I'm sure I'll be able to tie up the loose ends and have the Warren family-tree book ready by Christmas."

"My family is going to love it. It's a wonderful gift. Have I thanked you properly yet?" Charlie teased.

Decky chuckled. "No, I don't think so. How about a moonlit horseback ride and few hours on a blanket under the stars for payment?"

Charlie changed lanes again. Not looking at Decky, she replied, "Okay, but you have to promise to keep at least one eye open."

"Why is that?" Decky asked.

With a straight face, and to Decky's horror, Charlie said, "Somebody has to watch for rattlesnakes and tarantulas. They like to snuggle up to warm bodies at night."

"Tarantulas!" Decky exclaimed. "There are tarantulas just walking around?"

Charlie's expression remained serious, when she answered, "Oh yeah, they're everywhere, scorpions too. Be careful when you put on your shoes in the morning and always look under the covers before you crawl in bed."

"Tell me again why we can't stay in the house where it's safe," Decky whined.

Charlie countered with, "Well, at least I'm telling you what to look out for. You just let me discover the wildlife on my own when I moved in with you."

Decky chuckled. "You are never going to forget about that eel, are you?"

"No, I don't think I will," Charlie shot back, but she was grinning. "On a good note, there are forty-six different kinds of snakes in Oklahoma, but only seven of them are poisonous."

"You know, you have a mean streak," Decky pointed out.

Charlie laughed. "Oh all right, I'll let you off the hook. There aren't really any wolves, not anymore, and the cougars are gone."

"And the rest?" Decky asked playfully, a mood that quickly left her, when Charlie replied.

"Oh no, really, all the rest of it is true."

#

Charlie turned the car off I-40 a few miles back, heading northwest across the state. Decky finally stopped thinking about all the animals, reptiles, and insects awaiting their arrival, as the landscape began to change. Low, rolling, short-grass-covered hills and an occasional escarpment broke up

15

long straight stretches of flat farmland and pastures sprinkled with oil and natural gas wells. The only trees were huddled around the few water sources, mere dusty creek beds this time of year. Rain did not fall often in the Oklahoma summer. Everything looked kindling dry. One stray spark and another raging wildfire would start in a flash. Decky remembered the look of horror on Charlie's face last summer, while watching the news of wildfires burning out of control across Oklahoma. When the driver of the car in front of them threw a cigarette out his window, Charlie's reaction made perfect sense to Decky.

"You fucker!" Charlie shouted. "Use your damn ashtray." She looked over at Decky. "I'm sorry. That just makes me so mad."

"Entirely understandable," Decky responded, "but I think I've had a detrimental influence on your vocabulary."

Charlie forgot she was mad and smiled, replying, "Damn right! And when I slip up in front of my mother, I'm going to blame you."

The first towering red-clay bluff came into view, jutting out of the otherwise flat landscape. It was hard to believe all the surrounding land was once at that elevation. Thousands of years of wind and water erosion carved away layer after layer, leaving the tale of its past clearly marked in the bands of sediment under the hard cap-rock protecting this lone ridge.

Charlie pointed at the bluff. "Do you see that black silhouette on the edge up there?"

Decky squinted to see the profile of a Native American warrior astride his horse, lance in hand, surveying his domain. "That is very majestic and ominous looking at the same time," she commented.

Charlie changed lanes and passed the cigarette-tossing criminal. Decky was happy to see she resisted the temptation to flip the guy off. Instead, Charlie said, "That image always gives me chills. It's hard to reconcile my Native American roots with the pioneer ones. My family lives on land that was basically stolen from my own ancestors."

"Wasn't your ranch part of the Comancheria, Comanche land?"

"Yes, and Momma says her grandmother was half Comanche."

"That's part of what I have to clear up with your mother. This Meredith Ethridge, the one I have questions about, was the child of half Chickasaws. I don't know where the Comanche bloodline comes from, unless he married one, and I couldn't find any information on his wife. All I know is her name was Grace, and your mother told me that. He wasn't married to her long, because she never appeared on the official census. I don't know what happened to her. I know they had a child, your great-grandmother, but that's it."

"Well, Momma's gathered up all the family papers and sent out a call for pictures. You should have more than enough info after this."

"Your mom's been a little evasive about this Meredith character. I just know there is some deeply buried skeleton there. I can smell a family secret," Decky said, grinning.

"I have no idea what it is," Charlie said. "I know there was some outlaw activity and a few lynchings out here, back in the day. Who knows what you'll find out? We could be Sooners and that would be tragic."

#

They were halfway to Beaver County, when Decky saw her first cowboy. Charlie pulled into a gas station to fill up and use the restroom. She went inside, while Decky pumped the gas. That was when she saw him. The first thing Decky noticed

17

was his vehicle. A black monster of a pickup truck roared up to the pump beside her, sporting dual wheels on the back, a cattle guard over the front grill, and covered in prairie dust.

By mentally referring to it as a pickup and not just a truck, Decky had used the correct rancher terminology, according to Charlie's amusing earlier instruction. "It's only a truck if it has more than two axels."

Decky expected a sweaty, red-dirt covered ranch hand to step out of the cab. She was surprised to see the man that appeared before her. He was tall and dipped his blond head toward her, flashing a handsome smile, before slipping on the cowboy hat he retrieved from the seat. His temples were graying, so Decky thought he could be her age, maybe a little older. The crease down the front of each leg of his starched jeans was perfectly straight, before stacking just a bit where it landed on top of his shiny black boots. His jeans did not look painted on tight nor baggy and loose, but fit comfortably at his natural waist, a sight not often seen these days. The leather belt he wore was hand-tooled and fastened with a large silver buckle. His immaculately starched, western style, long-sleeved, white shirt appeared to have just come from under the iron. When Decky last checked the temperature, it was ninety-six degrees, but the man was not sweating. She watched him walk into the store, sure in her belief that the words tall, cool drink of water had been used to describe him at some point.

Decky finished pumping the gas and then went inside the store. She did not see the cowboy, but met Charlie coming out of the restroom.

"Do you want something to drink?" Charlie asked.

"A cold bottle of water sounds good. Thanks. I'll be right out."

"I'll be in the car," Charlie said over her shoulder.

Decky could not help but watch her walk away. Charlie's rearview was as mesmerizing as the front to Decky. Somehow knowing she was still standing there, Charlie looked back, laughed, and motioned for Decky to move it along. The cowboy came out of the men's room, just as Decky ducked into the women's. She saw him again a few minutes later, when she stepped back out into the blinding sunshine. She squinted at the scene, before lifting the sunglasses dangling from a cord around her neck up to her eyes. She refocused and saw Charlie standing at the side of the pickup, smiling, and chatting away with the "drink of water" while he filled his tank.

The next thing Charlie did startled Decky a bit. She stood on her tiptoes and reached up to hug the cowboy. He leaned down, kissed Charlie on the cheek, and lifted her off the ground a few inches, before setting her down. They exchanged waves and then Charlie got into the car, never noticing Decky approaching. The cowboy dipped his hat in a nod to Decky, as she climbed into the car. His handsome smile was not quite as appealing this go round.

Charlie waved at the cowboy again, before pulling away.

"Who was that?" Decky asked, trying desperately to keep jealousy out of her voice.

"That's Marty. He's a friend from home."

"Kind of wild to run into him out in the middle of nowhere," Decky commented.

"Not really," Charlie said. "There is only one main road out to the Panhandle and this is it. I always seem to run into someone I know."

"You must know him very well."

"Decky Bradshaw, are you jealous?" Charlie glanced over at Decky and chuckled. "Yes, I think you are. Honey, if you're going to turn green every time some good looking cowboy, or cowgirl for that matter, hugs me or kisses me on the cheek while we're here, then we might as well just call you Gumby."

Decky smiled, suddenly amused by her own behavior. She had been momentarily caught up in a little green-eyed envy, but theirs was a relationship built on trust and she knew Charlie would never give her a real reason to be jealous. To cover her embarrassment, she asked, "So, you're well-known in these parts, are you?"

Charlie chuckled again. "Everybody's well-known in a small town, for one reason or another. There were only thirty-four of us in my graduating class. Kind of hard to fly under the radar, if you know what I mean."

"I'm sure everyone loved you," Decky said, turning her attention to the prairie beginning to open up around her.

Along the tall ridges, she could see the giant white wind-turbines, constantly twirling in the Oklahoma wind. It really did come "sweeping down the plain" and there was certainly plenty of "waving wheat," just like the song said. Decky learned to spell Oklahoma listening to the musical when she was a child. Back then, she never dreamed she would wrangle her own cowgirl. She stared out at the wide-open spaces, with the original Broadway cast taking a turn on the jukebox, singing "O-K-L-A-H-O-M-A," while Charlie continued to chatter.

"Well, there is one person who isn't my biggest fan, my brother Bobby's third, and very new wife, Karen. She hates my guts. We were friends until Junior High and then she changed. She's my age, twelve years younger than Bobby. I guess he tried his generation around home and decided to dip in a different pool this time."

Decky looked out over miles and miles of seemingly uninhabited wheat fields and pastureland. If there were fences, they appeared to be there to keep the cattle and horses out of the road, not to restrict their movement over vast amounts of grazing land. A few houses popped up here and there, some inhabited, some long since abandoned. The iconic windmills Decky had seen in countless photographs from the dust bowl era dotted the landscape. In those pictures, the water pumps attached to the windmills had long since gone dry, during a climatic catastrophe brought on by poor farming practices and a historic drought. The scene of one of the worst disasters to befall the nation and immortalized in John Steinbeck's The Grapes of Wrath, the Panhandle had since been reborn out of The Dust Bowl.

Replacing those grainy black and white images of hopeless farmers, fighting a losing battle against clouds of killing dust, Decky could see rolling pale-green and golden hills, interspersed with the vibrant fields of a few sunflower farms. The big yellow-framed faces of the plants were turned, worshipping the blazing ball of fire slowly lowering over the western horizon. Occasionally, they would pass an irrigated field, the deep green of which stood out in contrast with the muted pallet of the prairie grass and cut hay fields surrounding it. Huge round bales of hay dotted the landscape, where it had been harvested, rolled up, and left to await a time when it would be needed. Other than the ones around the creek beds, Decky saw only lone trees on the tops of a few hills, with no other shade for miles around. The ground beneath those trees was crowded with lounging cows or horses attempting to escape the afternoon scald from the sun.

Decky was listening to Charlie prattle on about her new sister-in-law, while she took in the scenery. It appeared the dislike was mutual between the two women.

She asked, "Why do you think your brother has been married so many times?"

Charlie must have thought about it quite a bit before now. She answered quickly, "He's a simple man, undemanding. He is satisfied with his life and always marries women who find that boring. That's what I think, anyway."

Decky turned her attention to Charlie. "You're not going to get bored, are you?"

Charlie glanced at Decky and reached to squeeze her hand. "No honey, life with you has been anything but boring. I never know what you're planning next."

Decky grinned, leaning over to peck Charlie on the cheek. She whispered against Charlie's ear, "Keeps you on your toes."

Charlie threw her head back and laughed loudly. "Oh God, yes. You definitely keep me on my toes. Your plans always go so well. How'd that last one work out for you?"

Decky's last failed adventure involved finding a kitten companion for Charlie's ancient cat, Miss Kitty. It was a bad idea from the start. Decky had the scars to prove it.

She answered Charlie, "I've sworn off plans involving crazed animals and bloodshed."

Charlie slowed the car, making a ninety-degree right turn at a crossroads called Elmwood. They had been driving due west on an absolutely straight road for the last forty-five miles. Now they were headed due north. Decky was starting to see the pattern of the allotments from the land-run days. The land was divided into six-hundred-and-forty-acre sections, equaling one square-mile. The entire Panhandle was gridded out with graded dirt roads, running true in all four directions of the compass, creating a crossroads at every mile. The sandy paths looked like white stripes painted on the range, disappearing down the backside of hills, only to return again on the next one and the next, straight as an arrow.

She commented to Charlie, "Look at all the sand. I mean, I know this land was covered with ocean thousands of years ago, but I never imagined this much sand – and it's so white. Those roads make the pastures look like quilting squares."

"Now you know what all those lines were on the satellite image you were looking at the other night," Charlie said. "And those dark circles inside the squares were the irrigated fields."

Decky looked out Charlie's side of the car. It was more of the same. "Lots of space out here. Doesn't look like noisy neighbors are ever a problem. You can't see them, let alone hear them."

Charlie looked out over her homeland, the corner of her mouth curling into a smile. "We're pretty spread out, I'll admit, but it's a tight community. I'd bet you these people know their neighbors better than most of the folks living side by side in the city."

"Did you ever feel lonely or like you were missing out, living way out here?"

Charlie answered, "Who could be lonely with a family the size of mine? Plus, there was always work to do on the ranch, school stuff to get done, and I played every competitive sport available, we all did. I had no time to feel like I was missing anything. I was too busy to get into too much trouble."

Decky tilted her head to one side, trying to imagine Charlie as a young girl and the mischief she might have been involved in. She smiled at the prospects. "Too much trouble? Pray tell, what kind of trouble does a homecoming queen get into out here on the plains?"

Without missing a beat, Charlie replied, "Oh, nothing too serious. I only needed bail money twice."

Decky took the bait. "Seriously?"

Charlie snickered. "No. I never needed bail money. A deputy took me home once, for toilet papering a teacher's house, but really, I was a good girl. Sorry to crush your dreams of plying my family for dirt on me. I'm squeaky clean."

Decky had to laugh. "I think you're just saying that to keep me from snooping. There are bound to be some stories your brothers and sisters can't wait to share. It will just take the proper seeding to get them going."

Charlie's tone lost some of its playfulness, when she said, "Speaking of sharing, you have to promise me one thing."

"If you're going to ask me to leave any embarrassing stories out of my novels, I can't promise that," Decky said, trying to make Charlie laugh.

"No, I've given up hope of our lives staying out of your books, off your Facebook page, or your Twitter feed."

Decky only slightly defended sharing with her fans. "I only talk about the funny parts."

"I know, so I'm making a request. When you see the naked baby picture of me on the mantle, please do not take a picture and share my ass with the world."

Decky patted Charlie's thigh. "Oh, don't worry honey, I have no intention of sharing your ass with anyone."

"Good, then welcome to my hometown."

Charlie slowed the car through a series of speed zones, stepping down from sixty-five to twenty-five miles an hour. As they crested a hill, a very small town grew up out of the prairie, so small Decky could see from end to end.

Charlie added with a grin, "This is it. Beaver, Oklahoma, the Cow Chip Throwing Capital of the World."

Decky burst out laughing. "You're kidding, right?"

"No, honest. We have the World Champion Cow Chip Throwing contest every April. People come from as far away as Japan and Australia to compete."

"How could you withhold that little tidbit of information?" Decky asked, trying to control her laughter.

Charlie pointed out the window. Decky turned to see a ten-foot tall, fiberglass, brown beaver on the back of a trailer, proudly holding a giant cow chip in its paws. The hand painted sign on the front of the trailer said, "BEAVER OKLA – COW CHIP CAPITAL – WELCOMES YOU."

As Decky stared at the little town's pride and joy, she heard Charlie say, "Some things you just have to see to believe."

CHAPTER TWO

Decky had done a little research into the history of Beaver
County, Oklahoma, preparing for the simple narrative she was
writing to supplement the information she uncovered in
Charlie's family genealogy. Relying solely on historic
information, Decky had somehow overlooked the more
modern cow chip throwing fame of the town, a detail she
would not leave out of the family history, which would
definitely include a picture of the ten-foot fiberglass, smiling
beaver. It was undoubtedly a case of fact being stranger than
fiction.

Knowing the history of a place said a lot about its people,
in Decky's experience. Beaver County's history was as
colorful as any she had researched. The whole panhandle
outline fascinated her. On a map, it did not appear the land was
intended to be a part of Oklahoma, and as it turned out, it was
not. The rectangular shape came about when Texas ceded the
land to the federal government in 1850, supposedly to form

part of the southern border of the new Kansas Territory. The Cherokees called foul, because that would encroach on much of their reservation in Indian Territory. Decky could understand their concern after they had already been forced to walk the Trail of Tears. For once, the government listened. The Kansas border was moved further north, leaving the Panhandle unattached to any state or territorial government.

The area was labeled "Public Land" on pre-statehood maps. The inhabitants at the time were mostly outlaws, since there was no governing body to deal with them. The nomadic Comanche, the "Lords of the Plains," and their allies used the area as a seasonal home. That began to change, as forts sprang up to protect the ever-encroaching settlers. Decky had noticed a pattern akin to dominoes, as one tribe after another surrendered and assimilated. If the initial domino fell when the first non-native North American stepped onshore, then the loud clap of a tile falling was heard on June 27, 1874, at the Second Battle of Adobe Walls. The resulting Red River War ensured the rest of the dominos fell quickly.

Adobe Walls gave the government an excuse for concentrating its efforts to end the "Indian problem" forever. President Grant sent the man that brought the South to its knees during the Civil War, General William Tecumseh Sherman, to do his worst. Sherman approached the problem much as he had the southern insurrection. The Indians would submit, starve, or die. Never mind that the US government had promised the plains tribes the land would belong to them "as long as the grass grows and water runs." Decky thought most people would be surprised to know that what they called butchery in the south could not compare to the brutality Sherman unleashed on the Native Americans.

Despite having the same name, Tecumseh, as a great Shawnee tribal leader, Sherman advocated the wholesale slaughter of the plains tribes' food supply and never letting the renegades rest. Drive them, drive them, he encouraged, and they will submit. The last of the free roaming tribes were forced onto federal reservations in Indian Territory, during the summer of 1875. Decky remembered that year, because it was the year Charlie's great-grandmother was born and when her genealogy research hit a wall.

In the middle of the uprising, which Decky learned seemed to be part of allure, two enterprising former buffalo hunters seized the opportunity to get in on the bonanza that was the hide trade. Charles "Dirty Face" Jones and Joseph H. Plummer opened a supply post in the Panhandle of Texas in the fall of 1874, where they began hauling buffalo hides north to Dodge City, Kansas by the thousands, and supplies back down south to the hunters. The course they marked became known as the Jones and Plummer Trail. It also became a vital route for the military supply chain during the Red River War. As the demand for buffalo hides continued to rise, and emboldened by the enhanced military presence, hunters poured down the new route, hoping to get rich. Decky wondered if Charlie's ancestors came down the trail to settle here. She was desperate to know what circumstances led them to this place, at a time when no one was supposed to be there. Charlie's family had indeed homesteaded on the Panhandle before it was legally opened, but they were not alone.

The trail was so well used, during its twenty years of service, portions of it still remained visible in the pastures south of Beaver over one hundred and twenty-five years later. Decky could imagine the covered wagons coming right down the road she was traveling and crossing the Beaver River up ahead. The shallow, sandy-bottomed river flowed east, intersecting the trail where, in 1879, Jim Lane built the first business in Beaver. It was a sod house on the south side of the river, which served as a rest stop, restaurant, general store, and saloon for folks traveling north and south. More businesses and people began to gather at this trail stop, soon named Beaver City by these brave homesteaders. In 1886, the land opened for settlement, allowing those already there to make their claims legal. Eventually, using mile markers left by a government survey team, a one square mile section was platted out with streets, forming the present day town that was still contained within the borders set so long ago.

Charlie crawled the car through the one-mile main drag's twenty-five-mile-an-hour speed limit, as Decky observed her surroundings. It would have taken less than a minute to see the entire town at highway speeds. The "Andy Griffith Show" theme began to whistle through her mind.

Decky whispered under her breath, "The town that time forgot."

"What?" Charlie asked.

"I was just commenting on the Mayberry-like state of things," Decky answered, as they crossed the bridge over the river at the end of town and picked up speed. She looked up to see large sand dunes rising on the left side of the road. "Are those the Beaver Dunes?"

Charlie nodded. "Yes, those are the famous dunes, the Playground of the Panhandle. My nephew, Michael, Mary's son, said he'd take us out in the dune buggies later in the week, if we have time."

"Now, Mary is the oldest, right?" Decky asked.

"Yes, and Michael is only eight years younger than me. He was the first grandchild and my pet. I carried him everywhere when he was young."

Decky shook her head. "I'm never going to be able to remember all these names. I had a horrible time when I was teaching. 'Hey you,' became my saving grace."

"It's okay," Charlie said. "My mother is breaking out the name tags. She had one made for you."

"Name tags? Your family wears nametags?"

Charlie chuckled. "No, but that isn't a bad idea."

Decky knew she had to broach the next subject. She had hoped that Charlie would say something eventually, but that never happened. Decky was going to have to ask.

"What do you want me to say, Charlie, when someone asks who I am?"

"Did you have to explain who you were to my family last summer?" Charlie asked, putting on the turn signal and slowing the car.

Decky knew from an earlier map perusal that they were closing in on the ranch. Her heart quickened. She was nervous and uncertain, still learning to deal with people who did not approve of her sexuality. In the two years since she recognized her attraction to women, in particular Charlie, Decky discovered what it felt like to be discriminated against and hated because she loved someone. Once self-assured and confident in any situation, she could not help the anxiousness she felt among strangers. She tolerated the disapproving looks and pointing fingers. She watched in silent rage as the politics of her beloved state of North Carolina turned to ignorant hate speech, while an anti-gay constitutional amendment was used as a ploy to drive conservatives to the polls. She listened as "men of God" called for her extermination, naming her an "abomination." Decky knew firsthand the vicious passions these words provoked, but what she dreaded more than violence was the moment she would take the bait and respond. She feared her own rage and the purging destined to come.

Charlie's family knew Decky and Charlie lived together. They probably knew that Charlie was a lesbian, but they just did not discuss it. Charlie's older sister by three years and her

30

confidant, Franny, was the only person in the family that Charlie talked openly with about her sexuality. The three days Decky had been around part of the family were a whirlwind of activity and the subject never came up. Charlie seemed normal around them, although she never physically touched Decky in view of her family. That bit of distance indicated to Decky that Charlie was not entirely comfortable with what might be said, if they ever did discuss her sexuality. Charlie's philosophy was, "Don't ask questions you may not want the answers to."

Decky sighed. "No, I didn't have to explain anything, but what if someone asks who I am to you? What do I say?"

"Keep it simple. 'Friend' works," Charlie said, turning left and heading west again. She flipped down the visor, as the sun glared through the windshield. "They all think what they want anyway. Why spoil their fun?"

Decky flipped her visor down. Even the dark sunglasses she wore could not penetrate the rays setting the windshield on fire. "Doesn't it bother you? I mean, there are all your brothers and sisters proudly displaying their families. Don't you want people to know you are living happily ever after too?"

Charlie looked out her window at the pastureland on the left side of the road. "Oh look, there's Daddy."

Decky saw a man on horseback, trotting along the fence railing. Charlie slowed the car to keep pace with the horse, while she hit the button to lower her window.

"Hey there, cowboy," Charlie called out to her father.

Charles Warren stopped his horse and peered out from under his straw cowboy hat. He had the tanned weathered skin of a man who lived outside. He was thin, but looked to be in incredible shape for a man his age. He was wearing jeans and a short-sleeved plaid shirt, with pearl snap buttons. Authentic was the word that came to Decky's mind, and the theme from "Rawhide" started playing on her jukebox. He looked made for

31

the saddle. He smiled when he recognized Charlie, who beamed back with the exact same expression. There was no doubt this man was her father.

"Well, hello there, Little One," Charles said, calling Charlie by her family nickname, a fact Decky learned last summer.

Charlie brought the car to a stop in the middle of the road, seeming unconcerned that another car might come along. Decky looked in the side mirror and down the road in front of them. Not a car in sight. She had read somewhere there were less than three people per square mile in Beaver County. The likelihood of a car disturbing this impromptu meeting was slim.

"Hey, Daddy," Charlie said, and then leaned back so he could see into the car. "This is Decky."

"Nice to meet you, Decky. Welcome to the ranch," Charles said, with an easy western drawl.

"It's nice to meet you too, Mr. Warren," Decky answered.

"Call me Buck. Everyone else does, at least the ones I didn't bring into this world."

"You headed to the house?" Charlie asked.

Buck's horse pranced in place. He clucked to it and it settled down. "Yep, just ridin' the fence line with this youngin' here. He'll make a good cow pony if he calms down a bit. Go on to the house. Your momma's been waitin' on you."

Charlie grinned mischievously and taunted her father. "You wanna race?"

Buck met her grin with his own. "You have to go the speed limit," he said, before he yelled, "Ha," turned his horse, and galloped away.

Charlie laughed and started down the road. The race was on.

Decky was concerned. "Should your seventy-four-year-old father be charging across the field like that?"

Charlie picked up speed. "The day he can't ride a horse is the day we put him in the ground. He'll beat us too, if I try not to throw gravel on the back road." She glanced at Decky. "You did get full coverage on the rental agreement, didn't you?"

Decky grabbed at the console to steady herself, as Charlie made a left onto one of the section roads, fishtailed a little, and then stepped on the gas.

"Yes, I got full coverage," Decky answered, settling back against the seat and bracing herself better, "but that doesn't mean I want to end up in that fence over there."

Charlie concentrated on driving, but continued their conversation from before. "As far as happily ever after goes, I really don't care what people think. I know that is hard for you to believe, but I don't give it much thought. I've never discussed my sexuality with anyone in my family, except for Franny, because none of the others ever asked. If they do, I will tell them the truth, but other than that, my life is no one's business but my own. You'll find that is the prevailing attitude in my family. The people that matter to me know whether I'm happy or not. I don't have to tell them." She took another sharp left, throwing a rooster tail of sand in the air. "Relax, honey. I'm sure everything will be fine."

"All right then," Decky said, not convinced, but trying to sound that way. "Whatever works for you." She clutched the middle console tighter, adding, "I'm just along for the harrowing ride."

Charlie slowed the car and looked at Decky. "I love you. What other people think won't change that fact, so their opinions don't concern me. You just remember that."

33

Decky flashed a smile. She wanted Charlie to have a good time, so she dropped the topic. "I love you, too. Now give it some gas or your dad will beat us."

Charlie grinned at her and pressed down on the accelerator. On the crest of the tallest hill in sight, Decky saw the long, low profile of a large ranch house. The wide front yard could have held two football fields side by side. In contrast with the surrounding muted colors of the prairie, the lawn was a deep green. White steel fencing, made of round poles and rails, stood at least four feet high, separating the human space from the ranch animals on either side of the long driveway. Decky could see several Quonset style barns and a corral a few hundred yards behind the house. The horses grazing in the nearby pasture raised their heads when Charlie bumped the car over the cattle grate at the end of the driveway. They had arrived too late. Buck appeared on horseback up ahead, waved his hat in the air, and then rode off toward the barn.

"See, I told you," Charlie said. "He was born on a horse."

At that moment, people started pouring out the front door of the house. Decky recognized Franny and Louise leading the way, before the masses swallowed them. The Warren family lived up to the definition associated with its name. It did appear a rabbit warren was evacuating, as men, women, and children of all ages began to gather in the yard. It was like one of those clown car scenes, a never-ending trail of exiting people. Little One had come home and it appeared the entire family was there to meet her.

They were all gesturing some form of greeting and Charlie was waving back, as she slowed the car and rolled up the driveway. This was the land of her birth and these were her people. Unlike Decky's dysfunctional family, Charlie's relatives genuinely seemed not only to love one another, but to like each other as well. Children ran toward the fence line

34

repeating the phrase that undoubtedly started the stampede, "Charlie's here!" The adults formed a group with the smaller children and the teenagers that were too cool to be excited, moving around the side of the house to meet the car at the back.

"Did the whole family come to see our arrival? I thought I'd get them a few at a time, not all at once."

Charlie turned and winked at Decky. "They know I always bring presents."

Decky remembered packing the two boxes of Outer Banks souvenirs Charlie sent ahead and thinking she had gone a bit overboard. Decky thought buying every handmade wooden toy within driving distance was a little much. There were gifts for the adults, infants, and teenagers, too. Charlie took extra care to find the younger children things that would spark their imaginations and interest in Aunt Charlie's new neck of the woods. Among the items the boxes held were wooden pirate swords from Ocracoke Island, replicas of primitive games and toys of the English colonists on Roanoke Island, and kites from Kitty Hawk.

Now, observing the horde outside the car, Decky was not so sure there would be enough. "I hope we didn't leave anyone out. They seem very excited."

"I bought extra. This family breeds like rabbits. There are always more of them every time I come home." Charlie wound the car around to the nearly full parking area at the back of the house. There were enough vehicles already there to start a used car business. Charlie turned the engine off just before the family encircled them. The kids arrived first and plastered their faces to the windows, shouting Charlie's name.

Charlie said through laughter, "Oh good Lord, look at them, they're rabid. Are you sure you don't want to leave now while we still have a chance?"

Decky could see how glad Charlie was to be home with her family, even if she was pretending to be horrified.

"Too late, they have us surrounded," Decky said, laughing. "Welcome home, Aunt Charlie."

#

The family swarmed Charlie as soon as she opened the car door. Though her greeting was not quite as enthusiastic, Decky was subjected to a long series of hugs and "Welcome to the ranch" handshakes. There was no way Decky would remember all the names and relationships, so she quit trying. The "Hey you," method was looking like the way to go, as the never-ending stream of Warrens introduced themselves. Within seconds, Decky lost sight of Charlie, who was absorbed in the throng making its way toward the back patio.

Decky called it a patio because she had no other word for it. A slanted roof projected from the back of the house, extending over a large paved patio area. The roof connected to a thick brick wall, creating a room with big wooden barn doors on each end, folded back to let the air flow through. An interlacing belt system ran slow-moving, wide-paddle ceiling fans, more weapons against the oppressive heat. When Decky stepped inside, moved along by the family flock, she realized the brick wall was actually part of an outdoor kitchen. The cast iron double-doors of a large smoker were propped open next to a half-a-cow sized grill built into the bricks. There was a an old fashioned stone-oven for baking bread, and a commercial-sized gas stove with six top burners large enough to accommodate the huge steaming pots wafting the smell of chili through the air.

Cast iron pots, pans, and griddles, some the largest Decky had ever seen, hung along the wall over a long stainless steel countertop. One of the frying pans looked to be the size of a small car tire. Two big box-freezers, an ice machine, and a refrigerator stood in the shade of the main house, against the wall. Five long picnic tables were lined up side by side, down the middle of the floor. There were patio chairs and small tables scattered around. Decky had wondered how Charlie's family could all fit in one space. Now, she knew. They had their own mess hall and, at the moment, it resonated with conversations and laughter. Decky stood to the side, taking it all in.

A young girl, maybe eleven or twelve, sauntered up, looking much like Decky imagined Charlie had at that age. She eyed Decky up and down.

"Can you play softball?" The girl finally asked.

Decky smiled down at her. "Yes, I love to play softball. How about you?"

"Are you any good?" The inquisitor asked.

"I'm pretty good," Decky said, not sure where this was going.

"Aunt Charlie's friend, Lynne, was really good. She was on my team the last time she was here and we won."

"Decky can hold her own on the field. You didn't think I'd bring a bad player did you, Kayla?"

Decky turned to see Charlie had come to her rescue, but the miniature team manager's fears were not yet put to rest.

Kayla persisted. "Well, did she play college ball like Lynne did?"

Charlie knelt down close to the girl's ear. "Yes, she did, but I'm not telling which one. I don't want anyone to know how good she is, before we pick teams. Can you keep it a secret?"

Kayla took another look at Decky, obviously impressed. "Wow, she *must* be better than Lynne."

Charlie smiled up at Decky. "Oh yeah, she's much better than Lynne."

Kayla scampered off with her secret. Decky grinned at Charlie. "You didn't tell me Lynne was such a favorite around here."

Lynne was Charlie's ex. Decky only interacted with her twice, and neither experience was pleasant.

"Children see what they want to see," Charlie said. "Lynne spent time with Kayla, coaching her a little. You do that and you'll be her favorite soon enough. She lives, eats, and sleeps softball. You two should get along great."

"Now, who does she belong to?" Decky asked, trying to find some way to remember the kid's name.

"Kayla is my sister Debra's youngest. They live in Fort Worth." Charlie glanced around. "That's her over there." She pointed at a woman who looked a lot like Charlie's mother. Debra saw Charlie pointing and returned a wave, flashing a smile. Charlie redirected Decky's attention, pointing at a tall dark-haired man. "That's Daniel, her husband. They are both teachers." She pointed again, this time at a boy and a girl, about twenty-years-old, Decky guessed. "And that's Justin and Tiffany, her other kids."

Decky threw her hands up in surrender. "It's no use. I'm never going to figure this out."

Charlie's mother approached, reaching for Decky's hand. She patted it, saying, "We haven't overwhelmed you yet, have we?"

"No ma'am," Decky responded. "Thank you again for including me."

"What's one more when you have this many." Louise squeezed Decky's hand, smiling up at her. "I'm glad you could come. It's good to see Charlie happy again."

38

Charlie, who had been standing silently by, raised her eyebrows in surprise and then grinned at Decky, out of sight of her mother.

Louise released Decky's hand and turned to her daughter. "Why don't you show Decky around and then you two go get squared away in the RV? I'm going to start the steaks. Your Daddy and the rest will be coming in soon."

Charlie hugged her mother. "It's good to be home, Momma."

"I'm glad you're home, Charlie," Louise said, hugging her baby girl. "Now, go let Decky catch her breath. These kids are dying to know what's in those boxes you sent."

Charlie led Decky into the house, through the back door. They entered a mudroom with cowboy hats on a shelf above a row of neatly hung raingear and thick winter coats. Several pairs of thick rubber boots rested on a mat by the door. On the other side of the room, a heavy-duty washer and dryer sat beside what appeared to be a folding and ironing area. Freshly starched shirts hung from a rack near the washer, waiting to be put away.

Charlie commented, "I've sure done my time in this room."

Decky grinned. "You mean you can starch a shirt like that? You've been holding out on me."

"If you want your shirts starched or your jeans creased, we'll send them to the cleaners. I've ironed my last, believe me," Charlie said, leading Decky further into the house, describing what Decky was seeing. "That door leads to the pantry."

Decky could only imagine how big the pantry would have to be to store enough food for this crowd, because Charlie kept going through an archway that led into a large room.

"Just before I was born, all the walls were taken out in this area. Those posts are holding everything up," Charlie said, adding, "Kind of looks like a Cracker Barrel restaurant, doesn't it? I told Daddy they stole his design."

She was pointing at two large hand-hewed posts, connected to exposed matching beams across the ceiling. The immense wood-paneled room appeared to be divided for three purposes, food preparation, food consumption, and a place to relax when those needs had been met. Decky was standing in the kitchen area, which occupied a quarter of the space. Along the wall stood an upright freezer, a gigantic refrigerator, and two stoves. A wide tile countertop, covering deep large cabinets, created a preparation and serving area that included an oversized double sink. The counter took a right angle and connected with one of the posts, near the center of the room.

Charlie continued her tour guide spiel. "They needed a bigger kitchen because there were always so many people cooking and so much to cook. And then Daddy and the older kids made this table for Momma, so they needed a room big enough to hold it."

To the right of the kitchen area sat a long oak table, hand polished to a gleam, with twelve matching chairs. An antique buffet rested against one wall, with a pie safe and side table along the other. Over the buffet hung an oil painting of a young Native American man dressed in buckskins, with his arm around a beautiful young blonde wearing a Victorian nightdress. They stood on the bank of a shallow river against a background of bright stars, lit only by the glow of a small campfire at their feet. In the foreground, a man and child were silhouetted against the flames, their backs turned, gazing up at the smiling couple. Something about the smile on the buckskin wearing brave made Decky smile back.

"I like that painting," Decky commented.

"My mother's grandmother painted it," Charlie explained. "It's been hanging there since they built this house. Momma loves that painting. There are a few others around, mostly landscapes."

"Her grandmother was quite talented," Decky said, turning to see Charlie running the fingertips of one hand along the surface of table. "That is a beautiful piece of furniture," Decky said, admiring the craftsmanship. "Your father could make a living in woodworking."

"He had to find something for all those idle hands," Charlie said, as a way of explaining her father's talent. She was lost in the sentiment the family dining table held. "A lot of lessons have been learned here, and not just school work."

They moved on to the other half of the room. It was a large den area, with three couches grouped together in front of a sizeable TV on the wall. There were two matching recliners and a table with a reading lamp nearby. Decky surmised that was where Charlie's parents spent their time relaxing, watching over their brood. A very old upright piano stood in one corner, an acoustic guitar leaning in a stand beside it. Large cabinets were built into the long wall by the front door, with bookshelves above them filled with trophies, diplomas, pictures, and even some books. The other walls told the family history in photographs, ranging from the sepia tones of the eighteen hundreds to the vivid digital color of today. Charlie waited quietly while Decky slowly rounded the room, soaking up the images.

Decky stopped at the fireplace mantel in front of another oil painting, this one of a fireball-red Panhandle sunset. Under it was the infamous picture of smiling baby Charlie, naked on a white blanket, butt to the wind.

"Well, your description was perfect," Decky said, reaching for her phone. "That *is* a cute ass."

"I told you not to post that," Charlie said, trying to take the phone before Decky could take a picture.

Decky, at five-eight, was five inches taller than Charlie and easily held the phone out of reach. "I only want it for my screen saver," Decky said, laughing.

Charlie pawed at Decky's arm. "You will show everybody under the sun that picture, and you know it."

"Still in that can't keep your hands off each other phase, I see." Franny's voice caused both Charlie and Decky to jump away from each other, which made Franny laugh. "It's okay, it's just me."

"Stop laughing and help me get that camera away from her. She's going to show that picture to everyone," Charlie said, making a grab for the phone while Decky was off guard.

Franny, a slightly taller version of Charlie, refused to help. "Come on Charlie, that picture has been on the mantel for forty years. Why does it still bother you so much?"

Charlie made one more attempt to reach the phone, but Decky was watching and pulled it away at the last second. Charlie sighed, giving up. "Because I've been teased about it all of those forty years."

Decky could see that this was one of those childhood hurts that made no sense, but remained painful nonetheless. She put the phone back in her pocket. "Okay, okay, I won't take the picture."

Franny chuckled. "Oh, Decky, you are way too susceptible to her charms. You could have gotten mileage out of that picture. I know I have. I used to love to point it out to her boyfriends."

Charlie took her familiar pose when challenged – hands on hips, chin out. Decky usually agreed to or did whatever she was told, when the pose appeared. This time Franny was Charlie's target, to Decky's relief. It was also quite funny to watch the little sister defending her stance.

"Why am I the only kid with a picture like that? Where is yours?" Charlie demanded.

"I guess forty years is long enough for one joke," another female voice answered.

Decky turned to see a dark haired woman coming through the kitchen toward them. She looked like Charlie's mother, only taller. She opened her arms as she crossed the floor, smiling broadly.

Charlie closed the distance between them and clasped the woman tightly. "Hey, big sis. What took you so long?"

The woman hugged Charlie to her, answering over her shoulder. "Ranch business. I had to pay the boys before the holiday, so they'll be broke when they sober up and come back to work." She patted Charlie's back and then pulled her away to look at her. "You look fantastic, Little One. Are you ever going to get old like the rest of us?"

Franny winked at Decky, out of sight of the other two, and said, "Must be something in the water down there in Carolina, Mary."

"Must be," Mary said. "Would you bottle some and send it to me?"

"You look great," Charlie said, crossing back to Decky, pulling Mary with her. "Decky, this is the first born, Mary. She practically raised the youngest of us."

Decky extended her hand. "It's a pleasure to meet you, Mary."

Mary shook Decky's hand with a strong grip. "It's a pleasure to meet you, as well. I read your first two historical novels. I'm a fan."

Decky was not sure why it had never crossed her mind that someone in Charlie's family was one of her readers. She lived a very isolated life for a public personality. Decky did not travel much or do book readings often. She guest lectured at some local universities, but preferred to stay close to home. Her limited personal exposure to readers was through her public persona on Facebook, and other social networks. It always surprised her when she met a reader in the flesh. She sold books, so obviously she had readers, but still, she never expected to meet them, and certainly not in Charlie's living room.

"Thank you. I'm glad you enjoyed the books." Decky said, trying to remain calm.

Her mind, however, was racing. Mary said the "first two novels." That meant she either had not read the semi-autobiographical, coming-out novel Decky published about how she and Charlie met, or she had read it and chose not to mention it. If Mary had Googled Decky, then she knew for a fact that Decky was a lesbian and Charlie was her lover. Decky never identified Charlie completely, but it would not take much digging to figure it out. After the big court case, two years ago, Decky had no choice but to go public with her sexuality. Her publicist told her it did not appear to hurt Patricia Cornwell's image when she came out, so Decky went with honesty rather than subterfuge. It was a freeing experience, not having to pretend or hide, and up to the moment had not presented any problems. That was then, this was now.

Decky's worst fears were realized, when Mary said, "My kids gave me a Kindle for my birthday. I'll have to go online and order the rest of your collection. I really enjoy your humor. I read your blog."

Charlie's eyes widened. Evidently, she too had not thought of someone in her family looking Decky up on the Internet, let alone reading her very personal and politically liberal blog.

Mary added to the stress, when she said, "We're pretty conservative around here –" The pause was so long, Decky was sure she drew an audible breath before Mary continued, "but I have to admit you have opened my eyes on some issues and you made me laugh while doing it. Plus, I get a slice of Charlie's life." She turned to the shocked Charlie and hugged her again. "I sure have missed you. Don't stay gone so long next time."

Charlie looked past Mary, shrugging her eyebrows at Decky. She was as taken aback by all this as Decky was.

Franny interrupted the hug. "Well, Mary, are you going to tell her or am I?"

Decky was almost afraid to hear anymore. Things were going well so far. Charlie's mother seemed to have blessed their union, and now Mary was making a gesture of support. Neither of the women came right out and said they knew the exact nature of Charlie's relationship with Decky, but it was implied her presence was welcomed. However, Decky was a little too suspicious by nature. Growing up with Lizzie had made her cautious when things were going too well. The other shoe was bound to drop at some point. Apparently, her apprehension was rubbing off on Charlie.

"Tell me what?" Charlie asked, a bit of trepidation in her voice.

Decky was temporarily relieved of anxiety, when Mary walked toward the mantel and picked up the baby picture of Charlie.

She started dismantling the frame, while she talked. "Charlie, when you were a baby, you were enamored with this picture. When you were old enough to talk, you started announcing with pride that it was a picture of baby Charlene. Then one day a little friend made fun of it and you threw the biggest fit." She looked over at Franny, asking, "What was she, four or five-years-old?"

"I was seven, so she was four," Franny answered.

Charlie's jaw began to hang open.

Mary started working the picture out of the frame. "Momma wanted to tell you the truth, but the rest of us decided you needed a lesson in humility."

Franny giggled. "And it always got a rise out of you, so we just kept it going."

"What?" Charlie said, her hands back on her hips.

Mary wrestled the picture out of the frame and turned it around, showing it to Charlie. On the back, written in ink were the words, "Joseph, age four months, 1968."

Charlie was speechless. Franny and Mary burst out laughing, with Decky not far behind. Charlie raised her hands, as if she were going to make a point, and then just shook her head.

"Good one," Charlie said, laughing too. "You got me."

#

They toured the house with Charlie's sisters. The remaining rooms off the Great Room consisted of three bedrooms and two bathrooms. Decky wondered how the family managed with so few rooms during the full-house years. Her answer came when she was led to the fully finished basement bunkhouse. Three sets of bunk beds were arranged along one of the walls. Study and play areas were delineated by bookshelves filled with board games and the old version of an Internet search engine, a set of World Book Encyclopedias. The walls were decorated with more paintings depicting Native American and pioneer scenes.

The room was large and made larger by an additional space that Decky surmised was situated under the patio above. A thick, heavy door was standing open, revealing a locker room style bathroom with multiple showers and sinks. The tiled space was vault-like.

Charlie explained, "This bathroom is also the storm shelter." She pointed at a door at the end of the room. "That closet is stocked with everything we'd need to survive and get out."

"I guess this is a necessity out here in Tornado Alley. Sort of gives me a new perspective on Dorothy and Auntie Em," Decky said.

Mary commented, "If you ever see the damage left by an F-four tornado, you'll never look at that movie the same way. But then you have hurricanes to deal with on the Outer Banks, don't you? Do you and Charlie have a shelter to hunker down in?"

Charlie saved Decky from the sputtering she was about to do, answering, "Hunkering down is not the best idea out there, Mary. We'd drown from the storm surge."

Decky did not want Mary to think her little sister was in danger. She reassured her, "I built my house to sustain considerable wind and water, but I'd never ask Charlie to stay if it was life threatening."

Mary smiled, saying, "That's good to know."

Franny burst forth with, "Mary, you have got to see where Charlie is living. That house is unbelievable."

Charlie suddenly became uncomfortable with the conversation and started explaining the Warren family living arrangements. "My parents were upstairs with us girls, Mary and Debra in one room, Franny and me in the other, and all the boys stayed down here."

Mary took the hint and went along with the change of subject, saying, "There were different configurations over the years, but when we were all out of the crib, this was how we fanned out. The kids have sleepovers down here now and an occasional down on his luck cowhand will stay from time to time."

"Looks like your parents managed everything just fine with ten children. I barely survived one. I'm in total awe," Decky said.

Franny laughed. "I'm drawn to moments of introspection these days. I've decided, after much careful thought, and the living hell that is my life with a sixteen-year-old daughter, that our parents survived because they kept their sense of humor."

Laughing, the women ascended the stairs, Decky in the back of the pack. She observed the sisters chatting easily, as if no time had passed from their last meeting. Charlie's accent was showing a little more than usual. Years of trying to hide her native twang started melting away. Decky could hear the natural family harmonies, as Charlie's voice began to blend with her sisters' western drawl. Charlie had not stayed near home like most of the others, leaving at eighteen for college on the east coast, but part of her never left the Panhandle. Decky was seeing it now. Along with her accent, there were subtle changes in Charlie's body language. Decky could not quite put her finger on it yet, but she was sure she was about to see a side of Charlie she had never seen. Cowgirl Charlie held possibilities, which caused Decky to grin.

Charlie waited for Decky at the top of the stairs, while the other two walked ahead, out of hearing range. She tilted her head, smiling slightly, and whispered, "Why are you grinning?"

"No reason," Decky said, but her grin grew larger.

"You're not planning something, are you? You have that look and that means trouble."

"Nope, not planning a thing. Just taking it all in," Decky replied.

"Well, just in case you get any ideas," Charlie said, as they followed the sisters who had just exited out the backdoor.

"Riding bareback naked is not as romantic as it looks. Skin that never sees the sunshine chafes, if you get my drift."

Decky winced. "Ouch. Thanks for ruining that little romantic fantasy."

Charlie stopped at the door, turned, and smiled at Decky. They were alone for the moment. She winked and said, "Go ahead, keep working on those fantasies, just cross that one off your list."

Decky grinned. "Just tell me, when you did this naked bare-backing, were you wearing only a cowboy hat and boots?"

Charlie backed out the door, shaking her head. "I am so, so glad I cannot see inside your head. Really, I am."

#

After some of the nieces and nephews helped carry the luggage from the car to the RV, Charlie loosed the Warrens on the gift boxes. Leaving the family to their plunder, Decky and Charlie climbed into their temporary residence, and were finally completely alone. It was not a giant recreational vehicle, but it was modern and the space was theirs. A small couch, kitchenette, full bathroom, and a bed, what more could they need. The air conditioning was on and the blinds pulled tight against the still blazing sun. It was six o'clock in the evening, seven o'clock back home on the east coast where the sun was going down. It only seemed to get hotter as the day progressed, leaving Decky wondering if the sun ever set out on the Panhandle. Charlie had told her it could still be in the nineties at midnight. Decky decided her "living in a kiln" analogy was spot on.

She sat down with a heavy sigh at the small kitchenette table, not realizing how tense she was until she relaxed in the quiet, away from Charlie's family. When Charlie told her the numbers would be daunting, Decky had no idea how true those words would turn out to be.

Charlie stepped between Decky's legs, placing her arms around her shoulders. "I know you're tired. Everybody will go to bed or home early tonight. We have a lot to do tomorrow." She gave Decky a sweet little kiss, and then continued, "You only have to stay awake a few more hours."

Decky's lips curled into the grin that she seemed to have been wearing for two years. Charlie always made her smile. "I'll be fine," she said, pulling Charlie closer. "Just give me a kiss to tide me over."

"Just a kiss, right?" Charlie teased. "We wouldn't want you all hot and bothered while you're eating dinner with my family."

Decky's grin widened. "I've been a little hot and bothered since that cowgirl twang started creeping back into your accent."

"Well, it's a good thing I brought my boots, isn't it?" Charlie answered, and then leaned in for a kiss that threatened to delay dinner. She finally pushed Decky away, saying, "Okay, that's going to have to hold you for a bit."

Decky released her, not because she wanted to. She could never get enough of Charlie, but someone was knocking on the RV door. Charlie went to answer it. Decky heard Louise's voice before she could see her.

"Honey, your daddy's come up from the barn. It's time to eat." Louise climbed the two steps into the cabin, the aroma of grilling beef following her in. "And I brought this for Decky." She was carrying an old stationary box, which she placed on the table. "I think this might clear up those questions you've been asking about Merdy."

"Merdy?" Decky asked, not sure to whom Louise was referring.

"Meredith Ethridge. People called her Merdy."

Decky was confused. "I thought Meredith was a man. I thought he, uh, she was your great-grandfather."

Louise smiled, patting the top of the box. "It's all in there. Read it. You'll understand after you do."

"But you told me his wife's name was Grace," Decky said, trying to process the information rationally.

"When you've read everything in this box, we'll talk," Louise said, the gold flecks in her eyes sparkling with a secret. "I think it's time this story was told. I think maybe you are the one meant to tell it." She turned to Charlie, who was totally clueless, judging by the look on her face. "My grandmother always said the creator would send messengers into your life to show you what you already know, but cannot see. I have been haunted by dreams of her for weeks now."

Charlie stepped forward, reaching for her mother's arm. "Momma, are you all right?"

"I'm fine, Charlie, healthy as a horse. I'm not crazy either. I spent a lot of time with my grandmother. She believed there were spirits all around us, guiding us. I never talked about it much, but I believe we see things in dreams that warn us or point us down the right path."

Decky thought about the arrow through her heart and vowed to stay completely away from any canyons.

Charlie steered her mother toward the couch. "Sit down a minute. They can serve themselves if they get too hungry."

Louise resisted. "You know your daddy won't start without me." She pulled Charlie's hand from her arm and pressed it between her palms, turning back to Decky. "I was entrusted with this story by my grandmother, and told not to share it until the time it would be understood. I think that is why she came to me in my dreams. I believe that time is now." She released Charlie's hand and kissed her cheek. "Come on, let's go have a steak."

Louise exited the RV, leaving behind two speechless women.

"I had no idea your mother was so spiritual," Decky finally commented.

Charlie turned around, her mouth still hanging open. She closed it to say, "What in the hell was all that?"

Decky shrugged. "I don't know. She's your mother."

Charlie grabbed Decky's hand, dragging her toward the door. "Come on."

"Wait. I took my shoes off. Hang on," Decky said, trying to slip her feet back in her boat shoes.

Charlie was anxious. "Hurry up. The sooner they eat, the sooner they get sleepy and go to bed."

"Why the sudden rush?"

Charlie pointed at the box. "It's going to drive me nuts, until I know what's in there. I've seen that box in the fire safe. Momma said it was just family papers."

"Are you worried what we will find?" Decky asked, joining Charlie at the door.

"My mother is having visions that her long dead grandmother wants you to tell a story based on what you find in that box. Yes, I think that is cause to be concerned."

Decky tried to make Charlie laugh. "Don't worry. I have only a small niche following in Lesbian Fiction. It won't make the New York Times Best Sellers List."

Charlie froze with her hand on the door handle. "Lesbian what? She didn't say it was a lesbian story."

"Well honey," Decky explained, "she said Merdy was a *she* and she already told me *she* had a wife named Grace. What do you think the story is?"

Charlie crumpled in the stairwell. "Oh my, God. She's trying to tell me she knows. That's what all that 'glad to see Charlie happy again' stuff was, and Mary reading your blog. Shit, I do not want to have this conversation. I like it the way it is."

Decky doubted that was true, and said so. "You like it that your brothers and sisters can openly love their spouses, while you have to talk in code, calling me your 'friend.' Maybe your mom is trying to tell you that you don't have to do that anymore. Of course, your family knew Lynne was more than your 'friend' for ten years, and now they know I am."

"I know that, Decky. I'm not dense. It's just been so easy not to talk about it."

"What are you afraid of, Charlie? Are you afraid they won't love you? I don't see that happening."

Charlie answered honestly, "I don't want to deal with it, if it does."

"At least, I don't think we're in danger of having the windows shot out of the RV," Decky said, referring to her own mother's initial reaction.

Charlie laughed, despite her current state of panic.

"That's my girl," Decky said, smiling. "Remember, Franny said you had to keep a sense of humor."

Charlie stood up and brushed herself off, readying to exit into the fray. "Right now, I'd rather be dealing with her teenage daughter than this."

Decky remembered being a high school teacher and the mother of a sixteen-year-old. She nudged Charlie out the door, saying, "Trust me, this will be easier."

CHAPTER THREE

"No Man's Land. No truer words were ever used to describe a place. I find myself in the most dire of circumstances, torn between duties born of lineage and longing to be back in my adopted home. Oh Paris, the city of light, how I long for thee on this wretched dark night. The loneliness of the prairie envelops me and I dream of you. I was plucked from the very heart of civilization, where I was bearing witness to the birth of a new millennium, and summoned here to the end of the world. Tied here by blood I scarcely remember and, in all honesty, tried desperately to forget. This may be the land of my origin, but I have seen the world now, and this desolate strip of sand and prairie grass, this No Man's Land, is the last place under the heavens I would choose to be. Thora Ethridge, July 1, 1905, Beaver City, Indian Territory."

Decky stopped reading aloud.

"Wow, that's a bit dramatic, don't you think?" Charlie commented while seated next to Decky on the bed, leaning against the headboard.

"It wasn't unusual for a writer to be a little melodramatic in 1905," Decky said, adjusting the pillows behind her back.

They had recently retired to the RV, after filling up on steak and family stories. Decky had now met all the brothers and sisters, except the oldest brother, Bobby, and his wife, Karen. Louise made excuses for them, but Charlie seemed suspicious. She did not question her mother, but Decky could tell it bothered her. Franny had hinted that the new sister-in-law was at the heart of Bobby's absence, but there had been no time to elaborate in private. There were just too many people around.

Although she could remember few of their names, Decky's first interactions with Charlie's family had been enjoyable. They loved to laugh and treated Decky as if she were just another family member home for a visit. Some of Decky's earlier apprehension began to subside. Maybe Charlie was right, no one really cared about her personal life, but then there was the box and the unexpected conversation with Charlie's mother. Decky also had a strange feeling that Bobby's absence foretold of a storm brewing in the Warren clan.

Decky's background in theatre enhanced her observation skills. She spent the evening watching body language, recognizing some of Charlie's mannerisms in her siblings, like the tilt of her head when she was puzzled and the way her grin curled up higher on one side. They all seemed to enjoy each other's company, something unfamiliar to Decky's own family gatherings. From what she could tell, the brothers looked alike, except for Joseph. The two oldest sisters, Debra and Mary, favored the boys. The first seven born had Buck's tall, lanky cowboy body combined with Louise's light brown hair, darker skin tone, and warm brandy colored eyes shot through with honey-tinted starburst. Charlie, Franny, and Joseph, the youngest three, had Buck's startlingly big blue eyes and blond hair, a product of his Germanic roots, but they were shorter in stature like their mother.

When Decky commented on the last three siblings being blondes, Charlie replied, "Daddy says he finally conquered that Comanche blood with us last three."

Decky thought old Buck might be right, but she still wasn't sure about the Comanche bloodline, something she hoped to answer with the contents of the box waiting in the RV. Charlie must have been thinking about the box, as well. After a socially acceptable time, Charlie asked forgiveness for going to bed early, claiming to be too tired to stay awake one minute longer after the long day of travel. In reality, Charlie had torn into the box as soon as the RV door closed behind them. There were pictures, land deeds, old letters, and what appeared to be a handwritten manuscript. The passage Decky just finished reading was the lone paragraph on the first page.

Charlie waved a land deed at Decky. "What does all this mean? You're the expert. What do you see here in all this old paper?"

Decky lowered the manuscript to her lap and took the deed from Charlie. "Here's what I know, not what I'm guessing, but what I have seen evidence to suggest is true. Your mother gave me the family tree, which included Meredith Ray Ethridge, who had a wife named Grace and a daughter, Thora. That was all I had to go on. M. R. Ethridge was listed on the first territorial census of Beaver County in 1890, male, age thirty, living alone, and again in 1900, still alone. I could not find her after that, so I tried to find earlier records. I found a young Meredith on the Indian rolls, living in the household of Royal Ethridge. The entry listed this person as male and the age was right, but this was a Chickasaw family, living near Fort Arbuckle in the Chickasaw Nation. Your mother said she was Comanche. I have another record, just a note, really, found in the fort Quartermaster's journal dated, May 2, 1860. Here, let me show you."

Decky reached for the laptop lying next to her on the bed. Charlie yawned and stretched.

"Honey, you're tired. We can look at this tomorrow," Decky said.

Charlie snuggled up under Decky's shoulder. "No, I can't sleep now. Tell me what you found."

Decky positioned the laptop so Charlie could see. She opened a folder and then a file containing a scanned document. Decky paid a researcher to scour the Oklahoma archives in person a few months back, which produced the image they were now examining on the screen.

"Can you see?" Decky asked.

"Read it to me. My eyes are tired," Charlie replied through another yawn.

Decky knew Charlie would be asleep in a few minutes, but she read anyway. "The notation said, 'Babe born to Indian horse trader, Royal Ethridge, on the post last night. Much lamenting and wailing by the natives followed, as the babe's mother, Mary McGill Ethridge, passed shortly after. The child's name is Meredith Ray. God have mercy on the family in this time of sorrow.' That has to be her, but there is no reference to the baby's gender. Your mother was very adamant that Meredith or Merdy was a woman. I think the contents of this box might explain the discrepancy."

When Decky received no return comment, she looked down at Charlie, finding her already fast asleep. She gently rolled Charlie onto the pillow and slid out of the bed. Repacking the contents of the box, she moved it to the floor by the couch up front, taking her laptop along. She went back to tuck Charlie under the covers and turn out the lights, but she did not join her. The unread manuscript would never let her sleep. She knew she would lie awake wondering what secrets it held.

Decky sat down on the couch and pulled the manuscript out of the box. She read the first paragraph again, sensing the isolation of the author. She turned the page and began to read, drifting further back in time with each word.

#

I began this story with the paragraph on the preceding page, because I want to remember in the end, where I was in the beginning. My actual entrance into the world took place on July 5, 1875, thirty years ago today, here in this very room where I sit penning these words to paper. The candlelight, by which I write, dances shadows across the page and I can scarcely locate the ink. It is well past midnight. The rocker where I keep my silent vigil sways there in the corner, so recently was it abandoned. I must have drifted into slumber, only to be driven awake by a vision. So vivid was my dream, I sprang from my post and am seated here now, fulfilling the prophecy the images foretold.

Four days ago, when I returned to this place, I would have dismissed this dream as the product of my recent dietary vicissitudes. How naïve, how utterly untouched was I by the very blood that sired me. My ears were deaf, my eyes blind. I maintained a happy existence, with no thought to my heritage. I was content to play the part of the mysterious woman, flitting about Paris as some exotic creature of unknown origin. Shown the savagery of my people by well meaning Christians, I shunned the spiritual world of my ancestors. I buried my native past with each passing decade, distancing myself from

58

what I deemed a horribly ignorant society. I am shamed now, by my behavior. I have opened my ears. I have opened my eyes. I saw the visions clearly, and I know what I must do.

Tonight I dreamed of a child, a child that will someday come to hear this tale. It is to her that I write. I know not the time or place of its unveiling, but the dream made it clear, a record must be made of what happened here. And so, the tale opens where it began for me, the day I arrived from Paris.

"You sure you want me to leave you way out here, Miss?" The young man hired to drive my carriage asked, as we bumped down the dirt path.

Sand hills and prairie grass were all I beheld for miles. The utter desolation of the place contrasted with the cobbled streets and cafes of Paris still fresh in my mind, and rapidly darkened my already black temper.

"This is the last place I would choose to be abandoned, but alas, here I am and there is nothing to be done about it." I sighed heavily. "Nothing to be done, nothing at all."

"What could a lady like you want with ol' Merdy? You ain't exactly what I was expectin' when Mr. Lane hired me to drive you out here."

I adjusted my parasol and wide brimmed hat against the burning rays of the sun so foreign to my flesh, the tanned skin of my childhood having faded years ago. Even in this baking desert heat, I tugged upward on the long gloves covering my hands and forearms, fearful the dusky tint of my natural coloring would reappear. I could not return to Paris a dark skinned native. No, that certainly would not do.

"And what, pray tell, were you expecting? Mr. Warren, is it?" I asked with slight trepidation at what his response may be. I had no notion of what lay in store for me. I had not stepped a toe in this God forsaken land in twenty years.

*"Yes, ma'am, name's Warren, but you can call me Sam."
He tipped the brim of his hat as a way of sealing the
introduction, and then continued, "Mostly old Indians and
cowboys go out to Merdy's. Sometimes a woman comes to stay
for awhile, but they ain't like you."*

*"I will not be staying," I stated emphatically. "I will
conclude my business and be on my way in a few days."*

*Sam scratched his chin. "I reckon I could come back day
after tomorrow, unless you plan on saddlin' one of Merdy's
stock and riding back to town."*

*"I have not been astride a horse since I was nine-years-
old. I shouldn't think it would be necessary to amend that now.
Yes, two days should be enough time to settle my affairs."*

*"I seen that paper on your trunk. Says you come from
Paris, France." Sam's curiosity was getting the better of him. I
had yet to answer his inquiry as to the purpose of my visit. He
persisted, "Would'a never guessed Merdy knew a fancy lady
from Paris, and to come all the way across the ocean, must be
pretty serious affairs."*

*"Though you may have meant no impertinence, I do
believe the term 'fancy lady' applies to the women on those
French postcards base men are so fond of. I assure you I am
not one of those 'fancy ladies' from Paris, if that is what you
are inferring."*

*Sam turned shy and bashful. "I meant no insult, ma'am."
He was suddenly seized with enthusiasm, his words gushing
forward. "I just never met a woman like you. The way you
dress in them fine clothes, and you talk with big words. I seen
pictures of fancy – uh, refined women, but I never thought I
would meet one in the flesh." He quieted, embarrassed by his
confession.*

*"Thank you, Sam. I'm sure you meant no disrespect," I
said, to ease his mortification, and since he insisted on*

carrying on a conversation, I seized the opportunity to gather information about my soon to be hostess. "How well acquainted are you with Meredith?"

Sam chuckled. "Well enough to know not to call her Meredith. I'd advise you to do the same."

His smile lightened my heavy heart. I returned it, asking, "Shall I come to bodily harm if I call her by her birth name?"

"Ain't never known anyone that did and remained standing." He chuckled and then quieted, his tone turning somber. "O'course, that was before Merdy took sick. Word spread. People been comin' from up and down the trail. Payin' their last respects, I reckon. Seems like a lot of folks care a might bit for that tough old woman. I didn't know she knew so many people. Dropped a banker from Kansas out here, just a day ago."

My interest was piqued. "Oh? If that was a Mr. Lynch, my business may be concluded today and that would be grand." I could barely contain my excitement at the prospects. "You may very well have me as your passenger on the return to town."

"I believe his name was Lynch. Nice fella. Said he knew Merdy for years."

"That's wonderful news," I said, delighted that I may not have to stay out in this desert. My elation lasted only moments, as Sam pulled the buggy to the left and proceeded down an even more unkempt road.

"That's Merdy's house up there on the ridge," he announced.

There were horse stables and a corral on the ridge, but I could see no house. There was only a short structure, not more than four feet above the ground, near a lone tree. Memories flooded back to me of an old sod house cratered into the prairie, with just the top half of the walls and tiny windows visible above ground.

I gasped. "Surely she has built a proper home by now?"

Sam shook his head. "No ma'am. Merdy's been living in that same sod dugout long as I've known her, and that'd be all my twenty-five years. I was born in the back of a wagon, over yonder by the river. My ma was poorly. Merdy nursed her and brought me into this world. We stayed on, 'til Pa found a section to settle not far from here."

"I remember your birth. I was no more than a babe myself, around six I suppose," I said, recalling the kind young couple from Georgia, a baby, and a wet spring. I almost allowed myself to smile, before I remembered the wet muddy floors, the snakes forced into the house by high water, and the ticks and fleas that followed.

I cried out in desperation, "How could Mr. Lynch have requested I come back to such degradation, after keeping me in splendor all these years?"

My driver studied me carefully, his expression an indication he thought me indeed a "fancy" woman kept by a rich banker. I hastened to correct his impression.

"Mr. Lynch took pity on a poor girl and removed me from this squalor when I was nine-years-old. I was sent to the finest boarding schools on the continent, and upon graduation was allowed to pursue my education in the arts overseas. Though I have not seen him since he deposited me in boarding school, as my benefactor, Mr. Lynch provided a generous allowance and opportunities I could have only dreamed of without his benevolence. I am forever in his debt, and therefore, when he requested my presence here, I had no choice but to obey."

Sam commented, "That was right nice of 'im, but I don't think this Mr. Lynch is the man you speak of. This man would have been just a boy when you were a girl." He paused to make sense of his new knowledge. "You say this feller took you from here. Does that make you Merdy's kin? I never heard her speak of you."

"That should tell you exactly how much blood I share with Merdy, as you so fondly call her. I have no such tender memories of her." I strained my eyes forward for any glimpse of my benefactor. "Oh, I do hope it is the proper Mr. Lynch. Maybe he sent a representative in his stead," I said, with sincerity brought by a clearer view of my former home. My eyes fell on clumps of grass and dry weeds protruding from its sod roof. "Surely such a kind, civilized man would not propose I sleep under a dirt ceiling."

"Awe, it ain't so bad," Sam reassured me. "Merdy's covered the walls inside with plaster and blankets. The linen dropped-ceiling keeps most of the dirt out of the air. I helped her put clapboards around the outside, and we added some glass windows a couple a years back. Got a good solid door and no cracks to speak of. It'll keep the big critters off ya' at night, anyway. She's got horsehair ropes on the ground to keep the snakes out. Not much you can do about the spiders and scorpions gettin' in though."

I felt as if I would swoon. Nearly dropping my parasol, I grabbed at my companion's arm, pleading, "Do not leave me here. I will make my presence known to the parties present and then return with you to town. If anyone wishes to meet with me, they can call on me at the hotel."

"Whatever you say, ma'am," Sam said, trying to repress a grin.

I repaid his joviality at my expense with a sharp, "Apply the whip, Mr. Warren. I should like to end this endeavor as quickly as possible."

Had I known what lay ahead, I would have slowed the carriage, taking in every breath, every clump of prairie grass. Had I not been blind, I would have seen the horses resting in the shade of the lone tree behind the house. If my ears could hear, I would have listened to the hawk above, crying me home. For home I had come, unaware the circle of my life had rounded its course, bringing me back to the land of my creation to begin again.

#

Decky put the manuscript aside, stood, and stretched. Her eyes were growing tired and she needed a break. The author, Thora, stated she wrote inside a dark sod house by candlelight. While legible, the cursive handwriting took careful attention to decipher, as the low-lighting conditions must have caused Thora's pen to stumble at times. The pages were over one-hundred-years-old, but careful preservation and the manuscript's obvious rare handling kept the ink dark and the paper supple. Luckily, Thora used an expensive cotton rag paper, another indication of the style of life to which she was accustomed before returning to the Panhandle. If she had written on the more acidic wood pulp paper of the era, large portions of the document would have disintegrated to dust by now.

The clock on the microwave displayed the time, eleven-twenty-two. Decky had been awake nearly twenty hours with the time change, not counting the short nap on the plane. She needed to walk off all the heavy food from the day. If she were home, she would have gone down to the lap pool, but as it was, she had only the unknown prairie outside to burn a few calories and wake up. Despite all the warnings from Charlie, Decky thought if she stayed in the lighted areas, she would be safe. She checked on the sleeping Charlie and then stepped out of the RV.

It was still oppressively hot. She smelled the chili, removed from the gas stove earlier and now simmering over a bed of covered coals. All precautions were taken to prevent a dreaded escaping spark. The dry grass crunched beneath her shoes. Decky understood more fully the power of the rainmaker con men that traveled this country during the Dust Bowl years. Rain was a rare and welcomed commodity around these parts.

"Step back non-believers, or the rain may never come." Decky sang the words to the old Tanya Tucker song under her breath, which started the tune playing in her head.

The temperature gauge on the now silent patio read ninety degrees. The hot winds continued to blow up from the south, as they had all day. The trees and brambles around the property were slanted toward the north, an indication the predominant winds were southerly, and more than likely hot and dry. Charlie had talked about northwestern storms that blew down out of the Rocky Mountains, bringing blizzards to bury the Panhandle. At the moment, Decky could not imagine the weather here as anything but hot, and would have welcomed a snowdrift or two.

She headed down the dimly lit driveway toward the barns, counting on the heavily trafficked area to discourage any predators lurking about. The moon was full, but it was still extremely dark out away from the glow of civilization. The one streetlight, halfway between Decky and the barn, added a large pool of amber light to the smaller pool cast by the light over the barn door. There were more pools of light down the driveway, but Decky could not see much more than shadows. Dim light was better than no light in her book, so she stuck to the center of the drive and proceeded. She could smell the horses, both the pleasant and not so pleasant odors associated with them. It was very quiet, almost eerily so. Even the insects were barely audible. She could hear the soles of her shoes crunching the dry ground beneath her, the silence surrounding her amplifying the sound. A coyote yipped, off in the distance.

A much closer answer followed. Still, they seemed far enough away not to cause Decky alarm, or at least that was what she told herself.

The Warrens had two dogs. Decky met them just before dinner. They were large, muscular, Blackmouth Curs, one with a yellow coat named Dolly, and a red-coated one named Reba. Decky knew about the breed because her grandfather had one on his farm when she was younger. They were great hunting and herding dogs, in addition to being protective, loyal, loving family pets. She let them smell Dixie's scent embedded in her shoes, and once the greetings were over, she played with them for a few minutes. Then Jennifer, or maybe her name was Nicole, whisked them away to be fed and, Decky assumed, bedded for the night. She had not seen the duo with the Country Music Hall of Fame names since then. That's why, when the two large shadows came bounding out of the darkness beyond the barn, Decky froze in a panic, sure the coyotes she had convinced herself were a safe distance away, were instead about to have her for dinner.

"Don't run, they'll knock you down and lick you to death."

Dolly and Reba reached Decky about the same time as the warm baritone of the man's friendly warning. The dogs licked her hands, as she peered into the shadows for the owner of the voice. Decky saw the tiny red glow of a cigarette coming toward her, just before the tall man with graying temples below his cowboy hat stepped into view. She had never met him, but Decky was sure this was Bobby. She had seen enough pictures to recognize him, even if he had not looked so much like the others.

The growing loudness of the yipping coyotes momentarily distracted Decky from the imminent introduction. They were closer. Two yips followed one, then three, and then more, until the howling began. Dolly and Reba lost interest in Decky's hands, their ears alert, tracking the movement of the pack, as the howling seemed now to swirl on the wind from all directions. The chorus reached a crescendo and then subsided for the moment.

Bobby took a drag from his cigarette and then let it fall to the driveway, grinding it out. He reached down, picked up the butt, and dropped it in his breast pocket. "Nasty habit," he said, with the grin of a younger man. "Quit years ago. Been sneaking a few lately. You'll keep my secret, won't you?"

"I saw nothing," Decky responded, grinning back.

He reached in his jeans pocket, retrieving a pack of gum. "Would you like a piece? Have to cover up the smell or my wife won't let me in the house."

"No, thank you," Decky replied, and immediately wondered if she should have taken it.

In Native American culture, a gift offered should be warmly accepted. She wondered if she had offended him, and then pondered why she would apply that culture to Bobby, more so than the other siblings. It struck Decky how native Bobby's profile looked, when he turned into the light to glance at his watch. She had seen his picture, but out here in the flesh, with his ruddy tanned skin, squint lines around his dark brandy colored eyes, and thick almost black hair, Bobby could have changed into buckskins and Decky would have believed she was seeing the ancestors Louise spoke of. Her examination of Charlie's oldest brother was cut short, when the dogs turned together at some sound Decky was unable to hear. Reba whined, while Dolly's chest rumbled with a growl.

Bobby reached down and petted the Reba's head. "Easy girls," he said softly.

"Aren't you worried the coyotes will attack the dogs?" Decky asked, rubbing Dolly's ear, which the dog approved of with a grunt.

"They won't go far from home. They know they need to protect what's near, not run off after a pack of coyotes. One or two coyotes might wander close, but they are no match for a Cur. That's why Daddy's always had them. They're good herd dogs and smart."

A bright light flashed a few hundred yards from the barn.

Decky jumped. "What was that?"

Bobby tipped his hat back and looked off where the light had just been. "Motion sensor strobes. If the coyotes get too close, strobe lights flash. Scares them off most of the time." He took a good look at Decky. "You must be Charlie's friend. I'm her brother, Bobby."

"It's a pleasure to meet you. I'm Decky," she said, shaking his hand. "Charlie was disappointed you were unable to come by earlier."

Bobby looked down at the ground, a sure sign he was lying, when he said, "Yeah, Karen, my wife, had something we had to do at church."

Decky could feel the tension in the air. At the mention of the word "church," the hair rose on the back of her neck. Decky questioned religion long before she met Charlie. It was not the message of faith, hope, and love that she turned from. She still believed in a higher power and spoke with it often. Her problem with organized religion stemmed from human history riddled with bloodshed, in the name of one God or another. Every civilization had a creation myth, all strikingly similar. How could one story be more genuine than the next, if they were all based on the need for humanity to explain its existence? How could a religion that touted, "Judge not, lest ye be judged," do exactly that from the pulpit, condemning those who do not believe exactly as they do? In Decky's mind, we were all on this big blue marble together and we had better figure out a way to respect each other's beliefs, or the only thing we could really believe in was more bloodshed in the name of faith.

Although Lizzie accepted Decky and Charlie's relationship, she still believed Decky was a big ol' sinner, but being a Christian, Lizzie said she had decided not to judge. Saying and doing were two very different things to Lizzie. The last time she brought up religion and Decky's reservation in hell for not only being a lesbian, but also her lack of Christian devotion on Sunday mornings, Decky retaliated with, "Shouldn't your religion be more about your relationship with God than mine? You might want to think about saving your own soul."

Lizzie had flushed red at Decky's comment. "I go to church every Sunday and ask forgiveness for my sins."

"Are you going to ask forgiveness for that shrimp dinner you just consumed? I read somewhere that makes you among the unclean. Oh, by the way, I've been meaning to ask. Did you sacrifice a lamb at the temple when I was born? I believe that's proper procedure according to that ancient text you're so fond of quoting."

"There is just no talking to you. You cannot be rational," Lizzie said, before storming off.

"I know exactly what you mean," Decky had yelled after her.

Now, with the recent onslaught of hate filled violence aimed at the gay community, and calls from the pulpit for the extermination of homosexuals, Decky was a little more than unnerved by the word "church" coming into play during an introduction. Bobby was not exactly a stranger, but Decky could feel something amiss. She did not fear violence from him, just words she did not want to hear. She had grown tired of the venom "church" people spat at her, simply because she loved someone. Decky tried a veiled attempt at humor, to gauge the seriousness of the situation.

"Monday night church. Do they suspend that during football season? I hear you kind of like that sport out here."

Bobby laughed, to Decky's relief. It was short lived, however.

"I usually only go on Sunday, but now Karen, she's there if the doors are open." Bobby made eye contact, the torn feelings very clear in his expression. He continued, "She's a very devoted Christian."

"I see," Decky answered.

There was no use pretending this man was not wrestling with how to handle his devoutly Christian wife and his lesbian sister. "Devoutly Christian" was usually code for right-wing fundamentalist in Decky's experience. This was why the family had been reassuring Charlie that they really did not care one way of the other about her sexuality. Decky suspected there had already been a family discussion, and Bobby was the odd man out. Decky thought maybe she was reading too much into the conversation and held onto to that hope. The last thing she wanted was to be the source of Charlie's family discord. She had enough of that in her own.

A yip began the chorus of coyote howls again. The dogs growled, peering at something down the driveway. Decky was actually glad to hear the howling, because it changed the subject.

Bobby looked out into the darkness. "Got some new foals in the barn. Heard this pack moving through over at my place. Thought I should make sure everything was locked up tight. Coyotes get a little bolder in foaling season. They won't take down full grown horses or cattle, but they kill a lot of foals and calves every year in this business."

Another strobe light fired. The predators were on the move, circling the perimeter.

"So you live nearby?"

"Just over that ridge about a mile." He pointed south, toward the river. "Where I should be heading. Sun comes up early every day."

"Yes, it does. Is it okay for me to be walking around out here?" Decky asked, scanning the horizon for more flashes. "I'm trying to burn off all the food I consumed today. I'm too full to sleep."

"Coyotes are basically cowards. They don't want anything to do with humans, not grown ones anyway. They prey on the weak and small. Don't wander into one of the barns or corrals. A few of these horses will hurt you, especially if they don't know you."

Decky reassured him. "Don't worry. I don't usually go looking for trouble."

Bobby moved on with his warnings. "It's been real dry, so there are lots critters coming in close looking for water. Stay in the lighted areas, and you should do fine." Bobby petted the dogs. "These two will keep you company. They're smart. They'll keep you safe."

"Thanks, I don't think I'll be wandering too far. It was nice to finally meet you, Bobby."

"It was nice to meet you too, Decky," Bobby said, tipping his hat and backing away. "Tell Charlie I'll try to get by to see her. Good night."

He turned and walked down the long drive, disappearing into the darkness. Decky stared after him, "I'll try to get by to see her," echoing in her brain.

"I'll try," Decky repeated to Dolly and Reba, who seemed to understand this newbie to the ranch required their services more than Bobby needed an escort to his truck. She heard the truck start and saw the headlights before he turned south toward his home. "That, girls, is a man torn between loyalty to his family and his new bride. I just hope his baby sister doesn't get hurt in all this and that I can keep my mouth shut. The mouth shut part is really important."

Decky had taken a couple of steps, following the path Bobby took. The coyotes sang out all around her, while a strobe popped just where Bobby's truck had been. The dogs growled in unison, with Reba unable to suppress a warning bark to the invaders. Decky took it as a sign to retreat.

"I think we'd better head back to camp, girls. The natives are restless and I am an unarmed tourist. I would be no help to you."

The dogs padded along beside her, as she made her way back to the RV, where it was parked near the back of the house. She stopped at the door before going in. It appeared Dolly wanted to follow her into the air-conditioned cabin. Something on the patio had distracted Reba, but Dolly was ready for a cool down.

Decky looked down at the panting dog. "I know it's hot and if it were up to me, you would be welcome, but I don't think ranch dogs are allowed in here."

"Their kennel is air-conditioned. She thinks you have food."

Decky jumped, startled by the voice. Christ, these people just kept popping up out of nowhere. She focused on the patio, where Buck was relaxing in a chair with Reba at his side.

He realized he had frightened Decky, because he said, "I'm sorry. I should have let you know I was here."

"It's okay. The coyotes have me a little jumpy," Decky said, walking over to Buck.

"Yep, woke me up. They're close tonight," Buck commented, before indicating the chair next to him. "Here, have a seat." Decky sat down, while Buck continued, "It's the drought, drives the prey animals in closer for water and food. The predators naturally follow."

"I just ran into Bobby down at the barn. He said he was worried about the new foals."

"I'm surprised he isn't sleeping down there. Reckon that new wife of his would frown on that. Lost a many a good ranch hand to a spouse that didn't cotton to ranch hours," Buck said, the corners of his mouth tilting into a grin, so similar to Charlie's.

Decky smiled back at him. "And yet you've been married fifty-four years. I hear you're quite the ranch hand yourself. How did you manage?"

"Louise and the kids stayed with me in the barn in the beginning, during foaling season, at least until we could hire some hands. We didn't have anything but the land, a barn, and a little two bedroom house, when we started off, so we all had to work. When he was old enough, Bobby took over the horse breeding. He's got a way with them, has since he could walk. It's a gift. He hasn't had much luck with women, but he's a hell of a horseman. He trained them two girls of his to be just like him."

"That's Melissa and," Decky paused, trying to remember. She gave up quickly. There were just too many possibilities. "I'm sorry, I can't recall her name."

"Amanda. She and her sister both got degrees in animal husbandry from OSU. They came back here to work on the quarter horse breeding program. We board and train, too. Got a good line of champion cuttin' horses going," Buck said, his pride showing.

"Must be nice to be surrounded by family that loves this place the way you do."

"If you believe Louise, her people have been on this land for thousands of years. My people came later, but we stuck. The homestead sod house is under your feet, where you sit. Louise's grandmother, Thora, left it to her in 1958, just after we were married. She lived over the ridge in that first two-bedroom house I mentioned, where Bobby's stands today, but Thora was born right here in a sod dugout. That old woman loved this place, kept that sod house solid and livable all her life."

Decky remembered Thora's lament at returning to this land of "desolation." She smiled, saying, "It must have had a great deal of meaning to her."

"Thora was half Comanche. She'd bring us kids out to the sod house and we'd camp out like old times. She'd tell us stories about the Indians and the buffalo that roamed here before the white men came." Buck chuckled and continued, "Of course as kids, we didn't know we were the white men she was talking about. We all wanted to be great warriors and ended up cowboys."

"You knew Thora when you were a child?" Decky asked.

"I grew up on the next ranch over. Thora helped my mother bring me into the world. I've known Louise since we could toddle around together. Swore I'd marry her when I was seven," Buck said with a grin.

"You're a man of your word then," Decky said, grinning back.

Buck's smile slipped a bit, when he continued his story. "Thora went crazy there at the end, moved out of the ranch house after her husband died, and up here to the sod house. Louise found her laid out with all her Indian trinkets on. I guess that's the way she wanted to go. She just laid down and died."

Decky thought about the author of the manuscript. She imagined that was exactly how this woman would have preferred to leave this world. Decky did not know the whole story yet, but it was evident that Thora had undergone a spiritual discovery upon her return to the Panhandle. Buck's clues just made Decky desperate to read more.

"She must have been a very spiritual person," Decky said.

Buck nodded. "She was, and educated too. She used to read to us, show us artwork in books, and tell us about faraway places she'd been. She was an artist, painted pictures all the time."

"I saw a few of her paintings in the house. They are quite well done," Decky commented.

"Louise has them hung up all over the ranch and there are still more in the old storm cellar. Like I said, Thora loved to paint." Buck paused, seeming to reflect on a memory. "She dearly loved this place, too. We finally had to do something about that sod house. Louise was afraid it would collapse on the kids. We were looking to build a bigger house by then, so we dug out the sod house and made it part of the basement."

Dolly and Reba raised their heads from the patio deck, ears alert, scanning to the south. The yipping followed shortly after, further away now.

"They're moving back toward the river," Buck said, nodding his head in that direction. "They'll follow the bed down to the next ranch, then come back by here just before dawn. With all the ruckus for the next few days, I 'magine they'll move on off 'til the ranch settles again."

"I guess living out here you have to know a lot about coyotes," Decky said.

Buck nodded. "If they stay out of my business, I generally let them do as they please. Animals are creatures of habit.

They do what works until it doesn't. If you want them to do something different, you have to tell 'em."

"That seems to hold true for people, as well." Decky said, a yawn catching her last words.

Buck smiled. "That it does." He unwound his lanky frame, standing, concluding their little chat with, "Well, time to get some sleep. Sun comes up early every day. Go on, girls, see to the horses." With no further instruction, the dogs trotted off toward the barn. Buck turned to look at Decky one last time, before entering the house. "You have a good night, now."

Decky's "Goodnight," followed his, but she remained seated for a moment.

Was she being paranoid? Was she reading between the lines too much? All she really knew with any certainty was Bobby seemed to be struggling with something, probably Charlie's sexuality and his new wife's religious convictions. Hell, there was no probably to it, and Decky would bet good money that Karen was behind the conflict, whatever it was. Mary more or less admitted she was okay with Charlie's lifestyle. If she read Decky's blog, then there was no doubt she was completely aware of the situation. From Charlie's reaction, she had not known what to think of Mary's comment either. Charlie's father just had what might be considered a cryptic conversation with her, and Charlie's mother insisted Decky read a century old manuscript, claiming a vision told her to. It seemed the subject Charlie was perfectly happy never discussing with her family had indeed come up. The question remained, how would Charlie handle it? With the heat and all the innuendo, Decky was beginning to wonder if she had fallen off the panhandle and into the fire.

#

Out on the Panhandle

Back inside the RV, Decky checked on Charlie, who was sprawled across the bed, breathing deeply, lost in dreamland. Decky let her be and returned to the couch. Opening the manuscript again, she began to read.

My arrival at the sod structure aroused no greetings. I remained in the carriage, unable to move. For now, being in full view of the place, the direness of my circumstances became more grim. The memories I held of my former home were mere glimpses after so many years, reduced to a cloudy series of images in my mind. I saw them, as a stranger would view them, with pity for the poor, half-dressed child, living in the dirt. Only one memory moved me. I knew the fair-haired woman smiling broadly, holding me high in the air, was my mother, though this was the only recollection I had of her. The fogginess of my childhood memories limited my knowledge concerning my mother, for no one had mentioned her to me in twenty years. One hazy image and a name were all I managed to carry with me. Grace, her name was Grace, and she was beautiful.

The carriage driver dismounted and made a survey of the grounds. A fire smoldered in a deep rock pit, designed to prevent sparks from escaping to the dry grass. I remembered the fear of fire suddenly, the terror of a wild-eyed child staring up at a wall of flame and a rider galloping by on a great black horse, sweeping me from the ground. The memory ceased as quickly as it had begun, when the driver called out to me.

"Nobody here but Merdy. She's still lying where she was when I was here last. Tseena said she ain't been up in quite a spell."

"I'm sorry, to whom are you referring, Mr. Warren? Who is this Tseena?" I asked from my perch, still safely in the carriage.

77

"He's an old Comanche, lives out here with Merdy. He and Merdy were friends back in the warrior days." He led the carriage over to a watering trough for the horse, and then approached me as if to help me to the ground, all the while still talking. *"Tseena showed up here a few years ago. Said the spirits showed him how to find this place."* Chuckling, he added, *"He also says they sent him a vision message for Merdy and when he remembers what it was, he'll tell her, and go back home. 'Course, Merdy had to tell me that, 'cause Tseena only speaks Indian."*

He held his hand out for me to disembark. I looked around and saw not a soul for miles. I did not want to leave the carriage, but I had been bumped and jostled for the last two hours and wanted desperately to stand. The dilemma ended for me, when the outstretched hand turned into two, and the deceptively strong Mr. Warren plucked me from my seat. I was aghast at his freshness.

"Is it the custom here to remove a lady from a carriage in such a manner?"

Sam blushed. *"Yes ma'am. If I didn't help you, you could catch your dress up on the step and fall in the dirt. I seen it happen. Sorry if I offended you again. I keep doin' that and I surely don't mean to."*

I was not without some pity for the young man. He was merely six years my junior, but he had a boyishness, a certain naiveté, making him seem much younger. I eased his suffering, saying, *"I will be prepared next time, Mr. Warren – Sam."* I paused to smile, so he would know he was forgiven, and then continued, *"but I would suggest you learn to explain yourself before applying your hands to a woman's waist in the future."*

"Yes ma'am," Sam said, excitedly. *"And if you could just tell me when I'm doing something wrong, I wouldn't mind. I want to learn how to be a proper gentleman. I'm thinking of*

heading up to Dodge City. I want to know how to act so's I don't stick out like a sore thumb in a big place like that."

"Dodge City is hardly a big place, Sam, and I doubt very seriously you would stand out at all."

Hoof beats prevented any further conversation, as two riders approached at breakneck speed. The great black steed of my memory charged forward, carrying its rider straight toward us. Surely, this could not be the horse I remembered. That animal would have been much too old to run as if the devil himself were after him. The man on his back urged him on, shouting, "Ha! Ha!" The great beast needed no such urging. He won the race with fifty yards to spare, coming to a sliding halt in a cloud of dust, just before it would have been necessary for the rider and steed to take to the sod roof.

The rider dismounted, leaping to the ground in a fit of laughter. He led the horse to the watering trough, rewarding its performance with a pat on the haunches.

"My, but you are a damn fine horse," he said.

The dismounted rider was tall, wearing the dusty dungarees of a field hand, but I could see his white shirt was made of fine linen. He lifted his hat, the standard variety I had seen on the ranchmen of the area, revealing fair hair and the face of a man I assumed close to my age.

Sam leaned closer. "That's the Mr. Lynch I told you about."

I was crushed. This could not be the Mr. Lynch, the kind older man I remembered. The rider turned to me and smiled. Another memory seized me. That smile, I had seen it before on a boy in a carriage, leaving here all those years ago.

The second rider reached his destination. The young Mr. Lynch called out to him, "Tseena, you owe me two buckets of water from the well for that defeat. If you would, I'm sure our guests would appreciate a cold drink."

I beheld an old Indian astride a paint pony. His weathered skin was dark and deeply creased with age. He looked too feeble to have an able-bodied man order him about, and I said so. "Clearly that was an unfair race. You ride a superior horse saddled in leather. This man rides a pony and is practically bareback, with his flimsy pad and dangling stirrups. The saddle alone gives you unfair advantage."

The old Indian grunted and rode away toward what I assumed was the river. Young Mr. Lynch strode over with the confidence attractive men exude, one of those gentlemen who clearly felt superior to all in his presence. His display of plumage, so common among the male species, did not sway me, a woman who had been in the company of gentry.

"Ah, Miss Ethridge, I presume," he began. "I trust your journey was not too taxing."

"And you are?" I asked.

"John Lynch, Jr., at your service, ma'am. I'm sorry, but my father has been delayed. He asked me to see that you were made comfortable, while you wait. He should be here in a few days."

I hardly heard his words, other than the declaration that I was to stay and wait for the senior Mr. Lynch to appear. "I assure you I would be most comfortable awaiting your father's arrival at the hotel in Beaver City."

"I'm afraid that will not be possible. My directions were to keep you here until my father makes his appearance. Sam, would you unload the lady's trunk?"

"As you wish, Mr. Lynch."

How quickly my recent admirer turned against me, more than willing to assist in my abandonment on the prairie at the word of this man.

"Do not touch my baggage, Sam, unless and until I ask you to do so. Mr. Lynch, is it your intention to hold me here against my will?"

"No ma'am, not at all. You are free to leave, if that is what you wish. My father did tell me to remind you that no further payments to your trust will be forthcoming, should you chose not to await his arrival."

"Here? I must stay here in this wilderness? Surely you misunderstood him."

"No, he made it quite clear. How shall we proceed, Miss Ethridge? I'll pitch in, if you don't have enough to pay Sam here for the ride back to town, but passage back to France might be a bit hard to come by. I suppose with that fancy education you could find a job teaching and make the amount necessary in a few years or more, that is of course if you don't eat or have a roof over your head. Then it will take much longer."

"How is it that you know so much of my personal affairs, Mr. Lynch? Does your father make a habit of discussing my finances with you?" I asked, delaying my commitment either way.

"I have been employed by my father at the bank. I have handled your trust for the last ten years, since I returned from seeing the world much like you have. I too was given the option of obeying a summons, or finding myself penniless on the street."

I was, at that moment, silently adding the total amount of the funds in my purse. I was allowed to withdraw only what was necessary for passage to this place. I had been judicious in my spending, but still there was not the sum needed to defy the man who controlled the coffers. This tightening of the purse strings had been the result of my reply to the older Mr. Lynch's initial request that I come to this place at once. I *answered his invitation with a return wire, relaying that I really could not leave Paris in the summer. The light was simply too perfect for painting. His second request was hand-delivered with passage aboard the ship Baltic bound for New York, and instructions I was expected to follow or be cut off from my trust. Now, here I stood again, reminded that my life was at the whim of another, and I was helpless to do anything about it.*

"I see that I have been given no choice in the matter. Sam, you may remove my trunk from your carriage."

Mr. Lynch chuckled, proud of his victory. "Now that we have that settled, would you care to see the accommodations?"

"Before we enter, what is ailing the woman in there? Is it catching, should I take precautions?"

"Tseena says Merdy is in a vision state. She has no visible signs of sickness, and is conscious enough to eat and drink at times, but mostly she sleeps."

"I have no notion why your father would want me here. I owe nothing to this old woman. I have neither seen nor corresponded with her in two decades. What possible reason could there be for me to be here to witness her death?"

Mr. Lynch's expression turned sour. "You really don't remember who she is, do you? You carry her name, and yet you have no feelings for her. Why Miss Ethridge, you owe Merdy everything, your very life to be exact. You've known only luxury since leaving here, and for that you will now pay homage to the one that made it so."

"How could such a woman, here in a grass covered hole in the ground, afford to provide for me in this way? I was under the impression it was your father who arranged for my trust."

He cupped his hand under my elbow, and escorted me toward the sod house door. "You appear to have been under quite a few erroneous impressions, one of them being your observation about my saddle. Evidently, you have forgotten racing with a Comanche warrior. I assure you the leather saddle is of no advantage."

I scoffed at his pronouncement. "I have no such memory. What Comanche warrior are you referring to, if I may ask?"

He stopped moving me forward and turned me into the gravity of his hazel stare. He said two words that sent a chill down my spine, "Your father."

CHAPTER FOUR

Decky awoke to Charlie standing over her. She had fallen asleep on the small couch with the manuscript on her chest. Bacon – she could smell bacon cooking. Her eyes opened a little more and she began to come around. She was not sure how long Charlie had been trying to wake her. She was already showered and dressed, though Decky could not quite make out what she was wearing through her haze.

"Decky, look at me."

Decky squinted. The burning in her eyes reminded her she had little sleep.

Charlie smiled. "Ah, there you are. You were snoring when I came out here earlier. You can go back there and stretch out in the bed, or get up and have breakfast."

"Are you cooking bacon?" Decky asked, not moving.

"No, they cook breakfast for the hands and family outside in the summer. It keeps the house cool." Charlie poked Decky's leg. "Are you going to come eat? It'll be a long time before lunch."

Decky moved the manuscript off her chest and lowered her cramped legs to the floor. "I'm up, I'm up," she said through her hands, as she tried to rub the sleep from her face. "What time is it?"

"It's late. The hands have already been here and gone to work. It's seven-thirty. The sun comes up early every day on the ranch."

"I've heard that," Decky said, peeking out through her fingers. She rarely rose before nine a.m., unless there was a very good reason. She was trying to think of one. "Seven-thirty? I think I've had about five hours sleep."

"How far did you read? Do you know anymore than you did when I fell asleep on you?" Charlie asked, sitting down beside her on the couch.

"I only know Thora Ethridge was not a happy camper when she arrived here in 1905. I didn't read much more than that."

"Is it that difficult to read? Is it slowing you down?"

Decky lowered her hands, after rubbing her eyes back to life. She turned and smiled at Charlie. "It's not that hard to read. My eyes were just tired, so I took a walk and ran into a couple of your kinfolk."

"Oh, really?" Charlie said. "These were actual people, right? Not some vision from your reading."

"I met Bobby."

Charlie's smile slipped. "Bobby was here?"

"He came to check on the foals. The coyotes were close. And then I ran into your dad. The coyotes were bothering him too."

Charlie may have thought to ask for details, but following her policy of not wanting to know the answer to some questions, she only said, "I slept right through it."

85

Decky could have explained more about her activities last night, but at the moment, she had just noticed what Charlie was wearing. Her tight white, scoop-neck tee shirt was tucked into jeans that were relaxed just enough to still accent her assets. The boots really made it work. Charlie had transformed into the little blond cowgirl that once roamed this ranch. Decky liked what she saw. She liked it a lot.

"Where's your hat?" Decky asked, unable to control her grin.

"Oh, I have a hat. I just need to get it from the house." Charlie reached over and patted Decky's knee, laughing. "From the look on your face, I can see you approve of my outfit. Get used to the tight fitting jeans and shirts that leave not much to the imagination. It's standard cowgirl fare."

"I'll bet they don't all look like that wearing it," Decky replied.

"Thank you. Now, are you coming to eat or going back to sleep?"

"I'm up. Just let me get a shower. You go ahead. I think I can find you, since you said half of them were gone already."

Charlie gave her a kiss on the cheek, followed with instructions. "Wear your jeans. We're going horseback riding." She stood up and started toward the door, still talking. "I'm about to see if you can walk in those new boots you bought."

Decky thought about the boots. She made Charlie go shopping with her and point out a good ranch boot. She did not want to look like an urban cowboy or worse, a tourist. She'd made so much fun of visitors at home, who were trying to blend into the beach crowd and doing it badly, she'd hate to think of the locals around here having a laugh at her expense.

"Maybe I'll just wear tennis shoes. I should really break the boots in some, before I try to spend all day in them." Decky said, trying to think of a plausible excuse.

Charlie had a knack for reading Decky's mind. She shrugged and said, "They'll make more fun of you if you get snake bit on the ankle, with a perfectly good pair of boots in your suitcase."

"I'll wear the boots," Decky quickly replied.

"Good," Charlie said, her hand on the door handle. "You're not the only one with cowgirl fantasies."

Before Decky could respond, Charlie made her exit. That was inspiration enough to shake off the fatigue and send Decky into motion. Spending a day with Charlie on the ranch seemed like a fine idea, mighty fine indeed. Decky started to notice that her inner voice was sounding more and more like lines from a B western. She had always been a John Ford fan and made a habit of watching westerns with her dad. Through researching Charlie's genealogy, Decky discovered the western expansion was not quite as romantic as the movies and public school history books had made it seem. Reading from the Native American perspective about the removal from their homelands to Federal reservations was enlightening and heartbreaking. It was a no-win situation for the tribes. One point really resonated with Decky, one that was hard to ignore. The Native Americans were never the first to break a treaty with the US Government, not once, while the "great white fathers" failed to fulfill the promises they made in almost every instance. Even today, there were ongoing lawsuits filed by the tribes in an effort to recover what was promised them.

Decky showered quickly, her mind racing. Her attention deficit disorder was in high gear this morning. She flitted from one subject to another in rapid succession. From broken treaties, she switched to what she read last night. The story basically amounted to a spoiled, rich girl being called home to pay the piper, but it hinted at so much more. Abruptly, she remembered the coyotes howling all around her. Decky was back on the dark drive, listening to the pack as they circled the ranch looking for a way in. Then Bobby's anguished expression flooded her mind. He was definitely a man torn between two loyalties. Reba and Dolly were suddenly there, sitting with Buck on the patio. Charlie's father was anxious too. Maybe it was the coyotes, maybe not. Maybe he was worried about Louise's visions. Vision. Decky needed to have her eyes checked. It was probably time for reading glasses. She could not read as long as she used to without a break. Boom! Her thoughts jumped right back to the manuscript and the image of the man leaping from the great black stallion in a cloud of dust. She saw his boots first, before her reflection in the full-length mirror on the bathroom door interrupted her thoughts.

Decky was standing next to the bed. She was wearing a blue tee shirt with an Outer Banks logo across the chest, nowhere near as tight as Charlie's. Comfort was going to win out over fitting in for Decky. The shirt was fine, but the rest of her outfit needed work. Her missing jeans were the first clue, since she wore only underwear and boots beneath the tee shirt. While Decky's brain was hopping from one subject to another, she had somehow missed a step in the dressing process. This was her life now at thirty-nine. If her current state was any indication, Decky could see her middle-aged-self walking around without pants, blissfully unaware.

She leaned against the wall and took a deep breath. She needed caffeine to slow her brain down. ADD was both a blessing and a curse. When she was able to regulate it, Decky could accomplish many things, but when her mind ran so fast she could not pick a single thought to focus on, she could feel her anxiety spinning out of control. She took no drugs for the condition, choosing to manage the disorder through diet and exercise. When she left her home and more things were out of her control, the anxiousness rose and the symptoms worsened, one of the many reasons Decky hated to travel. Her normal solution to an onslaught of racing thoughts was a mile in the lap pool. That was not an option, so she was going to have to rely on coffee, and lots of it. While coffee sped most people up, caffeine slowed Decky's ADD brain down.

The uncertainty of what she would discover next in the manuscript and what was happening with Charlie's family fueled her apprehension. Decky just hoped she would not do or say anything to make the situation worse. After another deep breath, she removed the boots, slipped on her jeans, and put the boots back on. The heels were only an inch-and-a-half high, but they caused her to stand very erect, which made her feel much taller. She took a few steps and immediately noticed the difference in her gait. She decided right then that the cowboy swagger had a lot to do with the boots. With a hat, Decky thought she might be able to swing a little swagger herself, if she could just have some coffee and get a handle on her anxiety.

She saw her reflection in the full-length mirror on the bathroom door. She tipped an imaginary hat at her image, grinned, and quoted John Wayne's acting advice, "Talk low, talk slow, and don't say too much."

#

"Well, look at you. Half beach bum, half cowgirl, it looks good on you," Charlie said, when Decky took the first step out of the RV. "I was just coming to see what was taking you so long."

"I forgot my pants," Decky replied.

Charlie shook her head. "I'm not even going to ask. Come on. You need some coffee."

"Is it that obvious?" Decky asked, following Charlie toward the patio.

"You're in unfamiliar territory, you can't go jump in the pool, and you're anxious. Thank God, we left Lizzie home. You'd be climbing the walls." Charlie said, with a smile.

Decky laughed. "You know me pretty well."

They rounded the brick wall, where the aroma of breakfast on the prairie permeated the air. There were groups of adults standing around, chatting while finishing their coffee. The younger adults and teenagers, clumped together at the other end of the patio, looked less enthused about the early hour. An attractive brunette Decky had met before but could not name, walked toward them holding a plate piled high with scrambled eggs, fried potatoes, more bacon than one person should eat, and a biscuit the size of a fist, dripping butter from its edges. How these people stayed so thin was beyond Decky. Ranch life must have been hard work to burn all those calories.

"Here you go. Last plate of the morning," the woman said, setting the plate down on a nearby table. "Would you like some sausage gravy on your biscuit?"

Was she kidding? There was a heart attack waiting to happen already on the plate. Decky glanced over at the pans being readied for cleaning. They glistened with the remnants of the fat the meal was cooked in. Now this woman was suggesting Decky let her pour more flour and grease over the top of what was already on her plate. Since she and Charlie started eating healthier, the fat laden diet of her past had given way to more vegetables and lean meats. Maybe all of Lizzie's raving about the heart attack Decky was destined to have, since it "ran in the family," was finally getting to her, because what two years ago would have made her mouth salivate, at the moment looked more like first class ticket to the cardiac ward.

Decky smiled through the sick feeling the image gave her. "No, thank you. This looks great."

"Well then, could I interest you in a cup of coffee, or a glass of milk?"

Charlie spoke up. "I'll get it. Sit down, Kim. Talk to Decky. You've worked hard enough already this morning."

Decky sat down at the picnic table, the massive plate of food in front of her. Kim sat down opposite of her, looking tired already and it was barely eight-thirty. Decky knew she was one of the sister-in-laws, but that was as far as her knowledge went.

Kim pushed her graying bangs away from her face, smiling at Decky. "You go ahead and eat. Don't feel like you have to keep up a conversation. The quiet is just as nice."

"I hear I missed the crowd this morning," Decky said, picking up the fork, trying to decide what to tackle first.

"I don't even hear them anymore," Kim said. "I've been here cooking breakfast most every morning for twenty-five years, rain or shine. I could probably do it in my sleep. I 'magine I have scrambled a few eggs not fully awake a time or two."

Kim laughed and Decky noticed she was much prettier when she smiled. Decky swallowed the first bite of eggs, pleasantly surprised at the taste.

She asked, "Do you work here on the ranch?"

"I work here at the house. I loved Andy's momma from the first time I met her. I started hanging out with her in the kitchen way back when Andy and I were dating. It became my job after we were married."

Andy, Kim's husband's name was Andy. He fell somewhere in the middle of the pecking order. Decky was happy for the clues. She saw that Charlie had joined the people helping clean up after breakfast. Louise was still in charge, but other family members did the work, functioning together like a well-oiled machine. Decky continued to eat, while Kim, who had professed she liked the quiet, persisted with her monologue anyway.

"I know I may not look like it right now, but I love my life. Andy says it takes all day for me to look like I'm happy to be here. I've never been a morning person, but the sun comes up early every day here on the ranch."

Decky laughed between bites. "So I've heard," she said.

Kim chuckled. "Yep, you'll hear that a lot around here."

"Hear what?" Franny asked, joining them. She slid a cup of steaming coffee in front of Decky and sat beside Kim. "Charlie sent you this. She took my place at the sink, so she and Momma could spend some bonding time. Now, what is it that you hear?"

Kim answered, because Decky's mouth was full of biscuit. "The sun comes up –"

Franny finished for her. "– early every day. I know I've heard that enough in my life time, and that one up there, too"

Franny pointed over Decky's head. She turned to see a hand painted sign that read, "If you eat, you work."

"Didn't your dad put that sign up for Charlie?" Kim asked.

Franny answered, "Yep."

Her grin made Decky want to know more. She swallowed and prodded Franny, who she knew was dying to tell all the Charlie stories Decky had time to hear. "I know there is a story there. Do tell."

Before Franny could answer, the youngest brother, Joseph, joined them, bringing his own cup of coffee and his wife, Danielle. Decky knew their names, because they were part of the group that visited last summer. She recognized brother Jimmy's wife, Emily, from the beach trip. Through the greetings between the family members, as they were seated,

Decky was able to identify David, the second oldest brother, and his wife, Amy. Debra rounded out the impromptu family gathering, bringing along a coffee pot, and refilling Decky's cup with much needed caffeine.

Once everyone was seated, Franny pointed at the sign again. "Decky here wants to know the story behind that."

The general snickers meant this was a well-known story and one Decky now desperately wanted to know.

Joseph chimed in, "David should tell it. He was the oldest at home then."

Decky had only to sit back, nibble on her breakfast, and sip her coffee, while a group of older siblings, all too happy to rat out the baby sister, told their tale.

David began, "Charlie was in second grade. The school year had just started. She had a note sent home, because she wouldn't sit still in class."

Debra, the teacher, inserted the first of many interjections David would suffer. "Charlie finished her work too fast and they didn't know what to do with her. That was really the problem."

David picked up the story, seamlessly. He was evidently accustomed to the interruptions his siblings kept up throughout his story. "We were all sitting around the dinner table that night when the note came up."

Joseph leaned in on his elbows to add color commentary. "You have to know that family dinner was also when disciplinary discussions were held. That way, the rules didn't have to be repeated often."

"If you knew what happened to the rule breaker before you, it made you think twice before repeating the experience," Franny said. "It worked for the most part, but then there was Charlie."

Debra added, "By the time she came along, there was a pretty clear path of acceptable behavior lined out for her."

Joseph followed closely with, "Yeah, but Charlie thought she could make her own path. We all tried it. She just started a little younger with the boundary pushing than most of us."

They all laughed, including Decky. It did not surprise her in the least that Charlie began playing by her own rules at a young age.

David started again, when the laughter subsided. "That night at the table, Charlie decided to nip the discussion of her behavior in the bud. She announced that there was no reason to be concerned, she wasn't going back to school anyway."

Decky gave up trying to eat. She could not stop chuckling long enough.

David waited for a comment, but when none came, he continued, "Charlie was so sure of herself when she said, 'I can already read and add my numbers. Daddy says everything you need to know you can learn from watchin' animals, so I'll just stay here and watch the horses and cattle.' Momma didn't miss a beat. She said, 'Well, Buck, she's right. You're always saying that.' Daddy put his fork down and looked at Charlie. We were all kind of surprised when he said, 'Well all right, Little One, but 'round here, if you eat, you work. Them that don't go to school have to work on the ranch. I'll see you at sunrise in the morning. Sun comes up early every day for a ranch hand.' I think we all knew what was coming."

Franny jumped in when David took a breath. "She got right on up and went with Daddy in the morning, but you should have seen her when she got home that night. Daddy worked her so hard she fell asleep at the dinner table, just fell over in her plate. Needless to say, when he came into our room to get her at sunrise the next morning, she told him she thought she'd rather just be good in school, if that was all right with him. He

94

painted that sign and hung it up, should she ever forget. I don't think she did. She didn't get in much trouble at school after that."

David rounded out the story. "Yep, old Charlie knew pretty quick she wasn't spending her life being a ranch hand. Don't get me wrong, she worked hard out here like we all did, but she learned early on, if you eat here, you work here. She chose to take her meals elsewhere when the opportunity presented itself. We're all proud of her, first person to have a Doctorate in the family."

Decky wanted to say how proud she was of Charlie, too, but the invisible "don't ask, don't tell" wall prevented that. Instead, she asked, "Her nickname, is that one of those lessons, too? Is it because she's so touchy about being called short?"

Joseph laughed. "Oh, you've noticed that, huh? No, her name isn't because of her stature, but we did tease her about that. We figured other people would tease her, so if we did it first, she'd be used to it."

Debra answered the nickname question. "Little One came from her personality, not her size. From the moment she could crawl, she was gone. Someone was always asking –"

Every sibling at the table said in unison, "Where's the little one?"

"I'm right here," Charlie said, appearing suddenly at the end of the table. "What lies have you been telling about me?"

Kim answered her. "So far, it's all been the truth, Charlie. Very funny, but the truth."

Louise saved Charlie from any further embarrassing stories when she walked up and said, "Time to go to work, lots to do today."

Joseph was the first to stand. He stretched and announced loudly, "Come on folks, let's get 'er done."

95

The entire family went into motion, scattering in different directions, discussing plans and job assignments. Louise stayed behind with Charlie and Decky.

"I understand if I eat, I have to work. What would you like for me to do?" Decky asked, grinning at Charlie.

"I see my siblings have been telling you about my nap in the mashed potatoes," Charlie said.

Decky burst out laughing. "Well, they didn't tell me what was on the plate you fell over in, but thank you for that image."

"Lord, she was so tired, she didn't even feel me washing the gravy out of her hair," Louise said, laughing along with Decky. She added, "Maybe it was because she was the baby, but this child was cut from a different cloth from the beginning. The rest of them, well, you could tell them something and they took you at your word. This one," she paused and looped her arm around Charlie's waist, "this one, you had to prove it was true. Questioned everything, into everything. If my first ones had been like her, I never would have had time to have the rest."

Charlie kissed her mother on the cheek. "Saved the best for last is what I always said." A sheepish grin formed on her lips. "I guess I'm going to have to pay for all the stories I shared with their dates, aren't I?"

"You all tell on each other every time one of you brings someone new home." Louise chuckled. "I don't think Andy ever forgave you for asking Kim if she was friends with his other girlfriend."

Charlie snorted a laugh. "Oh my God, I was nine. I had no idea you couldn't have more than one girlfriend over to play."

"Charlie, tell me you weren't one of *those* little sisters. Did they have to pay you to leave them alone?" Decky asked, enjoying the teasing.

"No," Charlie said, "but they did start prepping me a little better. I knew a lot about the ends and outs of high school romance, long before I got there."

"I always thought that was why you didn't date much," Louise commented casually, reaching for Decky's plate.

"You know the real reason I didn't date much in high school, don't you?" Charlie said, beating her mother to the plate.

Decky held her breath. Surely, Charlie was not going to choose this moment to come out of the closet. Decky, frozen in place, was trying not to let her jaw drop. Charlie was smiling at her mother and appeared very comfortable with the conversation. Decky thought the pause Charlie took between sentences inordinately long, but it could have only been a split second before she continued.

"There wasn't a boy within driving distance that didn't know –" Decky cringed, before Charlie finished with, "my brothers, and sisters for that matter. It took a courageous young man to drive up that long driveway. There weren't that many with the guts to do it."

Decky let her breath out in a rush, causing both Louise and Charlie to look at her. She waved a hand in front of her. "Whew! It's already warming up."

Louise took the plate from Charlie, patting her on the shoulder. "Go on now, before it gets too hot. Don't keep her out in the heat too long and take some extra water." She turned to Decky. "I know you're used to being in the sun, but not this sun. You need to be careful out here."

"I'll take care of her, Momma," Charlie said, "and thank you for breakfast."

"Yes, thank you. It was delicious," Decky added quickly.

"Have fun," Louise said, and then chuckling, warned, "Don't work her too hard, Charlie. We wouldn't want her falling asleep in her mashed potatoes."

Charlie laughed and then grabbing Decky's arm, pulled her toward the driveway. "Come on, Daddy's waiting for us. We have a job to do." Decky had only taken a step, when Charlie stopped, and said, "Wait a minute." She walked to a table by the back door, picked up two straw Stetson cowboy hats, and returned, holding one out to Decky. "Here, I think this will fit you."

Decky watched Charlie slide the cowboy hat on her head and the fantasy was complete. She dipped her head and put on her own hat, raising her eyes to see Charlie smile. They started walking down the path toward the barns.

When she was sure they were alone, Decky said, "I'm really liking this Cowgirl-Charlie. You may need to bring that hat home with you."

"We'll order some when we get home. They don't travel well in suitcases."

"Some? Do you need special ones for different occasions?" Decky asked.

"Well, yes, there are different hats you wear at different times, but I was talking about getting hats for both of us." Charlie looked up at Decky and winked. "I'm liking my cowgirl, too."

Decky wanted to stop and kiss Charlie right then. Charlie saw the look and seemed to feel the same way, but instead said, "Hold that thought. We'll have some time alone later."

Decky was not going to pout. She knew they could not show affection anywhere but in their own home. If not danger, then disapproval waited around every corner outside of their little insulated world. They talked of lesbian cruises and vacation spots, but Decky had never been anywhere, other than

98

her own property and a few trusted friends' homes, where she felt comfortable or safe enough to hold Charlie's hand, much less kiss her. They experienced nearly dying together two years ago, simply because some jackass thought assaulting two lesbians was perfectly rational. Being cautious came as second nature to Charlie and Decky, now. Not getting a kiss in public was far less important than staying alive.

"I will hold that thought and let it percolate for a while," Decky said, and then to change the subject, she asked, "So, what are we going to do with your dad?"

Charlie broke into a wide grin. "We're about to break those new boots in, darlin'," she said, pouring on the drawl. "You are going on your first roundup."

"What are we rounding up?" Decky asked, not sure she wanted to know.

"Horses," Charlie answered, seemingly unconcerned that Decky had not ridden a horse in quite a while.

"Are you sure the first time I ride a horse in twenty years that I should be riding in a roundup? It's not like swimming or riding a bike. I do have to relearn a few things, namely staying in the saddle." Decky was genuinely concerned.

Charlie was having way too much fun with Decky's fish out of water struggle with ranch life. "Oh, you'll be fine, Decky. If you fall off, we'll wait for you to get back on."

#

Decky had not made it down the drive very far last night, as it turned out. Behind the two barns she had seen were more corrals, large stables, several out buildings, and an office. This was looking like a large ranching operation, but then it would have to be to support the number of families depending on it for survival.

99

"That is an incredibly beautiful horse," Decky said, watching a black stallion trot along the fence rail, paralleling their course toward the office. There was something familiar about him, as he snorted and pranced, excited by the cooler air of morning.

"That's Jack Five. He's a bit antsy. He's locked up away from his girls right now, because they have newborns. He might injure or kill a foal, trying to cause the mare to mate sooner," Charlie answered, nonchalantly.

Decky took a few precautionary steps further away from the fence. "Is he crazy?"

Charlie laughed. "No, he's a stallion. Nature drives them to breed. Some of them are more aggressive in that pursuit than others. Part of dealing with horses is managing their relationships."

"Do you miss it, Charlie, living on the ranch?"

"Sometimes, but I like the life I have. I made the right choice to leave. Besides, I would have never found you if I hadn't."

Decky smiled. "No, I don't think you would have run into me out here. Not enough water."

Charlie squinted out at the surrounding pastureland. "There is never enough water out here. I hope you won't be disappointed at not seeing any fireworks on the Fourth."

Decky looked at the dry yellowed stubs of grass on the sides of the path. "No, as a matter of fact, the thought of someone shooting sparks into the sky around here is petrifying."

"Do you know why our reunions are on the Fourth of July?" Charlie asked, leading the way up to the office door.

"I assumed it was because it was a natural time for everyone to be off work."

Charlie stopped before opening the door. "Momma and Daddy and most of the adults around here were up all night anyway, watching for fires. People started gathering and one thing led to another. I love fireworks as much as the next person, but when lives and livelihoods are at stake, I prefer to see them explode over large bodies of water. And don't get me started on cigarettes and campfires in the hands of idiots."

Charlie opened the door, the cool air from inside greeting them. Decky could already feel the sweat rolling down the middle of her back, just from the short walk to the office. She vowed never to complain about the humidity or heat at home ever again. She could use a good breeze coming off the water about now, but the respite in the office would have to do.

"I've checked the water pressure on all the pumps. We laid out the hose yesterday and the pumper trucks are full," another tall Warren brother was saying to Mary, who was sitting behind a desk.

"Thanks, Andy. I'm sure everything will be fine," Mary answered, giving Decky the much-needed clue to his identity.

Andy, Kim's husband, got it, Decky thought. She was patting herself on the back, when several more Warren men entered from the back of the office, deflating her moment of triumph. These were some of the nephews Decky met last night, all tall and in their mid to late twenties, with the same family eyes. One waved and the other two nodded in Decky's general direction.

One of them said, "Hey, Aunt Charlie," verifying Decky's identification.

Mary held up a finger, definitely in charge. "Just a minute, Charlie, and I'll walk you out to the stable." She turned to Andy and the others. "Are we are clear on who is on what shift?" All the males nodded that they were. Mary added, "Let's hope for an uneventful Fourth, boys."

Andy agreed with a nod, but added, "The rangers said they'd watch that back line to the park, but keep an eye out anyway. They'll only know they've got idiots shooting fireworks after the fact."

"Do you want those extra tanks up at the house now?" One of the nephews asked.

"Yep, take them on up to the house. I'll be along in a minute," Mary said, reaching for the cowboy hat on a hook by her desk.

Andy stopped Mary's progress, turning to Charlie. "Michael has your horses saddled in the paddock. I need to talk to Mary a second, and then we'll join you." He smiled to ease the brush off. "I'd like to ride along with you, if that's all right. Haven't been on a horse round up in years."

He laughed, so did Mary and Charlie. Decky was beginning to believe there was an inside joke she was not privy to.

"Okay, we'll wait for you," Charlie said, leading Decky back out the door.

The nephews followed them, exchanging a few words with Charlie, before heading off to finish their work.

"Is everyone that works here family?" Decky asked, as she followed Charlie to the next stop.

"Mary oversees ranch operations, which is divided into feed production, cattle, and horses. Bobby, John, and Andy split those jobs. Daddy is still the boss, but he lets Mary run things for the most part. Franny does whatever needs doing. She can rope a calf or add up the books. She'll probably take Mary's place when she retires. Seems like every child in our extended family has done at least a summer on the ranch. Some stick, some don't. I didn't."

"I think it's interesting that a woman runs the ranch, and her heir apparent is also a woman," Decky commented.

"It's worked so far. Momma did Mary's job until she came back from college and took over." Charlie said, steering Decky toward big double doors, opened to let the air flow through a large stable.

The smell of horses, leather, and manure blended into an aroma Decky was surprised to find was not offensive. It reminded her of walking through the big barns at the state fair when she was younger. The freshly washed concrete aisle down the middle of the stalls glistened in spots, still wet from the morning mucking. The matching double doors, open at the other end of the stable, silhouetted three horses, already saddled and awaiting their riders.

When Decky's eyes adjusted to the shade, she saw a large tack room off to her right. It looked like a locker room for cowboys. Saddles on stands sat in front wooden cubicles, where harnesses, coats, and dirty work boots joined other items a working ranch hand could need. Everything looked cleaned, painted, polished, or oiled, according to the material out of which it was made. Fresh hay and bedding had been added to the mostly empty, spacious stalls, the horses either out with a rider, or grazing.

Charlie explained, "This is the barn for the working horses. The boarding and breeding stock are in the other barns."

"Charlie, this ranch is huge, at least the buildings are, and everything is so organized and clean."

"Daddy says, clean equals safe and that's what we're shooting for. Less things to trip over and slip in if you keep things organized."

Decky chuckled. "I guess your insistence that I put things in the same place every time comes from your father's wisdom."

Charlie smiled up from underneath the brim of her hat. "Well that, and the fact that you can't remember where you put things when you don't put them back where they belong."

"You have a point," Decky admitted.

"Hey, Charlie," Michael called out.

Decky remembered him because he was a favorite nephew of Charlie's and they sat with him at dinner last night. Charlie was evidently Michael's favorite as well. He smiled broadly, as he stepped into the aisle with a water hose, just finishing washing down the rubber stall mat.

Charlie gave her much larger nephew a hug. "Hey cowboy. Never too old to muck stalls, I see."

"I used to hate this as a kid," Michael said, "but there is something therapeutic about it now. I think it's the fact the horses are generally quiet. Living in the house with two kids under the age of eight is noise enough for one person. I know why Grandpa was always down here building something or mucking stalls. He was trying to get some peace."

Charlie agreed. "Half the stuff on this ranch would not exist if Daddy hadn't been looking for an excuse to be out of the house, or a project to keep us all busy."

Mary's voice joined the conversation, as she walked up. "Daddy's philosophy was idle hands left time for mischief. You either found something to keep yourself busy, or he'd find something for you. This stable was built when he had his first five teenagers in the house. The one next door was built with the next set."

"Your father should write a book on parenting," Decky said.

"Oh, it's not a novel approach anymore." Charlie explained. "They have working ranches for wayward youth everywhere. We just weren't aware that we were part of the pilot program."

Decky suggested, "Maybe it's related to his Old Order Amish roots."

"Momma told me you've been doing family research," Mary said. "I can't wait to see what you've found out. I knew Daddy's people originally came from Pennsylvania, but I didn't know they were Amish, or how they got from there to Georgia to here."

That was not all Mary did not know, Decky thought, but said, "I was able to do a full history on your father's family all the way back to the German Rhineland."

Charlie apparently did not want to discuss the family genealogy at the moment. "Well, we should go find Daddy. I'm sure he's waiting. Where's Andy?"

"I'm right here," Andy said, jogging over to them.

"There's water in the saddle bags," Michael said. "I saddled up Jack's Lady for you, Charlie. I remembered you really liked riding her when you were here last."

"Thank you, Michael. Did I tell you you're my favorite?" Charlie asked, kissing him on the cheek.

Mary was ready to move things along, and took charge. "All right then," she said. "Enjoy your round up, Decky. Just trust Susie. She'll bring you back to the barn."

Decky was firing through her memory banks, trying to remember who Susie was. Charlie saw the confusion.

"Susie is Mary's horse. You're about the same height and weight, so we figured Mary's saddle would be a good fit for you."

Mary walked over to the trio of saddled horses. She nuzzled the gray one that was standing between two reddish-brown coated bays with black ears, manes, and tails. They were all beautiful and obviously well taken care of.

"Take care of my friend here." Decky thought Mary was talking to her, until she said, "She hasn't been on a horse in a while so be patient with her." She then turned to Decky. "Well, come on outside and hop on. I'll adjust the stirrups if I need to, but I think they're about right."

Hop on, Decky repeated to herself, as she followed Mary and the others out of the stable. Hop on, as if just wanting it to happen would propel Decky up into the saddle. She hoped she remembered how to mount and did not end up hopping on one foot with her other foot hung in the stirrup, while the horse walked in a circle.

Charlie was being no help. Her horse was tall, the largest of the three. Decky was mentally measuring the distance between the stirrup and the ground, in comparison to Charlie's height, and wondering how Little One was going to make that step. The size of the animal appeared not to bother Charlie, however. She took the reins of her horse and a handful of mane in her left hand, grasping the cantle of the saddle with her right. Andy stepped up beside her, cupped his hands in front of him, and bent his knees. Charlie stepped into his hands with her left foot, did a little bounce, and landed softly in the saddle, as if she did that every day.

"Come on, Decky," Mary said, checking that the cinch was tight. "Susie really is a good horse. You'll be fine."

Decky copied Charlie's movements, using the stirrup rather than Andy's hands. It took two hops, but she made it into the saddle. Mary checked the fit of the tack, judging everything to be in good order.

Apparently, Charlie was not the only Warren that could read Decky's mind. Mary stepped up close to Decky's leg and patted her on the knee. She asked softly, "Do you need a quick refresher?"

"Yes, that would be helpful," Decky said, smiling gratefully down at Mary.

106

"Don't pull the reins to make her turn, just lay them against the side of her neck and point both your knees in the direction you want to go. Find your center in the saddle. Use your abdominal muscles, but keep a soft back, and rock your hips with the rhythm of the gait. Your shoulders should be quiet. When you want to go forward, shift your center in that direction just a bit. You will automatically pull inward with your knees. Susie will feel your balance change, and in order to help you find it again, she will move forward. It's just nature. Trust the horse, she knows what to do. It's that simple. You've ridden before. It will come back to you."

"Thank you," Decky said. "I'm sure Susie will take good care of me."

"All right, cowgirl. You ready?" Charlie said, wearing a huge smile.

"I'm as ready as I'm going to be," Decky answered. "Let's ride."

Andy, who was now seated on his horse, led the way to the gate, while Michael opened it to let them out. Decky was simply a passenger and let Susie handle the exit. For the most part, that was how the first portion of the ride went. Susie just walked along with the other horses, which was fine with Decky. They rode three abreast down the sandy section road. Decky was concentrating on rolling the movement of the horse through her hips, and keeping her seat. She could not talk, because if she lost focus she began to bounce. Charlie was keeping an eye on her, but letting Decky work it out on her own. She chatted with Andy, while Decky and Susie became friends.

Well, chat was not exactly the right word to describe the conversation Decky was hearing. Charlie cut right to the chase, once they hit open pasture. "So, have you been elected to tell me the truth about Bobby? I know you didn't come on this little ride for lack of saddle time."

Andy turned to look at Charlie. "You always were too smart for your own good."

"Is it just that Karen is still the biggest bitch on the Panhandle, or something else?" Charlie asked.

Andy laughed, but glanced in Decky's direction. He looked uncomfortable speaking of family business in front her. He deflected Charlie with, "You really don't like her, do you?"

"She has made it her mission to screw with me since I was twelve. If I've ever truly hated anyone, it is Karen Ebert."

"Karen Ebert Hamilton Warren, to be precise," Andy said, stoking Charlie's fire.

It worked. Charlie set off on a tangent. "For the life of me, I do not know why she turned so hateful. We were friends for years."

"Best friends," Andy added.

"Yes, as badly as I hate to admit it, she was my best friend, but that was more because she lived close by than anything else."

"And then you started playing on the twelve-year-old All Stars," Andy prodded.

Decky had a suspicion that Andy knew exactly why Charlie and Karen's friendship hit the skids.

It became obvious that Charlie knew too, and just did not want to admit it, when she said, "I know what you're hinting at. I did not replace her with a new friend. Karen just could not stand it that I made the team and she didn't. She got mad long before Crystal and I became friends."

Decky chuckled. Charlie turned on her. "Why are you laughing?"

"I can't believe you've been hanging on to a junior high squabble for all these years," Decky answered.

108

Charlie was defensive. "It wasn't just junior high. It went on for years, even when I would come home from college, she was still harping about stuff that happened years earlier, always spreading some rumor or calling me out for a fight."

Decky was growing comfortable enough on the horse to relax and tease Charlie a bit. "You weren't brawling behind the rodeo bleachers on Saturday nights, were you?"

Andy seemed to be enjoying it, as well. He joked, "No, Charlie doesn't fight. She gets even."

"What did she do?" Decky asked over Charlie, who was riding in the middle.

Andy was more than happy to tell. "Well, she ignored her for the most part, which seemed to make Karen very angry, so that worked for a while."

Charlie interrupted. "Until –"

Andy did not let her have her way, and cut her off. "I'm tellin' this. Anyway, ignoring her worked most of the time, until their senior year and Karen's engagement to Bill Hamilton. You'd think Karen had enough to do without messing with Charlie, but she's just not drawn that way. She started a rumor about Charlie and Crystal."

Charlie's countenance darkened. "It wasn't true," she said, softly.

"I know," Andy said, then continued, "To shut Karen up, Charlie here flirted with ol' Bill until he dumped Karen and took Charlie to the prom, the social event of Karen's life to hear her tell it, and then dropped his drunk ass on Karen's doorstep the next morning."

Decky gasped in mock horror. "Oh Lord, you stole her man. You play dirty, Charlie, but you did give him back," Decky raised an eyebrow, "in one piece, I assume?"

Charlie smirked at Decky. "No, I did not sleep with him, if that's what you're asking, but it didn't stop Karen from telling everyone I did."

Evidently, it was a family skill to suffer interruptions and continue one's narrative. Andy resumed without a hitch.

"Bill and Karen got married anyway, but the prom incident eventually wore him down. He said Karen harped on it the entire time they were married. Said Karen's obsession with hating Charlie didn't leave her much time for anything else, despite the fact that neither of them had seen Charlie in years. He also said he had the time of his life at that prom and wouldn't change a thing." He winked at Decky. "I'd say the hatred between Karen and Charlie is mutual and long standing."

Charlie threw her hands up in the air. "And now my freakin' brother has married her. Was she the last available women within driving distance?"

"Karen found Jesus after she lost Bill," Andy explained. "Bobby met her at a single Christians' dinner at the church, last spring. She got him to stop going to worship with the family and switch to her church. He was either struck by the Lord's grace over there, or she gave him the best blow job he's ever had, 'cause he snatched that up quicker than flies on a fresh cow patty."

Decky's laughter tipped her forward, causing her to squeeze Susie with her knees, and since her hands were now on the horse's neck, Susie took it as a sign it was time to go faster, and go they went. The horse ran under Decky's center of gravity and then right on past it. Instead of tipping forward, Decky was now leaning back. The reins slipped from her hands, but fell together and curled around the saddle horn, leaving Susie to believe that someone was still in charge. That was about as far from the truth as one could imagine.

Decky grabbed at the saddle horn, but the bouncing had commenced at a steady pace, and she was unable to grasp it. While trying to right herself, she kicked Susie in the sides with both heels, not hard, but hard enough. Such behavior was a signal to Susie to haul ass. Decky's head nearly hit the horse's rump, as she fell further back with the sudden burst of speed. She was sure the next bounce would be her last, and her abrupt re-acquaintance with the ground imminent.

She felt a strong hand in the middle of her back, before she realized Andy was there. He pushed Decky into sitting position, just in time for her to see Charlie grab Susie's reins. They all slowed to a stop together, both horses and people breathing hard.

Decky caught her breath and said, "Thank you," but that was all she could say, as she tried to pull herself together.

Andy laughed. "It's okay. You'll get the hang of it pretty soon. When you want to stop, just lift the reins like this." He demonstrated and his horse lowered its head. "See how he drops his head? At the same time, sit back in the saddle and still your movements. They are trained to know that means stop."

Decky nodded that she understood and said, "I'll try sitting back in the saddle, if I can get my ass to stay there."

"You just have to learn ol' Susie's language," Andy said, and then grinned. "Now, when you kicked her, she interpreted that as skedaddle."

"I will certainly work on my communication skills. Skedaddle is not one of the signals I'd like to master," Decky said, through her slowing breaths, "but 'Stop' would be good."

Charlie was about to bust a seam, trying not to laugh.

Decky took offense. "It was not that funny."

"Yes, it was," Charlie said, followed by a burst of laughter, and then, "I didn't know your arms and legs could move in that many different directions at the same time."

"Well, I didn't fall off, did I?"

Charlie laughed harder. "You did everything but. It was like watching a paddle ball on a rubber band."

"Go on, laugh it up," Decky said, and then smiled at Charlie mischievously. She was enjoying Decky's little bouncing act just a bit too much. It was time for some laughter at Charlie's expense. "Hey Andy, did I ever tell you about the time Charlie caught the eel?"

Charlie tried to quiet her laughter. "Now, there is no reason to get ugly."

Both of their heads swung around to look at Andy, when he said, "You two are always laughing. I've noticed that." He focused his brandy colored eyes on Decky. "I'm glad Charlie has someone like you in her life. Everyone needs someone they can laugh with." He did not wait for, nor did he seem to need a response, before adding, "Are you good now? Got your breathing back under control?"

Decky nodded that she did.

Charlie took her cue from Andy. He said what he wanted to say, and Charlie was not ready to hear more if it was coming. She settled Susie's reins in Decky's hands. "Just relax. If a horse knows you're anxious, they tend to be a little uncertain themselves. Susie needs a strong leader, not because she would intentionally hurt you, but because she's a follower. Most horse control comes from the confidence of the rider."

"Well, that explains a lot," Decky said.

Charlie smiled, continuing to instruct her pupil. "Forget about your legs. Now get a good feel for Susie beneath you. Her legs are your legs, now. Tell them what you want to do. Start the movement from your pelvis."

Decky sat up erect in the saddle.

Charlie pulled alongside her. "Squeeze your butt cheeks together."

"What?" Decky said.

Charlie chuckled. "Just squeeze your butt cheeks and then relax them. Feel how it sits you down in the saddle?"

Decky did as instructed. It worked.

"Sit your weight solid, balance your upper body, and connect with the saddle." Charlie put her hand in the small of Decky's back. "Soften your lower back and find the rhythm with your hips." Charlie smiled and added, "It's like sex, just rock to the rhythm."

Decky smiled back at her, and then concentrated on connecting her body with the horse. She shifted her pelvis, as if she herself were about to take a step. The other muscles in her body followed the proper procedure, including the very slight lean forward in preparation for retaining balance. Decky felt the mare's muscles reacting to her own, as Susie took a step.

Charlie encouraged her, letting her hand slide off Decky's back, as Susie continued to walk. "Lead her. You can do this."

With Charlie believing she could ride the horse, Decky did too. She felt a wave of self-confidence wash over her. Unlikely as it had seemed, Decky had managed to stay in the saddle through that last little jaunt. She could do this. Decky focused her attention on Susie, and with the slightest shift of her weight, Susie increased the tempo of her stride. This time there was no bouncing, as Decky found the rhythm with her hips, and began to float along with Susie. She was no longer a reluctant passenger. Andy and Charlie remained behind, letting Decky control her horse without others to follow. When she finally felt the sigh leave her chest, Decky thought she felt Susie relax under the saddle, too.

She turned around and waved at the other two, calling out, "Come on, I don't know how long this confidence thing will last. So while I have it, we should move."

Charlie and Andy came up behind her. Decky could not see them but could hear them talking, because they wanted her to.

"She might make a halfway decent ranch hand, if you train her right." Andy said. "You stick around for a while and we'll have her ropin' cattle."

"She'll be all right for a week out here, but that is a fish out of water, a genuine Carolina beach girl. She can't stay on dry land too long, she'll quit breathing."

"Well, do you think we can get her to go faster now?" Andy asked.

Decky took that as a challenge and urged Susie into a trot. She mastered that gait, and then picked up the pace of her hip rocking and asked Susie for more. The horse immediately switched to a western lope and gained speed. The three hoof beats of the gait awoke a memory inside Decky. It had been twenty years since she was in a saddle, but she was remembering how to ride much more quickly than she thought she would. Decky was clipping along at a good pace and feeling proud of herself, but not ready to let Susie go much faster. Her moment of satisfaction was cut short when Andy and Charlie flew by at a full gallop.

"Show off!" Decky called after Charlie.

She doubted Charlie heard her. Decky's little blond cowgirl had one hand on the top of her hat, leaning into the neck of her horse, asking it to give her all it had. The legs of both horses were moving so fast, they appeared to float over the ground. The two horses disappeared over a ridge in a cloud of dust, Charlie giving her brother a run for his money.

Decky slowed Susie's pace and spoke to the back of her head. "Susie, I think we just got left behind. I hope you know where we're going."

Charlie reappeared, charging toward Decky at full speed. She made a big arc and then rode up to Decky, matching Susie's gait. Charlie was laughing, grinning from ear to ear, and to Decky, looking completely adorable.

"That was way too much fun. I haven't done that in a while," Charlie said, still chuckling.

"Did you win?" Decky asked, smiling because she could not help it. Charlie was glowing.

"No, Andy's horse is faster than Jack's Lady here, but I made him earn it."

"I saw pictures of you in the house on a black horse. Where is he?"

"That was my horse, Jackson. He died four years ago, when he was twenty-nine. He was a pasture horse of leisure by then. I got him when I was seven, as a foal. I haven't owned a place where I could have one since I left home, and I didn't want someone else feeding and boarding my horse so I can go ride it once a week. I couldn't have the kind of relationship I want with a horse and not be part of its daily life."

"We could have horses. We have plenty of land," Decky said. She would give Charlie anything she wanted, if it was possible.

"We'll talk about it. There is a lot more to owning horses than just land and a stable, but that's a good start." Charlie smiled at Decky. "Promise me you won't work up some kooky plan to surprise me with a horse. I really need to be in on this one."

Decky winked at Charlie. "The only plan I'm working on is getting you out of those jeans without taking your boots off."

"Big talk," Charlie scoffed. "When you get off that horse later, you'll be so sore you can't move. You're using muscles you don't even remember you have. You'll find out which ones in a few hours. The only thing you'll want between your thighs is an ice bag."

"I've been known to play through pain," Decky said, spurred on by her attraction to Charlie in western attire. "It'll take a lot more than sore muscles to keep me out of the game."

"Keep talking big girl. We'll see how you feel about physical activity in a few hours."

"I'm in great shape, Charlie. How bad could it be?"

CHAPTER FIVE

"Oh my God, this freakin' hurts."

"I told you," Charlie said, pulling Decky's boots off. "Do you have everything you need?"

"Yes, I'm just going to read and let the Ibuprofen go to work," Decky said, lying on her back, propped up on pillows with a large ice bag between her thighs.

Charlie leaned over and kissed Decky on the lips. She ran her fingers through Decky's hair. "I should have given you a couple before we rode. I'll remember next time. You'll be all right in a bit. We'll go for a walk and stretch you out some. It's the best I can do without a pool. Just rest for a few hours and then I'll come get you. You can catch me up on Thora's story then."

Decky started to reach up and put her arm around Charlie. That's when she discovered her ribs were sore, as well. She dropped her hand back to her chest. "Getting old sucks."

Charlie stood up. "It has nothing to do with age. You're just not used to it. It gets easier with time in the saddle."

"I don't think I can spread my legs wide enough to get back on a horse," Decky whined.

Charlie ran a hand up between Decky's thighs, which caused her to flinch.

"That was ugly," Decky said, through the pain.

"Just checking to make sure you can still spread 'em if you need to," Charlie said, a wicked grin curling the corner of her mouth.

"I believe your mean streak is showing, Little One."

Charlie gave her a quick peck on the lips, apparently done torturing Decky. "Okay, be back in a bit. I have to help Momma cut up potatoes."

She started to leave. Decky called after her, "Hey, thanks. I can now say I have been on a horse roundup."

Charlie laughed. "I'll back you up, when you tell Brenda. She doesn't have to know all the details."

"You have expanded my repertoire in so many ways, how can I thank you?"

"Finish that manuscript and tell me what my mother is up to."

"All right, but I can't guarantee that I won't fall asleep." Decky grinned. "If I do, would you wake me up wearing that hat? It's part of my fantasy."

"Should I be wearing anything else?" Charlie teased, backing out of the RV.

Decky looked down at the ice bag, and then back up at Charlie. "That will depend entirely on how well my recovery is going."

Charlie left the RV, her laughter cut off by the closing of the door behind her. It had been a morning full of laughter that only ended when Decky tried to stand after sitting down to lunch. That was when she felt her thighs catch fire. The pain seared up both legs and shot daggers at her rear end. Decky's boasts of playing with pain did not include having to walk with bowed tiny steps, as if she were still holding the horse between her legs. Lifting her leg for the first step into the RV was only possible because Charlie gave her a little push.

Decky had spent most of the morning on horseback, bringing in a small herd of horses. The roundup was not exactly what Decky thought it was going to be. She had envisioned a herd of wild horses like she saw in the movies, running behind a magnificent stallion, his mane and tail flying in the breeze. What she saw when she and Charlie crested the ridge was definitely a herd of horses, just not the mustangs Decky expected. Buck, Andy, Dolly, and Reba were lounging in the shade of some trees, several yards away from a herd of about twenty-five miniature horses. They looked exactly like normal sized horses, but the largest one was no bigger than the dogs that were waiting anxiously to herd them.

"They are so cute," Decky said, as they rode toward Buck and Andy.

"Don't let them fool you," Charlie warned. "They are full grown horses and some of them have much bigger attitudes than you would think, especially that black and white one. That's Old Turd."

"The horse's name is Old Turd?"

Charlie nodded. "He kicked Daddy once, and he yelled out, 'You old turd.' That became his name. He never learned any manners, but he's a good stud."

"How come we're moving them?" Decky asked.

"It's time to sell off the mature ones. Daddy always lets the folks that come to the reunion have first picks. He doesn't make any money off of them, barely breaks even really, but he's had a miniature horse since he was a small boy. He just likes them, but he doesn't sink a lot of money into them. It's kind of his hobby."

119

Decky noticed a house and barn a few hundred yards away. "Who lives there?"

"That's Andy's house. There are five houses on this ten square miles, counting Momma and Daddy's. All the brothers and sisters have a quarter section allotted to them for a house, if they want it."

"Where's yours?" Decky asked.

"Over by Bobby's house. Good thing I'll never use it. I could never live next door to Karen Ebert."

"Do you want to come back here, Charlie? I would come, if it's that important to you. I hope you know that."

They were nearing Buck and Andy, when Charlie said, "I used to think about coming home, but not anymore. I love you, our home, where we live, all of it. I have no romantic notions about living out my days anywhere but with you, on the beach."

"I love you, too," was all Decky had time to say, before they arrived at the trees, and the round up foreman, Buck, set things in motion.

Old Turd lived up to his name, scurrying about, causing the other tiny horses to rush excitedly behind him, as he crisscrossed the pasture. Decky giggled like a kid at the little horse's antics. He may have been small, but he had a huge ego, and a strong desire to prevent his capture. Buck set the dogs on him to break him out of the herd. It was a thing of beauty, watching the dogs work as a team to cut Old Turd from his mates. Then with one flick of the wrist, Buck let fly with a rope that landed perfectly around the little stallion's neck. Immediately upon feeling the rope, Old Turd turned into a well-trained horse on a lead, prancing proudly behind Buck's horse, and leading his lady friends and the others quietly out of the pasture. Decky followed Andy's instructions and watched Charlie closely for cues, while she rode to one side of the herd toward the main house. She would not soon forget the experience. Decky would like not to remember the pain she was in now, but the memory of Charlie smiling at her from under the brim of her cowboy hat she hoped was seared in her mind for all time.

In exchange for that wonderful adventure, Charlie only wanted Decky to find out what was in the manuscript. She flipped to the page where she left off reading last night, hoping to find answers to Charlie's questions.

"Well, Thora, time to reveal the family secret."

#

I was escorted into the sod structure from my childhood. It seemed small in comparison to my memory, but the smell of dirt was unchanged. It penetrated my senses as it always did, when a whiff of freshly broken ground infused the air, reconnecting me to this place. I harbored only torturous memories of the long dark nights, when I lay in this dirt abode, listening to my mother die. Now, I had been summoned to watch another take her last breath, or so it seemed. The smell of dirt brought nothing but pain, and I wanted to escape that place before my foot had thoroughly crossed the threshold.

Young Mr. Lynch's mere presence, so close behind me, propelled me into the darkness I dreaded. A lantern burned dimly on a small table in the center of the room, casting an amber glow that barely penetrated the shadowy corners. The four small windows were covered in heavy cloth, keeping the room dark and gloomy. I could see only shadows of the walls, but I knew they were there, heavy three-foot thick stacks of rectangle slabs cut from prairie sod. I hesitated at the door, causing my escort to step around me as he crossed to the table. He raised the wick in the lantern, brightening the room.

As if in normal conversation, he turned to a figure lying in the bed against the far wall and spoke. "Sure feels better in here, Merdy, out of the sun. Look who came to see you. Thora is here. She came all the way from Paris."

The figure made no move to indicate the words were penetrating her deep sleep. As Mr. Lynch raised the lantern, I stepped forward and beheld a face I had not seen in years, but remembered now as if it were yesterday. She was younger then, not much more than a child herself, and although it had been only twenty years, I expected to find an old woman in the last days of her life. What I saw confounded me. She had changed over time, but only matured into a more handsome figure. Her skin was tanned, showing just the slightest blemish of age. Her hair, still dark as night, was cut short, and combed by some loving hand while she lay sleeping. Had I not known who she was, I could have very easily mistaken her for an attractive man lying in peaceful repose.

"How long has she been like this?" I heard myself ask, not entirely sure why I was suddenly concerned with the woman's well-being more than my own.

"Tseena said Merdy sent the message to my father a month ago and then laid down. Comes out of it now and again, walks off toward the river alone, then comes back and lays down again. Doesn't talk. Doesn't seem to notice anyone is here. Tseena calls it a walking dream, says Merdy is somewhere between here and the spirit world. She will wake when she's ready to tell us what she has seen."

"Sam said she was sick, that people thought she was dying."

He reached into a bowl by the bed, removed a damp cloth, and dabbed the sleeping woman's brow. "Lots of people know Merdy. They've been stopping here for years when traveling through. She never turned people away and they remembered.

122

Word spread up and down the trail that Merdy had laid down. I guess people just assumed she was dying. I don't know what she's doing, but she can't survive like this much longer."

I was doubtful of the severity of the situation, and my previous concern turned to contempt. "Her color is fine, she has not wasted. I have volunteered in hospital, sir. This patient is malingering. She chooses to lie there and is up walking more often than you think."

"That's it, exactly. She does look better than she did when I was here two weeks ago. Could be the Indian medicine Tseena is feeding her."

"Dream states, visions, Indian medicine, have I returned to the dark ages? Are there no modern doctors to see to her?" I sat down in a small wooden chair at the table, too devastated to remain standing. "I've been taken away from my happy life to come here to witch doctoring and dirt floors. What have I done to deserve such treatment? I did as I was told. I learned, I excelled, I became what was asked of me."

I was bordering on hysteria when Mr. Lynch sat down opposite me, leaving the lantern on the edge of the table so he could see me clearly. "Miss Ethridge, you may hide your roots very well in Europe, but there is no need for that pretense here. I remember you in a hide dress with feathers in your hair. You did not shun your heritage as a child. I found that much more attractive than your spoiled little rich girl performance."

"I care not what you find attractive, sir," I said, with the full intention of finding Sam and leaving. "I'm sure your father did not send you here to berate me"

"He sent me here to close out your affairs. The bank's agreement with Merdy ends on your thirtieth birthday, which I believe is about to occur. What you do and say here will determine the style in which you live the rest of your life."

123

"Why was I never told of this condition? I would have been more prepared had I known I may have to support myself," I answered, incensed.

"You were not told, because Merdy insisted you be free to do as you please and then return here to make your decision."

Sam entered the room, interrupting our conversation, and bringing my trunk. He rested it on the floor, and said, "Ma'am, if there's nothin' else, I need to head back to town."

Mr. Lynch put his hand out, indicating the door. "Last chance," he said, as if I had a choice in the matter.

"You may go, Sam, but do come back in a few days." I turned to my captor, for that was how I had begun to think of him. "I hope that will be enough time for your father's arrival."

John Lynch rose from his chair and crossed to the door. He handed Sam a few coins and shook his hand. "When you hear of my father's arrival, be sure to tell Mr. Lane to have you bring him out."

"Yes sir, Mr. Lynch." The shiny gold in his hand bolstered Sam's enthusiasm. "Good evening, ma'am." He tipped his hat and was gone.

I was now alone with a comatose woman, a man I hardly knew, and an old Indian that claimed spirits and herbs were at work here. I was confused, tired, and a bit angry, but helpless to improve my situation. Mr. Lynch stood in the doorway, looking back at me.

He was kind when he spoke, which took me by surprise. "I know this has been a tremendous upheaval in your life. I wish I could make you understand what has happened, but if you will only trust me, the truth will be told and you will have the answers to your questions."

"Mr. Lynch," I began, before he cut me off.

"Do we have to be so formal? After all, we are old friends." He came to sit across from me again.

"I have some memory of a boy in a carriage, but that is all I remember of you, Mr. Lynch."

I insisted on the formality. I was an unmarried woman alone with a strange man, and my only chaperone was a reposing woman, who at that moment stirred beneath the bed covers, drawing our attention. I stared at her, the glow of the lantern just illuminating her profile.

"Don't you have any fond memories of her?" Mr. Lynch asked.

"I remember begging her not to put me in the carriage with you and your father. I cried for her at night when I was placed in the boarding school. I was told to forget that life, that it was a bad life, and that I was never to go back to the old ways. I did as I was told. I forgot about her and I assumed she had forgotten about me."

"Merdy never forgot about you. We talked of your travels often, over the years. I brought her the letters you sent my father, from time to time. She enjoyed reading you were doing well."

"Then why not contact me through your father? Instead, she let me think no one in the world cared for me other than a kind old man in Kansas." I broke down.

The pain of a lost child overwhelmed me and I began to weep, which infuriated me. I did not want to show weakness to this man, but I could not hold back the enveloping waves of sorrow. He did not speak, but handed me a handkerchief and sat quietly while I dabbed at my tears.

When I could, I spoke. "Forgive me. I had not thought of that time in quite a while. It was not a pleasant experience, but I grew to understand that I must succeed. I was driven to be just what the schoolmasters wanted, a completely assimilated young woman. It appeared to be my only opportunity to escape, and now I am back where I began, staring at the face of the woman who set all that in motion."

"Can you not even say her name?" He prodded gently. "That would be a start to unraveling your mystery."

"I called her Ahpʉ," I said softly.

"I remember that. It's Comanche for father," Mr. Lynch said, understanding in his voice, without the condemnation I expected.

"Yes, she was my father. I did not know she was an abomination until the boarding school matron told me. I was not allowed to talk about Ahpʉ or my mother. I was ashamed and began to tell people my father died before I was born."

"Your blood father did die before you were born. Merdy was the only father you ever knew."

I sat up on the edge of my chair. "I have never cared to know my true parentage, until this moment. Faced with someone that seems to know much more than I do and is not shocked by my relationship with this woman – Merdy – I will admit my curiosity is aroused."

He stood abruptly. "All in due time, Thora, if I may call you that. I will leave you to get settled. Your bed," he pointed at the accommodations on the opposite side of the room from the sleeping patient, "is over there. Tseena and I will sleep outside. The water in the pitcher is fresh and dinner will be served shortly. I hope you are not opposed to steak and beans."

I did not move, but stayed still, imagining all matter of things crawling in that bed. My expression must have betrayed my thoughts.

John laughed, heartily. "Fear not, your linens are fresh, and I took the liberty of purchasing a wardrobe more suitable for the prairie than Paris. It is in the case at the end of the bed.

126

I have paid your dressmaker for ten years. I was aware of the sizes required. I hope they will be suitable for you."

"You are kind, John Lynch. I may have misjudged you and I'm afraid I haven't made a proper impression. I will try to amend that, and since I have no choice but to see this adventure through, I am ready to face my fate."

He smiled and exited, closing the door behind him, and leaving me to my unpacking. I glanced around the darkened room, now devoid of the light from the doorway. A cave-like claustrophobia infiltrated the space.

"If I am to stay here, Ahpu, we will have light in this room and fresh air," I said to the figure in the bed, while I set about removing the dark curtains and opening the windows.

Alone with my thoughts, during the brightening of the place, I began to think of things I had shut from my mind, many years ago. How could this woman be my father? I was ignorant of the circumstances that made it so. I knew nothing of my mother's relationship to this woman. Of course, I had read The Bostonians, *the recent Henry James novel, and I had lived among women in such Boston marriages. I thought of afternoons shared with Gertrude at Rue de Fleurus, while we sipped wine, conversing of art and other beautiful things, including the coupling of women. It was not an unfamiliar concept, but my relationship with Ahpu was unique in my experience.*

Until it was explained to me, I had not seen my father as different from others. True, I had known few fathers and other children while residing in such isolation. I did, however, have vague memories of playing with travelers' children, while their parents fed and rested their livestock. I saw no distinction between those parents and mine, nor did anyone feel the need to point one out. Ahpu dressed as my father, acted as my father, and was perceived as my father by others. I knew she was a woman, but her role as my father was played so spectacularly, I was never concerned with her gender. My use of the pronoun "her," in reference to my father, caused quite a stir at the boarding school. I was whisked away, asked to explain myself, and when I did, was told of the abomination I had been forced to endure. I was taught to despise the thing Ahpu represented, and in turn, feel shame for having loved her.

As I gazed at Ahpu's face, now lit by the sun shining through the windows, I remembered her warm smile and the strong hand that held my tiny one. The words and beliefs of others, and my own willingness to forget, tainted those memories. To discover now that she, my Ahpu, was the source of the benevolence shown me these twenty years, brought a shame of its own. Her generosity had allowed me the hours spent discussing the value of art that by its very nature could not be defined. New bold steps being taken by Chagall, Picasso, and others, art outside the boundaries of accepted delineations. Yet, I had shunned Ahpu for living her life as she saw fit.

I also wondered what decision lay ahead of me. What conditions had Ahpu put on the trust funds that had been so readily available to me? What had she sacrificed of her life, so that I could live mine? My future was uncertain, but I knew in my heart this experience would alter me. In what way was unclear, but I was already changing in my feelings for this woman, who was sleeping soundly through my crisis. It was much easier to maintain my revulsion of her, when I could not see the cheeks that I had kissed so often as a child, when I could not touch the arms that held me tight. I had been so resolved in my opinion of her, the emotions welling up inside me now only contributed to my unnerving.

I touched the hand that used to soothe the tears from my cheeks. "What lesson have you brought me here to learn, Ahpu?"

She spoke so suddenly that I jumped at the sound. I recovered quickly and listened. Her dry throat prevented the words from coming clearly, as she repeated, "Petu," a word I had not heard since leaving this place.

I patted her hand and whispered close to her ear, "Yes, your Petu, your daughter has come home."

#

"Holy shit!" Decky said, looking around to see if anyone heard her, even though she was entirely alone. She fumbled on the bed table for her cellphone. She slid her finger across the screen, tapped it again, and put it to her ear.

After the third ring, she heard, "Do you need more ice or a stiff drink?" Charlie laughed into the phone.

"Uh, I'm not the one that's going to need a stiff drink. Maybe you should bring the bottle."

Decky could hear the fake smile in Charlie's voice, as she tried to cover her panic. "Okay, more ice coming up."

The phone went dead, as the beep-beep of the lost call sounded.

"This should be interesting," Decky said, as she lifted the thawing ice bag and moved to stand.

The excitement of the moment disengaged the warning bells that would have told her to take it slow. That became clear all too quickly. The last time Decky was this sore, she had cartwheeled off a slalom ski, ending in a douche inducing split-landing she would never forget. Horseback riding, for the first time in twenty years, was going on the list of notable traumatic events. She tried to straighten her legs, but they inevitably bowed out a bit at the knee to reduce the pain.

129

Decky was seized up tighter than a bowstring. She hobbled to the table, carrying the manuscript, and depositing the ice bag in the sink along the way.

Decky had just dropped the last two painful inches into the chair, when Charlie burst through the door, holding a large bag of ice and an open bottle of beer. She rushed toward Decky and handed her the ice. She then turned the beer bottle up and took a good long drink, before she sat down across from Decky.

"Where's my beer?" Decky asked, while gladly placing the ice across her thighs.

"You talk. I'll drink for both of us," Charlie said, pointing at the manuscript. "Well?"

Decky cocked her head to one side, unsure of exactly what to say.

"That confused puppy dog look does not bode well, and that grin creeping into your cheek is an ominous sign," Charlie said, indicating Decky's right cheek with the beer bottle.

"I'm sorry, I don't mean to grin, it's just –"

Charlie leaned closer. "It's just what?"

"Well, my family's interesting past doesn't look quite as colorful anymore. I'm not sure a few concubines and bastards measure up to a cross-dressing lesbian that your great-grandmother called father."

The beer bottle landed on the table with a thud, rocking back and forth before Decky caught it.

Charlie stared at her with her mouth hanging open, and then recovered enough to ask, "How do you know that she was a lesbian? Surely, this woman didn't come right out and call her a lesbian in 1905."

"I believe she used the terms 'Boston marriage' and 'coupling of women'. She also mentioned sipping wine in Paris with Gertrude at the Stein residence. I think it's a given she knew a lesbian when she saw one," Decky answered, trying not to laugh, and at the same time wondering why she found it so funny.

Charlie wanted to know the same thing. "Why do you find this amusing?"

"Well, Charlie, for a family that doesn't like to discuss your sexuality, your mother sure has opened a can of worms. What exactly am I supposed to do with this? Does she really want me to tell this story, or is this her way of telling you she's okay with who you are?"

Charlie turned a little pale. She sat back against the chair. "She's been in the kitchen telling half the family about giving you Thora's story, saying how she wants us all to understand exactly who to thank for the land we've lived on."

"I haven't gotten to that part yet," Decky said. "I just now got the gist of who is who, but I don't know anything about Thora's mother, or how she and Ahpu ended up way out here, together."

"Ah-pa?" Charlie sounded out, her brows knitted.

"I think that's how you say it. That's what Thora called Merdy. It's Comanche for father."

"So, it's clear she knew this person as her father," Charlie said, before taking the last swallow of the beer.

"Thora carried the Ethridge surname. She called Merdy father. Yep, I think it's pretty clear."

Charlie stood up.

"Where are you going?" Decky asked, not ready to walk just yet.

"While being drunk is frowned upon in my family, a good old fashioned I don't want to give a shit buzz is allowed. I'm getting another beer." Charlie pointed at Decky, as she walked toward the door, tossing the empty bottle in the trash on the way. "You read."

131

"Maybe I want a beer," Decky whined.

Charlie turned just before she exited. "Then read faster."

#

After her first words to me, Ahpu slipped back into a deep sleep. I spent the remainder of the day cleaning the sod house, making it livable for a woman. I changed my Parisian couture for the plain, but tasteful clothing of an American West woman provided by Mr. Lynch. I vowed to treat him more kindly. He was merely following the wishes of others, as was I.

We had a pleasant meal, while Mr. Lynch asked me of all the new happenings in Paris. He had lived there once and longed to return for a holiday. We did not speak of my situation, as we both agreed it had been a long day, and tomorrow offered ample time for discovery. He had set up a little camp table for our plates to rest on. I had not dined so crudely in many years, but enjoyed the stillness of the place. Since my early childhood, I felt as though the world never stopped turning, forever in motion. Here, everything seemed to have paused to take a breath. I began to feel that I had been called here to do the same.

Tseena sat away from us, intermittently entering the sod house while we dined. He eyed me suspiciously, on his comings and goings. I asked Mr. Lynch about this behavior, when Tseena was in the house.

"Why does he stare at me so?"

"Tseena doesn't trust women. Says they cause trouble. Can't say that he's too far off on that," he answered.

"And yet, his closest friend seems to be a woman," I pointed out.

"Merdy is his brother. They fought together as warriors. You should hear him go on about Merdy, except he calls her by her shortened Comanche name, Puku rúa. It means horse child

132

or colt." He laughed and I noted how easily it came to him. He exuded an air of relaxed confidence. "The Comanche called her Pihiso?ai puku rúa, which meant Angry Horse Child. She was evidently not happy about being captured when they first caught her in Texas. Tseena met her shortly after that."

This news stunned me. "Forgive me, but did you say Ahpʉ was captured by the Comanche? I thought she was Comanche."

My dinner companion turned toward me, his expression one of concern and pity. "You know nothing of Merdy's past? Do you know who your mother was?"

"I know only that she had golden hair and azure eyes. She died when I was five-years-old. Her name was Grace."

"I did not know her, but Tseena and Merdy spoke of her often. Hers was quite the story of survival, as is Merdy's. You would not be here, if not for those two very brave women."

"I would very much like to learn of their deeds. Will you be the one to tell me?" I asked, the need to understand my heritage growing by the second.

Tseena emerged from the house. He scowled at me as he passed, speaking to my dinner companion in a language I may have once known, but was unable to comprehend after so many years.

"Tomorrow, Miss Ethridge. Tomorrow, I will tell you what I know. Now, I must bid you farewell and see to the horses."

I wanted him to stay and explain so many things, but I left the two of them to attend to their chores and secluded myself in the sod house with Ahpʉ. A warm teapot rested on the table beside the pitcher of water, left by Tseena I assumed. He must have been feeding his patient, while Mr. Lynch and I conversed. I poured myself a cup of the tea, after hunting for a sufficiently clean vessel. It was not a brew I would have chosen, for its taste was bitter and dry, but it was warm and

133

some comfort. I had several servings over the course of the evening, only because there was nothing else to occupy my time. No books, no paintings, just blankets and plaster walls to gaze upon.

I found the inkbottle and paper packed away in my trunk and wrote the lament found on the first page of this manuscript. I wallowed in my misery, as the hours ticked by, and darkness fell. I heard movement outside, voices speaking in hushed tones. Then quiet overtook the place. Only insects called out to one another in the still oppressive balminess. Darkness brought little relief from the heat of the day.

I had not unlaced my corset, choosing to lie down with it in place. The warmth of the night forced me from my bed. I removed my nightdress and grasped at the corset laces, desperate now to be free of the binding.

"I can help with that."

The voice startled me from my struggle to rid myself of the breath-stealing contraption. I spun around to see Ahpu sitting on the edge of her bed, arisen from her death state. I stumbled backwards, shocked by what I saw.

"Not sure why women truss themselves up like that," Ahpu added, rising to her feet, and crossing to the table.

She poured a glass of water from a pitcher and stood there drinking it; all the while I gaped and covered myself, for I was in the presence of a man, or so it seemed. Her voice was soft, but carried the timbre of a young man's speech. I had not seen her clothing, as she was covered to her shoulders with blankets, even in the heat of the day. Now, she stood before me in men's trousers, suspenders hanging loosely from her hips. The sweat stained upper portion of a union suit protruded from her waistband, its buttons undone enough to reveal muscle, not cleavage. Her dark hair was cut short, in the style of a man. Her eyes were her most striking feature, seeming to sparkle with flecks of gold sprinkled in the deep green of her irises, and framed by dark brows. If it was possible to look more a mature handsome man, I was not aware of how it would be accomplished.

"Turn around," she said, after setting the glass back on the table. "And close your mouth before you draw flies." I did as I was told, following orders like a child, as she started toward me, continuing to speak. "You don't have anything I haven't seen of my own. I may dress like a man, but I'm the same as you underneath. Never saw a need to wear girly things." She laughed softly, while she untied the knot I had managed to create in the laces. "I was in a saddle before I could walk, racin' horses when I was seven. No, never saw a need to be bound up in all that drapery."

I waited while my laces were loosened, still as a statue. When she was finished, I slipped out of the corset, keeping my back turned. I redressed in my gown quickly, turning to see that Ahpu had moved to the corner. She removed a shirt from a peg on the wall, donned it, and adjusted the suspender straps into place. She picked up a pair of worn boots from the floor, carrying them to a chair at the table, and sat to put them on.

"If you're going with me, you should lace up your boots." She spoke to me as if my long absence had not occurred.

"Ahpu, do you know who I am?" I asked, confused by her sudden recovery and her apparent nonchalance at my presence after twenty years.

"You are Petu. You have come to hear the truth and it will be told to you. Hurry now, they wait for us."

Ahpu did not pause for me. She pulled on her boots, stood, and walked to the door before I could fully lace my own. I secured them as best I could and rushed after her, passing Mr. Lynch sleeping soundly on the ground near the door. He did not stir and I wondered how safe I was with him as my

135

guardian. It was a brief thought, as I ran into the darkness after Ahpʉ.

We walked for some time, not speaking, me trailing after her. She stopped near the river. I could not see it, but I could smell the water. I was startled into a yelp, when Tseena appeared out of the shadows.

Ahpʉ greeted him. "Aho!"

I remembered this was "hello" in my native tongue. I was happy the rest of Ahpʉ's greeting was in English, "My old friend, good to see you," because I was sure I could remember not much more of a language I was forbidden to speak, after I began my studies at the boarding school.

They clasped arms, Tseena saying something I could not understand.

Ahpʉ turned to me. "Come, the others are gathering."

We walked on to the river, where we arrived at a sandy bank. Three men sat around a small fire. They greeted my companions with smiles and shouts, offering pipes of tobacco and blankets to rest on. I could not make out their words, but their gestures were the ones of old friends. The three strangers were Indians. Two of them, one older than the other, wore breechcloths and leggings, with war paint adorning the upper half of their tanned bodies.

Ahpʉ introduced them. "Petʉ, this is Little Otter and Falling Tree."

"It is a pleasure to meet you," I managed to say, even as I was frightened of these savages.

They simply nodded and glared at me with cold black eyes. Silver hoops decorated with beads and feathers dangled from holes in their earlobes. Their cold black hair was parted down the middle of the scalp, captured in long ermine-wrapped braids, and hung over each shoulder. The part in the hair was painted black, along with fearsome black lines on their faces

136

and arms, giving them a very savage appearance. The third man was in his mid-thirties, dressed in trousers and a collared shirt, with neatly trimmed black hair. I recognized the manner and dress of a boarding school graduate, the assimilated Indian.

Ahpu did not introduce the trouser wearing man, but I knew it must be her father. The resemblance was uncanny. The six of us sat in a circle around the small fire. Only a trickle of water could be heard from the nearly dry riverbed. The men spoke with Ahpu, laughing and passing the pipe, while I sat silently in amazement, still attempting to gain a hold on my fear of the native warriors. My friends in Paris would never imagine the company I was keeping. I was having a difficult enough time on my own, believing what I was witnessing.

When Tseena passed the pipe to me, I waved him off. He shoved it towards me again. "Take. Smoke."

"You speak English?" I questioned.

"I speak so you may hear," Tseena said, shoving the pipe at me again.

I took it and puffed once on the end, before a spasm of coughing took my breath. The men laughed, as I passed the pipe to Ahpu.

Tseena held up a wooden cup to me. "Take. Drink."

I did not ask what was in the cup. I simply wanted the fire in my throat extinguished. I drank the concoction, realizing it was the same tea from the table in the sod house. This time I gulped it without compunction. Ahpu took the cup from me, before I could consume all of its contents.

"Easy, there. You will make yourself sick."

No sooner than the words were out of Ahpu's mouth, I was up and running to the bushes nearby, where I retched and became very disoriented.

Out on the Panhandle

Ahpʉ was at my side before I recovered my senses, leading me back to the fire, speaking softly. "Sit here and rest, while we tell stories of the past. You will see and hear things. Do not be frightened. These are merely memories." Ahpʉ turned to the men. "Who will tell the tale of how I became a human being?"

The man in the trousers spoke. "I will tell it. I am a mere shadow of the man I was, but I was there when you took your first breath, born to half Scottish Chickasaws, both father and mother, at the white man's fort on the eve of your mother's death. You were a poor babe with no mother, and a father who knew more about horse-stock than children. Your boarding school educated father and grandmother taught you to read and write. You knew both the white man and Chickasaw way of life. Your father traded horses at the fort with the Comanche, Apache, Kiowa, and the soldiers. You spoke many tongues, but mastered the language of the horse.

"You were raised with the horses, a wild colt, untamable and left unbroken. To the saddle you were born, your true parents the stallion and the mare, which bore you like the wind across the open ground. The fort closed in your tenth year. Your father's services were no longer needed, thus he wagered on your ability to ride his last great hope, a black as night beast that ran with the speed of wings. In the month of the flower, just after you began your eleventh year, he rode with you to Texas, taking along the great black stallion."

A rush of heavy hoof beats came at us from the river. I felt the ground shaking, when out of the dark rose the very horse of which the man spoke. The beast snorted and pawed at the ground, baring his great white teeth, and then up on his haunches he rose, clawing at the air, his piercing shriek filling the night. A child in knee britches appeared out of the darkness, palms held in the air, walking straight into the path of the beast. I thought the horse would surely trample the

138

child, but instead it dropped from its rearing, lowered its head, and surrendered with a nicker. The child led the great beast away with no rope, just a bond of understanding.

I was compelled to follow the child, as well. My heart beat out an unfamiliar rhythm, quickening as never before. The child appeared to be a boy with dark hair, cut to his shoulders, framing his delicate features. We crept through the low brush into a patch of trees. The boy turned to the horse, asking it for quiet with his startling green and amber eyes. He crouched, peeking at the scene unfolding below, for suddenly, the land beyond the trees lit up, as if day had come. A long wagon train, circled for defense, was under siege and on fire. Indians rode a cloud of dust around the remaining survivors, who were fighting with their last breaths, struck through with arrow and lance, bullet and club.

"You ride hard, if they see you. You don't stop until Jack gives out or you are shed of them." The trouser wearing man whispered the words, as he emerged from the shadows and crouched at the boy's side.

The boy turned to the man. "But that's White Bear and Big Tree. They are our friends, Pa."

"The Kiowa and Comanche have no friends on the warpath."

"Why don't we run?" The boy asked, and I had to agree with his suggestion.

"They are not all down there. The others watch from a distance, protecting the warriors from an ambush. We don't know where they are. They may have already seen us. Be still and hope they go and leave us be."

The warriors below whooped, the trills of their war cries and celebratory rifle shots filling the air. Some of them stood tossing goods out of the wagons to others loading the spoils on the now unharnessed mules of the train. When all but one of the men of the train was dead or dying, he was singled out and tied between two wagon wheels.

"Do not watch, little one," the man said.

I looked away too late. I was horrified to see a knife drawn across the man's scalp, while he was still breathing. His screams penetrated to my very bones. I covered my mouth for fear I would join him in his anguish. The other Indians set out scalping the dead and dying. The savagery was too much to endure, and when I thought I could bear it no longer, I was pushed over my limit. I fell to my knees, when the panicked shrieks of the scalped man intensified, as he was shot multiple times with arrows, and then set on fire to burn alive.

My horror turned to terror as the two savages from the fireside jumped from the bushes, and rushed toward us. I did not have time to question how the horse was now saddled, as the man suddenly stood and lifted the boy onto its back.

"Ride, little one. Ride like the wind."

"But you," the boy protested.

The man slapped the horse on the rump and yelled, "Ha!"

The stallion reared and leapt forward, the boy leaning into his neck. I could only watch for a moment, as the war cries of the warriors drew my attention. I turned in time to see the first arrow penetrate the man's chest. Two more followed quickly. I screamed with all the strength I had, as Little Otter turned, coming toward me, club held high in the air. I tried to stand, but my legs would not answer the call. I saw the nostrils of the warrior flare, as he narrowed the distance between us, his eyes dark and deadly. I raised my hands to shield the blow, closing my eyes.

Nothing happened. I waited, listening, but no blow came. I heard the crackle of a fire, opened my eyes, and had returned to the circle with Ahpu. Tseena was the only other person remaining at the fire. I tried to make sense of all I had seen,

140

but had no time to gather my thoughts. Ahpʉ stood and helped me to my feet.

"We must go now," Ahpʉ said. "The hour of the morning star is upon us."

"What of the boy, Ahpʉ? What happened to the boy?" I pleaded.

Ahpʉ answered, "When the moon comes again, you will know of the boy's fate."

This was all the answer I received, as Ahpʉ said his goodbye to Tseena, and led me back past the still sleeping Mr. Lynch, and into the sod house. She took off her shirt, hung it on the peg, removed her boots, and slipped back into the bed. The heavy sleep overcame her immediately. She was once again a silent prone statue. I stood over her, noticing the rosy youthfulness on her cheeks. The fresh air had improved her pallor. My eyes grew heavy and I left her to her dreams.

I took to my bed, examining the events of the evening. My last thoughts were of the boy, but not a boy at all. It was Ahpʉ. I had left her riding for her life, and so it seemed, my own as well.

#

Decky closed the manuscript, processing what she had just read. Thora described a vivid hallucination, more than likely drug induced. Something was definitely up with that bitter tea. What part, if any of the story was true? Were these simply the delusions of a drugged woman thrust into a place fraught with emotional memories? What about Ahpʉ, Merdy? She was a woman who dressed and carried herself as a man, but stated her womanhood with ease. She seemed comfortable in both genders, blurring the lines drawn by others. That was quite a feat of bravery for the time period.

141

Decky was so deep in thought, she jumped at the sound of Charlie opening the RV door.

"So, what do you know now?" Charlie asked, before the door closed behind her. She was wearing her hat again, which made Decky smile.

Decky stood and stretched her painful muscles. "I know I need out of this confined space."

"I was thinking the same thing," Charlie said, crossing to the mini-refrigerator, and pulling out two cold bottles of water. "Come on, we can talk about what you've read while we walk around. That should make you feel better."

Moving around had to be better than sitting here letting her muscles pull tighter and tighter. Decky threw the now melted ice bag in the sink, put on the cowboy hat and her boots, and followed Charlie to the side of the house, where a shovel and a wheelbarrow waited. Charlie grabbed the shovel with one hand, and finished off the bottle of water with the other. She tossed the empty bottle toward the house.

She turned to Decky. "Better hydrate. Just leave the bottle over there and we'll get it when we come back. You push the wheelbarrow."

"Come back from where and why do we need a shovel and a wheelbarrow? I thought we were going on a walk to loosen my legs up," Decky said, and then drank most of the water from her bottle.

Charlie started walking toward a gate that led to a pasture. "We are walking, but we are looking for something, as well."

"What, pray tell, do we need to dig up out in that pasture?" Decky asked, grabbing the handles of the wheelbarrow and following Charlie.

"In addition to a softball game that you will be participating in, we also have cow patty bingo and a cow chip throwing contest." Charlie said this as if everyone had these

142

activities at their family reunions. "You can also play horseshoes, if you can get a spot in the tourney, but they are pretty hard to come by."

Decky limped along behind Charlie, becoming friends with the wheelbarrow, and trying to avoid large rocks. "I see your competitive streak is genetic," she said, feeling her bowstring tight muscles begin to loosen. "Did you volunteer us to collect the chips for said throwing contest?"

Charlie scanned the ground in front of them as they walked, answering Decky's questions but concentrating on her mission. "No, everybody has to bring three cow chips, not less than six inches in diameter."

"You have rules?" Decky asked, as Charlie squatted over a pile of bovine feces of sufficient girth.

Just to make sure the patty met specifications, Charlie measured it using a small ruler she had tucked away in her back pocket. She explained her process, while examining the perspective contest projectile for hardness, tapping it with the ruler. "A good hard chip will go a hundred feet or more. It has to be compact and solid to get the best airtime." The chip must have met specifications, because she lifted it into the wheelbarrow with the shovel, and then went in search of more. "Everyone chooses the best chips to bring, because we put them all in a pile for the contest. You should be among the top contenders."

Decky looked down at the cow chip she was now carting across the pasture. "And what makes you think I'd be good at tossing cow manure? Is that some kind of commentary on my communication skills?"

"No, but you do have a great throwing arm and the best way to throw a cow chip is like a baseball. We're taking that women's title. You're going to practice." Charlie spied a good candidate for tossing, picked it up, and held it out to Decky.

143

Decky laughed. "You are not kidding, are you?"

"It's no different from the stuff you put in the garden," Charlie said, shoving the cow dung at Decky.

"I wear gloves when I work in the garden," Decky answered, setting the wheelbarrow down and backing away, no longer laughing.

"When did you turn into such a wimp? Here, throw the thing," Charlie insisted.

Decky straightened. She had a logical reason for her fear of cow chips. "Have you ever watched one of those mad cow disease videos?"

"I am cutting you off from YouTube. You can find something to scare you about everything on there. Now, here! Throw the damn cow chip."

Decky seized the cow chip and threw it in one motion, not wanting contact with it any longer than necessary. It flew a good distance, judging by Charlie's reaction.

"Hell yeah," she said, losing nearly every ounce of that Duke education. She slapped Decky a high five. "We are going to smoke that turd throwing wench."

Decky was confused. "To whom are you referring?" She asked, before she saw Charlie's expression. It was hard for Decky to maintain a straight face, when she added, "Oh, I see. This Karen person is a champion turd thrower. Is that the correct term for a cow chip throwing aficionada, turd thrower?"

Charlie picked up a nearby chip and handed it to Decky. "You're going to be the best turd thrower of them all, don't worry about why."

Decky could tell Charlie was serious about her old rivalry. Still, she joked with her. "Honey, has it come to this? Are we going to throw bull shit to see who wins the day?"

144

Charlie waved the cow chip at her. "That trophy is coming back to the family."

"You have a trophy?" Decky asked, unable to suppress a laugh.

"Yes, and I just found out she won it last year," Charlie said, a hint of middle school in the air.

Decky tried a bit of reason. "But if I win, it doesn't come back to the family."

"Yes it does," Charlie said, giving the cow chip another wave in front of Decky. "You are family."

"If I'm family, so is Karen."

Charlie wasn't going to be reasonable. "But I like you."

"Charlie, you're forty years old. It's ridiculous for you to act this way."

"This from a woman who makes me answer the phone when her mother calls," Charlie said, shoving the cow chip at Decky, more forcefully this time.

"Good point. Hold my hat," Decky said, and took the weapon she would use to destroy Charlie's enemy, if that's what she wanted, flinging it as far as she could.

CHAPTER SIX

"Oh my, but you don't smell at all pleasant," Charlie said, squeezing by Decky in the RV doorway.

"Hang on," Decky said, plucking a small piece of cow dung from Charlie's hat brim. "I've been tossing manure on the prairie, at your request. You didn't tell me they would explode like that sometimes."

"There is a fine line between throwing it hard and too hard," Charlie said.

"Thanks for the tip," Decky said, shaking her head one more time before entering the RV, trying to ensure all the stray chip pieces were expelled. "Who knew dried poop could blow into a cloud of dust? I think I swallowed some of it."

Charlie started removing her clothes right away, preparing for a shower. She had called first dibs, because she wanted to help her mother with the cooking. She cautioned Decky, "Don't sit down on anything we can't wash off. I'll hurry." She disappeared into the bathroom, leaving Decky alone.

Decky took a bottle of water from the refrigerator, unscrewed the top, filled her mouth with water, then thought of what she may have still in her mouth and was about to swallow. She bent over the sink and spit the water out. Mouthwash, she needed it in the worst way. To distract herself from imagining the bacteria colony hatching in her mouth, she walked over to the table, opening the manuscript.

Decky caught Charlie up on Thora's story during cow chip throwing practice. She commented occasionally, but for the most part, Charlie just listened.

"Peyote," she said, at one point. "I'll bet that's what was in the tea. They used to mix it with other herbs and make a tonic for illness, even fed it to the horses. In weaker amounts it does not cause hallucinations, but get enough, and off you go to lala-land."

"How do you know so much about Peyote?" Decky asked. "Have you ever taken it?"

Charlie shook her head. "No, it's bad medicine if you use it for the wrong purposes. It's for use in spiritual rituals and for medicinal purposes in the Native American Church. I've heard it will mess you up if you misuse it, plus it's illegal as hell to have it."

Decky stood over the manuscript, wondering if most of this writing would turn out to be peyote-induced ramblings, with no real answers. How would she know what was real and what wasn't? Decky found the place on the page where she stopped reading and began again.

#

I awoke the next morning to a tremendous headache and an exceedingly dry mouth. I drank freely from the water pitcher until it was almost emptied, the bitterness of the tea from last night still tainting my ability to taste. I checked on

Ahpu̶, who had not stirred from her resting state, not an inch. I dressed quickly, lacing my corset only as tight as I could on my own. Upon exiting the sod house, I found Mr. Lynch preparing something in a cast iron pot at the fire.

"Good morning, Miss Ethridge. I hope you slept well."

"Not as well as you, Mr. Lynch. A herd of elephants could not have disturbed your slumber. I walked by you twice and you never stirred."

He looked away from his task at the fire, examining me with an odd expression. "It is quite impossible that you exited that door last night. You did not set the bolt before you fell asleep. I secured the door from the outside and just now removed the catch."

Tseena came into my view. I pleaded with him. "Tell him, Tseena. You were there. We sat by a fire at the river."

The old Indian grunted at me and disappeared into the house.

Mr. Lynch laughed, before saying, "You're wasting your time. He isn't going to speak to you."

"He spoke to me last night, in English," I said, becoming more unsettled by the moment.

I was beginning to think I might have only imagined the events of the night. How else could I explain seeing the wagon train so clearly? I looked to Mr. Lynch. "It couldn't have been a dream," I paused, sighing deeply, "but it was, wasn't it?"

He tilted his head to one side and inspected me thoroughly, his expression one of concern. After a moment's appraisal, he asked, "You wouldn't by any chance have had a sip of Tseena's tea, would you?"

"If you mean the bitter concoction in the teapot left on the table, I had some before retiring."

Mr. Lynch laughed. "Well, that explains your confusion. That's Peyote tea, makes you see things. Unless you want to visit the other world, you should leave it alone."

"I had no idea I was consuming a hallucinogen," I replied in shock.

I was so certain it had all happened, I couldn't bring myself to tell Mr. Lynch that I also thought I spoke with Ahpᵾ, that she rose and led me from this place. He would think me mad, should I inform him of the images and savagery the drug-laced tea had conjured from my brain. I found myself walking toward the camp table, set for the morning meal. I took my seat and remained quiet for some time. Mr. Lynch chattered on, finishing his stirring of what appeared to be porridge, while I tried to understand why I would dream such things as scalping and that man's tortured screams.

"You'll be fine, Miss Ethridge. We'll get some food in you and you'll be good as new. I'd like to take you down to see the horses." He crossed to the table, placing a bowl of yellow mush in front of me, before continuing. "Merdy has some fine quarter horses. That magnificent animal you saw yesterday is a descendent of the horses you rode as a child. Are you remembering anymore of your life here? Surely, you recall the horses."

I stared down at the contents of the bowl. Cornmeal mush had not been on my palate since my early boarding school days. I lifted my spoon, hesitating.

"You must eat," Mr. Lynch suggested kindly. "It will help clear your head. I will speak to Tseena. He should take more care with his medicine."

I spooned some of the mixture into my mouth and was surprised to find it pleasant. I thanked Mr. Lynch and answered his question. "I have some memory of a black horse, one very similar to the one you rode."

149

"That would have been Jack. He was the sire for the line."

So there was a horse named Jack. My memories must have provided the name. I responded to Mr. Lynch, "I must remember him. He was in my dream."

"Merdy was riding Jack when the Comanche captured her. They probably wouldn't have caught her, if she had not disobeyed her father and turned back to look for him. She and her father were horse racing from town to town, just the two of them, when they came across a war party attacking a wagon train, just twenty miles from Fort Richardson, in Texas. General Sherman was there at the fort, at the time. That was May of 1871, just after I was born. They called it the Salt Creek Massacre."

My dream had been accurate. Had I been told the story as a child and manufactured the vision from long lost memories? Who would tell a child such atrocities? Surely, the gruesome details were not part of a bedtime story.

My confusion persisted, when Mr. Lynch answered, "I read stories about the attack when I was a young boy. Frightening, detailed stories, including a man scalped, shot through with arrows, stretched out between two wheels of a wagon, and burned alive. I cannot imagine Merdy seeing that happen at such a young age, and still she harbors no ill will toward the Comanche. She considers them her people and they feel the same way about her."

The last thing I heard was Mr. Lynch's voice, before the darkness took me.

"Miss Ethridge? Thora, are you all right?"

#

"Your turn," Charlie called out, as she left the shower. "Put those dirty clothes in the plastic bag I left in there."

150

Decky closed the manuscript. Thora would have to wait. She just caught a glimpse of a naked Charlie headed for the back of the RV. The cow chip procurement had loosened Decky up enough to consider chasing after her, but then she remembered she very much needed a shower first. Reluctantly, she gave up the thought of ravishing Charlie and went into the tiny bathroom. There was barely enough room for one person, so any thought of sex in the shower had been squashed when Decky first saw it, yesterday.

The first thing she did was brush her teeth and rinse with mouthwash, twice. Once Decky was satisfied any stray bacteria had been taken care of, she peeled off her smelly clothing, depositing it in the bag along with Charlie's. After adjusting the water temperature, she climbed behind the small sliding-glass door, and relaxed under the spray. Well, she relaxed as much as she could, having to suspend the little handheld nozzle above her head with one hand, because she was too tall for the wall-mounted holder. Knowing the small hot water tank would soon be empty, and with the thought she might catch Charlie half dressed, Decky rushed through the shower. She dried off quickly, wrapped the towel around her waist, and stepped into the cramped walkway between the bedroom and sitting area.

Charlie was right there, already dressed. Decky tried to hide her disappointment, but she did not have to for very long. Charlie wrapped her arms around Decky's neck and pressed her into the wall.

"Umm. You smell much better," Charlie said, between the little kisses she was planting on Decky's upper chest and neck.

Decky pulled Charlie closer. In response, Charlie pressed in against Decky's still damp body, raising her lips for a passionate kiss. It did not matter how many times she kissed Charlie, it still swept Decky away. Charlie wasted time getting dressed, because Decky was about to disrobe her, but just as surprising as Charlie's little ambush had been, so was her next move. She slid out of Decky's arms, winked, and cast a cocky grin at her.

"Didn't want you to think I forgot how to do that," Charlie said, and then turned to walk out of the RV, saying, "Have to go help Momma now. You just keep on reading and I'll reward you for your progress."

Decky stood against the wall, still breathless from the kiss. Just before the door closed, she called after Charlie, "Tease!"

While she dressed, Decky mumbled to herself about how Charlie's family was going to think she was some kind of eccentric author, staying shut up in the RV all the time. Charlie and her mother wanted Decky to read Thora's story, and it appeared she was not going to be allowed any other activities until she completed the task. She plopped down on the couch with the manuscript, found her place, and began to read.

#

I awoke to Ahpu standing over me, as I lay in bed inside the sod house. It took a moment for my surroundings to become familiar again, as it was dark, the only light coming from a lantern on the table.

"Did I sleep through the day?" I asked, and then suddenly remembered Ahpu may be a figment of my imagination. I reached for her, grasping her arm, feeling her warmth, and the solidness of her muscle. "You are real," I whispered, in astonishment.

She smiled warmly, her visage seeming to grow younger each time I laid eyes on her. She was not conventionally beautiful, but handsome would befit her, even striking. She had changed her sweat stained union suit for a fresh one and a clean shirt. Her trousers were cleaned and pressed.

152

Ahpu extended her hand for me to take, saying, "I am as real to you as you are to me. Come, our time runs short. There is much you have to see."

Again, we proceeded past the sleeping Mr. Lynch and into the night. As we neared the river, I could hear native drums and singing. The hair rose on my skin. I grasped at Ahpu's arm.

"Do not fear, Petu. These are your people," Ahpu said, as we broke through the trees to view an entire village caught up in celebration. "These are the Numunuu, the human beings." Ahpu sat near the bank of the river, patting the ground beside her. "Here we will watch. You will see how you became a human being, but first we will see what became of the boy."

I did not question her. I was by now aware that I was in a vision, but not a dream. I could smell the fire. The drumbeats pounded against my chest. All of my senses were alive. No, this was no ordinary dream. I could see Little Otter and his father. They were dancing to the drums, as they pantomimed the attack on the wagon and the boy's desperate attempt to flee, all while holding up the scalp of his father and others. I shrank from the hideous way they paraded the bloody trophies to the joyous shouts of their kinsmen.

"I could not be one of these savages," I protested.

Ahpu smiled. "All men are capable of savagery. All men are capable of good. You will see."

The boy came into view, as his part of the story unfolded. He was shoved and kicked into a circle of curious native children and women, who proceeded to abuse him more. This activity only ceased when four braves brought in the great black horse, each with a rope draped around the terrified animal's neck, but still he fought and reared. He was a froth of lather and caused considerable damage to the camp, as they

153

wrestled to control him. Little Otter charged at the horse, his lance held high. A shrill cry broke the air.

"Noooooo!"

The boy flew from his captors, throwing himself between the frightened animal and his would be assassin. Little Otter let fly his lance, sending it stabbing into the ground between the boy's feet. The boy did not flinch.

He shouted at the warrior, words I could not understand. The crowd hushed, as the horse calmed, walking up behind the boy.

"What did he say, Ahpʉ?"

"Listen and you will understand," he replied.

I leaned in to hear the warrior speak to the boy, his words becoming clear as I listened.

"Pihiso?ai puku rua. That is what I will call you, Angry Horse Child. You have courage. You speak to me as a human being, in my own tongue."

The boy took the lance from the ground, and holding it horizontally, handed it to the warrior. "I speak your tongue. My father, whose scalp you hold, traded many horses with the Comanche and the Kiowa. You have killed a friend."

This caused a stir among the villagers, as they discussed the matter among themselves. At that moment, eight warriors rode into camp, causing much commotion. They dismounted in the middle of the turmoil. One of them was tall, not much more than twenty, I suspected, but a great figure of a man. The Greek statues of antiquity paled in comparison.

The lance-bearing warrior spoke to him, "Quanah, my friend."

"Little Otter, it is good to see you," Quanah answered.

"Come, celebrate with us. We have many horses and mules from the white man, and this boy with the magic black stallion."

154

Quanah stepped forward. "I know this boy. Where is his father? He is my friend."

"That is his scalp, Quanah," the boy cried, his upper lip trembling. He was trying so hard not to give into his emotions, a brave little man.

The crowd hushed again.

Quanah surveyed the people in the village. They all seemed to cower under his cold stare.

I whispered to Ahpᵾ, "Is he a chief?"

"His time as leader will come. He is a great warrior and feared by many. No one will challenge him. They are afraid."

After what became a painful pause of silence, when it appeared Quanah had calculated his next move, he spoke, "For my friend's life, I will take the boy and his horse. In exchange, I will offer you this counsel. Do not go back to the reservation. One of the bluecoat star-chiefs was near the attack. He will see you all hang. The white invaders are angry and seeking vengeance for the wagon train. Join the Kwaharᵾnᵾᵾ. We go away from the white man's trails and live to fight another day."

The warrior contemplated his options. "We will go back to the reservation. Big Tree says no harm will come to us there. As for the boy, I will give him to you, but I keep the magic horse."

My own nervous laughter joined that of the villagers.

Quanah smiled at Little Otter's defiance. "It is not the animal that holds the magic. You may take the horse if you can ride it."

Loud laughter ensued, as no one could imagine anyone riding away on the wild beast.

Little Otter acquiesced, but to save face added, "Set the horse free. If he follows Angry Horse Child, he may go with you."

155

"You call him angry?" Quanah asked. He grinned at the boy, enquiring, "Merdy, did you fight them?"

The boy held back his tears, puffing his chest with false bravado. "I rode away like Pa said, but I had to go back. They caught me when I got off Jack, looking for Pa. I wailed on that big one there pretty good, 'til they tied my hands."

Along with the crowd, I found the boy's answer charming.

Quanah chuckled. "You have great courage. Your father's spirit is proud. We will speak his name no more, so that he may go to the next world unhindered." He turned to Little Otter. "Remove the ropes from the horse. You will see what magic the boy has. You should ask forgiveness of the horse spirits for your treatment of one who has been blessed with such power."

The boy removed the ropes one by one, as the braves who were once holding them had backed away, afraid of the magic of which Quanah spoke. The horse lowered his head, gentle now, as the boy freed him from his captors.

Quanah broke the silent gawking of the village with these words, "Behold the magic of the horse child." He turned to the boy. "Show them your power, little one."

The boy faced the horse, his arms hanging loosely at his sides. Though I could not see his face, I saw the boy make no gesture, nor did I hear him speak. The stallion raised his head high, eyes wide, and snorted. The onlookers leaned away, expecting the animal's wild frenzy to begin again. Instead, he shook his head, as if to free himself of any memory of his recent restraints, and then took a step forward. He lowered his head, eye to eye with the boy now, nickered softly, and then slowly folded his left leg under him, bowing to the ground. The boy stepped to the horse's side, leaned over the massive animal, and laced a hand through its shiny black mane. He threw a knee on the horse's back, and in one smooth motion

156

was lifted from the ground, as the stallion stood, head high, and proud. Hushed sounds of awe swept through the crowd.

Little Otter stepped to the side, allowing the boy and his horse to leave with no further protest. He spoke as the boy passed. "I will bury your father's scalp and sing for his soul."

The boy did not speak. He slowly walked the horse to the river, letting it drink away the exhaustion from its fight. He was so close I could have spoken to him, but I did not want to break the spell until I knew he was safely away with his protector. I could see that his cheeks were wet from tears he had held at bay for so long, a brave child as much as a broken hearted one.

Quanah rode up next to the boy. "This band goes back to the reservation near the fort. You may go with them. No one will harm you now. The men at the fort will find your family."

"My grandmother died last winter. Pa was all I had besides Jack," the boy answered, leaning over to wrap his arms around the stallion's neck.

"You will come with me. My people will be your people. You are now a human being."

I felt my heart would break for the boy, an orphan now, gone to live among strangers. The pain was as real to me as it was the day I was placed in a wagon and driven from my home. I watched the boy ride away with Quanah until I could see them no more. I turned my attention to Ahpu.

"The boy, he called him Merdy. That is you, but you are not a boy at all."

"I did not refer to myself as a boy. People assume what they will, from what they see," Ahpu said. "From an early age, it was clear that I was not fond of the things other girls were. I was allowed to choose my path. My Chickasaw grandmother believed that I was special, that I walked in two worlds, the masculine and the feminine. She said this was great magic. My

157

father went along because it was easier to travel with a boy, but he said when I turned twelve, I must dress as a woman and grow my hair long. He did not live to see that happen. I was eleven when he was killed."

"And yet, you love the people that murdered him. This, I cannot understand."

"I never saw Little Otter again, or his father. They went to the reservation. I was told they died there of a white man's disease. I went with the Kwaharᵾnᵾᵾ band, the Antelope Eaters. They were the last band of the people to move off the plains onto the hated reservation, but I get ahead of the story."

Ahpᵾ pointed across the river. I followed her gaze and saw that the scene had changed. The sun shone brightly on hundreds of lodges, covering the landscape as far as I could see, with smoke rising from the tops of the cone-shaped structures made of long poles and buffalo hides. An undulant green prairie served as the backdrop to a panorama very few white men had ever seen, a Comanche camp. A trickling river made its way down the middle of the nomadic tribe's temporary home, forming a series of shallow pools. Tall grass lined the banks of the pools, bending over the water, forming secreted places where children played hide and seek. Hundreds of natives went about their afternoon activities. A few of the women were talking and laughing, while hanging thin slices of buffalo meat on primitive drying racks made of sticks. Women cared for infants and toddlers, as they went about their duties, stirring large pots over fire pits, or scraping freshly skinned buffalo hides to be boiled in the pots, or stretching still steaming hides over stakes. Children of all ages ran here and there, entertaining themselves with childish games.

Their manner of dress, or lack thereof, captivated me. I had never seen so much human flesh at one time. For the most

158

part, the men were dressed as Little Otter had been, sans war paint. Some of the men wore shirts made of softened buckskin, so supple it fairly floated over their skin. Others paraded around in items traded for or stolen from white settlers and soldiers, ranging from a few women in US Calvary blue wool coats to the warriors wearing ladies' corsets and shaded by parasols. From birth, the boys appeared to wander unabashedly naked, until they reached pre-adolescence and took on the fashion of the adult males. The girls, however, did not go without covering. Even the toddler females were clothed in breechcloths up to young womanhood, when they joined the adult women in buckskin dresses, leggings, and moccasins, all decorated with beads and fringe.

A group of old men gathered around a fire, blankets tied around their waists, engrossed in each other's stories. Young warriors watched, as the more mature braves practiced lifting each other off the ground from the back of a galloping horse. The rider would place one foot in a loop at the end of a loose fitting rope around the horse's neck, drop his body on the side of the horse, and as he lay in this horizontal position would hook his other heel over the horse's back. He would ride like this with the horse lunging forward at full speed, reach out for his comrade, and pluck him from the ground. It was an amazing feat of strength and agility. All around the village people were occupied with living what seemed a happy existence, a peaceful pastoral life filled with love and laughter.

I saw Quanah before I noticed the two boys grappling in the dirt at his feet. He had grown into an even more imposing man. Quanah and the older man with him seemed amused by the dusty battle, taking place in front of them.

"Horse Child fights as though each battle will be the last," *Quanah said.*

159

It was then that I realized one of the boys was Ahpu, a little older than before, looking very much the young brave, with braids and a buckskin shirt. She gave no quarter to the boy she wrestled.

"Her mother gave up. Said Horse Child would not work like a woman, always racing horses, shooting bows, will not wear woman's dress. She fights like a boy so let her live as one, she said."

"I did not know when I brought her to you two summers ago that Horse Child was female," Quanah said. "She is like no other that I have seen, but male or female, her gifts are many. She reads the white man's words from their papers. Horse Child tells me what they say to us and what they write are not the same. She is a gift to us, a guide sent from the spirits, and there is not a horse she cannot charm."

The older man smiled. "Horse Child has been a blessing. Her mother loves her. I am quite fond of her too."

Quanah, his eyes on the battle at his feet, said, "She is strong like young warrior and better on horseback than the other boys. Why does Horse Child fight this one?"

"He told her he would beat her and put her in a dress," the older man answered.

Horse Child was pinned beneath the larger boy, but only for a moment. She bit the boy's ear until he released her. He backed away, holding his bleeding ear. Horse Child stood and spit on the ground, prepared for another onslaught.

The old man spoke to the injured boy. "It is best you go back to your camp. You may eventually overpower her, but you will pay a heavier price than just a bloody ear."

The sound of thunder drew everyone's attention, including my own. A cloud of dust rose in the distance, as the first sounds of gunfire reached my ears.

160

Quanah turned and yelled to the people. "The soldiers are attacking Shaking Hands's camp. Run! Get to the horses!"

In an instant, the entire village went into panic. The people ran in every direction. Horse Child followed Quanah's order, running swiftly out of sight.

Quanah continued to shout as he ran after him. "Fight them, warriors! We must give the women and children time to escape!"

What happened next destroyed any notion I had that white men were the more civilized race. Screaming Indian scouts, with bold black lines tattooed on their arms and faces, led well over two hundred blue-coated soldiers in a full gallop through the village, killing everyone in sight with no regard for age or threat. The attack caught the Comanche unprepared. They could do little more than run and hide. Close to a hundred natives were chased into a ravine. The soldiers fired into the inescapable confines of the chasm without mercy, quickly turning a fight into a shooting gallery slaughter. The trickling river, once filled with laughing children, was now crowded with the bodies of men, women, and those same young souls, dead or drowning in pools of water infused with their own blood. Some tried to hide under the grass overhang, but the soldiers fired repeating rifles into the reeds, making no distinction between babe and old man, neither of which was putting up any sort of a fight. The Indian scouts began to scalp and mutilate the dead bodies, butchering anything that still breathed. I gasped at their savagery.

With distinct hatred in her voice, Ahpu replied, "Those scouts are Numuruhka, treacherous thieves and man-eaters. White men call them Tonks, and hired our old enemy to hunt us."

I watched as Comanche warriors did what they could, counter attacking to distract the soldiers, giving some of the villagers time to escape into the river bottom brush. A woman appeared amid the dust and gun smoke, turning circles in her confusion, unable to decide which way to run. Horses galloped in every direction, the relentless gunfire deafening. Suddenly, Horse Child emerged from a cloud of smoke, riding at full speed toward the helpless woman, paying no heed to the bullets flying through the air. Dropping to the side of the horse, she extended her arm, which the woman grabbed. Using inhuman strength and the momentum of the horse, Horse Child swung the frightened woman up behind her, and rode away on the swiftest horse I had ever seen.

In less than a half an hour, what had been a village in peaceful animation was now a smoke filled, bloody killing field.

Ahpʉ began to speak softly, the emotion welling in her voice. "Some of the tribal bands had come together on the north fork of the Red River to camp with Shaking Hands's band, the Kutsutʉhka, the Buffalo Eaters. Shaking Hands was, at the very moment the soldiers attacked, in Washington talking peace with the Great White Fathers. This is the peace we received. We came back the next day to bury our dead. I saw children floating in pools of blood stained water. Bodies were scattered on the ground, some disemboweled, decapitated, limbs cut away, babies with bullet holes in their heads, all manner of wickedness. Our lodges were piles of smoldering ash. Everything we possessed was destroyed, or taken as a souvenir. The white soldiers took prisoner one hundred and twenty five of our people, mostly women and children, along with over three thousand of our horses. You see, Petʉ, savagery lives in all men."

The sounds of the summer insects grew much louder, seeming to come alive all around me and all at once. I looked back across the river to see it was now a dark night. Before me was a large herd of horses, being guarded by the same murderous scouts from the village.

"We followed the bluecoats. Our people were too closely guarded for a rescue," Ahpu was saying, "but the horses were left in the hands of a few scouts, a mile away from the soldiers' camp."

A rustle of grass on the riverbank revealed Quanah and several others, including Horse Child. They crept undetected in the shadows, until they reached the herd. Horse Child then waded among the horses, approaching a nervous gray stallion.

"What is she doing?" I whispered, speaking as if the young brave were not Ahpu herself.

"The gray horse is the leader of part of the herd. Where he goes, they will follow," she answered, intently watching the scene unfold.

With the confidence of one much older, Horse Child calmed the animal, and then leapt to its back. With precision timing, the rest of the raiding party crashed out of the brush on horseback, while Quanah and the others leapt on the backs of nearby horses. Horse Child gave a yell and led the stampede, on the back of the gray. The scouts were left on foot, as three thousand horses sprinted away.

Ahpu chuckled, but it was tinged with an edge of vengeance. "We did not catch all of the horses, but the ones we missed, we stole the next night. They took our women and children, but not our herd. We survived to fight another day."

I noticed the tight muscle in her jaw, the way she stared into the darkness. "You did fight, didn't you? Even as a woman, you became a warrior. Did you do these things to other people? Did you kill and maim in the name of righteousness?"

Ahpu turned to me, her expression a mixture of pride and sadness. "I went on many raids with Quanah for the next two summers. I stole many horses and mules, attacked wagons and settlements, repaying the white man for his arrogance. They hunted us, killed us like animals, destroyed the buffalo herds, and wanted us to trust them, come live on their reservation, where our people who went there starved on rancid meat and broken promises. We fought back to save ourselves."

"You have evaded my question, Ahpu. Did you kill and maim? Was this savagery in you?"

"I did what I was driven to do." Ahpu said, and then nodded toward the opposite riverbank.

When I turned to look across the river, the sun nearly blinded me. I raised my hand to shield my eyes, until they adjusted to the glare. Three young braves lounged on the red-clay bank of a small tree-lined pond, watching over about a dozen horses drinking from the muddy water. Hills rising up around the little oasis blocked my view of the horizon, the landscape differing very much from the earlier visions.

"Where is this place?" I whispered to Ahpu.

"Texas Hill Country," she whispered back, but did not take her eyes from the scene.

The young men began to stir, drawing my attention. I saw that Horse Child was one of them, appearing taller and stronger than before. I thought her to be a young teen now, and the very definition of androgyny, blending the masculine and the feminine so thoroughly there was truly no distinction. She was beautiful and handsome, the combination striking.

The other two young men appeared a bit older, with lanky bodies and the budding muscles typical of the adolescent male. One of them stood and stretched.

"I'm tired of watching horses. I want to go on the raids," he complained.

Horse Child squinted up at him. "Your time will come, when your father thinks you've learned enough lessons."

164

The standing young man continued to grumble. "I have mastered the bow, the lance, the club, and the horse. I have worked as a woman, serving the warriors on raids for three years."

The third young brave, reclining on his elbows, spoke, "This is what is expected of us on raids, take care of the horses, tend to the camp. This is how we learn the way of the warrior. Our fathers learned this way. It is tradition."

The disgruntled brave was not satisfied. "I am a man now. What lesson have I not learned?"

Horse Child rose to her feet, grinning at the lamenting teen. "Perhaps it is patience he wishes you to master."

This response angered the already sullen young brave. He lashed out, pushing Horse Child with both hands, chiding her. "You are but a woman in breechcloth. You are not a man and are contented to live among the horses. I want to fight like a warrior!"

Horse Child charged at the aggressor, planting her shoulder in his stomach so suddenly, he had no time to react and was sent sprawling on his backside into the water. She stood on the bank, smiling down at him. "Never antagonize an opponent unless you have anticipated the attack you may provoke. Another lesson you failed to learn."

The first gunshot startled all of us. It came suddenly and seemingly out of nowhere. It took only a second for my eyes to focus on the posse of cowboys pouring down the hillside, panicking the three young braves and their horses. My eyes darted back to Horse Child, who was by now in full stride, running with the stampeding small herd. The other two braves ran after her, trying to keep up. The deep mud along the edge of the pond slowed a few of the horses, giving Horse Child the opportunity to leap on one of them. The other two followed suit. *With gunfire blazing all around, Horse Child led them up a steep hill.*

Two of the dozen or so cowboys broke off from the main body, flanking Horse Child and her friends. The three bareback riders turned at the crest of the hill, away from the pursuers, and then split up, riding in different directions, diverting the posse again. The brave young warrior, who had been looking for a fight, was now fleeing for his life into the brush below the pond. More cowboys suddenly appeared in front of him, crashing out of the trees in his direction. He pulled his bow, gave a war cry, and started shooting as many arrows as he could. He fought valiantly, until his horse was shot out from under him. The brave went down in the tall brush with the next round of pistol fire, as the cowboys closed in and dismounted.

Horse Child did not fare much better. Just after her companions left her, the horse she was riding stepped in a prairie dog hole, sending it toppling head over heels. Horse Child was thrown through the air and landed on her back. She lay motionless so long, even as I knew she must have survived, I prayed she was not dead. The two flanking cowboys jumped off their horses and pounced on her, kicking and hitting her, while degrading her with vile language I shall not repeat. I gasped when one of them took out a large knife and slashed Horse Child across the chest, slicing her buckskin shirt open, revealing a thin line of blood across her tiny breast where the knife found its mark just above her pink nipple.

The man held the knife in the air, poised for another swing, when his companion grabbed his arm.

"Hold up, Pete. I think that's a white girl."

"That ain't no white girl," the man with the knife said.

166

The other one was not so sure. "You ever seen a squaw what didn't have brown nipples?" He leaned down to get a better look, asking Horse Child, "Do you speak English?"

She was barely able to speak, and only managed a breathy, "Y-es."

The men jumped back from her, as if she were on fire.

The one with the knife said, "Lord, all mighty. I was fixin' to scalp a white girl."

His companion ran to his horse, retrieving a blanket, and then helped Horse Child into a sitting position. He tenderly placed the blanket around her shoulders, speaking softly. "You're al'right now. We'll take you back to your family. You're safe with us. Can you tell me your name?"

Horse Child stared at the ground, not responding.

The cowboy continued to talk, as he helped her from the ground. "Come on now. You can ride with me. We'll just go down here to that pond and water the horses. The others should be back straight away. We'll get you home, don't you worry."

The other members of the posse had ridden away, some after the horses, and a few chasing the young brave that escaped, leaving Horse Child alone with her two would be killers turned rescuers. She put up no fight, as she was helped onto the back of the horse. They rode down to the pond, where they all dismounted again. Horse Child stayed near the horses, while the other two walked a few paces away.

The one who had been about to scalp her asked, "You reckon we can trust her, Zebediah? She looks like she's been Indian for some time. How do you know she ain't just some pink titty squaw that learned English somewhere?"

"Look at her eyes, Pete. Comanches don't have eyes that color."

Out on the Panhandle

Pete sneered at Horse Child. "What's she doin' dressed like a boy? I ain't never seen no squaw wear a loincloth. She don't act like no girl I ever seen, don't ride like one neither."

"We don't know what they done to her. Can't you see she's scared?" The one called Zebediah said.

Pete scratched his chin with the big knife. "She'd be better off dead than back with her folks. Ain't nobody going to want a thing like her around."

The other one smiled back at Horse Child. "She'll be al'right. She just needs cleaned up and a pretty dress, that's all."

The knife wielding Pete shrugged his shoulders and walked off toward where the other brave had fallen into the hands of the posse. Zebediah, the kind one, as I had begun to think of him, stayed behind watching Horse Child, but kept his distance. He seemed to sense she needed time to understand what was happening. A loud whoop from his companion drew his attention.

I turned to see Pete coming back toward his friend, holding the decapitated head of the young brave in the air, a handful of bloody black hair laced through his fingers. "Look here, Zebediah. They took his head, but left us his scalp to take."

To my surprise, Zebediah replied, "Hot damn!"

I was in the process of averting my eyes, when Horse Child drew my attention. She moved quickly, ripping the cowboy's rifle from its saddle holster, and letting out a shrill war cry. She began to fire repeatedly at the two cowboys, killing them both, and continued to fire until the rifle was empty. Her anger overwhelmed her, when she stepped into the brush and saw what had been done to her friend.

Accompanied with a scream from her soul, she ran back to the man called Pete, lifted the rifle in the air, and came down on the dead cowboy's head with the butt, again and again, as

168

he lay still clinging to the decapitated head of the young brave. The sound was sickening, her frenzy so violent that when she raised her head again, the blood of the dead man dripped from her face. In that moment, Horse Child looked every bit the savage she had been forced to become. I watched in horror, as she tied her friend's disemboweled body on the back of one of the horses, putting his head in a saddlebag. She took the cowboys' pistols and ammunition belts, then mounted the other horse and rode away, taking her friend with her as fast as she could go.

I faced Ahpu, unable to believe this gentle soul could be driven to such brutality. Yet, I could only question one of her actions. "The kind one, why did you kill the kind one?"

Ahpu's voice was distant, as if she were still caught in the emotion of the past. "He was only kind because he thought I was white. I let him keep his scalp so that his soul could find peace. That was my kindness in return."

I countered with, "But the blood of white men runs through your veins, as it does in mine. You had lived among the more civilized modern world. Could you not see that clinging to this nomadic culture was futile?"

"Freedom should be clung to at all cost, Petu. The Indians helped the white men fight a war for their freedom from the English government, yet they condemned the Indian for treasuring the same values. Give us the land the treaties promised, let us roam free on that land and govern ourselves, that was all we asked. The white man did not want to live in peace with us. We were told to be free of war we must go to his schools, worship his God, live in his houses, and forget all that made us the human beings. There is no freedom on the white man's road."

"But the murder and brutality could not be allowed to continue. You must know that," I argued.

169

"Blood lust gets in the souls of men of any race. There were very few examples of man's goodness during those years leading up to the Red River War, native or white."

My mother's face appeared in my thoughts. "Did you capture my mother on one of those raids, Ahpʉ? Is that how you managed a white woman as your consort?"

Ahpʉ turned to face me. I was surprised to find a smile on her lips, which seemed to grow as she spoke. "I did not capture your mother's heart through force, but I did steal her from your uncle. He came here to my home many years ago to avenge that theft."

"Did you kill him too?" The words left my mouth as I thought them, taking no time to consider how accusatory they sounded.

Ahpʉ took no offence. Instead, she smiled a boyish grin and turned to the darkness behind us, calling out, "Come out, old man. Your brother's daughter would like to speak to you."

I saw the source of Ahpʉ's good humor when the old man stepped into view. This man was no stranger to me and I spoke to him. "Good evening, Tseena."

#

Decky raised her head from the manuscript. She needed a break from all the brutality. Like Thora, she was trying to see the conflict from both sides. The Native Americans fell victim to the march of civilization, yet it seemed so cruel and heartless. Decky supposed all conquered cultures had their own horrible history. It did not make the manuscript any easier to read.

Decky picked up her cellphone and dialed Charlie's number.

Charlie answered, "I was just coming to get you. It's time to eat."

170

"Oh, thank God. I thought you were going to keep me prisoner in here for days," Decky said, with a tinge of whining in her tone.

"Think of it as a labor of love," Charlie said, just before the door opened and she entered the RV, with the phone still pressed to her ear.

Decky broke into a smile when she saw her, and said into the phone, "I've been laboring. I'd like a down payment on the love part."

Charlie set her phone on the table and granted Decky's wish with a long, deep kiss. When she pulled her lips away, she asked, "Better now?"

Decky smiled and nodded that she was.

Charlie took her by the hand, dragging her toward the door. "Good. Now, come on and meet some more of the family."

Decky froze, which jerked Charlie to a stop. "More of them? They are here already?"

"Haven't you heard all the vehicles coming and going this afternoon?" Charlie asked.

"I guess not," Decky answered. "I was too busy reading about bloody massacres to notice."

"You'll have to tell me all about it later, but if you want to eat, we need to go now, before all the food is gone." Charlie walked over to the blinds on the big window behind the couch, pulling them up to expose what had been an empty grass lot leading down to the corral. Pop-up campers and tents covered every inch of grass, with a few more RVs parked down toward the barns.

"Damn!" Decky exclaimed. "It looks like a campground."

Charlie lowered the blinds and turned to face Decky. "I told you, this is a big party. Come on, you'll be fine. I've seen you work that southern charm."

Decky did not move.

Charlie came closer, wrapping her arms around Decky's waist, asking, "What's the matter, honey?"

Decky thought a minute before answering. Her instincts were telling her something was coming in that manuscript, something more than a simple cross-dressing, Comanche warrior in the family tree. She had always trusted her instincts. This was not the time to change that policy.

"Charlie, I think your mother is going to have that conversation with you very soon, the one you've been avoiding. I also think her need to have it now is related to your brother Bobby's absence. Thora's story is going to play a pivotal part in this somehow."

Charlie smiled up at Decky. "I see it coming, too, but I've come to terms with it. I'm forty years old. I'm way past defending my lifestyle to anyone. I'm pretty sure the only one it's a hang up for is Bobby, and that's Karen's doing."

Decky drew Charlie close again, hugging her tightly. "Just be careful, sweetheart. Don't get baited into a confrontation." Charlie started to laugh against her chest, prompting Decky's, "What's so funny?"

Charlie pulled out of the hug and started for the door. "Coming from the girl that let my ex bait her into breaking her nose, I consider that funny."

"She deserved it," Decky protested, even if she was embarrassed by her lack of self control the night Charlie's ex said just one thing too many. It was not Decky's finest hour.

"You have to promise me one thing. You have to –" Charlie said, her expression serious.

Decky cut her off. "I know, I know, let you fight your own battles."

Charlie shook her head in agreement. "Yes, that too, but I was going to say you have to let me be the one to punch

172

Karen." She broke into a smile and opened the door, adding, "Of course, only if she deserves it."

"All right, Laila Ali, go on with your bad self," Decky said, chuckling.

Charlie stepped out of the RV, saying over her shoulder, "If I haven't hit her by now, it'll take a lot more than bible thumping to push me over the edge."

Decky followed, closing the door behind them, Horse Child's words echoing in her mind, "Never antagonize an opponent unless you have anticipated the attack you may provoke."

Decky mumbled to herself, "I hope Karen has learned that lesson already."

CHAPTER SEVEN

When Decky stepped out of the RV, the Warren ranch had taken on a carnival atmosphere. There were white tents staked out across from the patio and down the drive, with more chairs and tables set up in the shade they provided. Because of the constant wind, the tents were tethered to fifty-gallon plastic drums Decky presumed were filled with water. One of the largest tents covered a temporary stage made of plywood and wooden pallets. A steel guitar, electric piano, monitor speakers, and a bank of microphones sat on the front of the stage, with amplifiers and empty guitar stands surrounding a drum kit at the back. Stacks of speakers framed the stage. A shaded table at the back of the tent was covered on top and underneath with all sorts of instrument cases, including violins, both electric and acoustic guitars, banjos, and perhaps a mandolin or two. The soundboard mixer rested nearby. To an old stagehand like Decky, it was easy to spot a country music concert in the making. The old washboard leaning against the drum set was a dead giveaway.

Decky poked Charlie to get her attention, as they walked toward the patio. "Is a band coming to play for the reunion?"

"No, that's just family stuff. I'm one of the non-musical Warrens, a rarity," Charlie said.

"You can sing. I've heard you," Decky said.

"Not like you, and not like the rest of my family. You'll see."

"Yes, but you have other talents," Decky whispered next to Charlie's ear.

"Well, hey there, Charlie," a tall, dark-haired, gorgeous woman said as they turned the corner onto the patio.

Charlie immediately hugged her. "Crystal, oh my God! Momma didn't tell me you were coming."

The two women gazed into each other's eyes for a second, before another hug. Crystal patted Charlie's back, saying, "Well, Momma said your mother called and wanted me to know you were coming home. I just had to drive up from Amarillo to see you. It's been too long."

Charlie smiled up at the woman and said, "Yes, it has. I'm so sorry we lost touch," and then she hugged her again, adding, "I've missed you."

"I've missed you too." Crystal said, and then held Charlie at arm's length so she could look at her. "Damn, girl, you look fantastic. I haven't seen you since that last reunion I came to. What was that, four or five years ago?"

"How are Dale and the kids?" Charlie asked.

"It *has* been a while," Crystal said, with a smile. "The kids are great, but I divorced Dale four years ago. What about Lynne? Is she here?"

Charlie laughed. "No, I divorced her, almost three years ago. We do have a lot of catching up to do."

Decky was beginning to wonder if Charlie remembered she was there. She could tell these two went way back. Didn't

Andy say that Charlie and Crystal's friendship was the beginning of the problems with Karen? Was it a coincidence that she would show up now, or was Louise's hand in this as well? Crystal said Charlie's mother called hers. Decky was seeing conspiracy in the air. She tried to temper that with the knowledge she was just a bit jaded by her experiences with her own mother's manipulative behavior.

Just when Decky was sure she had been forgotten, Charlie turned to introduce her. "Decky, this is Crystal, my best friend in junior high and high school. Crystal, this is Decky. I'd marry her just for the tax deduction, but the state won't let me."

Decky grinned. That was the first time Charlie introduced her to anyone in Oklahoma as anything other than a friend. Strange that such a small thing meant so much. That was what some people did not understand. The things they took for granted, like introducing a spouse, were rare and longed for occasions in Decky's world.

"I'm going to make her marry me anyway," Decky said, while shaking Crystal's outstretched hand. "It's very nice to meet you."

Crystal flashed perfect white teeth, returning a hardy handshake. "Nice to meet you too, Decky, is it?"

"Yes, my brother could not say Becky when we were small, so it kind of stuck."

"I like it," Crystal said. "So, you must be from the beach."

Charlie laughed. "How can you tell? Is it the sun bleached hair or the boat shoes that give her away?"

"She just has that suntanned surfer girl thing going," Crystal said, turning back to Charlie. "You forget I'm a photographer. I know these things."

The two old friends turned and headed for the end of the food line, and just that quickly, Decky was relegated to third

176

wheel. She didn't mind, really. It was fun watching Charlie laugh with Crystal through a meal of grilled chicken and salad, a lighter fare than Decky's previous ranch meals, and a welcomed sight. Decky did notice Crystal's resemblance to Charlie's ex, Lynne. Crystal lacked the olive skin, but she could pass as a close relative of the ex. She'd seen pictures of Charlie, from her twenties, with various short-term girlfriends. They too were of the dark haired variety. Hum, a pattern maybe? Decky's fair hair, blue eyes, and sprinkling of freckles on her cheeks certainly broke the mold. She listened to Charlie and Crystal catch up on each other's lives, commenting when prompted by Charlie, but as they began to talk about old friends and things Decky knew nothing of, her mind wandered to people watching.

A wider variety of guests were scattered around the patio and under the tents than before. Decky smiled and waved at the few people she knew, and spoke to the ones that stopped by the table to welcome Crystal home. She had an honored place among the siblings. From what Decky picked out of the conversations, Crystal and Charlie basically came as a set for a number of years. Decky had been that way with her best friend, Dara. They went their separate ways after high school, Dara moving to the west coast. They stayed in touch through email, but rarely saw each other. Decky was happy Charlie was having the chance to reconnect with someone that obviously meant a great deal to her. She vowed to send Dara an email when she got home, just to check in.

The clank of steel on steel caught her attention. Across the driveway, a serious game of horseshoes was unfolding between a foursome of old men in cowboy hats. A child ran by, soaking wet. Decky followed the little wet foot prints with her eyes to a couple of large, molded plastic, stock tanks, placed in the side yard near the other end of the patio, and filled with splashing preschoolers. Decky was jealous of the children. She would have loved to jump in that water, if only for a few minutes. She really missed her pool. Maybe she should join the adults supervising the water play. If nothing else, she would definitely end up soaked, with all the splashing and heavy water-pistol action.

Two-sided, wide-step, wooden ladders, appearing custom made for the tanks, allowed easy access in and out of the makeshift pools for the smallest toddler. The tanks were connected to pumps equipped with filters to keep the water clean, a necessity when dealing with baby pools. Decky also noticed large hoses coiled next to the pasture fence, near the pumps. From her research into stock tanks, for a previous theatre production, she knew those containers were ten feet in diameter and two feet deep, and would hold about a thousand gallons of water each. Smart move, she thought, easy access to two thousand gallons of water near the residence, in the middle of a prairie one spark from igniting. Even without power to the pumps, the hoses could be hooked up to the drain holes in the tanks. That much water pressure reduced to the diameter of the hose would push the water out with enough force to knock back a flame. Fear of fire, it was a constant in these people's lives.

Decky heard a guitar being tuned and looked to see part of the younger adults grabbing instruments, preparing to play. As she surveyed the scene, Decky saw all the various age groups beginning to demarcate seating areas. The oldest were in the tent farthest from the amplifiers and electric guitars, but closest to the house. The young families with babies and small children huddled at the other end of the patio, near playpens and food supplies, and close enough to watch the pool play. The middle-agers were scattered here and there in small groups. There was a distinct absence of teenagers and preadolescents, indicating there must be a "cooler" place on the ranch than this to hang, or they were out selecting cow patties for tomorrow's competition. Everyone present seemed happy to be there and engrossed in amusing conversations. Smiles, everywhere smiles, it was a heartwarming sight. Decky's own family reunions usually ended in slamming doors and squealing tires. Of course, the party was just getting started and she had not seen much alcohol about.

Like a prayer being answered, Franny swooped in holding a cold beer in each hand. She stopped at the end of the table, addressing her sister. "Charlie, I'm sure you've been ignoring Decky here, so I brought her a beer and I'm taking her with me." She handed the beer to Decky.

"I'm sorry, hon –" Charlie caught herself and corrected quickly. "Decky. I didn't mean to leave you out of the conversation."

Decky stood up, smiling so Charlie would know she was fine. "It's okay. You see me all the time." She turned to Crystal. "It was a pleasure to meet you. I look forward to talking with you after you two catch up. Right now, I'm going to mine Franny for more embarrassing Charlie stories."

Crystal commented, "Oh, I have a few I'll share with you."

Charlie looked momentarily stricken with fear. Decky saw her shake it off, and wondered what that was all about. She got her answer when Charlie said, "Make sure the statute of limitations has run out on some of that stuff, before you shoot your mouth off."

Crystal laughed. "Like the time you let all the air out of Karen's tires and she didn't realize it." She looked up at Decky, laughing loudly now. "That dumbass drove nearly a mile on rims, before she pulled off the road and set the grass on fire from the sparks. We saw it and went to call the fire department. They got it out pretty quickly, but Karen's car had a bit of heat damage in the paint from then on."

Franny started laughing too. "Charlie was sixteen and scared to death she was going to be blamed for the fire, even though it takes a real idiot to drive on four flat tires. After she told me what happened, she made me swear not to tell. I never did, until now."

Charlie smirked at her sister. "So secrets with you have a time limit? You know if Karen finds out it was me, she'll make a big deal out of it."

Franny did not miss a beat. "She has bigger issues these days, Charlie, but I won't tell if you don't."

Decky thought she caught a bit of double entendre in Franny's words. The look on Charlie's face said she heard it too. Decky managed only a wave at Charlie, before she was whisked away from the table. Charlie smiled at her, but Decky could see the wheels turning in that little blond head. The makeshift band of Charlie's nieces and nephews finished tuning and launched into "Mommas Don't Let Your Babies Grow Up To Be Cowboys." Decky turned to see Michael was the one at the microphone, doing a great rendition of the Waylon Jennings tune.

"He's very talented," Decky said.

"You should hear his momma sing. Mary is the best of all of us," Franny said, leading Decky still further away from the main party. "I heard you sing last summer, when Joseph brought his guitar out on the beach. You should sing a few tunes with us."

"I think I'll just lay low this trip. I don't want to draw attention to myself," Decky said, and then sipped from the ice-cold beer, before asking, "So, when is this Karen going to make an appearance and how much damage is she about to do?"

"I see you've been paying attention," Franny answered. "In the six months that Bobby has been married to that bitch, she's managed to disrupt this family in ways I never thought possible."

"What's her problem?" Decky asked.

"Let's see, she's been running around trying to get someone to agree that the ranch should be restructured, so the kids living off the ranch would be cut out of any shares and lose claim to the land. She thinks Momma and Daddy should go ahead and sign over the ranch to Bobby, claiming it would save so much in taxes when they die, which I'm sure she's hoping will be soon. You see, the way things are set up, none of us will ever own the ranch out right. It belongs to all of us. Should a person want to opt out, then they have to sell back to the ranch. The land will never leave this family. You can bank on that, but Karen wants it so bad she can taste it. She's pushing Bobby to take control, which is laughable. Bobby could have been ranch manager, but his first love is horses. He doesn't care about the other ranch operations."

"What does Bobby have to say about all this?" Decky asked.

Franny shook her head. "I love my brother, but he let her feed his ego. He changed there for a while, and by the time he came back to his senses, Karen was running wild with her campaign. I think he reined her in some, but then it just kept snowballing. He'd rather ignore her, than have a confrontation. It drives me nuts."

"What does all this have to do with Charlie?" Decky asked, adding, "Other than her ranch share, which I know she just sends to Mary to put back in the ranch."

Franny held up her hand. "Wait, I'm getting to that, but first, Karen decided that Bobby's two ex-wives should not be involved in any of our family gatherings. Joanne, his first, is

181

the mother of his two children. She and Bobby remained friends and she's always been at every family event, even after he married Barbara. Joanne and Barbara get along fine, and they are both wonderful, they just couldn't live with a man who loves horses better than people. Bobby's girls told Karen to F-off, which caused a rift between them and their father."

"Sounds like she's trying to isolate him, so she can manipulate him more," Decky commented, recognizing classic psychopathic behavior. She was not willing to call Bobby's wife one just yet, but she was leaning that way.

"When she couldn't keep Bobby's exes away, she decided it was her duty to inform everyone that Charlie was a lesbian and should not be allowed around children. Karen started calling all the relatives, encouraging them to ask that Charlie be banned from the reunion. She even suggested that if Charlie was permitted to attend, over the 'good Christians' objections, then safe zones should be created, where you and Charlie would not be able to interact with children or people who found this 'abomination' unacceptable. Karen used copies of newspaper articles about your court case and a few of your blogs as proof that Charlie is a lesbian. And I should add, there is quite a bit of "I told you so" in Karen's tirade. So really, there's no need for Charlie to pretend anymore."

"Oh, God," Decky said, under her breath.

"Oh, he's on Karen's side too, if you believe the vile crap coming from her mouth," Franny added.

"And Bobby is just letting her do this to his sister?" Decky asked.

Franny was angry. Decky could hear it when she said, "I'm so disgusted with him, at this point."

"Why didn't you warn Charlie? She would have never come, if she knew what was waiting for her," Decky said.

"That is exactly why I didn't warn her, and Mary threatened anyone else who might tell her. Charlie needs to be here and we're not letting some jackass keep her away from her family."

"Franny, Charlie's been through a lot, we both have. We try to avoid situations like this. We nearly died because of people like Karen."

Franny turned to face Decky, tears welling in her eyes. "I know, and it broke my heart when that happened. Charlie told me what you did. Knowing you would die for my sister was all I needed to know about you. Thank you, and thank your father for pulling that trigger. I'd have done it myself, if I was there."

Decky let the traumatic memory of Charlie's bloody face flash by in her mind. She used to try and stop it, but had finally realized fighting it was counterproductive. She learned just to let the images flicker by quickly, and fade on their own. She saw them less frequently now and the nightmares were abating, but she would never forget the pain that seized her when she saw Charlie's battered body on the floor. When Decky thought back on that night, it was not the beating she herself took or the gun pointed at her temple that she remembered. It was the all-consuming panic and pain she felt when she thought Charlie was going to die. That was why she begged that asshole to kill her first. Decky had not wanted to live past that moment, if Charlie was not going to be with her.

Decky swallowed hard and said to Franny, "There isn't anything I wouldn't do to make Charlie happy and keep her safe. I don't know why some people can't just let us be. We're not hurting anyone by loving each other. I just don't get it."

Franny stopped just in front of the barn Decky had been in earlier. "You are safe here. No one is going to harm you."

"Words, Franny, words harm too, and they incite violence. I don't want Charlie hurt by words anymore than I want her

183

physically harmed. I have no desire to stand by and watch some misguided fundamentalist take pot shots at her. Maybe we should just go, before the shit hits the fan."

"No, you can't let Charlie run away from this. It's time, Decky. She has to stand up now. Charlie has avoided this conversation with the family for years, and I'm ashamed to say we let her. It hasn't been a big secret or really the topic of conversation. We all love Charlie and want her to be happy. We should have told her that years ago."

"You might be right," Decky said, "but she should know what's coming, what's been done and said. I'm not going to let her be blindsided by this. You know I have to tell her."

Franny winked at Decky. "Why do you think we're taking this little walk? Come on, I have something to show you."

Decky walked alongside Franny, continuing to gather information on what she and Charlie might be up against. "So, what was the result of Karen's phone campaign?"

"Of course, somebody called Momma and told her what was happening. She had a private conversation with Bobby. I don't know what was said, but the calls stopped. I don't know if she found a soul that agreed with her, but Karen is not going to let an opportunity to mess with Charlie pass. This long feud between the two of them is about to come to a head. My money is on Charlie. You should get in on the pool. The pot's getting pretty big."

Decky was stunned. "You have a betting pool on how this is going to go down?"

Franny chuckled. "Yep, and it's growing by the minute." She led Decky to the side door of a bigger barn, where they both finished their beers and tossed the empties in the trash before entering. Franny opened the door and motioned for Decky to follow, while saying, "I have no doubt that Charlie will handle this situation with class and intelligence, neither of

184

which Karen possesses. Don't worry about Charlie. She has nine brothers and sisters watching her back, and she knows that."

"Nine? Are you including Bobby in that list?" Decky asked.

Franny smiled. "Charlie and Bobby have always had a quiet respect for one another. She adored him when she was little, and he doted on her. He always looked out for her, never minded Charlie tagging along after him on the ranch. He loves her, Decky. You'll see."

Decky let her eyes adjust to the lower indoor light, as they walked down the center aisle of an incredibly impressive stable. The warm, honey-stained wood paneled stalls combined with the cold gray of the metal bars and hardware to create a beautiful space. High velocity fans, equipped with evaporating mist cooling systems, kept the oppressive heat from outside at bay. All the Dutch doors in the stalls were closed, restricting any predator's access, but allowing the horses to look outside through barred windows. Decky suspected that was because most of the stalls contained mares and foals. She thought of Bobby, knowing he was somewhere watching over these animals as if they were his children.

The top halves of the stall doors were open on the aisle, with several curious heads poking out to see who was visiting. Decky peeked into the stalls as they passed one fine-looking mare after another, either with a young foal or about to drop one. She stopped to look at a very tiny baby, whose shaky, spindly legs looked entirely too long for him to manipulate properly.

"Now that is just precious," she said, pointing at the little guy, whose wide-eyed expression seemed to indicate he was still trying to get his bearings.

"He was born this morning," Franny said, moving forward.

185

The mare moved, blocking Decky's view of the foal. She was not threatening, just unsure of a stranger. Decky whispered, "That's a good momma," and then followed Franny toward the other end of the stable.

"Will Bobby be coming to check on the foal later?" Decky asked, wondering if she should worry about an appearance by Karen.

Franny indicated the back of the stable where they had entered. "He's probably back there in the office watching us."

Decky turned to see that she had walked right past a small walled-off area. A window allowed her to see a corner of a desk and a portion of a bank of small computer monitors displaying images of the stalls.

Franny continued to explain. "He's either back there or watching on a computer somewhere." She waved at one of the cameras that Decky could now see everywhere. "The girls set up the monitoring system. Welcome to the new age of horse husbandry. He can hear us too. Hey Bobby, get your head out of your ass," she shouted at the camera, causing a few of the mares to raise their heads and snort.

Decky had to laugh, though she tried not to make it too obvious. She did not want to give Bobby another reason to dislike her.

A woman's soft, soothing voice came out of speakers concealed somewhere in the large barn. "Dad *is* an ass, but don't scare the horses, Aunt Franny. I have two more about to foal."

Franny waved at the camera again, and in a much softer voice, said, "Sorry, Melissa," and then pulled Decky to the door of the last stall on the right.

Inside, Decky saw a gorgeous mouse-gray mare with a dark black stripe down her back, matching her mane and tail. Standing beside her was a young foal with a solid black coat,

186

so deeply pigmented it appeared to emit a blue sheen, except for the one mouse-gray colored sock on his left back leg.

Franny spoke, in almost a whisper. "He's three weeks old. His name is CJ, short for Charlie's Jackson."

Decky turned to face Franny. "Charlie's horse was named Jackson."

"Yes, this is his son and he looks exactly like him." Franny said.

Decky was confused. "How is that possible? Charlie said he died four years ago."

Franny's smile broadened. "Bobby. Bobby froze Jackson's sperm a long time ago. This mare is JoJo's Blue Babe. We call her Beebe. Her great-grandmother was Jackson's dam, and Beebe here could be her twin. Short of cloning, which he is opposed to, Bobby damn near created the same horse, right down to the gray sock. He did this because he loves Charlie. He will do the right thing."

"I certainly hope so," Decky said, marveling at the little black foal. "I just have one question."

"What is that?" Franny asked.

"Well, two questions really. First, how long do I have to clear the land and build the stable?"

Franny's answer indicated she had thought it through. "The mare is part of the deal and of course you'll need another horse, if you both want to ride while CJ matures. Charlie can help you pick one out. I'd give CJ at least six months on the ranch, before we travel him. Melissa can help you with stable design and technology. I've seen your house. I know this stable will be unbelievable. Next question."

"How will I recognize this Karen, so I'll see her coming?"

Melissa's same soothing voice sounded behind Decky, but not over the speakers. She turned to see the pretty brunette approaching, who was saying, "You can't miss those Tammy

187

Faye Baker eyelashes. If you can make her cry, you'll get the full effect."

Melissa leaned into the stall window. Both Beebe and CJ came over for a rub. She seemed completely at home in the stable, having inherited her father's love of horses. The horses responded to her, eagerly seeking her loving hand. Melissa was also very funny.

She started chuckling, but kept her voice calm and even. "Heads up, by the way. Got word from Carmen down at the Klip and Kurl. Karen's gone Reba-red and teased her hair like she's going to Dallas. She was also passing out Family Research Council flyers and ranting about Aunt Charlie this morning."

Melissa started laughing harder and struggled to gain control, before she disturbed the horses. Decky was trying to see the humor in some woman passing out a FRC flyer she knew to be full of blatant falsehoods without even reading, and probably not speaking too kindly about Charlie.

Franny wanted to know too. "What's so damn funny, Melissa?"

Melissa took a series of deep breaths and then finished the story. "Carmen said that Mrs. White, the old math teacher, was in for her weekly curl, and finally got an earful. She stood up and told Karen she'd always been jealous of Charlie, and that she was a sour little girl and well on her way to being a bitter old woman." Franny and Decky started laughing but Melissa held her hands up. "Wait, that's not the best part."

"I'd like to know what can top that," Franny said.

"Carmen said, Karen came back with, 'Charlie was always your favorite, because she liked math.' Then old Mrs. White – damn, I wish I had known she was so cool – anyway, she said, 'You're right, Karen. I did like Charlie better than you, because she had two things, my dear, I'm afraid you will never

188

have, a brain and a lack of self-absorption.' Karen stormed out after that."

Franny was nearly doubled over, laughing. Decky laughed too, but in the back of her mind she was wondering about the flyers being passed around the community, and whatever else was spewing from Karen's mouth. From all her years of studying human behavior, because that was what creating a believable dramatic character required, Decky knew there was a deep seeded motivation for Karen's actions. Something happened all those years ago. It could have been a big deal, something Charlie just chose not to talk about, or it could have been a small hurt that festered for nearly thirty years, fueling a loathing that was now out of control. One thing Decky knew for certain was the church was not driving Karen's venom. This was hatred in its purest form. Karen could dress it up in religious conviction, but this was personal, and not the least bit Christian. Yep, this was going to get ugly.

#

After coming back from the stable, Decky found Crystal and Charlie seated under the tent where the band was playing, cold beers on the table, and surrounded by people. Franny and Decky pulled up chairs to the already crowded table. After an exchange of smiles with Charlie, Decky once again became the observer. The band played a mix of modern and classic country, with a few rock and pop songs thrown in, changing musicians and singers frequently from a seemingly endless pool of talent. They were good, but loud.

Crystal got up to take pictures, but there was no way for Decky to have a conversation with Charlie, unless she shouted in her ear. Between songs, a few sentences were exchanged, as people continued to come by the table to say hello to Charlie, some offering words of encouragement that left Charlie baffled, by the look on her face. After the last notes of "All My Exes Live in Texas," a white-haired woman squeezed Charlie's shoulders, leaning in close to her ear.

"It's good to see you home, Dr. Warren," she said.

Charlie turned in her chair, and when she recognized the woman, stood up immediately. "Mrs. White, it is so good to see you," she said, hugging the older woman enthusiastically.

Decky recognized the name from the Klip and Kurl story, and Charlie's reverence for the woman was obvious in her inflection and body language. The band tuned up for another song, hurrying Mrs. White's next comment.

"I just wanted to tell you again how proud I am of you, and nothing anyone else thinks would ever change that."

The band kicked into the first notes of the next song, ending Decky's ability to hear the rest of Charlie's conversation with Mrs. White, but she could see the worry lines forming in the corners of Charlie's eyes. It was time to fill in the gaps for her. When Mrs. White moved away from the table, Decky stood and grabbed a couple of beers from a nearby cooler, motioning the stunned Charlie to follow her. Charlie excused herself and joined Decky outside of the tent.

"How many beers have you had?" Decky asked.

"One, why?" Charlie said, her eyebrows knitted.

Decky handed her a beer. "Not enough. Come on, let's take a walk."

Charlie opened the beer and took a swallow. "I'm not going to like this, am I?" She asked, as they started walking toward the barns.

"Nope, but let's get some distance between us and the rest of these people before I tell you."

"That bad, huh?" Charlie said, and took another swallow of beer.

"Well, I've got good news and bad news," Decky said, looking over her shoulder to judge the distance Charlie's voice might carry, should her reaction be volatile. She decided a few more paces were in order, so she stalled a bit. "Are you going to come clean about what really happened with Karen?"

Charlie started to dodge the question again. "I don't know why she –"

Decky cut her off. "Come on, Charlie. You know exactly why she turned on you. You know the exact moment. Tell me what happened."

Charlie sighed. "I knew she thought of me as her best friend, but I had other friends, she just stuck to me like glue. I really think she liked being part of my family more than being my friend. I think she used my house as a refuge from her miserable home life. Her dad was real mean. I didn't mind, until the summer we turned twelve and I met Crystal. Her mother moved back here to live with her parents, so she started going to school with us. We became inseparable and Karen became increasingly jealous."

"I can see that happening. You and Crystal seem to be very close, even now," Decky said.

Charlie grinned, tossing a glance Decky's way. "I knew that green-eyed monster would show up eventually, and no, Crystal and I were never a couple. I told you my first girlfriend was in college."

"I'm not jealous," Decky said, and then winked at Charlie. "Well, maybe a little."

They walked slowly, Charlie kicking at the gravel. Decky waited, knowing Charlie was gathering her thoughts.

After a deep breath, Charlie continued. "I was twelve, Decky. Looking back, I probably should have handled it differently, but Karen changed after Crystal moved here. She became a bully. She was constantly trying to drive a wedge

191

between Crystal and everyone else at school. Most people ignored her, but some didn't. I finally told her she couldn't come over to the house anymore. From then on, Crystal was no longer Karen's target, I was."

"Maybe that's what this is all about," Decky commented.

Charlie stopped walking, demanding, "Are you going to tell me what's going on? I'm sure Franny told you."

"Okay," Decky said, looking around to make sure they were alone. When she was sure Charlie's reaction would not be witnessed, she spilled the beans. "Honey, you know how you said your family just doesn't talk about your sexuality? Well, that isn't true anymore. From what I've gathered, Karen decided it was her duty to make sure everyone knows you are a lesbian."

Charlie waved a dismissive hand in the air. "It wasn't a huge secret. I think if it really bothered my parents or siblings, they would have said something by now. I doubt anything Karen had to say would sway them against me." Charlie paused, tilting her head and knitting her brow. "It didn't, did it?"

"No, I don't think so, but that's not all of it, Charlie," Decky warned.

"What else could she do?" Charlie asked, unaware of the depths to which her old adversary had stooped.

Decky had to break the news. "She pulled some articles from our court case off the Internet, along with my blogs, as evidence that she was right about you. She then proceeded to make everyone coming to the reunion aware of your homosexuality and tried to have you banned from attendance. She suggested that if you could not be kept away, areas should be roped off to prevent children and God fearin' folk from being exposed to the 'abominations.' I think that's me and you. Anyway, it didn't stop with the reunion guests. She's been all

192

over the county passing out Family Research Council flyers, and telling anyone who would listen that the former homecoming queen and hometown pride, Dr. Warren, is a lesbian menace. It sounds like she's on a mission to run you out of town. She may be organizing a stoning, as we speak."

Charlie's mouth was hanging open. She closed it only to say, "You have got to be fucking kidding me."

"There's more," Decky said.

Charlie narrowed her eyes. She was becoming angrier by the second. "What else?"

Decky gently placed a hand on Charlie's elbow. "Come on, keep walking." Charlie complied, but her jaw was set hard. Decky told her the rest. "I can't decide if Karen is more like the women on 'Dallas' or Sister Woman in 'Cat on a Hot Tin Roof.' Either way, she's power hungry. She wants the ranch restructured, cutting out all the siblings that do not live and work on the ranch, which gives Bobby a bigger piece of the pie. She suggested that your parents hand over the deed to the ranch to Bobby and step aside, because of their age. Karen would also like his two ex-wives banned from the ranch and family gatherings, and I'm assuming you as well. Of course, none of that is going to happen, but she's kept things stirred up pretty good since they got married."

"What in the hell is wrong with my brother? Did she castrate him, or what?" Charlie said, her face flushed red with anger.

"Charlie, I'm just an observer here, but even with the limited knowledge that I have, I think your brother is out of his league on this one. He's so passive, he'd never imagine that Karen married him to get inside this family, and I think that's exactly what she did. She saw him as her way in and her chance to get back at you. If he's figured it out, then his pride won't let him finish it."

193

Out on the Panhandle

"Why would a forty-year-old woman hold a grudge like this for so long? It was exactly this type of behavior that made me not like her in the first place." Charlie shook her head. "You know, I think she might be nuts, Decky. If she really planned this to get back at me, or envisions herself owning this ranch, then she must be certifiably psychopathic."

"I've thought about that," Decky said, "but she's not too bright from what I've heard. Psychos tend to be smart. I think she might just be your run of the mill bitch with a score to settle. Either way, I think you can handle it, now that you know what you're up against, but if you want to leave, we can do that. It's up to you."

"Oh, hell no!" Charlie said, with plenty of emphasis on the "no." She continued, "I'm not letting her run me off, and if Bobby ever shows his face, I've got a few choice words for him too. Like, grow a set!"

"You might want to hold that thought, until you've seen what's inside this barn," Decky said, pointing at the door.

They had reached the breeding barn. She knew Melissa was watching from somewhere, because she told Decky to bring Charlie down to the stable. Decky had argued with Melissa and Franny, that it was Bobby's place to show Charlie the foal. They both insisted that Charlie needed to know that Bobby was still her big brother and cared deeply for her. Decky took the beer from Charlie, tossed both cans in the trashcan, and opened the door, waving Charlie in.

Decky followed, commenting, "His wife might be an ass, but I think Bobby deserves a bit of a break. You and I have both been duped by people we thought were in love with us, so don't get too indignant about his behavior."

Charlie walked down the aisle, stopping to look at a few of the foals. She paused the longest at the newborn's stable, quietly watching as he nursed. Decky knew Charlie was working out the pros and cons of her situation like a math problem, as she always did. If they were somewhere with pen and paper, she would be making a list, analyzing data, formulating her argument, and approaching the issues rationally. She could be hot tempered when provoked, but for the most part, Charlie was as passive as Bobby, avoiding confrontation at all costs. Decky left her to her thoughts, slowly guiding her toward the last stall. Just before CJ and Beebe came into view, Decky stopped Charlie in the aisle.

She put both hands on Charlie's shoulders, facing her. "How bad is it, really? Franny and the rest of the family seem to have a handle on the ranch, and don't plan to accommodate any of Karen's wishes. So, that's all just hot air. You've been outed and possibly slandered. Well, if she's using the Family Research Council materials for her argument, then I'm pretty sure you've been slandered. Anyway, I think you were always afraid of what people would say, and now you know. They love you, Charlie, the ones that matter. They've been telling you that since you got here. And if I'm not mistaken, your mother has a plan to nip all this homophobic crap in the bud. You might want to just be patient and see what happens."

Charlie was calmer now. She spoke softly. "Do you have any idea what to expect, from Karen I mean? When is she going to make her appearance?"

"I think she'll probably show up tomorrow. She's set you up for a showdown. That's probably what people expect anyway, but I don't think you'll be facing her alone. Just be proud of who you are, Charlie. Your family cannot stand up for you, if you don't stand up for yourself. The rest, I think they can handle." Decky turned Charlie toward the stall, giving her a gentle nudge forward. "And as far as Bobby goes, I don't think there is any doubt how he feels about you."

Charlie stepped up to the window of the stall. Beebe stuck her head out, blocking Decky's view of Charlie momentarily. She heard Charlie's sharp intake of air, and knew she had just seen CJ. Beebe pulled her head back into the stall. Decky could now see Charlie and the tears beginning to stream down her cheek. She stepped over and put her arm around Charlie's shoulders.

"His name is Charlie's Jackson. They call him CJ. Bobby did this for you. The mare is Beebe and she is yours too."

Charlie did not take her eyes off CJ, when she said, "He's perfect. He looks just like Jackson when he was small." She turned to Decky. "But how? Bobby told me Jackson's samples were destroyed."

Decky shrugged her shoulders. "I don't know. Maybe he didn't want you to get your hopes up, or he wanted to surprise you. Either way, he did a very sweet thing."

Charlie looked back at the foal. "He certainly did." She took a deep breath to clear her emotions, and wiped the tears from her cheeks. She looked up at Decky. "Okay, I've got this, but you have to finish that manuscript tonight. I need to talk to Momma, and I want to know what else is in that story she thinks will help shut Karen up."

Decky hugged Charlie to her. "It's going to be okay, honey."

Charlie stood on her tiptoes for a quick kiss, and then said, "Thank you. You know I love you more than anything in the world, don't you?"

"Yes," Decky said, and leaned in for a longer, deeper kiss.

Melissa's voice sang softly from the speakers, "Get a room, Aunt Charlie."

CHAPTER EIGHT

"Sit down and tell lies, old man," Ahpu said with a chuckle.

Tseena folded himself down beside Ahpu, acknowledging me with only a grunt. I was still attempting to absorb the information that this was my uncle. Did my sire look like him, dark and brooding? I had thought myself far removed from my native blood, but here before me was a pure savage, separated from me by a small branch in my family tree. I needed no more proof, nor would my denials make it untrue. I was a Comanche.

"Petu," Ahpu said, jarring me from my thoughts. "My time with you is passing quickly. There is much you must understand." She pointed across the river, at a prairie filled with sun-bleached bones as far as I could see. "It was late fall of my fourteenth year, after the summer of much blood, the last days of the free roaming bands of the Comanche. The buffalo hunters were many and slaughtered the beasts, leaving the *prairie littered with the bodies, taking only the hides and heads."*

Tseena interrupted. *"Our brother the buffalo gave us life and we thanked him. The taiboo killed them and left them to rot."*

"Taiboo?" I asked.

"White men," Ahpʉ *answered, and then continued, "Earlier, in the June month, Quanah and many warriors, Comanche, Kiowa, Apache, attacked the sekwʉ kahni, the adobe house, where the buffalo hunters camped. It began what the soldiers called the Red River War. We were hunted day and night, fought many battles, and went on many raids. When the weather began to cool, we settled in our refuge. The white men call it Palo Duro Canyon, on the Prairie Dog Town Fork of the Red River, a place we had always been safe."*

She directed my attention to the orange-red glow of the rising sun, as it painted shadows on the lodges that now lined the riverbank. A sleeping village was revealed, nestled on a wide canyon floor between steep walls of banded rock, striped with reds, yellows, oranges, earth tones far too numerous to count. The breathtaking landscape was covered in green grass and low, full bushes, with cedars and cottonwoods strewn along the banks of the river. The only movement came from the trails of smoke puffing out of the cone shaped lodges, with their door flaps closed tightly against the dew of the cool morning. An old man crawled slowly out of a lodge, stood, and pulled a thick buffalo robe around his shoulders. He looked to the east, raised his hands as if to pray, but quickly jerked his head to the south. He shouted at the lodge, as he ran to grab a rifle, and fired a single shot into the air.

I was not forced to watch the carnage this time, only given snippets of the soldiers' attack. The old man was the first to die. The people ran out of the lodges and those that were not

198

killed escaped up the canyon walls, leaving behind all they owned, including most of the horses. I saw Horse Child on Jack's back, riding for their lives.

Ahpu commented, her voice tight with emotion, "The horses we did not catch and ride out of the canyon were left behind, almost fifteen hundred."

A shot rang out, as horses began to scream. I jerked my head toward the terrified animals' cries, only to see one of them fall to the ground, dead. Soldiers held ropes tightly pulled around the other frightened horses' necks, as they began to shoot them in the head, one by one. I could not watch and covered my eyes.

Ahpu only whispered, "They took a few hundred, but killed over a thousand."

Tseena led me to the next vision. He pointed across the river. "My people needed horses, so we took them from the white man moving into our lands."

The scene unfolded before me, a night so dark I could make out only shadows at first. A nicker from a horse drew my attention to a clump of trees. A painted warrior sat on horseback, holding Jack's reins. He looked to be nearing his twenties and too masculine to have been Horse Child. He peered through the trees with anticipation. The drumming beat of horses' hooves became clear in the distance, growing louder. The beats turned into a rumble as a dozen or more horses came into view, hot breath blowing smoke from their nostrils. Horse Child was mounted on one of them, bareback, driving them through the trees. She slowed her horse and jumped from its back, took two running steps, and hopped on Jack, instantly urging him forward.

Horse Child shouted at the warrior, "Come, Tseena. We must move the horses quickly."

199

Tseena looked back through the trees. "Where is my brother?"

"He goes to count coup, burn the camp, and get his scalps. Quanah sent us for horses, and those he shall have. Your brother and the others will meet us there."

I watched as the scenery moved with them, changing as they rode into the darkness. Soon, a horse galloped out of the night, a larger, young warrior on its back, holding a terrified, blond young woman in front of him. Her clothes were torn and disheveled, her lip dripping blood, the red impression of a hand still imprinted on her cheek. Horse Child and Tseena slowed at the warrior's approach, but kept the moving herd in sight. The warrior rode up beside Horse Child.

Tseena shouted over the hoof beats, "Brother, did you bring me a wife?"

The warrior chuckled as he answered, "You must find your own, little brother. This yellow hair is mine. I found her hiding in the tall grass."

Just then, the girl struck out at him and screamed, "Release me, you wretched heathen!"

The warrior snatched the young woman by the hair and slapped her, drawing fresh blood from her lip. "You will die like the others, if you do not behave," he said, angrily.

Although I could understand the warrior, the young woman could not. I realized this when she said, through tears, "I do not speak your tongue."

Horse Child spoke to her. "Bear Runs said stop fighting or he will kill you."

The young woman stared in amazement at Horse Child, saying, "You speak English?"

"Yes, and you must not fight him. He does not make an idle threat," Horse Child answered.

200

Out on the Panhandle

Bear Runs lifted the young woman, as if she weighed no more than a feather, and while still moving at a steady pace, placed her in front of Horse Child on Jack's wide back. "Take her to the camp. You will keep her until I return. Let it be known that she is mine. Look between her legs and see the blood. I have claimed her."

The young woman sobbed, as Horse Child wrapped her arms around her and whispered in her ear. "Stay close to me, I will protect you. What is your name?"

The sobbing woman said, "Grace. My name is Grace Harrell."

I turned to Ahpu. "Is that my mother? Is that how I was conceived?"

Ahpu took my hand. "Yes, that is your mother and father. Do not ponder the source of your beginnings. Your mother welcomed you with open arms as a gift from the spirits. Your father's cruelty was of little consequence. He did not live long enough to abuse your mother again."

Tseena said with pride, "He was a great warrior. You should be proud he chose your mother to bear his seed."

Before I could retort with how barbaric and grotesque I thought his brother was, Ahpu said, "Forgive him. The love of his brother and the loss of his culture blind him. He cannot see, as with so many others, that we are all human beings. Your mother taught me that forgiveness frees the soul. You shall see."

She nodded back toward the river. I saw now that more time had passed, and the night had turned into gray day, the ground covered in light snow. Horse Child sat by a fire in front of a buffalo hide lodge, braiding leather strips into a rope. Her gender ambiguity was more prevalent now. Her features were too pretty to be called masculine, but her body was one of an adolescent boy, long and lanky. Her hair hung

201

down to her shoulders, unbraided, and tucked behind each ear. Nearing fifteen, if I've kept up with her age correctly, she should have blossomed with femininity by now, but her buckskin shirt fit so loosely, any feminine traits were obscured. Had I not known she was a woman, I should never have guessed.

Young Tseena approached with several other young men. "My brother is dead. These warriors say he was taken in with their band when he was shot, shortly after we last saw him. He died many months ago. Your promise to look after the woman is done. I have to come to claim her as my wife, as is my right."

Horse Child did not look up from her task. "She will not go with you."

"She must!" Tseena shouted. "She bears my brother's child. She will be my wife."

Unmoved by Tseena's declaration, Horse Child continued to braid the rope, speaking calmly. "Your brother had many wives. I know, because I have fed them while you chased after his ghost all winter. Go now, and take care of them, as is your duty. I save you from two more mouths to feed. Oha Tso'yaa' is happy here with me. Leave her be."

"I've asked you to use my Christian name," the blond young woman said, backing out of the lodge. "My name is not Yellow Hair. It is Grace and yours is Meredith." She turned to see Tseena and the others. "What does he want?"

"He has come to claim you as his wife," Horse Child answered.

Grace took a step closer to Horse Child, frightened now. I could see her small round belly, where I was at that moment growing into the child I would become. She was wearing a buckskin dress, a blanket wrapped around her shoulders, her blond hair combed and glistening in the sun. She blinked her blue eyes, placing a hand on Horse Child's shoulder, and rubbing her belly unconsciously with the other. A graying older woman emerged from the lodge. I recognized her as the woman Horse Child had rescued in my earlier vision.

"What noise is this?" she asked.

Horse Child did not look up, answering nonchalantly, "Tseena has come to claim Yellow Hair, mother. What do you think of that?"

The old woman patted Horse Child on the shoulder on the way to stand closer to the fire. She grinned mischievously at Tseena. "It is a brother's right and duty to take care of his fallen brother's family. Of course, if you want her, Horse Child, you could offer Tseena an exchange."

Tseena objected loudly. "Horse Child dresses like a man, but she is not one. She cannot have a wife."

The old woman laughed. "I have prayed to the spirits about Horse Child. They tell me she was given the soul of a warrior and the cleverness of a woman, the best of both. She has power over Yellow Hair, like her magic with the horses. You should make the exchange and save yourself the trouble. The spirits joined Yellow Hair and Horse Child. You must not be angry with them. I have seen it happen, not often, but who are we to question what the spirits have made?"

Tseena would not be moved. "She will be my wife. I will come for her in the morning. Prepare her for our marriage night."

"What are they talking about?" Grace asked, nearly in hysterics.

Horse Child stood to face Tseena. "You come in the morning. Your yellow-haired woman will be waiting for you." She turned and pulled Grace into the lodge.

By a trick of the vision, I followed them. Horse Child held Grace at arm's length, bending to look into the shorter

203

woman's eyes. "Tseena is claiming his right to you. He will not trade with me. I will take you to the fort and leave you with your people. It is the only way. We must go now."

Grace stepped back and dropped her eyes to the floor. "I have no family to return to. I carry a native child. We will both be shunned. You must come and stay with me, keep us safe, as you have done these five months."

Horse Child shook her head. "I was told by my Chickasaw grandmother that the white man does not allow people of two spirits to exist. I am unlike others. I know this. I too would be shunned. The supplies run low. Come summer, Quanah and the people will go to the reservation. I will not follow and be forced to live as the white men see fit."

"Where will you go?" Grace said, wringing her hands.

"I am one quarter Indian, by the white man's law. I do not have to go to the reservation. There is a land no man owns near the Beaver River. I have been there with Quanah. There are no laws, no rules, and fewer people. I will live alone and be happy."

Grace's voice softened. "You love me too deeply to be alone. You would come find me."

Horse Child became shy, as a young suitor did for me once when I teased him about his affections. I completely dismissed from my mind that these were two women. I saw the tenderness between them, with no physical touch. What may have begun as dependence for survival had changed these human beings, as only love can. I glanced at Ahpu beside me. She regarded the scene with a smile, mirroring the shy Horse Child's expression under her sweetheart's gaze.

Barely lifting her eyes from the floor, Horse Child said, "Then will you come with me?"

Grace extended her hand. "If we are all to be shunned, then let us be shunned together." She waited for Horse Child

204

to take her hand. When she did, Grace continued, "I am as Ruth, in the story I told you from the bible. Where you go, I will go. Meredith Ethridge, you are my people now."

Tseena drew my attention away from the young lovers, when he said, "Horse Child tells lies. She said Yellow Hair would be my wife in the morning." He grunted, and added, "Horse Child has no honor."

Ahpu threw her head back and laughed. "I left you a yellow haired woman," she said, "and more."

I followed her gaze to see a golden palomino mare with a mane and tail of long, flowing, yellow hair tied outside the lodge. The old woman stood in the early morning light, holding five other grand animals. She smiled, and chuckled to herself, as a single tear flowed down her cheek.

It seemed Tseena still held a grudge. He complained, "You play with words, like the taiboo that you are. A human being does not steal another man's wife, or he will die."

"Tseena, you have been here many years now," Ahpu said playfully. "If you were going to kill me, I think you've had your chances."

"I wait for you to bring the yellow haired wife you promised, and then I will go," Tseena stated, crossing his arms defiantly.

Ahpu reached out, squeezing the old man's shoulder. "Then we wait for her together, my friend." She turned back to me. "We rode for many days, avoiding well traveled trails as much as we could, but we neared a new trail cut through the prairie, heading straight toward our destination. We came across a sod house tucked next to the trail."

She directed my attention to Grace, peering into a dark sod house dug into a low hill. Horse Child was checking the load on a travois, attached to a bay mare, assuring what lay under a large buffalo hide was secure. Jack and a smaller horse, I

205

surmised Grace had been riding, munched lazily on grass beside the mare.

Grace said, "I don't think anyone has been here in some time," just as she was about to enter the sod house.

Horse Child was suddenly at her side, grabbing her arm. "Stop!" She pulled Grace out of the doorway and slipped inside, lance in hand. After several minutes, she emerged holding two large rattlesnakes by the tails, minus their heads. She grinned at Grace. "Dinner."

"Dare we stay here?" Grace looked around cautiously.

"No, we must keep moving, but I found something else inside." Horse Child dropped the snakes on the ground and disappeared into the sod house. She came back out bearing a small trunk and set it on the ground. "This was under the bed in the corner." She plucked the feathered end of a broken arrow from a sash tied around her waist, holding it up for Grace to see. "The Kiowa have been here, but they did not find this box."

Grace dropped to her knees and opened the trunk. She held up a simple farm dress of drab gray material, as if it were the finest of Paris fashion. "Oh, Meredith! It is a proper dress." She held the dress around her, checking the fit. "The waist is high. I think it may fit still." She dug deeper into the trunk. "And a petticoat, too! And look, a shirt, vest, and trousers for you." Grace unloaded the trunk. "Even suspenders. I don't suppose you found any shoes in there?"

Horse Child smiled at Grace's joy over the dress, but when the shirt and suspenders came out, her mood soured. "I will wear buckskin," she said, rejecting the white man's clothes.

Grace stood, still clutching the dress above her swollen belly. She explained her position. "Meredith, we cannot travel as a white woman and an Indian. If white men find us, they will take me and kill you, before they stop to find out you are

206

woman. You have been away from the white man's world too long. You must trust me in this domain, as I have trusted you in yours."

Horse Child kicked at the dirt with a moccasin toe. "I do not wish to costume myself as a white man."

Grace's hand flew to her hip, a trait I noted in my own behavior when faced with an unreasonable opponent. She held out the dress to Horse Child, saying, "One of us must wear the dress. We grow nearer to a trail. I see it in the wagon ruts we pass. Soon we will see white men. I will not venture farther dressed as an Indian to be the target of some overzealous farm boy from Kansas seeing his first native, but I do not think the trousers will accommodate my girth."

Horse Child bent to pick up the men's clothing and the snakes. Her only comment was, "I will wear the trousers."

Tseena chuckled. "See, Horse Child is not a man. Her woman tells her what to do."

Ahpu watched the scene change before us, while asking, "Where is your woman, Tseena?"

The smile on Tseena's face turned to a scowl. "I left her on the reservation. She is an old woman with many children to keep her busy. Yellow Hair will be my new wife."

"We shall see, old man," Ahpu said, a sly grin on her face, but staring straight ahead, as if she could not tear her eyes from the view.

I saw why, when before me the soft moonlight illuminated Grace, her back turned slightly, wading in the shallows of the river completely unclothed. It was a scene I should like to paint someday, if only to attempt to capture the beauty of womanhood. She hummed to herself quietly, as she splashed water over her glistening skin. Her hair was freshly washed, dripping rivulets down her chest. She shivered against the cold, before Horse Child approached with a buffalo hide robe.

"Come Grace, you must get warm. The fire is burning."

Grace turned, facing Horse Child, who gazed unabashedly at her naked body. I covered my mouth to mask my gasp, when Grace moved toward Horse Child, pushed the robe aside, and began to undress her. Grace untied the sash around her lover's waist, dropping it to the ground. She then slid her hands under the buckskin shirt, lifting it slowly over the taller woman's head. Horse Child removed it and dropped it to the ground, revealing small pink budded breasts atop a torso worthy of sculpture. She did not speak, but watched as Grace removed the breechcloth, and then knelt to remove her leggings and moccasins.

I could feel my own heartbeat pounding against my chest, but I could not turn my eyes away. I marveled at the tenderness with which Grace led Horse Child to the water, where she lay in a shallow pool, pulling her lover down with her. I should have been horrified, at the very least scandalized, but I was neither. This was not an act of wanton lust, but the consummation of what I already knew. These two women loved each other beyond the rules and boundaries of others. Their coupling was too beautiful to have been an abomination. I understood now and knew how alone they must have felt, and I cried tears of joy because I knew they had each other. The young lovers were left to their intimacy, as the blackness of the night folded around them.

Ahpu spoke, her words trembling with emotion, tears slowly falling on her cheeks. *"It is important that you know the bond between your mother and I. It is a bond that remains today, and shall never be broken, from this life to the next."*

I placed my hand over hers, my own emotions causing my voice to come out in a whisper. *"I understand, Ahpu."*

We then joined Horse Child and Grace by the fire. They were dressed now, in the white man's clothes. The dress was too large for Grace's shoulders, but her belly still protruded under the ample material. The trousers hung off Horse Child, held up only by the suspenders, and rolled up at the cuff. The shirt and vest draped on her lanky body were obviously made for a larger man. They appeared as small children dressed in their parents' clothes. Grace's face was aglow, smiling contently, as she used a large knife to finish trimming Horse Child's hair. The effect accentuated Horse Child's Caucasian bloodlines. With each clump of hair falling to the ground, she transformed into a young white man before my eyes.

"You have beautiful hair, Meredith. I have trimmed it to your chin. You will look like any other young farm boy from Kansas." Grace looked down at her mate's feet, sighing. "Except for the moccasins."

"If I am to be called by my Christian name, and pretend to be a man, then I would like to be called Merdy, as I was when I was a child."

Grace trimmed the last long strands of hair. "Well then, Merdy it is." She stepped back to admire her work, saying, "My, but aren't you handsome." She tugged at Merdy's vest. "If I had thread and needle, I could make this fit, but as it is, it covers your femininity well. We cannot mask your native inflexion when you speak, however. No matter, should we encounter anyone, I have a plan for us."

The scene dissolved as Ahpu said, "Your mother was merely a year older than I, but she had lived longer in the white man's world. Her father brought the family from Virginia to Fort Smith, when she was but a babe. Grace went to school, could read and write. She was clever. When her father bet his last dollar that a homestead in Texas would bring the wealth he craved, he instead met his death along with every member of his family, except Grace. She survived on her wits. She kept us alive the same way."

Out on the Panhandle

The brightness of day broke through the night sky, illuminating Grace and Merdy crossing an open pasture. They no longer had the native travois, just the small trunk, a buffalo hide, and a few blankets tied on the back of one of the mares. Four riders approached them from the east, coming fast. I was pulled into the scene, as though I rode beside Grace, while she watched the riders.

She smiled and spoke calmly. "Merdy, remember my plan."

I glanced at Merdy. She pulled at a white bandage tied around her neck. Dried blood appeared to have seeped from a wound beneath it. She stared nervously in the direction of the riders, dropping her hand from her throat to the pistol at her waist.

Grace cautioned, "Remain calm."

The riders arrived in a cloud of dust, four cowboys on lathered mounts. They tipped their hats or nodded toward Grace, and eyed Merdy suspiciously. One of them acted as spokesman for the group. He scratched his stubbly chin and squinted in Grace's direction.

He inquired, "What in tarnation are you young folk doing out here in no man's land all alone?"

"Our group was attacked by Indians," Grace said, with a great deal of sadness. "Everyone was killed, but me and Merdy here. We were in the river when they attacked at night. We hid in the reeds. One of the men with us ran into the river and they shot him. A piece of the bullet came right through him and hit Merdy in the throat, that's why he can't talk, but the Indians didn't see us. We are lucky to be alive and are headed back to Kansas. We want no part of these Texas savages."

The cowboy chuckled. "You look like your wearin' your pa and ma's clothes, 'cept for them bare feet, there."

210

Grace put on a show of being bashful. "We left our boots and things on the riverbank, while we were bathing. These clothes are all that those heathens left to us. They burned or took everything else." She worked up some tears, adding, "It was just horrible what they did to those folks."

"We're sorry to hear that ma'am. Lucky you found some horses. Indians usually take them too, and ain't them Comanche saddles?" He seemed sincere, but still wary of their story.

"Merdy found his horse, because no one can make Jack mind but him. These two mares go everywhere Jack goes. I guess some of our men got a few shots off before those savages killed them. Merdy took these saddles off some dead Indian ponies. All we have to our names is this little trunk and some blankets."

Another of the cowboys spoke up. "You're risking your life out here with a mere boy. You should ride with us back to camp and wait for a freight wagon heading north."

Grace rubbed her swollen belly. "He was man enough to do this and he's gotten me this far. I'll not sleep here on this prairie one more night than is necessary. We will catch up to a freight wagon at the Beaver River crossing tomorrow. Merdy said he'd rather go back and face my pa than deal with these Indians."

"Well, sounds like your fella knows where he's going," the spokesman said, seeming to accept their story, and anxious to continue the errand he was on before stumbling on the couple. "Good luck with her pa, son. You're doing the right thing."

Merdy nodded to the men and grunted at Grace, who played the prompt perfectly.

"Well, he's ready to get moving. Thank you for checking on our welfare. If only all of Texas was populated with men like you, instead of those savages, I would gladly stay."

211

Out on the Panhandle

The cowboy tipped his hat again. "Stay near these wagon ruts and you'll probably do all right. The Camp Supply soldiers patrolled through here yesterday. You take care now. Watch out for those Indians."

Grace smiled and waved good-bye. "We sure will."

"She was brilliant," I exclaimed to Ahpu on the riverbank.

She smiled back at me and said with pride, "Your mother had the power of the charm. She was also kind and giving. All that knew Grace loved her." Ahpu paused, gazing up at the stars, lost to her memories, I supposed. I studied her, while waiting for her to continue. The moonlight on her face showed a still younger visage, as her age seemed to abate with each memory. She remained focused on the sky above, as she began to speak again.

"There is not time to show you all your mother was in this way of the vision. Close your eyes and fly now."

I had no reason to ignore Ahpu's request. The visions had opened my heart to her. As my mother had seemed to feel, I found comfort in her calming presence. My fears and inner turmoil paled when she was near. I felt safe, as I had when I was a child. I felt a sense of belonging, and had not known how desperately I had yearned for it. With no more hesitation, I turned my eyes to the stars and closed them.

The images flew by too quickly, at first. I caught only glimpses of Grace on the trail with Merdy, how they found the place they would call home, and the work that went into building a new life. I saw laughter and smiles, tender moments of embrace, as my mother grew heavier with child. I was in the sod house when the images slowed and I could hear their voices again.

There, lying on the bed was my mother drenched in sweat, a newborn suckling at her breast. I was witnessing the moments following my birth. Merdy lay behind my mother, holding her, gazing at the babe. Outside, a storm raged, lighting the sky with bolts of blue, followed by ground rumbling thunder. The three souls in the sod house paid no attention to the tempest, burrowed there together in their home.

"She is beautiful," Merdy said, placing a finger in the babe's tiny hand. "She is strong too."

Grace turned her head to look at Merdy. "She must have a name of strength. She will face many trials in her life."

Thunder rumbled through the sod walls. "The thunder spirits herald her birth. She should honor them with her name," Merdy suggested.

Grace smiled at the babe. "My grandmother's name was Thora. She said it meant thunder in her mother's native home."

"Then welcome, little Thora," Merdy said, gently touching the baby's cheek.

I was suddenly drawn back, the images speeding by again. I watched, as the baby became the toddler of my faint memories. It was an odd sensation seeing the child I was, happy and contented with my life. That child had no knowledge of her circumstances. She was loved and cared for by two devoted parents. Years passed by quickly. The herd on the property grew, as I saw Merdy return time and again from the prairie with horses she wrangled. I watched as she helped foals be born, gentled the wild ones, and provided for her family, while my mother was contented to make a happy home. The images slowed again, as I saw myself, a child of four or five, riding on a wagon seat with my mother, as she drove the supply laden vehicle across an unmarked field of tall grass.

Merdy rode beside the wagon on Jack. I could see that she had aged even more handsomely. She would have been nearly twenty by now. The life of a homesteader had made her strong,

213

her lanky frame incased in hard muscle. Merdy looked the part of a cowboy, a pistol at her side, boots on her feet, and a wide-brimmed beaver skin hat to shade her eyes.

I heard the child I was ask my mother, "How much further, Pia?"

I remembered that was my name for her. I now know that it is a Comanche word for mother. She had blossomed into a beautiful woman, wearing a calico patterned dress that fit her perfectly. She wore a hat with flowers pinned about its crown, her blond locks tucked beneath it. My memories had not captured her exquisiteness well enough. My Pia and Ahpɨ made a stunning couple. I no longer thought of them as Merdy and Grace. From that moment on, they were, in my vision and in my heart, my Ahpɨ and Pia, my father and mother.

Pia answered the child. "We will be home by sundown, little one." She smiled over at Ahpɨ. "We did very well at the market. Your breeding skills are highly sought after. You will make a name for yourself yet, I do believe."

Ahpɨ's attention was elsewhere. She stood up in the stirrups of her black leather saddle, peering ahead to a small stand of trees. She put up her hand to signal my mother, who pulled back on the reins of the mule team, bringing the wagon to a stop.

"What is it?" Pia asked.

"I smell smoke. We are not alone," Ahpɨ said, her eyes never leaving the trees.

Pia dismissed Ahpɨ's concerns. "It is probably another lost, broken down family this far off the trail. We will help them and then be on our way."

"There are no tracks. They come from the west, down the river," Ahpɨ said, removing a rifle from its saddle holster, and handing it to my mother. "Wait here," she commanded, and then rode toward the trees.

214

"I want to go with Ahpu and Jack," my childish voice rang out.

"Quiet, Thora," Pia said, watching Ahpu for signs of trouble, her brow wrinkled with worry.

Ahpu disappeared into the trees, emerging a few moments later, waving her hat for Pia to bring the wagon. I heard the rush of relieved breath from Pia's chest, as she put the rifle down and prodded the mules to move forward.

"Is everything all right, Pia?" The child asked.

Pia answered her, "Your Ahpu is very brave, but she worries me sometimes," she smiled, *"as do you. You inherit your fearlessness from Ahpu."*

I chuckled, as I heard my childish reply. "I will be just like Ahpu when I am big. I shall wear boots and trousers and ride horses all day."

Pia's face lit with a smile. "Yesterday, you asked me to buy material to make you a dress like the princess in the story I read to you. One day you dream of princess gowns and the next you sit astride a horse, galloping across the open prairie. You have many years to make up your mind to do either, or both. Your path will come clear to you, in time."

Pia pulled the wagon to a stop where Ahpu waited. She had already dismounted and was still peering into the trees.

"What is it, Merdy?" Pia asked.

Ahpu helped my mother from the wagon, saying, "Three men, outlaws. Two dead, one nearly so. Looks like they got into an argument and shot each other, from what I can tell." She looked at the little girl on the wagon seat. *"Stay in the wagon, Petu. If someone comes, signal like I taught you."*

"Yes, Ahpu," young Thora said obediently.

The vision carried me with Ahpu and Pia into the shadows. In a small clearing beneath a heavy canopy of summer foliage, two men lay dead, a campfire still smoldering at their feet. It

215

appeared they had just begun to make camp, when the carnage took place. Their bedrolls were tightly bound, lying near the fire. Two mules were still harnessed to a small wagon. Three horses were staked out, only one having had the saddle removed. The one surviving man sat leaning against a tree, blood soaking through his shirt at his stomach, drawing his last shallow breaths. He seemed to be the youngest of the three, in his early twenties. Pia went to him, while Ahpu removed the team of horses from the men's wagon, and the tack from their saddle mounts, setting them free to graze and drink from the small creek nearby. Pia concentrated on the dying man. I could tell by her expression that she knew that was his fate. She forced a smile and knelt beside him, offering comfort.

"Hey there, cowboy," she said. "Looks like you got yourself in a bit of trouble."

The man opened his eyes for the first time. He blinked and coughed, blood dripping from his lips.

"Lord, he done sent an angel to carry me to heaven," the man said, through shortened breaths.

"My name is Grace. Is there anything I can do to help?" Pia asked.

The man tried to lift his hand, but he was too weak. "In my vest pocket," he said.

Pia reached into the man's pocket, pulling out a tiny, framed picture. She looked at it and then placed it in the man's hand, asking, "Is that your sweetheart?"

"That's my Mary. She's gonna be awful upset when I don't come back. She didn't want me to go with Jake and Amos. I wish they'd never come by the farm to fetch me. Look at me now, rich as forty thieves and a dying man."

Ahpu approached, asking, "What happened here?"

216

The man looked up at Ahpu. "That one over there," he pointed at one of the dead men, "that's my oldest brother, Amos. He used to run with ol' Bill Coe back in his outlaw days, till the soldiers come and destroyed the roost."

He tried to take a deeper breath, but it was no use. He continued his tale, as Pia wiped his brow with a handkerchief she produced from her waistband.

"Amos swore he figured out where Cole hid his gold up in Blacksmith Canyon, 'fore he was hung in Colorado. Damned if he didn't too. It's yonder in that wagon, more gold than three men could spend in a lifetime."

He stopped talking and winced in pain. Pia looked under his vest at the gaping wound, and then folded the vest back down. She found a blanket and placed it over the man.

"Lot a good that gold will do me now. Jake and Amos got into it over that money, just after we made camp last night. Jake shot Amos and I shot him. I thought he was dead, but he knifed me in the gut when I turned him over. I had to shoot him two more times." He coughed up more blood and looked down at crimson stained shirt, before adding, "I'm a rich dead man. Now, ain't that a kicker."

Pia leaned in closer. "Tell me your name and where I can send word to Mary. She should know you were thinking of her."

"Name's Tom Skinner, ma'am. Send word to my pa, Big Amos Skinner, Joplin, Missouri. They'll know him there."

"I'll do that Tom. I'm going to sit here with you," Pia said, reaching to hold the man's hand. "Shall we say a prayer, Tom? Would you like that?"

"Yes, ma'am, I would," he answered.

Pia began, "The Lord is my shepherd, I shall not want."

217

Out on the Panhandle

Tom joined her, *"He maketh me to lie down in green pastures: he leadeth me beside the still waters. He restoreth my soul —"*

The man clutched tightly to Pia's hand. With his last breath, he struggled to sit up, and said, *"Tell Mary she was right. We could have been happy without that gold."* He exhaled and slumped to the ground.

Pia reached and gently closed his staring eyes. *"Rest in peace, Tom Skinner. God have mercy on your soul."*

Ahpu stepped to the back of the dead men's wagon, lifting a tarp that covered supplies for prospecting and five wooden lock boxes. The latches were all broken open, busted with pick or shovel, the locks still fastened to the hanging hasp. Such was the zeal of the now dead, gold crazed trio. Their excitement was understandable, as Ahpu opened lid after lid, filled to the brim with shiny gold and silver Spanish coins and solid gold bars.

Pia approached and peered over the side into the wagon. *"Oh — my,"* stammered from her lips. She slowly took her eyes from the golden splendor and settled them on Ahpu. *"Merdy, what are we going to do with all this gold? Who does it belong to?"*

Ahpu looked around nervously. *"Bill Coe was a bad man. The warriors talked of his horse and cattle thieving. His gang robbed many stagecoaches and made them look like Indian raids. He took a big Mexican pack train they said, and buried many boxes full of gold. He was hung before he could return to claim it."*

"This must be it," Pia said, whispering as if she could be heard out here on the prairie.

Ahpu put the lids back on the boxes, in a hurry now. *"Go, bring the wagon to the other side of the trees. We must hurry."*

218

Out on the Panhandle

Pia did not hesitate to follow Ahpu's instructions. The trust they shared was deep, depending as they did on one another for survival. They set about arranging a decent burial for the men, albeit a hasty one. Pia rolled the men up in blankets, while Ahpu rolled her sleeves up and sweated through digging a shallow pit. They laid the men side-by-side and covered their bodies with rocks. Little Thora helped carry some of the rocks, while Ahpu explained to her the natural way we returned to the earth. Pia burned Amos and Tom Skinner's names into pieces of wood she tied into makeshift crosses for the graves. She made one that said simply, Jake.

It took both of them to move the heavy lock boxes to their own wagon, where Ahpu now stood in the back, covering them with supplies to hide them from any prying eyes. Pia began gathering the dead men's belongings in the back of their wagon, where the gold had been. Little Thora tried to help, dragging a much too heavy saddle behind her.

Ahpu turned and said, "Take the saddle to Pia, little one. The men that come looking for them will know them by their tack. We will leave it with their wagon."

"What's in those boxes?" Little Thora asked, dropping the saddle at her mother's feet with a final mighty pull.

Pia scooped up the saddle, and threw it into the wagon. "It is food that will spoil, if we leave it."

Thora was satisfied with the answer and went to fetch another saddle. Ahpu gave Pia a puzzled look.

Pia answered the look with a whispered, "She cannot speak of what she does not know."

Ahpu climbed down from the back of the wagon, securing the tarp over the load. She spoke softly and in code, as parents do when little ears are about. "If you would rather leave the food here, I would not object."

219

Out on the Panhandle

Pia glanced back at little Thora, struggling with her load. "We will take it home and decide what the future holds for us."

Instantly, I was flung headlong into darkness, soaring above the trees. I felt that my heart would leap out of my chest, before I came to rest inside the sod house. It was late at night, the only light a small candle by the bed, where Ahpu and Pia lay facing each other, speaking in hushed tones, a sleeping little Thora between them.

"Then it is settled," Ahpu said. "We wait a month. If no one comes, then we will go, as you wish."

"I would go tomorrow," Pia replied. "We did not steal the gold. If others had found it, it would have disappeared just as quickly. We will send some to Tom's father for his Mary. No one need know where it came from." She paused, biting her lip in thought, before she said, "I know you don't want to leave, Merdy, but I want Thora to learn about the world, not just in the books I read to her. I want to experience that with her, and you. We can live the rest of our lives, not caring what people think, living where we can love each other without fear of discovery."

"Are there such places?" Ahpu asked.

Pia reached to push a lock of Ahpu's thick dark hair from her forehead. She smiled, winking mischievously. "We certainly have plenty of funds to travel the globe and find out. There is enough to bring Jack and a herd of horses." Her enthusiasm began to overcome her and she giggled with glee, then quieted, whispering again, "We could buy an estate in England, where you breed magnificent stock. Thora will have the finest education. She will study art in Paris, history in Rome." She giggled again. "In one month, we begin our adventure, my love. In one month, our lives will be changed forever."

Out on the Panhandle

The two lovers kissed sweetly, while their sleeping child lay unaware of what the future held for her. I knew what was to come and my heart began to ache. My vision became blurry with tears, but cleared at the sound of a man's voice outside the sod house. Time had passed when I looked up from my moment of anticipated sorrow. Little Thora danced in and out of the sunbeams cast through the small windows, the wooden shutters thrown open to light the room. She twirled around the dirt floor dressed in a homemade princess gown.

Pia looked up from her sewing, as the man called out again, "Mrs. Ethridge, are you there?"

I followed Pia out of the house, as did little Thora. Two men stood beside a buckboard, hats in hand. One of them was tall, his hair salted with gray, and wearing a badge. He stepped forward and spoke, "Mrs. Ethridge, I was wondering if Merdy was around."

"Good afternoon, Mr. Clayton. I see they have made you the lawman, now. What do you want with Merdy?" Pia asked, smiling, but her eyes darted toward the sod stables in search of Ahpu.

Mr. Clayton explained, "Oh, it's nothin' to do with the law, Mrs. Ethridge. This here is a census man. We're tryin' to get a regular government going out here and we need to start a list of folks that live here. Came by the last week, found no one home but the man you hired to watch the horses."

Pia seemed relieved. She smiled sweetly. "We were at the market in Liberal, selling off some stock."

The other man stepped forward. He was dressed in a black suit, with a bowler hat tucked into one hand, and papers grasped in the other. He began to cough uncontrollably, dropping his hat, and reaching for a handkerchief in his pocket to cover his mouth. When he regained his composure, he finally spoke.

221

"Please forgive me. I am not accustomed to this climate, or so the doctor in Dodge City told me. My name is Borden, Alfred Borden. The territory hired me to survey the homesteads. Is the head of the household at home?"

"My husband is out with the horses. He won't be home for another hour or so," Pia answered.

Mr. Borden became flustered. *"Well, I suppose I could take the information from you. May we go inside, out of this oppressive swelter?"*

Pia showed the men inside the sod house, but remained outside with little Thora. When she was sure the men could not hear, she bent to the little girl's ear. *"Go tell Ahpu men are here. Stay with her. I will come when they are gone."*

I could hear the man coughing from inside, as I watched the child run toward the river and dissolve into darkness. I was momentarily disoriented, when I heard the cough again. This time it was a softer sound, a woman coughing. My heart leapt to my throat. *"No!"* I cried aloud. No, I would not be made to suffer this again. I fought against the vision. *"Please,"* I begged, *"do not make me witness this."*

I heard Ahpu's soft voice floating on the air. *"You must see to understand, Petu. You must have strength now, the end is nearing."*

The vision took me straight away into the gloom of the sod house. It no longer brimmed with life, but foretold of eminent death, with its dank odors and somber occupants. Little Thora slept on a pallet on the floor, her face still damp from the tears that cried her to sleep. I remembered it all very clearly, the pain I had forced myself to forget. Ahpu sat on the edge of the bed, gently dabbing the sweat from my mother's pale, drawn face. She struggled to breathe, her chest rattling with congestion, between coughing bouts.

Pia spoke in whispered sentences, clipped by her lack of oxygen. "Promise me – she will – go to school."

Ahpн's answer trembled from her lips. "She will go to school. She will see Paris. She will see the world, as you wish."

Tears began to stream down Ahpн's face. My childish heart was not the only one broken that night.

Pia gathered strength to comfort her. "My sweet Meredith. I have loved no one but you. I leave you with my most precious gift, our daughter."

"I – I –" Ahpн stuttered, unable to form words.

Through her pain, Pia managed a smile. "If you say my name every day – my spirit will never leave you." Her voice grew weaker, the breaths more ragged. "Until we can walk – the path together – to the next world – say my name every day – I will wait for you."

I forced the vision away, squeezing my eyes tightly shut, knowing what was to come next. I was spared the witnessing of it, but the sound still quakes my bones as I write of its happening. From the bottom of Ahpн's soul came a primal scream of anguish, a shattering wail, the sound of a heart being torn in two.

#

Decky closed the manuscript. She could hear the band still playing outside. She could not go out there looking for Charlie, because of the tears streaming down her face. She lifted her cellphone from the table and took a couple of deep breaths, trying to gain her composure. After a moment, she knew she would not be able to speak. She typed a text to Charlie instead.

"Come now. Bring Kleenex. Bring the box."

CHAPTER NINE

"Oh my God, Decky," Charlie said, tears cascading down her cheeks.

Decky handed Charlie the box of tissues, grabbing another handful before relinquishing it. She sniffed, and wiped her nose again, saying, "See, that's why I couldn't read it to you. It's heartbreaking."

Charlie slid over closer to Decky on the couch, slipping under her shoulder for a much-needed hug for both of them.

"They only had five years together. I just can't imagine how horrible that was, losing her so soon," Charlie said, softly.

"It makes you think," Decky said. "Life can turn so quickly. The future was bright for them one minute, and the next, it was over." She squeezed Charlie tightly to her.

Charlie sniffled, and wiped her tears again. "Say my name every day, that was so sweet."

Decky kissed Charlie on the top of her head, and said, "I read about that in one of the stories the captives told. The Comanche did not say the name of a person who had passed, because they feared it would tie them to this world and not allow their spirits to move on to the next."

Charlie sighed deeply. "She didn't want to leave her alone. Grace knew Merdy would remain isolated, distancing herself from a world that could not understand her."

"Isn't that what we do now, all of us, the ones that don't fit the mold society tries to shove us in? You and I hide in our own little world, insulating ourselves from those that would shun us, just as Merdy and Grace did."

Charlie looked up at her. "And for good reason. I'm not making myself a target, if at all possible."

Decky pulled her arm from around Charlie's shoulder and stood up. She began to pace the floor, attempting to give voice to her thoughts. "Those women showed incredible courage. Do you think that's the message your mother is sending you? I mean, I know she's telling you she's okay with your sexuality, but there is something more to this story, something she needs you and everyone else to know."

"I don't know, Decky. What happened after Grace died?"

"I didn't read anymore. I was too busy trying to get my shit together," Decky answered.

"Well, then read it to me," Charlie said, standing and crossing to the sink. "I'll make some coffee. No way I'm sleeping until I know what happened."

#

I returned to the riverbank to feel Ahpu holding me while I sobbed. She stroked my hair and calmed me with these words, "Grace. I have said her name every day. She is with us still, you shall see. But first, I must show you the rest."

I rested my head on Ahpu's shoulder, not looking, but knowing her cheeks were wet with tears, as well. I closed my eyes and flew again, above the trees, soaring in wide circles over the sod house now. A red-tailed hawk joined me in my circuit, dipping so close, I could see its yellow eye blink, before I was plunged into a dive and deposited in the middle of a developing scene. A carriage with a burly dark man at the reins was parked near the sod house.

Young Thora leaned on the sod wall, just outside the door. She resembled more the child from my memories, dirty from head to toe, hair unkempt, in a too large buckskin dress that drug the ground. Such was my state at nine years of age, just before I was sent away. I was no longer a well-kept child, but one who lived the shadow of a life that once had been. Ahpu̶ stood by the fire pit in front of the house, her clothing no cleaner than the child's, and looking haggard.

A red-haired, attractive woman approached in the fancy dress of the day, made of black silk with cashmere puffed sleeves and smocking, and an exquisite embroidered trail of yellow roses nestled in a shaded green vine down one side of the skirt. Her matching hat, parasol, and gloves were of equal elegance, but I immediately had the impression that she was overdressed in the manner of a middle-aged parlor madam. Her manner of speaking to Ahpu̶ confirmed my suspicions.

"Merdy, have you brushed that child's hair since the last time the girls fixed her up? It wouldn't hurt to take some soap to yourself either."

"We've been working in the stable," Ahpu̶ answered.

"I'd still kiss you, if you'd let me, and not charge you a nickel, you handsome thing," the woman said, patting Ahpu̶ on the cheek. She turned to the child. "She's a pretty little girl. You could at least put some clothes on her that fit."

"It was her mother's dress. She likes to wear it," Ahpu̶ said, defensively.

"Oh, your dearly departed. Still pining I see."

226

"Is something wrong with one of your horses, Rose?"
Ahpu asked.

*"No, the stock's all fine and the girls, too." Rose batted
her eyes flirtatiously, continuing, "I never got to thank you
proper for patching up Lilly when that cowboy went wild on
the girl. That scar on her cheek is nearly healed now."*

*"I'm glad she is better," Ahpu said, ignoring Rose's
advances, and asked, "If all is well, then why have you
come?"*

*"I like you, Merdy, always have, since you stumbled drunk
into my place three years ago, draggin' that child behind
you."*

*"I have had my moments of weakness," Ahpu answered,
looking down at the ground, seeming ashamed.*

*Rose chuckled. "No honey, what you have is the worst case
of heartbreak I've ever seen, and I've seen my share come in
off the trail. Ain't never known one quite like you though. That
woman of yours must have been somethin'."*

*"She was. That is not why you are here, to talk about
Grace," Ahpu said, growing impatient.*

*"No, I've heard you talk about her plenty, when you've
had a few. I came to give you a warning." Rose hooked her
arm in Ahpu's, glancing back over her shoulder, and moved
them away for more privacy. "That lock box you had me send
to Missouri some years back, well it's stirred up some trouble.
Three men showed up asking about it, said they tracked it to
Beaver City, and Lane sent them down the trail to my place.
One of them said he was looking for his brother Jake. He
thinks that box might have come from someone that knew what
happened to him. One of them damn girls let slip she thought
she might have seen you with a box like that once."*

Out on the Panhandle

"You did not tell them the box came from me?" Ahpu asked, appearing surprised that Rose would protect her identity.

"Honey, I been around enough to spot trouble a mile away. These men got evil on 'em so thick you can smell it. They mean to do harm to the person that sent that box. I believe they'll be comin' tonight. I just thought you should know."

"Thank you, Rose. You were kind to warn me," Ahpu said.

Rose faced her, placing a hand on Ahpu's cheek. "I would not want to see anything happen to such a sweet soul." She dropped her hand, shaking her head. "I don't know what it is, but you've got magic, Merdy Ethridge. Stole my heart first time I met you, but I know I'll never have yours."

Ahpu pawed at the ground with the toe of her boot, uncomfortable under Rose's wanton gaze. Rose let the subject drop and turned them back toward the carriage. She had one more piece of information for Ahpu.

"That girl told those men you are a woman dressed like a man. I didn't like the look in that one fella's eyes. Why don't you take the girl and go on over to Warren's place for the night, 'til I can get Clayton to run 'em off."

"I can't leave the horses," Ahpu said, helping Rose back in the carriage. "Thank you for coming to warn me. We will be fine."

The woman smiled down at Ahpu. "You be careful, Merdy Ethridge. I'd hate not to see you again."

After the woman left, Ahpu flew into action. Little Thora followed her into the sod house, as did I, floating above them, watching their every move. Ahpu slid a little trunk from under the bed and knelt beside it. I recognized it as the one that contained all she and my mother owned, when they first

228

journeyed to this land. She pulled from it the old breechcloth and leggings she had once worn.

Little Thora asked, "Why do you take out your warrior clothes, Ahpu?"

Ahpu looked up, holding her old buckskin shirt in her hands. "Tonight, I must be a warrior, again."

"Can I be a warrior, too?" Little Thora asked.

Ahpu smiled, placing a hand on the child's shoulder. "You must promise to do exactly as I say and I will show you the way of the warrior."

"I promise," little Thora said, excitedly throwing her arms around Ahpu's neck. "I love you, Ahpu."

I watched as Ahpu pulled the child close to her and whispered in her ear. "I love you too, little one."

I knew why I was shown this image. It was to be reminded of the bond that I had allowed the words and beliefs of others to break. I had burned her letters, under the watchful eye of the boarding school matrons, until they simply burned them without my knowledge. Even as I aged to a woman with a mind of her own, I made no attempt to rekindle the relationship. I had selfishly forgotten the love and care she lavished on me, because of its "unnatural" label, and irrationally blamed her for not trying to break through my shunning of her. I let the pain of being separated from Ahpu turn to malice, for which I now felt devastating remorse, and anger toward those who had encouraged it to happen.

I was sure I was about to learn the reason Ahpu sent me away, as I joined her and little Thora outside of the sod house. I was beginning to remember more of what I was witnessing, but from a perspective foreign to me as a child. I smiled at my little face, painted black from my nose to my hairline. My mother's large dress had been cut to my knees, the excess material fashioned around my calves in makeshift leggings.

Out on the Panhandle

With two braids hanging down my shoulders and a scalp lock decorated with a feather, I was a miniature warrior, complete with tiny bow and blunt arrows. Ahpu's buckskins strained against her frame, taller and more muscular now than the juvenile that last wore them. A hat perched on her head made of buffalo horns, with braids of ermine attached to replace the long hair Ahpu no longer had. Her face painted in black and white vertical stripes, bow and lance in hand, arrow filled quiver, Ahpu appeared quite the intimidating savage of the white man's nightmares.

I would have been taken aback by her transformation, were it not for the smile she cast at little Thora dancing around the fire, acting out her imagined conquest. I remembered that we danced. We danced in joy and sorrow, for rain and good grass, for thankfulness and dreams we danced. My breast swelled with a rush of emotion, as I was led to feel it all, all the things Ahpu and I had been to each other. She had been my teacher, my playmate, my friend, both mother and father, and we had been each other's solace while we mourned the loss of the woman we both adored.

Jack's nervous whinny drew Ahpu's attention. He stood nearby, white lightning bolts painted down his legs, a circle painted around his eye, the old Comanche saddle and neck rope tied securely in place, a warrior's steed ready to do battle. A similarly adorned paint-pony waited next to him for its miniature warrior to mount. Ahpu closely observed Jack's behavior, gleaning the direction from which the enemy approached.

"Come, Petu, it is time," Ahpu said.

"I am a warrior now," little Thora declared. "You must call me by my warrior name."

Ahpʉ hid a slight grin behind an affected seriousness for the child's benefit. "Forgive me, Thunder Child. Come now, we must hurry."

Mounting their war ponies, the two warriors rode into the darkness toward the river. They stopped to turn a small herd of horses out of the corral. Ahpʉ put a lead rope on a gray-blue mare, while speaking softly.

"Do you understand your duty, Thunder Child? It is a great duty. If they get our horses, we are on foot."

"The Comanche on foot is a pitiful thing," the little warrior recited. "I remember, Ahpʉ."

Ahpʉ handed the mare's lead to her, asking, "And if I fall, do you remember what to do?"

"I take Blue Bell's lead, turn the horses to Warren's, and ride as fast as I can," Thunder Child answered with confidence.

"The rest will follow the mare," Ahpʉ said, and then reached to touch little Thora's cheek. "Do not look back. If I do not come for you, say my name every day. I will never leave you."

They started the small herd in a slow wide circle, coming out of the trees by the river, and east of the sod house. The moon was but a sliver in the sky. The only illuminated area was near the blazing fire left burning in the pit. Ahpʉ kept her eyes on the shadows just out of the firelight, increasing the tempo of the herd when she saw the men approach and dismount about a hundred yards out.

She turned to her small warrior and said, "Drive them, Thunder Child. Make the men hear a thousand hoof beats. Make them fear, so that they will never return."

With that pronouncement, Ahpʉ wheeled Jack in the direction of the men, letting loose a war cry that split the night air. Thunder Child attempted war cries of her own to add to the confusion of the startled men. Ahpu galloped past them at full speed, stabbing her lance in the ground at one of the frightened men's feet. Her first pass was so surprising the men fired not a single shot. The sound of the unseen herd disoriented them, as Thunder Child tightened the circle. I remembered being quite good in the saddle as a youth, and as I watched my younger self drive the horses, I cheered her on her quest.

Ahpu began riding a smaller concentric circle in the opposite direction, drawing the first rounds of gunfire. The men fired where she had been, not where she was, unable to see her clearly as she darted in and out of the shadows. One of the men broke for his horse, stumbling and falling most of the way, firing into the air blindly. He was allowed to flee, as Ahpu focused on the remaining two, racing by them, hanging from Jack's side, and firing arrows from under his neck. The shafts buried deep in the soil around the men, driving them back toward their mounts. When they finally turned their backs to run, Ahpu charged at them. I watched in utter amazement, as she forced Jack to leap into the air between the two men, while she kicked them each to the ground as she flew by, their weapons falling harmlessly out of reach.

Ignoring Ahpu's instructions, Thunder Child joined in the fray. She came screaming out of the woods behind the now panicked herd. Her cries were so passionate, the men cowered face down in the dirt. She loaded and shot her bow as fast as she could, while continuing her attempts at blood curdling, warbling war cries. The men's staked out horses began to drag the log to which they were tied, terrified by the fleeing herd. Ahpu fell out of character momentarily to chuckle at her little warrior's antics. A few of Thunder Child's blunt arrows hit the men while they lay on the ground, and then she disappeared into the darkness after the stampeding herd.

232

One of the men rolled over, picking up one of the offending arrows. "What in the hell is this?" He asked, looking at the blunted projectile.

Ahpu turned Jack and let him rear above the man's head, clawing at the air as if he would stomp him to death, before she brought him down.

"I will speak English, so that you will understand. This is sacred land," Ahpu shouted. "Do not come here again. The horse spirits have blunted the arrows and let you keep your scalps. Do not tempt them a second time."

The men scrambled to their feet and ran after the horses.

Ahpu patted Jack on the neck. "Let's go find Thunder Child. She's probably halfway to Texas by now."

I recalled how Ahpu finally found me that night, the herd having given up their frantic flight about a mile down river. I was seated on the bank, still trembling from the adrenaline of my charge. The vision took me there, just as Ahpu sat down beside the shaken little warrior.

"I'm sorry, Ahpu. I saw you charge them and then I don't know what happened. I just started hollerin'."

"The war spirit visited you," Ahpu said, patting the child's little knee. "You did very well. Let's get the horses back and get cleaned up. No one must know that we did this. We must hide our warrior beings until they are needed again."

"Yes, Ahpu. I'm scared of my warrior being. She is too powerful."

"You will learn to control her in time," Ahpu said, helping Thunder Child to her feet.

Suddenly, she thrust the child behind her, turning to stare at the opposite riverbank. A sound had come from the thick bushes and reeds near the water. Ahpu turned, holding a finger to her lips, signaling for Thunder Child to step back quietly. She then pulled the pistol from her gun belt and crossed the shallow river. Aiming the barrel at the bushes, she cocked the trigger back, and crept toward the noise.

"Oh, sweet Jesus, Indians!" A scared boy exclaimed. He waved his arms in surrender, repeating, "Friend, friend."

"What are you doing here?" Ahpu asked.

"You speak English?" The terrified youngster said in dismay.

"Yes. Now, what are you doing here?" Ahpu asked again, this time accenting her words with the barrel of the pistol.

"I'm hurt," the boy said, and began to cry. "All I wanted was to shoot a buffalo. Those men robbed me and I think they broke my leg." His tears fell harder now. His words were barely understandable, when he added, "I crawled here. Look at my hands."

He held up bloody hands, sobbing uncontrollably now. I could see that he was badly bruised about his face, one eye black from the beating he had taken. Ahpu lowered the gun and returned it to the holster. She knelt down beside the boy.

"How old are you?" She asked.

"Fourteen," he said, after gasping for air.

"What is your name?"

He gasped again, trying to bring his sobbing under control. "John Lynch, Jr. from Dodge City. I just want to go home."

Ahpu stood and motioned to Thunder Child. "It is an injured boy. Gather the horses. We must take him with us."

She whistled to Jack, who came to her side obediently. She looked down at the boy.

"Well, John Lynch from Dodge City, let's see about getting you home then."

"Are you a real Indian warrior?" The calming boy asked.

"Only when I have to be," Ahpu said.

Out on the Panhandle

The vision switched to the next afternoon. The sky was dark to the west, a heavy thunderstorm brewing on the plains. The warriors were cleaned up and the buckskins put away. John Lynch reclined on a makeshift cot by the door of the sod house, his right leg splinted below the knee, and hands freshly bandaged. His facial wounds had been tended to and he was wearing clean clothes, probably Ahpu's. Little Thora was also freshly dressed in clean clothes and seated in a chair beside the boy, reading to him from a well-worn storybook, while Ahpu worked at trimming a horse's hooves by the fire pit. The man I knew as Clayton, the lawman who brought the sick census taker that killed my mother, rode up on his horse.

"Good day to you, Merdy," he called out.

"Clayton," Ahpu said, acknowledging him with a nod of her head.

"Who is this young fella?" Clayton asked, dismounting and walking toward Ahpu. "Looks too young to be one of them drovers you're always patchin' up."

Ahpu put down her tools and slapped the horse on the rump, sending him off to graze. She pulled her hat from her head and wiped her brow. Before she replaced the hat on her head, I saw faint traces of the war paint at her hairline.

She answered Clayton's question. "Found him in the bushes by the river. Name's John Lynch, a banker's son from Dodge City. Says some men told him they would take him on an adventure. Instead, they took his money and left him for dead, out on the trail."

"You are a fine human being, Merdy. Don't know what folks around here would do, if not for your kindness and doctorin'. You sure enough saved my life. I regret to this day bringing that diseased man to your home. Grace was a very special woman."

235

"She was," Ahpu replied and moved on. "What brings you out this way, Clayton?"

"Seems three men from Missouri ran into a whole mess of wild Indians out this way, last night." He pulled one of Thunder Child's blunt arrows from inside his boot top, smiling, and showing it to Ahpu. "Damndest thing though. The Indians were shooting blunt arrows." He handed the arrow to Ahpu. "I don't reckon you know anything about this, do you?"

"Looks like a child's arrow," Ahpu said, innocently.

"Those fellas looked like trouble, so I sent them on their way. They were happy to oblige and warned everyone in the saloon to prepare for attack by ruthless savages."

"Not too many wild Indians around here, unless you count the little bit of Chickasaw in me," Ahpu commented, handing the arrow back to Clayton.

The lawman turned to the boy. "How about you? See any Indians last night?"

The boy shifted his gaze from Clayton to Ahpu, saying in a strong voice, "No sir, haven't seen a real Indian since I left Dodge City."

"And you, Thora," Clayton asked, squatting in front of her chair.

"No sir, I haven't seen a real Indian either," she said bravely, even though she looked very much the half Comanche she pretended not to be.

Clayton reached and rubbed a smudge of black paint from the child's ear, smiling, and winking at her. He stood and turned back to Ahpu.

"Well, I guess them boys just mistook the wind for howling Comanches. Either way, they're on the way back home with a story to tell." Clayton cleared his throat and removed his hat. "Merdy, you done right by me, nursing me when I was sick, even after I brought death on your house. I know some don't

236

understand the way you live, so if you ever need help, if someone comes to threaten you and yours, you call on me. Sometimes folks can use a little help, and I'm damn proud to come to your aid whenever you need."

"That's good to know, Clayton. I'll keep that in mind. I could use your help reaching the boy's father. Do you think you could help with that?"

"I'd be glad to do it, friend," Clayton said. "You bring Thora by for supper sometime."

He put his hat on his head and extended his hand to seal the conversation.

Ahpu took his hand and shook it with a strong grip, smiling when she said, "It is good to have friends."

Thunder sounded in the distance. Clayton looked up at the sky.

"Let me get his particulars and be on my way. Looks like that's a mean one. Tinder dry as it is, we need the rain, but that lightnin' might set the whole prairie to blazin'. You're smart to keep it down to dirt around your house and stables."

Ahpu stared off at the horizon. "Fire is a hungry animal. It must feed or starve."

Clayton spit in the fire pit. "Them Comanche used to control the fire out here, I'm told. You wouldn't know anything about that, now would you?"

Ahpu smiled over at the man. "The Comanche used to control a lot of things out here. Much of that power was lost to the white man."

"Well, if a fire does come, we might be hoping that band of wild Comanche them fellas saw is around," Clayton said, with a wink.

Ahpu laughed. "There may yet be a few of them wandering around. You just never know."

A flash of light blinded me. I realized the vision had jettisoned me to the center of a pasture, a few miles away. A bolt of lightning splintered the only standing tree, sending a shower of sparks in all directions. The ground rumbled with simultaneous thunder. The sparks landed on dry leaves and grass, sheltered from the rain by the fallen tree. A few dead leaves began to smolder, as the rain passed overhead, not leaving enough moisture to extinguish the fire it started.

Another flash and the interior of the sod house became visible again. The visions were coming quickly, switching from scene to scene as my tension mounted. I remembered the fear of fire and how it was born in me, but now I was to see the effect my actions had on others. It was the afternoon after the storm. The grass beyond the sod house was burning out of control. John Lynch stood on a crutch made from a tree branch, staring at the smoke billowing into the sky. Ahpu appeared in the doorway, looking back over her shoulder.

"I set a break fire. If the wind keeps blowing out of the south, it will turn the flames around us." She looked around the sod house. "Where is Thora?"

"She isn't with you?" John asked.

Terror filled Ahpu's eyes. "No, she did not come with me. I told her to come to the house and wait with you."

John peered out at the high flames licking at the pasture, turning the earth a scalded black. "She did come to the house, but then she ran out again. Said she left Pia's book down by the river."

"The river is the other boundary of the fire break," Ahpu shouted, leaping the three steps out of the sod house, already in a dead run. "She will be trapped!"

"Look at the flames," John called after her. "You can't get there now."

238

Out on the Panhandle

Jack was tied near the doorway, in case they had to make an escape. His mission had now changed. Ahpu grabbed a soaking wet blanket she had placed on the roof of the sod house earlier, and threw it over Jack's back. She took off her over-shirt, dipped it in the water bucket, and tied it over Jack's nostrils. She then dipped her handkerchief in the water and tied it around her face. Ahpu was about to ask of the horse something few others would do, follow her commands and plunge headlong into the flames, risking both of their lives. She climbed up into the saddle and looked back at John.

"If she returns before I do, stay in the house. The sod is wet. You should be safe."

Ahpu did not hear John call out, "God speed."

She was already headed into the flames. I rode with her, feeling my body slip into hers, sharing her emotions. My heart raced, thundering against my chest. An ache began to grow in the pit of my stomach. It was not fear of the fire, but the terror of loss that I shared with Ahpu. I physically felt her fight against the panic, as she urged Jack to go faster.

The first flames were small. Jack cleared them with ease and landed in an area yet to burn. I could feel the heat burning my skin, Ahpu's skin, while she pranced Jack back and forth, looking for a way through the next wall of flames. Cedar trees, packed with now boiling oil, began to explode near the river, announcing the main fire was approaching its banks. Somewhere between Ahpu and the riverbank, a child sobbed in terror, desperately seeking a way out of her nightmare.

I heard the voice, as if it were my own, when Ahpu cried out over the roaring inferno, "Grace, I need you. Help me find her."

I saw through Ahpu's eyes, as the wind kicked up the flames behind us, forming a wave about to break and consume all in its path. At that moment, a scorched page of the

239

storybook fluttered above the fire, directly ahead. Through the flames emerged the image of a frightened little girl surrounded by fire.

Ahpu shouted, "Fly, Jack. Fly!"

She leaned into his neck and that magnificent animal charged into the flames without hesitation and at full speed. Ahpu slipped to his side when the first wall was breached, extended her arm, and snatched the child off the ground. Pulling them both up into the saddle, Ahpu covered little Thora's body with her own, and urged Jack to go faster into the next line of scorching flames. After three long strides, at a speed I never knew a horse was capable, we emerged from the inferno and plunged into the shallow riverbed. We were not out of danger, merely momentarily clear of the flames, as they lapped at the banks on both sides. Ahpu turned Jack east down the riverbed, outrunning the blazing ball of flames, as the two fires met.

We came to rest in the sand hills, where we could see the prairie burning for miles. The sod house appeared to be out of danger, as the winds drove the fire north away from it. I separated from Ahpu and became a bystander again, watching as she lowered the child to the ground. Not speaking to little Thora, Ahpu dismounted and checked Jack for injuries, whispering praises to him softly, thanking him for his bravery and courage. The air was thick with smoke, so she left the shirt tied over his nostrils, but untied the one she wore, and finally turned to the frightened child. Ahpu approached her, knelt down, wiped the tears and soot from her cheeks, and then tied the handkerchief around the little girl's face.

"This will keep the smoke from your lungs," Ahpu said, gentle now that her fears had subsided. She pushed a stray lock of hair from the child's forehead, saying, "You disobeyed

240

me, Petu. It almost cost us both our lives. You must listen to me always."

"I forgot Pia's book," little Thora offered as her excuse, bursting into new tears, as she added, "I dropped it in the fire."

"We will find a new book. Pia would understand," Ahpu said, pulling the child into her arms. I could see in her expression the imagining of the loss of a child, as it filled Ahpu's eyes with tears. She squinted them away, squeezing the little girl tighter, whispering to her, "Pia wanted you to have many books."

The child sniffled and pulled back to look into Ahpu's eyes. "I saw her in the fire, Ahpu. I saw Pia in the fire. She said, 'Stay here. Ahpu is coming,' and you did."

Ahpu smiled and said, "She has kept her promise to never leave us." She paused, her expression changing to sadness, before embracing the child again and saying, "It is time that I kept mine."

I did not need the vision to tell me what came next. Several days passed, spent cleaning up after the fire and returning neighbors' stray stock that wandered onto the property. Ahpu was quiet, almost sullen, and spent many hours at night down by the river alone, while I stayed with John Lynch in the sod house. I remember thinking as a child that she was angry with me. I understood now that she was gathering strength for what must be done.

The vision resumed in the sod house. It was four days after the fire, when John Lynch's father arrived to take him home. At the time, I had played outside, unaware that my fate was being decided within the sod walls. On this occasion, I was present for the conversation.

John Lynch, Sr. sat at the small table with Ahpu. I realized now how much he favored his son, with his hazel eyes and fair hair just beginning to gray at the temples. John, Jr. sat on the edge of the bed Ahpu had made for him, looking rather forlorn as his father spoke softly.

"John, I know you only wanted an adventure, and I can't fault you for that. Your mother and I want you to have many adventures in your lifetime, but son, you have to go back to school."

"But I hate the boarding school, Papa," John, Jr. answered.

"It is a good school, and from there you will go on to University, travel the world, learn from all types of people. Our wish is that you will gather that knowledge and then come back here to share it, if you choose. You may find other places more exotic and adventurous than here on the plains."

"But I want to be a rancher, Papa. That is the adventure I seek."

"You are only fourteen, my boy. You have years to decide what you want out of life. Your mother and I simply want you to have the knowledge to make an intelligent choice. You do as we ask, and I'll set you up on a ranch upon your return. Can we shake on that, man to man?"

"Yes, Papa," John Jr. said, extending his hand. He was not happy about the decision, but accepted the restrictions on his future for the moment.

He hobbled outside, leaving John, Sr. alone with Ahpu. The older man shook his head and chuckled.

"His mother made me promise before I moved the family from Boston to Dodge City that I would send him back east to school. Hell hath no fury like a woman hanging on to a promise. He has no idea how I would love to be in his shoes today. A young man with a future waiting to be conquered."

Out on the Panhandle

"We must help the children make choices that are difficult, at times," Ahpu said, carrying the weight of a decision of her own.

"I owe you a debt of gratitude for saving my son's life. Should you ever need anything at all, please do not hesitate to ask," John, Sr. offered.

"I do have a request, Mr. Lynch. I too made a promise to a child's mother. She asked that Thora go to school, see Paris, and travel the world, much as your wife asked. I would like to send her back with you."

Mr. Lynch became flustered. *"Are you asking me to provide an education and travel for your daughter? Why, I'd have to talk to my wife, of course, but if that is what you wish in return for the care of my son, I must try to accommodate you."*

Ahpu smiled at the man. *"You are an honorable soul, Mr. John Lynch. I do not need your money, just your knowledge of the world. If I supply the funds, would you manage them and see that Thora lives the life her mother wanted for her, the one I promised to provide?"*

"You do realize you are speaking of quite a sum. Have you not looked into the Indian boarding schools for her?"

Ahpu stood, got down on her knees, and pulled one of the small lockboxes from under the bed. She opened the top, exposing the gold. *"I have more,"* she said to John, Sr., who was gaping at the sight. Ahpu looked down at the gold. *"Her mother wanted only the best for Thora. Will you help me fulfill that wish?"*

John, Sr. stammered out, *"It isn't stolen, is it?"*

Ahpu shook her head. *"It was stolen and buried by outlaws many years ago. The men that found it are dead by their own hands. The other men who have knowledge of its true ownership are all dead, as well. There is no one to return it to."*

The older man stood and waited for Ahpu to join him. "I am honored that you would trust me with your daughter and your fortune. May I ask, what makes you think so highly of me?"

"You were kind to your son. You want only what is best for him. I treated him as my own. I have no doubt you will treat my daughter the same way," Ahpu answered.

John, Sr. extended his hand. "I will do that, my friend."

And he did. Mr. Lynch saw to my every need for the next twenty years. I lived the same privileged life he provided for his own son, under the mistaken impression that I was the beneficiary of his benevolence. I do not know why that belief was never questioned and the actual source of my funds not identified. I had no time to ponder the answer, as the last of my visions began.

The tearful words I had spoken the day of my departing rang out, as Ahpu placed me in the carriage with John and his father. "Please, Ahpu! I will never disobey you again."

She placed both hands on my tear stained cheeks, her own tears flowing freely. "This is not a punishment, Petu. I must keep my promise to Pia. You will come back. Say my name every day. I will never leave you." She kissed my forehead. "I will always love you, Petu."

I saw her turn her back and walk away that day, as the carriage began to move, and my desperate cries to stay filled the air. What I had not witnessed as a child, I saw now. Ahpu collapsed to her knees inside the sod house, her body shaking with sobs, and the moan of another heartbreak welling from her chest. In all the years I had been gone, I never considered how devastated she must have been, left alone there on that dirt floor, having given up the one thing she had left and loved most of all – me.

"Ahpu̶, I'm so sorry," I said. "Please forgive me, Ahpu̶. I am so sorry."

"Thora, Thora, wake up," I heard a male voice say.

My eyes fluttered open to find the adult John Lynch, Jr. hovering inches from my face, his brow wrinkled with concern.

"What happened? Where is Ahpu̶?" I asked, trying to sit up.

"Whoa. Wait a minute. Don't try to move too fast," he said, gently pushing me back on the pillow. "You've been out for two days. Tseena confessed to spiking the water with Peyote. He won't be doing that again."

I turned my head to see Ahpu̶ asleep in her bed, just as I had left her. "Has she not stirred?" I asked.

"Not a bit. Hasn't even awakened to take food or water from Tseena. He says she will wake soon. We shall see."

Mr. Lynch, or John, as I had begun to call him after my visions helped me remember our long ago friendship, nursed me until I was able to regain my strength. We then kept watch together over Ahpu̶, while I shared my visions with him. His father arrived the next day, a handsome older man nearing his seventies, and stooped now with age. He regaled me with stories of his friendship with Ahpu̶ for hours, before revealing the reason for my summons.

"Thora, Merdy had me call you home because she found out she was dying. There's no easy way to put it, so there it is. It was important to her that she tell you who you are and how you came to be her child. I wanted to tell you numerous times that you had shunned the one who kept you in your finery, but Merdy would not let me. Her idea was that you would find your way home. I am sorry you did not arrive soon enough to hear what she had to say. It seems the cancer has taken its toll

245

already. I will tell you what I know of your background, if you like?"

I exchanged looks over the small table with John, before addressing his father. "I am aware of my beginnings, Mr. Lynch. I am also thankful that I was called here to remember the love with which I was nurtured. I believe Ahpu has succeeded in her wish that I will cherish those memories forever."

Mr. Lynch's eyebrows rose. "That's quite a transformation from the woman who simply could not leave Paris in the summertime. I'm sure my friend would have been pleased with the woman you've become, if she could wake to see it." He shuffled some papers on the table, and then continued. "Thora, you are a moderately wealthy woman. With my help, Merdy bought up five square miles of land around this house. With the remainder of your trust and the breeding stock that comes with this ranchland, you can live a comfortable life here on the prairie. Should you decide to leave, Merdy has left the land and the stock to John here."

John spoke up. "I bought the ranch next door." He smiled. "I'm finished with the banking business and about to begin my lifelong dream. I'd be proud to call you neighbor."

I smiled back, while his father explained further. "The remainder of the trust funds will be yours to do with as you wish. It was important to Merdy that this land would never fall into the hands of strangers. She called it sacred land."

"My mother is here," I said.

"Yes, she has shown me Grace's grave. I know it was important that the site never be disturbed."

Mr. Lynch did not comprehend that I meant my mother was literally with us. I knew it without doubt. I had the same faith as Ahpu that Grace waited to walk the path with her. In my visions and even now as she lay sleeping, Ahpu had grown

246

younger, as her time to meet her lover approached. I smiled because I knew she was not dying, at least her soul was not. Merdy Ethridge was simply waiting for her Grace to come. It struck me that my parents may have been waiting for their daughter to understand, and I did.

"Mr. Lynch, I will be staying here. I went in search of my place in the world, only to find it was here all along. This is my home, where I have learned the value of promises kept and the true meaning of love everlasting."

That was where we left our business, for there was nothing left to do but wait. While John and his father slept outside, anticipating the death of a friend, I rejoiced for Ahpu. I learned from Mr. Lynch that Ahpu was suffering from a female cancer, one that killed painfully and quickly. How ironic that her feminine nature would ultimately take her life, but more importantly, I believed it would also set her free. Her pain would be gone soon, her heart would be healed, and she would walk with my mother once again.

Mr. Lynch had transported provisions down with him to begin work on John's ranch. Among the bundles of wood, my new neighbor intended to use to build a proper house, was the rocking chair he carried into the sod house for me. It is there that I have been patiently waiting for the rest of the story, for I am sure there is more I am to see. The dream that drove me to pen and paper also left me with the knowledge that the ending was near.

I have been writing now for hours. I am sure the morning star will be visible soon. I look at Ahpu and she seems to smile now, resembling more the young warrior who stole the heart of the fair-haired maiden. Was it a trick of the light? Was it the remaining Peyote in my blood? Had the visions forever altered how I saw Ahpu?

Someone stirs outside – It is but Tseena, beckoning me to come with him. I shall write more when I return.

#

Decky turned the page over. There was nothing there. She looked back where the writing stopped, in the middle of the page.

"That's it," she said to Charlie, who was reclined with her head in Decky's lap.

Charlie shot up into a sitting position in the middle of the bed. "You're kidding. That cannot be it."

"It just stops. Are there any other pages in the box?" Decky asked.

Charlie bounded off the bed and ran to the kitchenette table, retrieving the box, and returning to dump its contents on the bed. They sorted through land deeds, old pictures, letters, even a few old homemade Mothers' Day cards Louise had thrown into the mix, still no more pages. Decky lifted a marriage license dated July 1, 1906, one year to the day that Thora had returned to the Panhandle.

"Hey, look at this," Decky said, holding the license up for Charlie to read along with her. "Thora Grace Ethridge married John William Lynch, Jr. I guess that's how the ranch went from five to ten square miles. They merged."

"You make it sound like a business deal. It takes all the romance out of it," Charlie said, taking the paper from Decky's hand. "Did you see this?" She pointed at the bottom of the page, where the bride and groom listed their parents' names.

"Well, I'll be damned," Decky said, and then read aloud, "Mother, Grace Harrell, and father, Merdy 'Horse Child' Ethridge."

"That's just incredible for the time," Charlie said.

"What are you talking about? That's incredible for any time," Decky said. "That Thora was a hell of a woman, and determined not to erase the role Merdy played in her life."

Charlie sat back against the headboard, thinking, then sprang up suddenly, saying, "Oh crap, is this fraud? I mean Merdy is listed as the head of the household and a man on the homestead deed, the census, and this marriage certificate. Can the government take the ranch?"

"Whoa, relax. I know there was no law preventing a woman from homesteading, but if it will make you feel better, I'll shoot Molly an email."

"Do it now. Maybe she's still up," Charlie said, handing Decky her laptop.

Decky typed what she thought was as short a description of what had happened that she could come up with, without it turning into a historical fiction piece. Charlie made herself busy in the kitchenette, returning with another cup of coffee for them both just as Decky hit send. The music had quieted outside, as it approached the midnight hour. Acoustic guitars had replaced the louder instruments a while ago, and now some woman was singing an a-cappella rendition of Patsy Cline's "Sweet Dreams" to round out the night.

"Who is that? She's really good," Decky asked Charlie.

Charlie handed Decky her coffee, while she climbed into bed to lean on the headboard beside her, answering, "That's Mary."

They listened, as Mary's voice echoed off the barns, sweetly singing the ranch to sleep. Decky's cellphone sounded the notice for a new text message. She clicked on it and read, "Call me. I'm up. Molly."

Decky found the number for Molly in her contacts. The extremely talented lawyer, who saved Decky and Charlie's butts and got them some cold hard cash in return for their

249

troubles, had become a friend, and was always helping Decky with legal stuff for her novels. Molly picked up on the first ring.

"Decky, are you working on a novel, or did this really happen?" She asked, without the formalities of a hello.

"It really happened, and how are you, by the way?" Decky responded.

"I'm better than I've ever been," Molly said, her tone reflecting the newfound love in her life, and then moved right along to, "You have to write this story, Decky."

"Tell Leslie hello for me," Decky said, very happy her friend had finally met the woman of her dreams. Then she explained, "I can't write it until you tell me whether any laws have been broken. It's Charlie's family ranch in question. Wait a second, I'm putting you on speaker, so Charlie can hear too."

Molly waited for Decky to give the okay, and then launched into her legal opinion. "My first impression is the statute of limitations on a tort usually does not begin to run until the tort is discovered. I am assuming we are in the tort world because the ability to prosecute a crime dies with the defendant. The statute of limitations on fraud is usually longer, because it is more difficult to discover. However, there has to be some injury for a tort. In other words, someone has to be able to prove damages. If the State of Oklahoma and, or the US government was intending to pass the land to the homesteader, regardless of gender, no tort. If they were not intending to pass regardless of gender, they have to show some damages. I think Oklahoma and the Feds would have a hard time proving any damages. Finally, to pursue a fraud claim you must prove specific intent. They would have to prove Charlie's relative specifically intended to dupe everyone into thinking she was a man for the purposes of defrauding the government. She took no action in the scenario you gave me.

The people doing the paperwork simply made the assumption, or took the word of someone else. The only action taken by this Merdy Ethridge was no action, or at best, an omission. Proving a negative is damn near impossible in the legal world. Again, I don't think it is an omission because she did not omit anything. She simply did nothing. She did not actively participate in the fraud."

Decky started laughing. "Are you done?"

"Yes," Molly said, beginning to chuckle, as well.

"I think you said it's all good. We're in the clear," Decky asked.

"I just looked at the Homestead law of the time. I found nothing that would indicate my initial analysis was in error," Molly said, adding with a laugh, "Yeah, it's all good."

"I love it when you talk all lawyer like," Decky teased.

Charlie jumped in the conversation. "Don't get her all hot and bothered. We're living in an RV in my parents' backyard. The walls are thin."

"What, they won't let the gays stay in the house in Oklahoma?" Molly joked.

"There are at least twenty prepubescent children in the house," Charlie said. "Thank the Lord for this RV."

"It's not bad, Molly," Decky commented. "We should rent one, load it up with women, and hit the road."

"We're going to need a bigger one and more bathrooms, if that happens," Charlie said, laughing.

"I'm game, as long as you don't let Leslie drive," Molly said, and then added, "Seriously, Decky, I'd love to read this Ethridge woman's entire story."

"How about you bring Leslie down to the house? We'll sit on the back deck, drink beer, and I'll tell you all I know," Decky offered.

"Sounds like a plan," Molly said.

251

"Thanks for answering my email so quickly, and in person. I'll call you when we get home, and we can set a date." Decky concluded the conversation with, "By the way, what are you doing answering emails at this time of night with a hot, new woman in your house?"

"You have to let them sleep sometime, Decky. You don't want to wear that new off too fast."

Charlie threw her hands up, saying, "I've been telling her that for two years."

"Wait a minute," Decky said. "Between the two of you, there are at least forty years of full on lesbian lifestyle. I have a lot of catching up to do, and I don't mind at all having my new worn off."

Molly started laughing loudly. "God help you, Charlie, and with that, I bid you good night."

CHAPTER TEN

"There's a bright golden haze on the meadow," a crisp clear tenor voice rang out over the prairie. Gordon MacRae stepped into Decky's view, spurs jangling, his hat tilted back enough to let a few blond curls peek out above his brow.

He continued to sing, "The corn is as high as an elephant's eye –"

Decky sang along, "and it looks like it's climbin' clear up to the sky."

Gordon turned to begin the next verse, "Oh, what a beautiful mornin'," as Shirley Jones hung clothes on a line to dry. Wait, Decky thought, that isn't Shirley. It's Charlie.

Decky blinked her eyes open to see Charlie sitting up next to her in the bed. Gordon kept right on singing. Charlie stared off as if she were listening to him, too. Suddenly, it dawned on Decky that the voice was coming from outside and someone was actually singing the opening number to the musical, "Oklahoma!"

Out on the Panhandle

"Who is that singing?" Decky asked, rubbing the sleep from her eyes.

The corners of Charlie's lips curled into a little smile. "That's Bobby. He's been singing that song at the crack of dawn on the morning of the reunion, since he played Curly in high school."

Decky sat quietly, listening to Bobby croon the song that changed American musical theatre history, something she was sure no one within earshot cared about but her. Rogers and Hammerstein literally rewrote the book on Broadway musicals, when they opened the show with a lone tenor and a nearly bare stage. Up to then, a big production number always started a show and the dances and songs were not necessarily tied to any storyline. All that changed with "Oklahoma!" in 1943, but Decky doubted anyone was thinking anything at the moment other than, "Damn, that man can sing."

When Bobby finished, Decky said, "Why Charlie, I had no idea I had married into the family von Trapp. Who knew they were secretly living the quiet ranch life on the Panhandle?"

"He's really good, isn't he?" Charlie said with pride.

"Yes, he is, and Mary, and Michael, all the others, and they play instruments, too. How did you not inherit this performance gene?" Decky asked, pulling Charlie back down on the bed and into her arms.

Charlie snuggled up to Decky, nuzzling her neck. "By the time I came along, the only instrument left was a tambourine."

Decky chuckled. "What would you play if you could?"

Charlie leaned up so Decky could see her grin. "I would love to have played the drums."

"So, why didn't you?" Decky asked.

"Andy inherited them from David, and Joseph got them next. There was a line. By the time I could play them, no one was around to play with me. I lost interest and discovered ball,

254

ball of any kind, and trail racing. I loved trail racing with
Jackson. I was busy doing other things, so I just hung out, beat
the tambourine, and sang harmony when asked. The band thing
was really the older kids deal."

"They had a band?" Decky asked.

Charlie crossed her hands on Decky's chest and rested her
chin there, so they were face to face. She grinned broadly.
"You, my dear, are in for a treat, the once a year reunion of the
Keeps 'Em Busy Band. Instead of KISS, they were KEBB."

Charlie's head began to bounce with Decky's laughter.
Decky asked, "Where did they come up with that name?"

"People used to ask Momma and Daddy how all the kids
were so good at music, and they would say, 'Keeps 'em busy
and out of trouble.' The band didn't play much outside of
home, but they played a few dances at the school and some
rodeos."

"So will I get to see you perform with the band?" Decky
said, grinning at the prospects.

"Maybe," Charlie said. "You win that cow chip throwing
trophy and you can have whatever you want."

Decky pulled Charlie in closer. "What if I need inspiration
now?"

Charlie raised one eyebrow, questioning Decky. "How do
your legs feel this morning? Have you recovered from the
horseback riding?"

Decky quickly responded, "Yes, I'm good. Not on injured
reserve anymore. How about a nice workout to get the morning
started?"

Charlie rolled off Decky and right on out of the bed,
landing on her feet to stand over Decky. "Nope. You need
incentive to win, so you don't get any until you do."

"Damn, Charlie, is it that important to you?"

Charlie put her hands on her hips. "Yes, as a matter of fact, it is."

Decky pulled the covers back and slid her feet to the floor. She stood up in front of Charlie, wrapping the little blond in her arms. "Hey," she said, softly, "just relax. I know you are worried about what this day will bring."

Charlie put her head on Decky's chest, answering, "I knew this moment would come, but I envisioned a nice quiet talk around the dining room table, not a public outing in front of hundreds of people."

Decky patted Charlie's back, soothing her. "Honey, I think the outing has already happened. The absolute best thing you can do today is just be happy. Let them see who you really are and that you are no different from the girl they have all loved for so long." She pushed Charlie back so she could look her in the eyes. "You have to look at this as an opportunity, not a brick wall you have to run through."

Charlie tilted her head to one side, wearing an expression of confusion.

Decky explained, "Charlie, there are nearly three hundred people expected at this shindig. You don't think for one minute that you and I are the only gay people here, do you? How many of those young nieces, nephews, and cousins of yours are looking to you to see how to handle someone like Karen? The best example you can show them and the worst thing you can do to Karen is not let it bother you. Just have a good time, and if she confronts you, I have no doubt that you will know exactly how to handle it with class. I have money riding on that in the betting pool."

Charlie's mouth fell open. "What?"

Decky laughed and pulled Charlie into tight embrace. "Yep, they have a pool on how this is all going to go down. There are betting options now, because no one was putting any

256

money on Karen. You can bet on varying outcomes, like whether there will be punches thrown, how many bible verses will be quoted, and how many cuss words will come out of your mouth. There's even one that says you will use words that Karen has to look up. I put an extra twenty on that one and fifty on you not using profanity in front of your mother. Because of the nature of the discussion, they did allow for at least two cuss words before I lose my money, but you can't say fuck or I automatically forfeit."

Charlie pulled out of Decky's arms and went to her purse on the nightstand. She dug around for her wallet and produced a hundred dollar bill. She handed it to Decky, saying, "Tell Franny, and I know she's behind this, double or nothing that I don't cuss." She reached back in her wallet for another bill. "And tell her, here's another hundred that you take the chip throwing trophy back from Karen by at least ten feet."

Decky took the money, saying, "I can't just beat her?"

Charlie smiled mischievously, saying, "If you want me to have a good time, then you will crush her."

#

Charlie showered and dressed quickly. Decky gave her a kiss and told her how much she loved her, before letting her go help with breakfast. Decky stayed behind to shower, but first she had to call her son, Zack. He was playing host to six of his friends. Decky could only imagine what shape he would be in. He answered on the fourth ring, still groggy.

"Mom, it's eight thirty," were his first words.

"Good morning to you. It's only seven thirty here," she said, knowing he was still trying to come fully awake. He had always been a sleepyhead in the mornings.

257

"You know how you hate it when Granny calls and wakes you up? Well, I'm beginning to understand," Zack said with a yawn.

Decky teased the half-awake boy, now in the last months of his teenage years. "Oh, that's low, comparing me to my mother. I might have to leave all my possessions to Dixie. She would never say something like that."

Zack moaned.

Decky eased up on him. "Okay, I'll let you go back to sleep. Just checking in. Is everything going okay?"

"Yes, except Miss Kitty keeps killing my socks. How does she get the drawer open? She's like a cat burglar."

"I don't know, but I bet several pairs of mine are spread out in the master bedroom. She's obsessed with socks," Decky said, and then changed the subject. "You guys are being safe on the water, right? And I'm not naïve enough to think there isn't some alcohol being consumed. You do have a sober person or two in charge, preferably you."

"I've been sober, Mom. Between Brenda, Granny, and Papa coming around to check on me, I haven't had time to drink. Brandon is the only one trashed, anyway, but I guess he earned it."

Brandon was Zack's friend who just returned from his first tour in Afghanistan. Decky commented, "If he's old enough to die for his country, he can have a beer at my house, just don't let those high school kids in the booze. You remember our rule, right?"

Zack laughed. "I got it, Mom. Don't do anything you could go to jail for or let anybody die. And if it makes you feel better, I asked Papa to come and help out with the fireworks."

"You know that means Lizzie will be there, so clean up the house and save yourself the pain of listening to her rant,"

258

Decky said, with the voice of experience. "And thank you for being smart enough to call him."

"No worries, Mom."

"How's Dixie?"

"She's fine. She's sacked out on my other pillow. Anything else?" Zack asked through another yawn.

"No, I think that about covers it. You good on food?"

"Yeah, we're good. Tell Charlie thanks for all the frozen meals. They have come in handy. Glad you found someone that can cook."

"Well, you can thank her yourself by helping me with a little plan," Decky said.

Zack groaned.

Decky ignored him and asked, "Is your old drum set still up in the loft of the guest house?"

#

Decky came out of the RV, her newest plan in the works and ready to see what the Warren family reunion held in store. Her immediate impression was, "Holy shit, look at all these people and it's just barely eight o'clock," which she mumbled under her breath.

More cars and trucks were arriving by the minute, anxious guests springing from the doors, sometimes before the vehicle stopped completely, running to the open arms of a relative coming to welcome them. Breakfast was in full swing under the patio roof. The tables were filled with plates piled high with biscuits and gravy, a staple of Oklahoma breakfast, Decky had learned. The hungry mob eagerly assaulted platters of eggs and bacon.

Decky caught a glimpse of Charlie, wearing an apron and stirring eggs at the stove, before the cellphone ringing in her pocket distracted her. She pulled it out and looked at the

259

screen, knowing before she did it had to be Lizzie, and it was. She stepped outside the patio, trying to find a quiet place to answer the call.

"Good morning, Mom," Decky said into the phone.

Lizzie launched into her right away. "You've been gone three days and have not called your son."

"I just talked to him," Decky answered.

"Oh," Lizzie said, momentarily deflated, but not completely defeated. She added, "Well, it took you long enough to check on him."

"Happy Fourth of July, Mom," Decky said, not wanting to get into another long conversation about what a terrible mother she was.

Zack graduated in the top of his class and was doing very well at college. He was a great kid and their relationship was a good one. Decky did not need parenting advice from a mother that drove her own children nuts.

"Happy Fourth to you too," Lizzie responded. "What all have you got planned for today?"

"Well, there's a softball game, cow patty bingo, and a cow chip throwing contest lined up. Not sure what else they might be planning," Decky said, trying not to laugh before her mother's reaction.

"Cow patty bingo? Cow chip throwing? Decky, you are not throwing cow manure, are you?"

"Why, yes I am," Decky said, snickering. "As a matter of fact, if I don't win, Charlie may never speak to me again."

"Well, you be sure to wash your hands," Lizzie said, as if Decky were still six.

Decky ignored her, and redirected the conversation, again. Sometimes her attention deficit came in handy. She could jump to so many different topics, it would fluster her mother, who would give up and leave her alone.

260

"Hey, tell Dad thank you for going over tonight to help out with the fireworks. That makes me feel a lot better. And I'll thank you in advance for the cleaning you will do, but it really isn't necessary." That's good, Decky thought, praise her, but now reinforce the boundaries. "The master bedroom is off limits to everyone, and Zack knows that. So, you won't need to go up there. I invoke my right to privacy here, Mom."

"What in the world could you have in your house that I could not see?" Lizzie asked, trying to cover what Decky knew to be a fact. Given the slightest hint that there was something Decky did not want her to see, Lizzie would hunt like mad to find it.

Decky was feeling a bit frisky, and of course, that had a lot to do with the fact that Lizzie was halfway across the country. There was absolutely nothing in their bedroom that either she or Charlie felt the need to hide, but Decky decided to poke the bear. "Besides, you wouldn't want to accidently open that one drawer."

In the moment Lizzie was temporarily occupied, her brain spinning out of control with imagining what the lesbians could be hiding, Decky made her exit.

"Hey, I have to go or I'm going to miss breakfast. Give Dad a hug for me. Love ya'. Bye."

Decky was laughing when she hit the end call button. Zack could thank her later. She had just insured him a Lizzie free evening down on the dock, because his grandmother would be busy inside, tearing through Decky's house, hunting for something that wasn't there. The best part was Lizzie would not be able to ask about what she was not supposed to be looking for. It would drive her nuts.

"Why are you smiling like the cat that ate the canary?" Charlie said, arriving at Decky's elbow with eggs and bacon on a plate.

261

"I just sent Lizzie on a snipe hunt," Decky said, still pleased with herself.

"Oh, honey, you should not toy with her. You know it makes her crazy." Charlie handed Decky the plate. "I was looking for you. Here's your breakfast. Do you want coffee or milk?"

"Thank you. Coffee would be great, but where should I sit?" Decky asked, seeing no space opened up under the patio.

Charlie pointed at one of the tents. "We finished cooking. Go over to that tent. We'll be over there in a minute," she said, already walking away.

Decky called after her, "Who's we?"

Charlie did not hear her. Decky made her way to the tent, avoiding losing her plate, while navigating children gone wild. They darted about, the fresh air seeming to have the same effect as a bag of Halloween candy. Once out of the fray, Decky found an empty table in the corner of the tent and sat down. The china of the day was paper and plastic. She had just released her spork, a combination spoon and fork, and napkin set from its plastic wrapper, when little Kayla walked up.

"Hey, Aunt Decky, you're on my team."

The title took Decky aback, but she smiled and said, "Great! Okay, Coach, what position do you want me to play?"

"Everybody plays everywhere. You'll see," Kayla answered and then ran off.

Decky chuckled to herself, saying under her breath, "Aunt Decky. Now, that's a new one."

She was just about to put the first spork-full of eggs in her mouth, when Charlie and Louise arrived at the table. The "we" became clear. Charlie was on a mission to talk to her mother about Thora's manuscript. She handed Decky a steaming cup of coffee and immediately began her inquiry.

262

"Momma, we finished Thora's story. Well, we read what was there. It seemed to just stop."

Louise smiled over her coffee cup. "There is more."

This excited Decky. "Really? May I read it?"

"Yes," Louise said, her smile widening. "I will give it to you, but first I believe I owe my daughter an apology."

"You don't owe me –" Charlie began to say, but her mother cut her off.

"Hear me out, Charlie," Louise said, taking her daughter's hand in hers. "I tried to let my children make their own way, choose the path they were destined to follow. I never interfered or commented unless I was asked," she chuckled, "or the train wreck was so obvious and I had to step in."

Charlie smiled at her mother. "You saved my butt a few times."

Louise's smile slowly slipped from her lips. Decky felt very much the third wheel, but sat completely still, a piece of bacon poised in front of her mouth where she had frozen.

Charlie's mother continued. "From the very start, I knew your journey would be the most difficult. There were no walls that you would not climb, no fences you wouldn't jump." A bit of her smile returned, as she focused on her baby girl. "I knew you had the courage to be just what God had made you, and that you were the child my grandmother spoke of. You see, Little One, I knew you were coming."

Decky dropped the bacon. Her eyes filled with tears, as she saw the words hit Charlie, who sat stunned, staring at her mother.

Louise let that sink in and then went on to explain. "My grandmother entrusted that story to me, just before she died. I read it to her over and over in her final days. Her last words to me were, 'She is coming.' When you finally arrived, I knew the moment I set eyes on you, but I had to be patient. When

263

you read the rest of the story, you will understand why I waited to share it with you."

"Why didn't you say something?" Charlie asked, fighting back tears.

Decky knew that question had nothing to do with the manuscript. It came from years of having to hide who she was, guard her conversations, and play the role of lonely, unmarried Aunt Charlie. Louise felt the weight of Charlie's pain. She looked down at the table.

"I'm so sorry. I waited for you to come to me." Louise lifted her welling eyes to look at Charlie. "I assumed you knew that you could. I should have told you that whom you loved was no concern of mine, or your father's. My only hope for you has always been that you would find the spirit I believed was destined for you." Louise looked over at Decky. "I think you've done that." She smiled, causing a tear to spill to her cheek, adding, "I certainly knew it wasn't Lynne."

Charlie chuckled and wiped her eyes. "I could have used a heads-up on that one."

Louise looked from Decky to Charlie. "I also know all about the attack you both endured." She turned back to Decky. "I think you might have a bit of that warrior spirit yourself. I have thanked your father, and now I'm thanking you for saving Charlie's life."

Decky made eye contact with Charlie and replied, "I think your daughter saved mine. Thank you for keeping at it until you made her."

Louise grabbed one of each of their hands. "I am telling you now, there will be no more hiding in this family. If it wasn't for the love of two women, none of us would be here."

She narrowed her eyes, a look that Decky had seen on Charlie's face a few times. It meant the person on the other end was about to get an earful. Thankfully, it was not Decky this time.

Louise placed Charlie's hand on top of Decky's, and concluded with, "If anyone has a problem with that, you just let me handle it."

#

After breakfast, various musicians and singers began what would be a non-stop parade of performances. From the smallest little Garth Brooks and Reba wannabes, to the oldest white-haired pickers, the Warren reunion guests were treated to some fine entertainment. There was hardly time to sit and listen, though. Charlie marched Decky off to the cow patty bingo corral to write her name in a square.

She explained the game to a mystified Decky. "See how they've marked off squares on the ground? Later on, they will put a cow in here and whatever square it drops a patty in wins. It's simple."

"You people will bet on anything, won't you?" Decky commented.

"Yep, pretty much," Charlie said, signing her name in square thirteen. She handed the marker to Decky. "Your turn."

"What about these squares with more than one name?" Decky asked, seeing that someone had signed under her favorite number already.

"Everyone in the square splits the prize," Charlie said, as if Decky should know that.

"What's the prize?" Decky asked, signing under Bobby's name in square twenty-one.

"The cow," Charlie said, looping her arm through Decky's, and turning her back toward the patio. "Of course, that's after it has been dressed."

265

"By dressed, I'm assuming you don't mean in a costume," Decky said, enjoying the relaxed Charlie. "You're not about to spring some bovine drag show on me later, are you?"

"No," Charlie said, throwing her head back and laughing. "Have I told you I love you, today?"

The conversation with her mother had lifted a heavy burden from Charlie's shoulders. Decky was unsure Charlie ever grasped the magnitude of that weight, until it was no longer there. There was a new lightness to her voice, more strength and confidence in her step. No matter what age a child achieved, the affirmation of a parent had healing properties, and knowing the folks back home had your back could work miracles. Charlie was a walking example of that.

There was also the matter of the arm looped through Decky's. This public display of affection might look like a small thing to others, even mistaken for just two old friends walking arm in arm, but to a gay couple, feeling secure enough simply to touch one another in public was a very big deal. Something as innocent as holding a lover's hand was another privilege the straight world enjoyed without fear of reprisal, while the LBGT community stands by, envious of such a simple act of acknowledgement. Only someone whose life had been threatened, because of whom they fell in love with, could possibly fathom how much it would mean to move freely among the masses unbranded. Decky had only been dealing with the stigma for two years. Charlie carried that load for twenty.

"I love you too, Charlie Warren. I'm going to win you that trophy."

Charlie spun out of Decky's arm and started walking backwards in front of her, putting on a sultry expression and voice to match. She really did understand how to motivate Decky. "You win and I promise to make it worth your while."

266

"Oh yeah," Decky said, upping the stakes. "Let's say I get another one of those wet tee shirt strip tease demonstrations, if I win."

Charlie's face flushed crimson, but she laughed. "You are incorrigible. What am I going to do with you?"

Decky did not answer. Her attention had been drawn to the crest in the drive, near the patio. The midmorning sun glowed through a woman's teased red-hair, turning her skull into a flaming orange ball of fire. Medusa could not have made a better entrance.

Decky's expression must have given something away, because Charlie said, "What? What is it?" and then turned around. "Oh shit, it's Satan's bride."

"I haven't seen hair that big since the eighties," Decky commented, mesmerized by the lighting effect.

The glowing orange head moved under the patio and out of sight.

Decky stepped up beside Charlie, who had stopped and was squinting up toward the house. Decky could swear she heard that whistling sound from "The Good, the Bad, and the Ugly" theme song. She stared into the sun with Charlie, and said, "I'm going to paraphrase Doc Holliday from 'Tombstone.' Make no mistake. It's not revenge your after – it's a reckoning. You go on now, Marshall Earp, lay down the law. If you need any help, I'm your huckleberry."

Charlie turned to look at Decky, shaking her head in bewilderment. "What's it like in your head with all those characters floating around? Never mind, I don't want to know." She started walking again.

"Come on, who could resist?" Decky said, playing at defending her reference. "It's the showdown at the OK Corral. I couldn't make this stuff up."

267

They were almost to the patio, when the orange-flamed head reappeared. The two opponents locked eyes, and Decky was sure everyone in view froze to see what would happen next. Decky thought Charlie would just walk by Karen, like her mother asked her to, and let Louise handle the problem. After all, Charlie was not the type to go looking for a confrontation, but Decky's assessment of the situation was in error, which became apparent rather quickly.

Before Decky realized what was about to happen, Charlie walked up to Karen, who blinked back at her with exceedingly long false eyelashes caked in mascara and turquoise painted eyelids. Decky almost laughed when the jukebox in her brain started playing, "I like my women just a little on the trashy side." She imagined that song was written about a woman just like Karen, and figured she must have wiped out the local Wal-Mart beauty counter to acquire that much makeup. The crowd held its collective breath, as Charlie squared off against her nemesis.

Hands on hips, Charlie never gave Karen a chance to speak. "My girlfriend, Decky here, is fond of slipping quotes into conversations. While I am not one for pastiche interpolation during normal discourse, in this instance, I could not have expressed the veridicality of my cathexis toward you any more succinctly than Coco Chanel, and I mean this from the bottom of my heart, Karen, when I say, I don't care what you think about me. I don't think about you at all."

Charlie then proceeded to walk away, not giving Karen an opportunity to respond. Decky followed after her, smiling at Karen and saying, "Nice to meet you. I'm the girlfriend." She could not help but giggle a little as she scurried after Charlie.

When Decky caught up with her, Charlie said, "Did I include enough big words to win the bet?"

Decky was still giggling. "Yes, I think there were a few I need to look up. What is a cathexis?"

"The process of investment of mental or emotional energy in a person, object, or idea," Charlie answered, and then asked, "I didn't cuss, did I?"

"No, you didn't say a single cuss word. I won that bet too," Decky said, already adding up the winnings in her head.

She stopped doing the math, when Charlie said, "Don't count your money, yet. The day is young."

Crystal caught up with them, as Charlie led them to the front yard. Crystal was beside herself with glee. "Oh, my God, Charlie. That was priceless. She was still standing there with a mouth open long after you left. I took a picture," Crystal said, giggling and showing them a digital shot of Karen's gaping expression. She looked back over her shoulder, reporting, "Her minions are comforting her now."

Decky asked, "Karen has minions?"

"Some things never change," Charlie said, sighing. "I didn't see Tammy and Sue Beth, but I should have known they were here. They've always traveled in a pack."

Crystal continued to laugh, as she said, "I'm not sure what all you said to her, but I totally got that you told her you didn't give a shit about what she thought of you. I just wish I had it on video. I'd like to replay that from time to time."

Charlie finally came to a stop in the front yard. She turned to Crystal and Decky. "From my past dealings with Karen, I know that was just round one. She won't be able to resist making a scene. I just wanted to get my two cents in, before she made me too mad to think."

"I thought you agreed to allow your mother to handle this," Decky pointed out.

Charlie grinned. "Oh, I'm sure Momma is going to give her a piece of her mind. Just be prepared for the usual Karen

269

tactics of snide remarks under her breath, so that when you respond she reacts as if she's done nothing."

Crystal agreed. "Been there and done that. How many times did we get in trouble for saying something back to her, while she denied she'd said a word?"

Decky spoke up. "I think you both should do your best to ignore Karen and let Louise follow through with her plan. Everyone is going to get a little enlightenment today, if you'll just be patient."

Charlie smirked. "That's easy for you to say. Wait until the first whispered 'pussy licker' hits your ears and talk to me then."

Decky's jaw dropped.

Crystal shook her head in agreement with her friend. "Yep, all through high school. Charlie and I got that every day from Miss 'Who Me?' Why, she would never use such language."

Decky taught high school. She had observed a lot of adolescent behavior. It prompted her to say, "Wow. That's aggressive. She really hates you, Charlie. That kind of emotion and venom is deeply rooted and not just from a middle school snub. What did you say to her when you told her she couldn't come to your house anymore? Better yet, what made you finally reach that point with her?"

"Oh, this is good," Crystal said. "Charlie has met her match, someone to call her on her shit."

Charlie really did not want to answer. Decky could see it in her body language. She pawed at the ground with her tennis shoe toe.

Decky prodded her. "Come on, Charlie. It can't be all that bad."

Charlie exhaled, her shoulders slumping. Defeated, she gave up and said, "After I told her she couldn't come over anymore, she accused me of having a crush on Crystal, and I

270

did not deny it." She turned to Crystal, "I did have a mad crush on you."

Crystal hugged Charlie. "I know, honey. I had a mad crush on you too, but c'est la vie, I just wasn't drawn that way."

Decky was thinking she was glad Crystal was not gay. She might not have ever met Charlie.

Crystal released Charlie from the hug, saying, "It's a good thing too. You would have just broken my heart." She winked at Decky. "It appears that you were destined to meet this surfer girl and have your heart stolen."

Charlie smiled and put her arm around Decky's waist. "Yeah, I think I'll keep her."

Decky threw her arm around Charlie's shoulder. "Just try to get away. I'd stalk you, you know."

"I know you would," Charlie said, laughing, relaxed now after her confession.

Decky summed it all up. "So, basically what you're saying is, Karen ran with that tidbit of information and blew a twelve-year-old crush into a lifelong character assassination. Did it ever occur to you that she wanted you to have the crush on her? I'm not saying she's secretly a lesbian. Little girls have crushes on girls, boys, adults, fictional characters, and teen heartthrobs. Maybe your admission scared her, because you broke her heart."

"I've thought about that, and whatever her reasons were for declaring war on me, it turned into a personal vendetta, which was mine to deal with," Charlie said. "Now, she's involved my family in her attempt to run me off for good. That, my friends, is not going to happen."

Decky smiled down at Charlie. "Thunder Child would be proud. Shall we go find some war paint?"

"Who is Thunder Child?" Crystal asked.

Charlie turned to Crystal. "My great grandmother."

271

#

Lunch and softball were interrelated, as it turned out. There were so many people wanting to play, over the years the Warren reunion had devised its own set of rules. The bases were laid out in the front yard according to regulation, but that was the only resemblance the competition had to a traditional softball game. Everybody played in the field at the same time and everyone got a chance to bat in no particular order. The teams were divided up into red, white, and blue loyalties, duly marked by the colorful bandanas tied around various parts of the players' bodies. Gloves were optional, but Decky was thankful that Charlie packed theirs in her suitcase.

Points were awarded for each base a player reached, one point for a base hit, two for a double, and so on. Players could also score points for their team making defensive plays that were awarded points on merit, not to exceed the four points one would receive for a homerun. The debates over scoring were as much fun as the play. Although physical contact was not allowed, opposing players could do anything else to distract each other, and they did. The smaller kids were of course assisted and cheered for their efforts, but the adults went all out to make each other laugh so hard, many balls hit the ground or went through player's legs.

Decky became a victim herself while camped out under a high fly ball, waiting for it to come down, when Charlie's brothers, Jimmy and Joseph, started doing an exaggerated Tango around her, complete with lip trumpet accompaniment. She did not know what was more amusing, the dancing, or sounds they were creating. She took her eye off the ball, which allowed Charlie, who was on another team, to jump in front of Decky and swipe the catch from her. Charlie collected two points for her team, and her brothers received one for their efforts. Kayla was the only one not laughing. Her team was behind. The Warrens were a competitive and athletic bunch. There were a number of spectacular catches and amazing plays. Decky reacquired some of Kayla's respect with a diving catch, earning three points for their team. After that, Kayla pretty much stuck to Aunt Decky like glue.

The game flowed freely, with players leaving to fill plates with Fourth of July picnic staples. Almost everyone brought a covered dish to add to the food Charlie's family provided. In addition to Louise's very popular chili, there were hotdogs, hamburgers, more barbecued ribs than Decky had seen in her entire life combined, fried chicken, assorted baked beans, potato and pasta salads, and some very creative uses of Velveeta cheese Decky chose to avoid. There were other dishes, but she decided to stick with the ones she could name.

Decky had wandered over to grab some food, after her turn at bat. She scored three points for her team with a triple, which seemed to satisfy Kayla, who then agreed that she was hungry too and accompanied Decky through lunch. They spent the time between bites talking about softball hitting and throwing techniques. Decky did not mind hanging out with Kayla. She was that girl at twelve-years-old, the one that did not care about what other little girls were doing. Decky only wanted to play ball, or surf, or ski, anything but dress up and play with dolls, to her mother's constant consternation. It warmed Decky's heart when Kayla's mother, Debra, stopped by the table to chat with her daughter.

"Are you milking Decky for information, K-Bear?" She asked, winking at Decky.

"Yes," Kayla said, excitedly. "Aunt Decky is going to show me some things I can do to get more speed on my throws without hurting my arm, and she said I could come to her house and learn how to surf."

273

"Well, that's very nice of your new Aunt," Debra said, smiling at Decky. She patted her daughter on the shoulder. "Don't wear her out, K-Bear. Let her play with the adults once in a while. Have you seen your Aunt Charlie? I need to talk to her."

"She was still in the field when we left her. Kayla and I were hungry," Decky said. "I appreciate her keeping me company."

Debra kissed her daughter on the top of her head. "She's going to be the best softball player in the world, if dedication has anything to do with it. She's smart too, makes great grades. We're very proud of her."

"Mom," Kayla whined, embarrassed by the attention.

Decky smiled, knowing one day Kayla would realize how much those words of encouragement really meant to her. Decky's affirmations from her mother were always tempered with a "but." She could hear Lizzie's voice, even now. "Congratulations on graduating in the top of your class, but you were not Valedictorian," or, "Great job on the Master of Fine Arts, but you could have been a lawyer in the same amount of time," and more recently, "I'm glad you've found the love of your life, but I just wish it wasn't a woman." Yes, Kayla would appreciate her mother's support one day, more than she could ever know.

Debra went to find Charlie, and Kayla went to get a ball so she and Decky could play catch. Decky was standing over one of the dessert tables trying to decide between chocolate cake and pecan pie, after eliminating all the other choices. There were so many people, one more person coming to stand next to her did not draw her attention. The words aimed at her were what turned Decky's head.

"I've read your blogs, Ms. Bradshaw," Karen said, emphasizing the Ms. a little more than necessary. "I'm

274

troubled by your lack of concern for how your lifestyle will affect your son. It's bad enough he had to grow up without a father."

Decky noticed two women behind Karen. No doubt, these were the minions, Tammy and Sue Beth. One was short and plump, the other tall and too skinny, both emulating Karen's makeup and fashion trends, with matching sneers on their faces and bibles clutched in their hands. They had cornered Decky alone, as pack animals do, thinking she was the weaker of the herd members. They were mistaken. After years of dealing with Lizzie, Karen would be a piece of cake. With that in mind, Decky plucked the chocolate cake from the table and spoke to Karen.

"I've read the Family Research Council's blog. I'm troubled by their lack of concern for facts, so I guess we're even."

Karen was probably not half-bad looking under all that plumage, but with the huge red-orange hair, turquoise eye shadow, and too many trips to the tanning salon, she resembled a horribly mutated combination of Wynona Judd, Reba McEntire, and Tammy Faye Baker. It was not a good mix. Karen ignored Decky's remark and took another shot at her. The slight smile on her lips did nothing to conceal her wicked intentions, or improve her appearance.

"I would think that having a messenger of God sent to destroy you would have opened your eyes. Don't you see, he sent that man to steer you away from your sin and back to God's love. You were saved from death so that you may repent your sins."

The minions, Tammy and Sue Beth, nodded their heads, simultaneously saying, "Amen. Praise him."

Decky's first thought was Karen would look much better with the chocolate cake smeared all over her face. She pushed

275

Out on the Panhandle

the anger back down, and said instead, "I believe that bullet crashed through his skull before he got to the God's love part of his message." She took a bite of cake, savoring it lavishly for effect. She pointed at the table and swallowed. "Umm, this is really good. You should have some. It might help with that nasty bullshit aftertaste."

Kayla came running up. "Come on, Aunt Decky. Let's go play some catch, before the cow chip throwing starts."

"I'm sorry, Kayla honey," Karen said. "You must be mistaken. This woman is not your aunt. She would have to be married to your Aunt Charlie and that is not legal, and is against all of God's teachings. Your parents should have told you that."

Decky was about to step in and take Kayla away. Involving a child in this mess was not Decky's idea of fair play, but she did not have time to intervene.

"She's more of an aunt than you'll ever be," Kayla said, adding, "Besides, my mom and dad said you're a bigot and I shouldn't listen to you."

Not to be outdone by a twelve-year-old, Karen resorted to middle school tactics by encouraging her minions to gang up on the girl. She turned to her flock. "We must pray for this child. Her parents have given her over to be recruited by the evil forces of homosexuality. Open your bibles, ladies, we have to read God's word."

Decky put her hand on Kayla's shoulder, already moving her away, while saying, "Why don't you ladies reflect on first Timothy, chapter two, verse nine, before you get to little Kayla here. I wouldn't want you to overlook anything."

Decky walked away with Kayla, while the three bible thumpers furiously turned pages in search of Decky's reference.

Kayla looked up at Decky. "What does that verse say?"

Decky smiled down at her new little friend. "It says that women should adorn themselves in respectable apparel, with modesty and self-control."

Kayla threw her head back and laughed, reminding Decky of Charlie again. "Good one, Aunt Decky."

Decky laughed with her, saying, "Come on. I need to warm my arm up really well. I have a cow chip throwing trophy to win."

CHAPTER ELEVEN

After warming up with Kayla, and teaching the future All-Star a few things, they went in search of Charlie. Kayla told Charlie all about Decky's chat with Karen as soon as they found her, at least the part she witnessed.

When Kayla ran off to tell her mother the story, Charlie said, "It looks like you have a fan, Aunt Decky. Nice choice on the bible verse, by the way. How'd you pull that out of thin air?"

Decky grinned. "I can't take credit for that. Every time Lizzie would see Tammy Faye Baker on TV, she would shout that verse at the screen. It seemed appropriate."

Charlie raised one eyebrow, searching Decky's face. "Is that all that happened?"

"Who won the softball game?" Decky said, dodging the question, but Charlie was not as easy to redirect as Lizzie.

"My team, by one point," she answered, but was not finished. "What did Karen say before Kayla walked up?"

"Damn, Kayla will be disappointed," Decky said. "Did the cow declare a winning square yet in the bingo game?"

"Yes, neither of us won. Answer my question," Charlie demanded.

Decky stalled again. "Good, I made the mistake of seeing the cow and I couldn't have eaten it anyway, after seeing that face."

"That's not a real popular stance on a cattle ranch," Charlie said, and having had enough of Decky's evasive tactics, added, "If you ever want to have sex again in your lifetime, quit pretending like you don't hear me."

"Wow, pulling out the big guns already," Decky said, still not answering.

Charlie's warning tone, when she said, "Decky," indicated she was not amused.

Despite not wanting to add fuel to Charlie's fire, Decky really did not want the little blond angry with her. She spilled her guts. "Karen said she was concerned about my son, that the guy who almost killed us was a messenger from God, and we were saved so that we might repent our sins and go straight. I remained calm and used only one cuss word."

Charlie looked genuinely surprised. Decky could not imagine why. Surely, Charlie expected something like that from Karen. Charlie's astonishment turned out not to concern Karen's remarks.

"I can't believe you stayed composed through that, unless the cuss word you used was cunt."

"No, I offered her some cake to alleviate the bullshit aftertaste," Decky said, smiling broadly and beginning to chuckle.

Charlie matched her smile, saying, "I think Thunder Child would be proud of you, too."

\#

Crystal moved around taking pictures, documenting the reunion. Decky talked to her about using some of the shots in the Warren family history book, but now she wasn't sure exactly how that story was going to play out. How much of Merdy Ethridge's true history would Louise want distributed to a very large extended family? Decky would have to wait and see. At the moment, she was lined up to pick her cow chips for the contest. Kayla was at her side, explaining the best way to find a good flyer, while Charlie smiled at her niece's crush. It was cute, harmless, and Decky remembered a certain young softball-playing teacher she had followed around like a puppy one summer. Besides, the girl knew her cow chips.

"If it looks like it has dried air bubbles on top, that's not a good one," Kayla said. "It will be too light. A good chip is solid and heavy with lots of grass in it, but not too wet. The wet ones are nasty when they explode."

"Why don't you pick a couple out for me?" Decky suggested.

Franny appeared at Charlie's elbow. "Hey, guys." She smiled over at Kayla. "Our little friend has been telling everyone how hard you can throw. The money is running hot on Decky."

"Franny, you really should have been a bookie," Charlie said.

When the sisters exchanged smiles, Decky was reminded again how alike they were and how they cherished one another. Growing up in the same bedroom, there were not many secrets between the two. Franny had been Charlie's hand to hold, partner in crime, and shoulder to lean on. She had taken to heart the attack on her little sister's character. The side betting was probably not the only thing she had going, if the glint in her eye was any indication.

"So, I hear you've been spouting bible verses, Decky," she said with a chuckle. Decky tilted her head, expressing her wonder at how Franny could know that. Franny's eyes shifted to Kayla. "Your fan club sent out tweets. Good one, by the way."

Decky was momentarily stricken. She often forgot she was a public personality. She began to survey the crowd for cameras pointed her way. Her facial expression must have revealed her fears.

Kayla quickly said, "I only tweeted it to my cousins. They won't retweet it. It's not like you're famous."

"See Decky," Charlie said, trying desperately not to laugh. "You really should write that young adult book. These kids don't know who you are well enough for a retweet."

"Let's keep it that way," Decky said.

Kayla's eyes grew large. "Did I do something wrong?"

Charlie tussled the young girl's hair. "No. Your Aunt Decky is just paranoid, but she is kind of famous, so let's not put any embarrassing stuff on the Internet, okay?"

"Okay," Kayla agreed, but needed clarification. "Was what she said to Uncle Bobby's wife embarrassing?"

"No," Charlie said, smiling up at Decky. "It was brilliant."

#

Decky did not win the trophy, but it was a successful adventure. Age groups and gender divided the contestant pool. Each participant was given two chances to throw. The top five distances in each division moved on to the finals. Decky had the longest distance in the women's division first round, followed closely by Karen. Charlie made the finals too. They survived being in close proximity to each other without another incident. Decky decided that was due to the fact Karen

281

was concentrating so hard on making sure everyone was following the rules.

They cheered Kayla through her division, which she won handily, and watched the other finals as time for their last throws approached. The crowd fanned out along the boundaries marked off in a long rectangle. If a chip strayed into the crowd, which happened often and dodging them seemed to be part of the charm of the competition, it was deemed out of bounds. The wind caught some of the longest throws of the day, and sent them sailing into the crowd, creating a mad scramble and lots of laughter, but no points for the competitor.

Decky could feel the eyes on her, as she stepped up for her first throw in the women's final. Out of the corner of her eye, she saw Franny slip a twenty in her pocket, just after taking another last minute bet. The first two competitors, cousins of Charlie's, threw short of their earlier distances. Charlie's chip set the new benchmark, which Karen quickly exceeded by a few inches. It was now Decky's turn.

Charlie encouraged her. "Come on, Decky. Give it a ride."

Decky did not want to disappoint Charlie and she was also hoping to be rewarded for her efforts. She took two running steps and put everything she had into the throw. The bovine feces projectile flew high and long, catching the wind for a little extra distance. The crowd roared when it landed a good four feet in front of Karen's best throw. Evidently, there were quite a few people in the crowd with a vested interest in the outcome.

The cousins tried to improve their rankings, but fell way short. That left Decky, Charlie, and Karen still fighting for the lead.

Just before Charlie took her turn, Decky whispered into her ear, "You don't need me to beat her. Do it yourself."

Out on the Panhandle

Charlie grunted with her throw, nearly crossing the foul line with her momentum, but she did not. Karen was there to make sure her toes stayed behind the line. Charlie's chip flew past Decky's best throw, putting her in the lead. The crowd cheered, but Charlie only smiled at Karen, stepping out of the way so she could have her last throw. Karen held out her hand to Tammy or Sue Beth, Decky had never figured out which one was which. The shorter one handed Karen her prized chip, the one the minions had guarded throughout the competition. Karen studied it, looking for just the right grip. Decky never knew one could study a cow chip for that long, but then Karen was a bullshit-slinging expert.

When she finally loosed the chip, Karen's throw looked long and high enough to take the trophy with room to spare. It was sailing along, on track to set a record, when a gust of wind came out of nowhere and sent it crashing to the ground, just short of Charlie's best mark. A hush fell over the crowd as Karen stomped into the throwing field, demanding a re-throw due to the sudden burst of wind sheer. The judges were able to move her to the side, so that Decky could have her final throw, but she continued to argue just inside the boundary line.

Decky turned to Kayla and whispered something in her ear. Kayla smiled and ran back to the pile of leftover chips, searching for just the right one. She returned quickly, grinning from ear to ear.

"This should do it," Kayla said, handing the heavy chip to Decky.

Charlie took one look at the chip and started shaking her head, a "No" forming on her lips, but it was too late. Decky focused on her target and let the soggy chip fly. Some of the outer edge blew off within the first few feet, but the heavy middle stayed intact and continued on course. Karen had her back to the field. The two judges she was yelling at started

283

backpedaling quickly. Karen turned to see what they were evading, just as the chip exploded at her feet, showering her with bits of wet manure in the process. She was far enough inside the boundaries for Decky to claim it was an accident, but she doubted a single person there believed that it was. There was a moment of hushed anticipation, as the crowd waited for Karen's reaction.

She looked down at her body, spattered with little black dots of manure. She threw her hands up in the air, and shouted, "Shit!"

Someone in the crowd yelled, "Yep, that's what that is," before the place erupted in laughter.

Charlie was declared the winner, and received a plastic cow chip replica with the words "Warren Reunion Women's Champ" painted on the top with what looked like gold fingernail polish. She grinned with the pride of an Olympic athlete. People collecting on their bets surrounded Franny. Karen stomped off and went inside the house, with her minions running along beside her, picking chip fragments from her hair. Crystal steadily took pictures, which Decky was hoping she would get copies of.

Decky leaned close to Charlie's ear. "Now, doesn't that feel better than me winning?"

Charlie laughed, and said, "Yeah, but you cost me a hundred bucks."

Decky broke into a wide grin. "Seeing her covered in shit wasn't worth a hundred dollars?"

"No," Charlie said. "That was priceless."

#

There was a lull in the activities, while everyone cleaned up after the cow chip throwing and prepared for the evening festivities. Charlie went into the house to shower and change,

284

because she needed to rush to a sibling meeting. On her way out of the RV, she stopped to kiss Decky.

Letting her up for air, Charlie said, "You didn't win, but I'm going to reward you anyway. Just hold that thought."

Decky grinned. "I've been holding that thought for a few days now."

Charlie pecked her on the lips again. "Good things come to those who wait, besides I think you'll be more inspired later."

"Why, what's about to happen?" Decky asked.

Charlie turned to walk away, speaking over her shoulder, "You only thought you loved me. Just wait."

Decky showered and changed clothes inside the RV. If she had not, she would have been fixated for the rest of the night on the bacteria possibly growing somewhere on her body. Redressed in fresh tee shirt and shorts, she headed back out into the masses. Immediately, Chely Wright's song, "Sea of Cowboy Hats," started playing in Decky's head. Most of the crowd, from the smallest child to the oldest adult wore cowboy hats, boots, and tight jeans. A great number of the western-attired crowd was seated in the band tent or standing near it, while the driveway served as an impromptu dance floor. There seemed to be great anticipation building in the air.

Two of the sister-in-laws, Danielle and Heather, found Decky wandering near the food tables. After filling her plate, they ushered her to a table in the band tent, near the stage. Melissa and Amanda, Bobby's daughters, were already seated there with their mother Joann, who was introduced to Decky, along with their step-mother, Barbara, who was also seated at the table. As it turned out, all of the spouses belonging to the Warren siblings were seated together at the two long tables nearest the stage. All except Karen, who was several tables back.

Out on the Panhandle

On stage, Louise and Buck, along with a few others from their generation, were playing a Bob Wills standard, "San Antonio Rose," and doing a hell of a job. Decky knew now where the musical talent in the family came from. Louise was playing the electric piano. Buck handled the vocals and accompanied her on one of the twin fiddles carving out the Texas swing anthem. The old man on the steel guitar was making it sing. Charlie had been right. Decky loved this. She was tapping her toe under the table and chewing her food to the rhythm, while listening to the family as they shouted over the music around her.

Carl, Franny's husband, whom Decky had met last summer, sipped a beer, and declared, "Well, I imagine we're about to have our own brand of fireworks. Franny has been too secretive. She is up to something."

Heather, whose husband was Charlie's brother, John, and who also worked on the ranch, spoke up, "Oh, she's been up to something for weeks, getting packages in the mail she won't let anyone see. Yep, don't mess with Franny's baby sister."

Josh, Mary's husband and a hardened cowboy, with callused hands and deep set crow's feet wrinkles in the corners of his eyes, chimed in. "If Bobby don't wake up soon, I don't know what all is going to happen, but God have mercy on the person that messes with one of that Warren brood. They'll circle the wagons around each other and take on all comers."

Kim jumped in. "I think we're about to find out just how far you can push Momma Louise."

Decky was observing that the spouses did not mind at all discussing family business. It became quite clear that she was among her own kind, the one in the relationship who asked the questions, even if the answers would not be pleasant. They each loved a Warren, a member of a tight-lipped, tight-knit

286

clan. They also had one other thing in common with Decky, a distinct dislike for Bobby's current wife.

Debra's husband, Daniel, leaned up and spoke to the table. "I think Karen is about to get what's coming to her, and I for one am glad. Maybe Debra will stop spending hours whispering to Franny and Mary on the phone."

Emily said, "You know, if Bobby had gotten drunk instead of gone to church, we wouldn't be in this mess."

Josh spoke up again. "When Bobby woke up and pulled the bag off, I bet he wished he'd got drunk instead of saved. Time to chew the arm off and get outta there, before she wakes up."

Decky tried not to just all out guffaw, but these people were funny.

Melissa pointed at the back of the house. "Well, we're about to see what happens next. Here they come."

Decky looked up to see the Warren children coming toward the stage. When they were grouped together like that, there appeared to be more of them and quite imposing. Charlie was walking beside Bobby, smiling up at him, as they shared a laugh. Whatever was going to happen, Decky was glad to see Charlie with the big brother she obviously adored. Other people noticed the two of them together, too.

Amanda, Bobby's youngest, said, "Daddy just talking to Charlie is sending Karen in to orbit, and you can bet he knows that. Yep, there's about to be a showdown. I think Bobby Warren's bucket just got full."

There was a consensus of "About damn time," pronouncements, just as the song ended to a rousing applause.

The older folks took their bows and then relinquished the stage to the Keeps 'Em Busy Band. It seemed this was going to be the highlight of the evening, as the crowd squeezed into every available space under the tent and spread out on the grass around it. The band members grabbed instruments and began to tune. David tapped on the drums, adjusting the seat, while Debra tuned her fiddle, as Joseph worked with both acoustic and electric guitars. John sat down at the steel guitar. Jimmy plucked the strings of his bass. Decky watched as Bobby checked first an acoustic guitar, then an electric, and finally tuned a banjo to his liking. Mary listened closely to her mandolin, turning the tuning knobs slowly, while Andy cut loose on the piano keys. Franny was ready to go with her acoustic guitar. She was standing near Charlie, who stood by watching the others, holding her lowly tambourine.

Amy, David's wife, spoke to Decky. "This is your first time hearing them, isn't it? You're going to be surprised."

"I'm surprised already. I didn't even know they had a band," Decky said, just as the tuning stopped and the band members took their places.

Bobby stepped up to the center microphone, a guitar draped over his shoulder. The girls grouped together near a bank of mics on the right side of the stage. The others were busily adjusting their own microphones, ignoring the restless shouts from the crowd. A gentleman on the soundboard gave Bobby a nod that he was ready. When everyone was settled behind him, Bobby counted off, "one, two, three, four," Joseph started picking the strings of his electric guitar, and John cut loose on the steel. The first notes of Meryl Haggard's "Mama Tried" filled the air, along with cheers from the crowd. The rest of the band joined in, Bobby started singing, and Decky started grinning.

She sat back and said to no one in particular, "I can't believe she never said a word."

Heather leaned in to say, "They are like that. If you want to know, you have to ask."

When they reached the chorus, the pure family harmonies Decky had recognized in their speech rang clear through the night air. Louise had come to sit at the end of Decky's table with Buck. She tapped her fingers and smiled up at her children. Louise had every right to be proud, they were not only good musicians, but Decky had learned they were good people too. She saw where Charlie came from, the roots she had put down, and Decky loved her even more. It was a privilege to be with Charlie's family, to be one of them.

She now saw what Karen envied so much in Charlie, what drove her hatred. No matter what Charlie faced, she would never do it alone. Karen tried to use Charlie's sexuality to drive a wedge between Charlie and her family, an attempt to disrupt the happiness Karen herself so desperately craved. The really sad part, as Decky saw it, was this family would have welcomed Karen with open arms, if she hadn't been such an ass. Despite their childhood feud, Charlie had been willing to accept Karen as Bobby's wife. It was Karen who could not abide Charlie as Bobby's sister. It appeared that Karen had misunderstood the bond between the Warren clan. She showed her cards, and apparently had been asked to leave the table.

Decky glanced back at Karen, finding that the glowing hair was much less teased, probably due to the manure removal. She also found that Karen was staring back at her. She must have been trying to bore holes in the back of Decky's head, before she turned around. Decky smiled and waved just to antagonize her. What could Karen possibly do in a tent full of people, except make a bigger ass of herself than she already had? Surely, she had admitted defeat by now.

Melissa was looking at Decky, when she turned back around. She shouted over her father's voice, as he was rounding out the last verse. "Don't let her fool you. She's like a rattlesnake backed in a corner. They think they have no choice but to strike."

The song ended to applause, but Bobby took no time to bow. The band launched right into Toby Keith's "I Should Have Been A Cowboy," with Bobby singing the words that sounded as though they were written for him. Again, the background vocals were superb, like they rehearsed together every day. Charlie knew the words to almost every country song she and Decky listened to. Decky never imagined she learned them singing with her family.

When the song ended, Bobby spoke for the first time. "It's good to have the whole family back together again."

Whistles and cheers erupted from the crowd. Decky's table was especially raucous.

Bobby continued. "Happy Fourth of July, everyone." More cheers, and then he said, "I'd like to ask my –," he paused, then went on, "Joann, if she'd come join me for a song."

Melissa turned to her mother. "Go on, Mom. You know you loved to sing with him."

Joann stood and walked to the stage.

Amanda snickered. "Oh yeah, Dad's bucket is full. He is totally messing with Karen now."

The music started and Decky recognized the song immediately, "You're the Reason God Made Oklahoma." If Bobby was intentionally trying to piss Karen off, the performance that followed was a well-aimed first salvo. The voices of the former married couple blended beautifully. It was obviously not the first time they sang together. The emotions the song evoked seemed too real to be staged dramatics. Bobby was going to force Karen to ask the question, to choose between his new life with her and his old one. She suspected Karen would not like the answer. It seemed to Decky his choice was clear.

Barbara, the second wife summed up what everyone in the tent was probably thinking. "They should have never split up."

Decky watched Charlie standing on the stage with her sisters, while they took in the scene, all smiling. There was little doubt what they thought, or the other brothers for that matter. Decky glanced back at Karen. Both Tammy and Sue Beth were whispering in her ears, while she glowered at the stage. Nope, it would not be long now. If the tone of the evening's musical choices continued, there would definitely be a reckoning. The song ended to loud cheering and Bobby's daughters, along with everyone else at the front tables, on their feet clapping loudly and whistling.

Bobby thanked the audience and Joann, and then said, "We're going to turn it over to the girls now."

He backed away from the microphone and exchanged his guitar for the banjo. Mary stepped to the center microphone. She smiled out at everyone, while the others adjusted their positions and instruments behind her.

"You all having a good time out there?" She asked, receiving a hardy affirmation of cheers and shouts. She looked back at the others, finding they were prepared to move on, and faced the crowd again. Mary raised her mandolin to playing position. "This one's for my cowboy."

She waved at Josh and then nodded to Franny, who started picking her guitar. Decky's eyes snapped to Charlie's within the first few notes. Charlie winked at Decky, knowing it was one of her favorite songs and one she sang to Charlie all the time. Debra touched the bow to the strings of her fiddle and the Dixie Chick's "Cowboy Take Me Away" came to life. Mary made the song her own, and when she reached the chorus, the sisters' voices melded so completely Decky was simply blown away. These girls were the Dixie Chicks before the country music megastars were even born. She smiled up at Charlie, who was singing right to her. Yes, she was right again. Decky had only *thought* she was in love with her.

291

Decky was the first one on her feet when the song ended. Mary took her bow and switched places with Franny during the applause.

Decky heard Carl say, "Hold onto your hats, boys. It's about to get hot in here."

Decky thought he was speaking about Franny's impending performance. He was, but when Decky heard Joseph slide the first notes of the song on his electric guitar, she knew Jake's warning had a double meaning. Franny chose another Dixie Chicks song, this one with a very different message, and Decky was sure it was aimed at Karen. The first words of "Sin Wagon" roared out of the speakers with attitude, causing Decky to begin to laugh uncontrollably. The rest of the family onlookers were cracking up too. When Franny got to the part about mattress dancin', Decky nearly fell off her chair.

Franny pointed at Karen and said, "That's right, Karen, I said mattress dancin'."

The song required amazing instrumentals, which they pulled off without a hitch, each solo demonstrating the incredible caliber of the musicians in the Keeps 'Em Busy Band. Charlie just grinned and sang harmony, enjoying the show as much as everyone else. By the time they brought the song to an end, both audience and band members were spent, requiring a break.

Over the sound of applause and laughter, Decky heard Louise say, "Y'all wait right there. I want Crystal to take a picture."

Crystal appeared at Decky's side, camera in hand. She had been taking pictures. She said, "I got some great shots of Charlie. I'll make you copies."

Decky stood around with the rest of the band groupies, namely the spouses, waiting for their respective musician to leave the stage. She was enthralled at how Charlie and her

292

siblings automatically assumed their customary family picture pose with ease. Charlie knelt down front with Franny, and the rest formed rows according to height. She guessed they had worked out the details long ago. Decky had seen pictures of them posed that way all over the house.

She thought Charlie would be coming off the stage after the picture, but Louise asked for one more.

She turned to the spouses and said, "Now, y'all go stand by the one what brung ya'."

Louise then winked at Decky. The little glint in her eye told Decky the time had come. She smiled back at Louise and followed the rest of the in-laws onto the stage. Decky stepped up beside Charlie, as the new posing position was acquired. In all the other pictures like this one in the house, Charlie stood at the end of the line alone. That was not going to be the case anymore, if Louise had anything to say about it, and she did.

Louise got her chance to speak her mind, when Karen pointed at Charlie and Decky and announced loudly, "I will not be captured in an image with those abominations!"

The ranch fell silent. Everyone froze in position, except Louise. She had made it onto the stage and was standing near the center microphone. She turned to it and began to speak.

"Well, I knew it was coming and I reckon most of you did too. Those of you with little ones, go on over and feed them some snacks on the patio. The rest of you, come on and sit back down. I have something to say, and I only want to say it one time."

The crowd moved to find seats and quieted quickly, all eyes on the stage. One brave young voice, sounding a lot like Kayla, called out, "You tell 'em, Grandma," which caused a ripple of nervous laughter. Decky felt Charlie take her hand. She squeezed it and smiled down at her.

"It's going to be all right," Decky whispered.

293

Louise cleared her throat, and directed her first comment to Karen, who was still standing. "Sit down, Karen. I'll address your concerns in a minute, but first I'm going to address my own."

Karen slowly lowered herself back down in the chair. Louise turned and smiled at her children and their spouses behind her, and then spoke to the rapt audience.

"These are our children and the ones that they love. Buck and I couldn't be prouder of each and every one of them. We raised them to be proud of themselves as well, and I think they are. I'm going to tell them and you something tonight that I have never shared with anyone but Buck, until a few days ago when I shared it with my youngest daughter. I'm doing this, so there will be no question of where I stand."

Decky felt the muscles in Charlie's hand tighten, as Louise began the story.

"It is appropriate that I tell this story on the anniversary of the founding of this country, the land of opportunity. While my Native American ancestors would not look on this day with the same celebratory notions as my white pioneer predecessors, they would embrace the idea of freedom it represents, freedom to walk the path of one's choosing. That's what my grandmother's parents did in 1875, when they first staked a claim on this land. The remains of their sod home lie under the house over there. I saved some of the dirt from it, so I would always remember from where I came."

Decky watched Charlie's jaw muscles tighten, as the passion welled in her mother's voice.

Louise swallowed the emotion and returned to the story. "Merdy Ethridge and Grace Harrell were the names of my great-grandparents. I never met them, but according to my grandmother, Thora, they loved each other without end. Merdy was of Chickasaw-Scottish descent, parented by half bloods.

294

Grace was a blond haired, blue-eyed girl from back east. They met while both were captives of the Comanche tribe. They fell in love and decided to make a life together. A fifteen-year-old Indian and a sixteen-year-old white girl would have had it hard enough, without the other added complications of their lives, but they managed to make a life here in No Man's Land, away from laws that would have kept them separated."

Decky admired the way Louise was crafting her story. Louise left the "other added complications" dangling like a rabbit in front of greyhounds at the track. The crowd was hooked. She could lead them where she wanted now.

"Although my grandmother was the product of Grace's original abduction and her biological father was later killed, Merdy was there when she was born and the only father she ever knew. Merdy and Grace raised my grandmother together for five short years. My grandmother told me they were happy years, filled with love and laughter. They may have lived in a sod house, but they had more than most folks today, each other. My grandmother spoke of her parents' abiding love, saying it surpassed all that she ever witnessed, including her own marriage, and I assure you, my grandparents worshipped each other. What she spoke of was a love destined to be, and one that even the death of her mother, Grace, could not end. Merdy stayed on this land, my grandmother called sacred, for twenty-four more years, loving Grace. The two of them are buried on a rise down by the river, together forever. I stand here today, the proud descendent of those two people, because they chose to follow their hearts, no matter what they had to face."

Karen could contain herself no longer. "Marrying an Indian is not the same as homosexual behavior. We've all got some Indian blood in us somewhere, there's nothing wrong with that, but being queer is a sin. Even the Indians knew that."

Out on the Panhandle

Decky wanted to shout at Karen that the same bible she was using to condemn her and Charlie was used against interracial marriage too, but it would be pointless. Karen was an idiot. Bobby took a step forward, but Louise raised her hand to stop him. She had it under control.

Louise glared down at Karen. "The reason we all have some native blood is because some white man somewhere decided the only good Indian was a dead Indian, and it was assimilate or be extinguished. And if you knew anything about Native Americans, you would know that for the majority of the tribes, a person's sexuality was a matter for the creator, and not theirs to question. Many tribes looked on it as a gift, an ability to see the world from both sides, one human formed of two spirits."

Karen was not impressed. "It's because they were ignorant heathens, before they heard God's word. They were not Christians."

The crowd drew a collective breath, only exhaling after Louise began her retort.

"Some of those same stories from the bible, the ones some Christians claim explain their existence, were being told around the heathens', as you call them, ancestral campfires before the bible was written. I may be part ignorant heathen Comanche, but I am also a Christian. That doesn't mean I can't recognize a creation myth when I see one. You can pick and choose what you want out of the bible to back up your narrow view of the world. It's been done repeatedly throughout history, or rewritten to suit the whims of religious leaders at any given time. You know, the powers that be used that book as evidence the universe revolved around the earth. They were wrong then, and you are wrong now, but whatever your religious beliefs, you are welcome to them. The fact remains, religion in this county should have no bearing on basic human rights. So if you would, please, shut the hell up, Karen."

While the crowd giggled and whispered to each other, Decky leaned over to Franny, saying, "Hey, no one mentioned a bet on how many cuss words your mother would say."

Charlie shushed Decky, as Louise addressed the audience again. "Merdy Ethridge was a well respected horse trainer, breeder, and neighbor. The majority of the horses on this ranch are direct descendants of a sire named Jack, who was a descendant of Piomingo, a legendary Chickasaw racehorse named after a great Chickasaw leader. The land you stand on now, the horses we breed, the training methods we use, were all passed down by my great-grandfather, Merdy, who passed it to my grandmother, who for reasons of her own, passed it solely to me."

Louise laughed, looking down at Buck, who was still seated at the table taking it all in.

"Buck here got a sweet deal, he just didn't know it was going to come with so many mouths to feed."

The audience laughed, along with the occupants of the stage. Louise took the kind of breath a speaker takes when they are about to wrap it up and drive the point home. Decky stepped closer to Charlie, squeezing her hand, just to let her know she was still there. Charlie was focused on her mother, who began to speak again.

"My grandmother passed the land to me, my mother's only daughter for one simple reason, I was the only female heir. That may sound strange to you. Most people are used to equal division among the siblings, or male heirs being sole beneficiaries. My grandmother had a really good reason for leaving this land to me. You see, this land has never been in a man's name. Merdy Ethridge, who served as my

297

grandmother's father and only parent from the age of five to twenty-nine, was a woman."

The reactions from the crowd ranged from stunned silence to an enthusiastic, "Hell, yeah," from the back of the tent. Louise silenced everyone with her next sentence.

"If your politics and, or your brand of religion prevents you from seeing that what the creator has made when he joins two spirits in love is one of his greatest gifts, then I've enjoyed having you on the place, but you are not welcome here. On this ranch, this sacred place to me and mine, there is no one, and I mean no one, who need fear judgment for loving another human being."

Franny stepped forward and shouted, "Now!"

Suddenly all the siblings started removing their shirts. It took a second for Decky to realize they were all wearing tee shirts underneath with the words, "I LOVE MY GAY SISTER," splashed across the front. All except for Charlie's, that said, "I'M THE GAY SISTER." Louise was the last to remove her over-shirt. Her tee shirt proudly proclaimed, "HATE: NOT A FAMILY VALUE."

Almost everyone in the crowd cheered. A few people slinked away, understandably. Decky knew there was no way Louise's message would be acceptable to everyone, but the majority of the people present were on her side. And then there was Karen and her support personnel, Piggly and Wiggly, as Decky had started to think of them.

Karen stormed toward the stage after building up enough rage, her cronies following closely behind. She screamed up at Bobby. "Take that shirt off this instant! No husband of mine will support this repugnance."

Franny elbowed Charlie, saying, "I bet she had to look that word up."

Bobby walked slowly to the edge of the stage. He squatted down in front of Karen and spoke to her softly, so that no one else could hear. Whatever he said, Karen was not pleased. However, to everyone's surprise, she turned on her heels and exited without another word. Franny, never the shy one, was not afraid to ask Bobby what he had said when he walked back over to his brothers and sisters.

He looked down at Charlie and smiled, then made eye contact with the rest of them, before saying, "I told her she was right, the man wearing this shirt wouldn't be her husband, and I mean to rectify that as soon as the courthouse opens after the holiday." He chuckled a little, and then added, "She wasn't mad about that. I think she knew it was coming."

David said, "Reminded her of the pre-nuptial agreement, huh?"

Bobby nodded, answering with only one word, "Yep."

Mary spoke for the entire family, as they shared a collective sigh of relief. "Welcome back, Bobby."

CHAPTER TWELVE

Laughter and music filled the rest of the night. The band played for two more hours, different people from the crowd joining them for a song or two. Decky was even coaxed on stage for a duet of "Oklahoma Swing" with Joseph. The music slowed and softened to acoustic ballads toward the end, as quiet overtook the ranch. Peals of laughter occasionally punctuated the muffled conversations at the tables. Decky's tablemates changed often, as she met more people than she could ever name. Charlie, alternating from the stage to the table, received hugs and words of support from one person after another. A few people pulled Charlie aside to talk. She whispered to Decky once that the gays were coming out of the woodwork. Otherwise, neither the topic of Karen, nor Charlie's sexuality ever resurfaced. That business was done and the Warren family was moving on.

The only negative comments were reactions to the sporadic popping of fireworks throughout the evening. Each pop turned all heads in its direction, but did not receive the "oohs" and "ahs" of most firework displays. Instead, heads shook and prayers went up, with a few not so devout expletives thrown in. These folks had a deep-rooted fear of fire. A wildfire made no distinction between good or evil, treasure or trash. Fire was an all-consuming force almost impossible to control once it found its fuel. Being on constant alert for fires caused by nature or accidentally was part of being a rancher. Having to guard against fires caused by people ignoring burn bans or tossing cigarettes out of car windows, and those that would fire rockets into the air, showering the tinderbox prairie with sparks, was maddening.

The crowd began to thin, the reunion guests tuckered out, and the ranch slowly started to fall asleep. Decky and Charlie excused themselves for the evening, exchanging hugs with every one of Charlie's siblings before departing. Decky even got a hug from Bobby, and a whispered, "Take care of my baby sister," in her ear. She promised him she would, took Charlie's outstretched hand, and walked away contented.

Before they reached the RV, Louise caught up with them. "I left the rest of Thora's story on the table in the RV," she said. Then she hugged Charlie to her tightly. "You have been nothing but a blessing, Little One. I've always known you would walk your own path, and I'm very proud of how you've done it." Louise released the hold she had on her daughter, and pulled back to look into her eyes. "Had you asked, I would have told you that years ago. You chose not to talk to me about parts of your life, and I chose to let you. We have both learned from our mistakes." She hugged Charlie again, saying into her ear, "Now, will you come home more often?"

Charlie was in tears, answering through sniffles, "Yes, Momma, I will. I love you, and thank you."

Louise smiled over at Decky. "And bring this one with you too. Anyone that can aim a cow chip like that belongs on a ranch." She turned to walk away, and then looked back. "I believe you two will understand the depths of the love between Grace and Merdy. I am so happy that you've found each other, but then the story foretold it would happen."

Louise winked and left Charlie and Decky scrambling to get into the RV. They had to read the rest of the story now.

#

Several days have passed since I last wrote. Only Tseena keeps me company, but we are not alone. I will never be alone, for I will always have Pia and Ahpu by my side. When I left the sod house with Tseena, leaving Ahpu asleep in her bed, I did not know it was the last breath I would see her take, but this does not sadden me, as one would think. I am saddened for the time I spent away from her, the time I missed at her side, but not for her passing. She has left this world and crossed to the next, once again to stand with her love, her Grace, and my Pia. Who could not rejoice at their reunion? I saw it with my own eyes, and I can tell you now, there is no greater power in the world than true love.

When I followed Tseena two nights ago, he did not speak until we reached the river, and then it was only a grunt to get my attention. He handed me a cup I knew would cause the visions to reappear and I drank it willingly, without question. I wanted desperately to talk with Ahpu again. I felt the effects almost immediately, and knew I was under its spell when Tseena spoke and I could understand him.

"Horse Child is ready to sing her death song," he said, seated by the fire. "We must prepare for our mourning."

I sat beside him, watching as he leaned over the fire and lit a small bundle of sage, leaving it to burn in an ancient looking shell. He turned to me, a small leather bag in his hands. He

302

pulled from it sprigs of different herbs and tobacco, speaking as he dropped them into the fire.

"Father in heaven this is our friend coming," he prayed. "By these words, I ask that our tears of mourning be wiped away so that we may see again."

Fragrant smoke billowed into a cloud and was lifted into the sky by the wind. When it had disappeared, Tseena dropped more herbs in the fire.

"By these words, I ask that our mourning cries may be silenced so that we may hear again."

Again, the wind took the smoke into the night sky.

Tseena raised his hands to the heavens. "When our friend crosses to the next world, the stars will fall, leaving us in the dark. Help us to lift up the stars and replace them in the sky, so that the spirit of our friend will have light at her crossing, and the path for us here on earth will remain clear."

The air around me filled with Ahpu's voice, though I could not see her. "Nothing lives forever, Little One, but love."

The sky turned ink black. Before me, the stars fell from the heavens, trailing tails of white dust behind them. I felt the pain of loss, as it took my breath away. I was frozen in a place of mourning so deep, I knew the stars would never shine again.

In that moment, Ahpu's voice said to me, "Say my name, I will never leave you."

I cried out, "Ahpu!"

I closed my eyes and felt the agonizing pain of loss double me over, as I sobbed for her passing, for I knew it had happened. She no longer breathed in the sod house. I would never again touch her warm face.

The hand on my shoulder startled me, the voice even more so.

"Don't cry, Petu. I am at peace."

Out on the Panhandle

Her voice was close now, next to my ear, as she pulled me up from my keening. I opened my eyes to find Horse Child, fully clothed in her native costume, young and vibrant as the first day she brought Grace to this place. She was smiling and wiping the tears from my cheeks with her thumbs.

She spoke softly, "Take the tears from her eyes so that she might see. Take away her cries so she might hear. Lift up the stars, so her path will be clear, for she is loved."

The stars reversed their course, illuminating the heavens, and with them, they lifted the pain of loss, replacing it with joy of knowing that love knows no end. I smiled at Ahpu, signaling that I was ready to see and hear what she had come to tell me. She understood. Standing, she walked to the edge of the river, extending her hand to someone I could not see. The flutter of heavy wings reached my ears. Out of the darkness a red-tailed hawk appeared, lowering itself to Ahpu's arm.

This truly amazing sight quickly became unfathomable, when the hawk began to transform into the beautiful blond young woman I recognized immediately. When the metamorphosis was complete, Ahpu took her hand, and gazed into her eyes for a moment. They were silent, but the look exchanged between them said all it needed to say. Ahpu slowly reached to touch the face of the woman she loved for the first time since she laid her body in the ground, but not her soul. The soul of her lover had stayed with her and was now here to walk beside her forever. There would be no more good-byes, no more broken hearts. I watched as Ahpu took my mother in her arms and kissed her sweetly, her healing complete.

They turned and came towards me.

"Hello, Petu," my mother said, kneeling beside me.

"Pia," whispered from my lips.

"Yes, I am here, Petu. I have always been here."

Out on the Panhandle

Ahpu smiled down at me, standing beside my mother. "Say our names every day. When it is your time to walk the path, we will meet you here. We will be with you always, little one."

Pia spoke again. "We leave you here to live the happy life that awaits you. I have seen it, Petu. You will know love beyond bounds."

"Will I be able to see you, talk to you?" I asked.

Ahpu raised her hand and gestured all around me. "We will be in the river, the trees, the hawks that fly above you, the land beneath your feet. All around, you will see the signs of our presence. You will hear our voices in the wind, in the song of the birds, the whinny of a new foal. All you need do is look. All you need do is listen. You will know that we are near."

Pia touched my cheek, the warmth of her hand so soothing and calming, a feeling I had ached for since the dark night she left me.

"I have missed you, Pia," I said.

"Because you did not remember who you were, you could not know that I was near. Ahpu has helped you see, Petu. Never forget the love that accompanied you into this world. It is a love without end."

"I understand, now." I said. "I will remember."

Pia pointed across the river. "I need to show you something."

I looked where she was pointing to see a golden haired little girl with big blue eyes, staring across the prairie. It was the girl from my dream, a child of the future, the one I felt compelled to tell of my visions, but how could Pia have known?

"Who is she?" I asked.

Pia smiled. "One day this child will come. She will be of two spirits and walk a different path than others." She reached

305

to take Ahpu's hand, saying, "When the time comes, she will need to know our story. It will give her peace and strength."

Ahpu added, "Tell this story, Petu. It must be told so that others will understand. Love is sacred. It knows nothing of man's rules."

I looked at the tiny girl. She appeared to be searching the horizon. "What does she look for?" I asked Pia.

"She is waiting for her love to find her," Pia said. "She will come."

Just then another young girl appeared. She was taller and thinner, but near the same age, with yellow hair and freckles. She took the smaller girl's hand and they began to walk a winding path together.

Pia commented, "Some spirits spend many lives together in this world. Their souls are bound forever in the next. These two will find each other again."

Ahpu cautioned, "You must keep the story close, until the time of its unveiling. Should it be given too soon, it will not be understood. Guard it well, Petu. Pass it on to one you trust. She will know the child when she sees her. She will know when it is time to reveal the story."

Pia stood beside Ahpu, who slid her arm around her waist. They were beautiful together, young and in love, the amber glow of the fire seeming brighter where they stood. They looked down at me, their daughter, with contentment. I felt the peace they finally enjoyed, the peace of knowing that what the creator destined had now come to pass. Merdy and Grace, Horse Child and Yellow Hair, my Ahpu and Pia would be together forever.

Pia gazed into Ahpu's eyes, saying, "As it was ordained, so shall it be."

The amber glow began to engulf them, turning a blinding white. They stood there embracing, smiling into each other's eyes. Ahpu turned just before she faded out of sight. She smiled down at me, and left me with the words I shall leave you with, as well.

"Believe in love. It never ends."

So, for you, child of the future, I have recorded this record of two souls that found each other, of the life they built together, and the love that they shared. They foretold of your coming, and a great love you will find. I bear witness to its truth. I believe you will come and this missive will find its way to you. I will keep it for you, treasure it with all my heart, because I believe, I truly believe, Ahpu was right. Love never ends.

#

Decky set the manuscript pages together on the nightstand. Her other arm was around Charlie, who was softly crying into her shoulder. Decky pulled Charlie in close, wrapping her in her arms. They were both too stunned to speak.

The ranch was quiet, except for an occasional coyote yip and an answering bark from Dolly or Reba. Decky listened to the wind blow against the RV and thought of Merdy. Where was she tonight? Were she and Grace watching over them now, knowing their story had found its home? Did they know that Decky found Charlie, that the future they foretold came true?

"I believe," Decky whispered.

Charlie tilted her tear stained face to Decky's. "I do too," she whispered back.

#

Decky awoke to a naked Charlie crawling onto her chest. She had fallen asleep with the bare skinned blond in her arms, after a long and quite passionate night of lovemaking. The

307

Out on the Panhandle

discovery of their predestination had inspired Charlie in ways that had Decky whispering, "I believe, I believe," just before she finally collapsed. Now, it appeared Charlie was back to reconfirm Decky's faith.

Charlie took her time squirming up to Decky's lips for a quick peck, before saying, "Good morning."

Decky had a decision to make, both choices concerning things she had little control over. Deal with Charlie, naked, and purring like a kitten on her chest, which woke up parts of her body she was sure had been satiated a moment ago, or answer the call of her screaming bladder as Charlie's bodyweight bore down on her abdomen. The one activity clearly took precedence over the other.

"Good morning to you, and as much as it pains me to say this, the pain you are inducing is worse," Decky said, rolling Charlie off her, and hovering over her for just a second, saying, "My bladder thanks you. Hold that thought, back in a sec."

Decky ran off to the bathroom. She stayed a few minutes longer than she had planned, brushing her teeth, washing her face, combing her hair. She did not think she was gone that long, but when she came out, Charlie was fully dressed.

"What are you doing?" Decky asked.

Charlie grinned. "I needed to get you up. You're up. Mission accomplished."

Decky squinted at the blinds. From the color cast by the sunlight, she knew it was early. She asked Charlie, "Why are we up at the crack of dawn? And that was tacky, by the way."

Charlie ignored the tacky comment. "We need to go pick out a horse for you. Bobby said meet him down at the barn early this morning. We can shower when we get back. Put on your boots, we're going for a little ride."

308

Decky grabbed the boots without further comment. If Charlie insisted on going riding, Decky needed coffee and stalling would shorten her caffeine intake time. She only looked up from her task when she heard Charlie chuckling.

"What's so funny?" Decky asked, unable to stop the smile that curled her lips.

Charlie leaned over and kissed her on the forehead, before saying, "Put your pants on, honey."

#

Pants on, Decky was treated to a quick breakfast and two cups of coffee with the ranch hands. It may have been a holiday for some, but there was work to be done, namely restoring the ranch to pre-reunion status. The tents would come down today, the stage would be disassembled, the guests would start leaving, and ranch life would go on. The pools were being drained, the water used to irrigate Louise's prized green grass in the front yard. It was a luxury on the prairie, but one Charlie explained was all that her momma asked, a green yard to look out on. The rest of what she wanted out of life, Louise said she had in abundance.

Down at the stables, Bobby picked out a three-year-old mare for Decky, explaining she was smart and learned quickly. He talked to Decky while she mounted the palomino with the golden mane. Bobby was telling her all about the horse named Daisy, but all Decky could think about was Yellow Hair. She could tell by Charlie's expression that she was thinking the same thing, while already mounted again on Jack's Lady. Decky had to wonder if Thora's manuscript had been as secret as Louise thought. She snapped out of her pondering when Bobby stepped between the two horses.

"If you like her, she's yours," Bobby said to Decky.

Decky smiled at him. "I'm sure I will. She's beautiful."

"She and CJ should have some nice foals, when he's old enough," he said, patting Daisy on the neck.

Charlie leaned over in the saddle and pecked her brother on the cheek, a move that would have sent Decky tumbling to the ground. Yep, Charlie had some Comanche blood, that was for sure. The horse culture lived on in this family, through its horses and its people.

Charlie said, "Thank you again for CJ. He's amazing, Bobby. Really, you outdid yourself."

Bobby grinned up at his sister. "Every cowgirl needs a horse, Little One." A man of a few words, he backed away, saying, "Y'all have a good ride now."

Bobby opened the gate for them and they rode away, south, toward the river. Decky felt more comfortable in the saddle today. Not only did the saddle fit better, she had the confidence of belonging on the ranch to seat her solidly. Daisy seemed relaxed too, content to walk along beside Jack's Lady. Either Decky's skills had improved, or Daisy was a very intuitive horse, understanding Decky's desires almost before she expressed them with a slight adjustment to her body weight.

"I like this horse," she said to Charlie.

"She's beautiful and I'm sure you thought about Yellow Hair when you saw her, but make sure you're comfortable with her and not letting the romance of it affect your decision," Charlie said, ever practical. She glanced at Decky, who was smiling broadly. "Never mind. Welcome to the family, Daisy."

Decky patted Daisy's neck. "We're going to be great friends," she said and then asked Charlie, "Where are we headed, as if I didn't know?"

"I want to see them again, now that I know who they are," Charlie answered.

Decky knew she was talking about Merdy and Grace's graves. They rode on in silence a few more paces, when Decky

310

said, "You know, Charlie, I knew. I knew from the first time I laid eyes on you, but I bet your momma flipped out when she saw me."

"Why do you say that?" Charlie asked, leading them toward a lone tree on a ridge.

"Because all of your other girlfriends had dark hair." She grinned over at Charlie and winked. "I, on the other hand, walked out of a prophecy."

"You took your time getting here," Charlie tried to say with a straight face, but failed and started to laugh.

"You needed the practice, evidently. I seemed to have picked it up rather quickly," Decky said, proudly.

Charlie laughed harder. "Yes, you have," she said, "Yes, you have."

They quieted as they neared the old family graveyard and dismounted. Decky tied her horse to a short cast iron fence, bent askew by age and what appeared to be a run-in with a piece of farm equipment. It marked out a square plot of land holding six well-manicured graves. Someone took care of this little square of prairie. Decky suspected it was Louise's task, which would be passed to Charlie in time. The oldest two graves were side by side at the back of the plot.

Charlie read the inscriptions on the matching headstones. "Merdy Ethridge, born May 2, 1860, died July 7, 1905, age forty-five. Forever with Grace." She moved on to the next one. "Grace Harrell Ethridge, born February 16, 1859, died July 14, 1880, age twenty-one. Love Never Ends."

"I guess Thora replaced these with granite headstones after she settled in," Decky commented, pointing at the back of the markers.

Charlie moved around to see what Decky was talking about. Decky squatted in front of two old wooden crosses, tucked up to the headstones, and repaired repeatedly over the

311

years. The one on Grace's grave was much more worn than Merdy's.

"Looks like somebody has been keeping these together. They were probably the original markers," Decky said, running a finger over Grace's cross.

"Can you imagine how Merdy felt when she made that?" Charlie asked.

"No, I can't," Decky said, standing up next to Charlie. "I can't and don't want to think about pain like that." She took Charlie in her arms. "But knowing I will be with you forever, that I can and will think about for the rest of my days. I love you, Charlie Warren. I apparently always have."

They walked around to look at the other graves. John and Thora Lynch rested at Merdy and Grace's feet. Thora died at age eighty-three in 1958. John passed a few years earlier in 1956. They were married for fifty years before his death. John lay on Thora's right side. On her left, lay the grave of someone that apparently came to mean a lot to Thora. The marker read, "Tseena, Gray Coyote, born 185_, died November 30, 1934." Decky laughed when she read the inscription at the bottom. "He finally went home."

There was only one stone left. It sat alone just off to the right of Merdy's grave, and appeared to mark off a large burial mound. Thora must have placed this marker too, because it matched the others, but was in fact older than Merdy's. The inscription was simple, "JACK. 1867-1895. Fastest Quarter Horse on the Panhandle. Fly Jack, Fly."

Decky was just about to say something, when she notice Charlie was distracted.

"What is he doing out here alone?" Charlie pointed at a black horse on the top of the next ridge. "That looks like Jack Five."

"Maybe it's a vision," Decky said, laughing, but Charlie did not join her.

Charlie's brow wrinkled with concern. She tilted her head and turned her nose up to the air.

Decky became concerned too. "What is it, honey?"

"Do you smell smoke?" was Charlie's reply.

Decky sniffed the air. She did smell smoke. "Yes, I do," she said. "It's coming from that direction." She pointed at the ridge where the black horse was standing. "The wind is bringing it to us."

Charlie moved quickly toward the horses. "Come on. We need to see where that is coming from."

They mounted up and headed toward the source of the smell. The black horse disappeared over the ridge. When they crested the ridge, Decky expected to see the horse down below them, but he was not there. She quickly forgot about the horse, as the first puffs of smoke became visible. Charlie urged her horse to go faster, forcing Decky to keep up. They crested the last ridge before the river. Charlie paused for just a second and then kneed Jack's Lady into a full gallop. Decky looked down and saw two barely teenaged, bare-chested boys, attempting to beat back a small grass fire with their shirts. It was growing quickly, too fast for the boys to stop it. Decky forgot that she did not really know how to ride a horse and leaned into to Daisy.

"Ha," she yelled, and off they went, tearing after Charlie.

Charlie arrived on the scene just a few seconds ahead of Decky and was already off her horse, running up to one of the boys.

"What happened, Travis?" Charlie shouted.

Decky dismounted, looping Daisy's reins around the only thing she could find, a large rock, and ran up to Charlie in time to hear the boy say, "I tried to stop them, Aunt Charlie. These

313

damn city kids thought it would be funny to set off firecrackers in the prairie dog holes. I was camping down on the river and heard them. I ran over here, but it was too late. I sent one of them running back to the house, but it's a long way."

"We didn't see any kid," Charlie said, panic in her voice.

Travis panicked too. "Then nobody knows this fire is burning, yet?"

Charlie turned to Decky, at the same time she was ripping off her shirt. She was stripped down to her sports bra, before Decky knew what was happening. "You have to ride back to the house. Get us some help," she shouted at Decky, already starting to beat at the flames.

Decky grabbed Charlie's arm, spinning her back to face her. "You go. I'll stay here. I can't ride that fast."

Charlie stared at Decky for a second, long enough for it to sink in that Decky was right. She handed her now scorched shirt to Decky. "Watch the wind. Don't let the fire jump behind you. You'll be trapped."

"Go!" Decky shouted, beating back the flames that were now lapping at her heels.

Charlie looked at the fire again, torn between leaving Decky and the others behind and getting help fast. A gust of wind kicked up the fire, spreading it toward the ridge, and doubling its fuel. If it reached the top, where the wind was always blowing, Decky knew that it would fan out much faster. The smoke began to thicken, making it harder to see and breathe.

Decky yelled, "Ride, Charlie. Fly!"

Charlie ran to her horse without further hesitation. She needed no help getting on the horse. Charlie leapt, her hands grasping mane and saddle, yanking herself from the ground, and was racing away at a full gallop in a flash. She disappeared, as the smoke thickened around Decky. The fire

314

was already out of control. She needed to pick her battle and fight that line. The ridge was her only choice. Decky looked over at her fellow fire fighters, already exhausted from their efforts. She glanced toward the river, the only source of refuge should the fire make it out of this little valley.

Decky heard the other boy cry out, "Hey, look!"

He was pointing into the thick smoke at the hottest part of the fire. Decky saw what he was seeing, and her heart leapt into her throat. The boy Travis had sent to get help must have become lost. He looked about twelve, small and wiry, and completely freaked out. He had somehow circled back around into the fire. Little fires were springing up in all directions, as the wind fanned the sparks out over the dry grass. Disoriented by the smoke and his terror, the boy turned circles, holding his shirt over his face, searching for a way out.

Decky shouted at him, "Go toward the river!"

Travis and the other boy began to shout as well. "Go to the river. Run!"

It was no use. The confused and frightened boy could not hear them over the ever-increasing roar of the fire. Decky saw something out of the corner of her eye. The black horse had reappeared and was cutting through the smoke, showing Decky a clear path to the petrified child.

She called out to Travis, "Don't let it come up this ridge!"

Decky ran to Daisy and climbed up in the saddle. She patted Daisy's neck. "Okay girl, show me how it's done."

Decky leaned forward and squeezed her knees, adding a "Ha" to set Daisy in motion. Decky steered the golden horse to mimic the path of the black one, riding headlong into the smoke, trusting that the sign she thought she had received was the right one – follow the black stallion. She broke clear of the thicker smoke and saw the boy ten feet in front of her. She slowed Daisy. Although she was feeling more confident in the

315

saddle, she did not think she was capable of lifting the boy onto the back of the horse at a full gallop.

She shouted at him, "Give me your hand," as she came nearer, her arm extended to the boy.

Daisy seemed to perceive the situation without Decky doing anything. She came to an abrupt halt next to the boy. Decky could see that he was crying and frozen in place, unable to help her help him. She hopped off Daisy and joined her hands like she had seen Andy do for Charlie.

"Step up," she shouted to the boy.

He stared at her, unmoving.

"Get on the goddamn horse!" Decky shouted, which evidently was a language the boy understood.

He stepped into Decky's hand and landed in the saddle, just before Decky hopped up behind him. Daisy did not wait to be told to go. Once Decky's weight hit the saddle and her hands were on the reins, Daisy took off for the river, the only patch of land not currently on fire around them. Decky held on to the boy and the saddle horn and let Daisy do her thing. She was doing very well so far.

They reached the tree-lined riverbank, when Decky suddenly remembered the exploding cedar trees in Thora's story. She looked left and right, trying to decide which way to turn. She saw the black horse again through the smoke. This time he led her down the bank and past the fire's edge. When she broke out of the smoke, Decky saw pumper trucks coming through the pasture, and could finally breathe a little easier. Daisy evidently was relieved, as well. She slowed to a trot and carried her passengers safely out of harm's way.

Decky was sitting on the ground, Daisy standing quietly beside her, when Charlie walked up. The ranch hands, with Bobby and Andy in charge, had fanned out around the fire with hoses from the big tanks on the back of the trucks, and drowned the flames into submission. Their embarrassed father had duly chastised the firecracker-throwing, fire-starting, city boys, whom Decky discovered were cousins from out of state. Travis had been thanked for his courageous efforts. Decky sat quietly by through it all, trying to process what had just occurred.

Charlie plopped down on the ground beside Decky. "Travis just told me what you did. Why am I not surprised?"

Decky looked around. "Did you see that black horse? It came back."

"No," Charlie said. "I asked Bobby. Jack Five is still in the stable. He said there shouldn't be any horses in this pasture. He'll look for it after the fire is out."

"He won't find him," Decky said, turning to Charlie. "I don't think he was real."

Charlie chuckled. "Of course he was real." She looked past Decky toward the river. "Look, there he is now."

Decky turned to see the black stallion standing just inside the tree line, barely visible in the shadows. Decky was about to give up her fantasy that the black horse was Jack sent by Merdy to help her, when her heart caught in her chest. A dark haired figure stepped out of the shadows and leapt on the black horse's bare back. Another horse emerged, peeking out from the darkness, a blond woman in the saddle. Decky could have believed it was a just some neighbors come to see what the smoke was about, except she could clearly see the expression on the blond woman's face. She smiled up at Decky and Charlie, as if she knew them. Just as quickly as they appeared, the horses turned back into the darkness and were gone. Right after they vanished, two more horses flashed by in the shadows, carrying a tall cowboy and a dark haired woman in braids. The woman turned at the last moment and smiled at Charlie, before she too was swallowed by the trees.

317

Decky stared after them, struck silent by what she had seen. She was afraid to say anything, in the off chance that she was hallucinating from smoke inhalation. She had almost convinced herself that her oxygen-deprived brain had created the whole scene, when she heard Charlie speak.

"Did you see that?" Charlie whispered.

Decky never took her eyes of the trees. She simply said, "I believe."

#

Their last night on the ranch was spent with Charlie's immediate family, which was still a fairly large crowd. Neither she, nor Decky said a word to anyone about what they had seen, except Louise. They figured she would not think they were crazy, and she didn't.

"I see Merdy sometimes," Louise said. "She looks after the place."

Louise's belief in Merdy's presence made Decky feel much better. At least if she was hallucinating, Charlie and Louise were right there with her. They could share a room at the loony bin together.

Before Louise let them go to bed that night, she took them both by the hand, and said, "What the Lord has joined together, let no man put asunder. People should think about what that really says. It gives me great comfort to know your spirits found each other." She turned her eyes to Charlie and quoted Thora's manuscript, "As it was ordained, so shall it be."

Charlie completely lost it and fell into her mother's arms. Decky tried to fight back her tears, but gave up and let them flow. She got in on the hugging and "I love you" declarations, too.

318

They left Louise to find Buck waiting by the RV door with Dolly and Reba. He called Charlie off to the side for a private chat, while Decky played with the dogs. Charlie came back wearing a grin and Buck said his goodbyes to both of them.

"Come on girls," Decky heard him say to the dogs, as he walked away. "Sun comes up early everyday on the ranch. Let's get some sleep."

Once inside the RV, Decky asked Charlie what Buck wanted to talk about.

"He said, 'Charlie, is there anything else we need to clear up?' I said no and he said, 'Well, you know I love you.' I said yes, and he said, 'Well, all right then.' Daddy is a man of few words, but he gets his point across."

The next morning, all packed and ready to head back to "the City," Decky felt something she had not expected. She was really going to miss the ranch and the people who lived here. Charlie's family had taken her in as one of them, and Decky felt more belonging here than she had ever felt with her own family. She promised every sibling, during a long line of hugs and handshakes, that she would return their sister to them more often, and extended invitations to everyone to come enjoy the Outer Banks of North Carolina with her and Charlie.

Kayla was draped around Decky's waist, giving her another "one last" hug, when her grandmother stepped up. "Kayla, honey, you have to let Aunt Decky go now, they have a plane to catch."

Kayla reluctantly relented. Decky bent down to look her in the eyes. "Your mom says you can come learn to surf next summer. Aunt Charlie and I would love to have you visit."

"Next summer is a long time from now," Kayla whined.

Charlie offered a solution. "Maybe you can come during Christmas break."

Kayla brightened. "I'll ask my mom. Thanks for teaching me those throwing tips, Aunt Decky." She turned back to Charlie. "I'm glad you're gay, Aunt Charlie. I hope you keep this one."

Charlie laughed loudly, and then said, "I think I'll do that, Kayla. I'm glad you approve."

Crystal was next, promising to send copies of the pictures and to come visit Charlie in North Carolina. Decky had a feeling Charlie would do a better job of staying in touch, not only with Crystal, but everyone. While her family had been guilty of allowing it to happen, Charlie had kept them at arm's distance for many years. Decky knew they would be seeing a lot more of the Warren clan and she was genuinely happy about it. Not only did she have a new family, but they had a band.

With a few tears and more goodbyes behind them, Charlie pulled the rental car out onto the road, heading back toward Beaver. They were both quiet. Decky assumed Charlie was processing all that had happened in the last five days, as was she. At about the same location they saw Buck on their arrival, Decky saw a black horse and rider charging down the fence line, paralleling their course. The rider wore buckskins and carried a lance, full feather headdress blowing behind him. Decky was really getting worried now. Charlie did not seem to notice the fully armed Native American warrior galloping along just in front of them. Finally, Decky had to say something.

"Do you see that?" She asked.

"See what?" Charlie said.

"You mean to tell me you don't see that warrior riding down the fence line on that black horse," Decky said, astonished that Charlie couldn't see it.

Charlie looked where Decky's finger pointed, and said, "Decky, are you going to be seeing things from now on? You know how susceptible to suggestion you are."

The horse continued to tear across the pasture. Decky was beginning to sweat. She was really loosing it. She blinked her eyes, but the horse and rider were still there. Her heart started beating rapidly, and she was about to go into a full-blown panic attack, when she heard a muffled chuckle from Charlie. Decky's head snapped around to see Charlie trying to cover her giggles with her hand over her mouth.

Decky narrowed her eyes. "What did you do?"

Charlie burst into peals of laughter, barely able to explain, "That's Bobby. He likes to dress up and confuse the tourists sometimes, with Comanche sightings."

"And you arranged for him to make me think I was seeing wild Indians?" Decky asked.

Charlie could not answer. She was laughing too hard.

Decky rolled down the window and waved at Bobby, who had finally come to a stop at the end of the pasture. He reared the great black stallion into the air and shook his lance.

Decky turned back to the woman she was destined to love until the end of time. "Good one, Charlie. You got me."

EPILOGUE

Decky saw the mail truck coming down the drive and went out to meet it, Dixie at her heels. The truck only came down the path if there was a package to deliver. She welcomed the break. Decky had her head buried in research since she and Charlie came back from Oklahoma, two weeks ago. Today, she had been immersed in the Red River War and all it entailed. Thora's visions had been accurate according to eyewitness accounts, which lent even more credence to the truth of her retelling. Decky saw a novel in the story and would write it one day, but at the moment, she could not stop learning. The research was just too interesting and drove Decky to want to know more. Luckily, Charlie was otherwise occupied these days, which was all too evident when Decky stepped out of the house.

The postal worker and an old friend from high school, Carol, stepped out of the truck. She motioned toward the garage apartment, and asked, "I thought Zack was off diving."

Decky smiled. "That's not Zack Charlie is in there living the dream."

"I didn't know Charlie played the drums," Carol said, heading to the back of the truck.

Just then, there was a calamitous sound of crashing symbols and pounding, out of sync beats.

"Well, she's learning," Decky said, chuckling.

Carol slid the rear door of the truck open, saying, "She's got the loud part down, anyway."

Decky took the long, flat package Carol extended to her, saying, "That's why she's out here and not in the house with me."

Decky read the sender information. The package was from Louise.

Carol turned to retrieve a second parcel. "Hang on, there's another one." She reached in and pulled another flat package out, this one smaller and from Crystal in Amarillo. "Saw Charlie pick up cowboy hats last week, more packages this week. Liked that Wild West stuff out in Oklahoma, did ya'?" Carol asked.

Decky smiled. "Yes, I did. We had a great time." She remembered Carol had horses. "Hey, we're building a stable and should have the horses in by spring. We'll have to go riding together."

Carol handed Decky the delivery notice to sign, commenting, "When I saw Charlie, she showed me CJ's picture. He's gorgeous. Can't wait to see him." Carol started laughing, adding, "She also told me about you bouncing around in the saddle like a rubber ball. I'da paid good money to see that."

"I didn't fall off," Decky said, defending herself, but she was laughing too.

She said goodbye to Carol, and then Decky took the packages to the garage apartment, braving the loud banging. Dixie turned to leave.

Decky called after her, "She's getting better."

Dixie was not at all impressed with Charlie's improvement and headed around the house toward the dock. When Decky opened the door, Charlie was in the throes of her own concert, Dr. Dre headphones on, eyes closed, pounding on the drums in an almost steady beat. Decky thought she had improved in two weeks and was so happy that one of her plans had actually worked. Charlie was thrilled to find a drum set waiting for her, when they came home. Zack spent a few days working with Charlie on technique, before he took off for Hatteras Island with some friends to go wreck diving. Charlie was like a kid with a new toy at Christmas. It made Decky smile just to see her enjoying it so much. She stood and watched Charlie, until the little drummer finally noticed her.

"You're getting better," Decky said, when Charlie removed the headphones.

Charlie grinned. "This is so much fun. Have I thanked you enough for this?"

"Yes, and you are welcome," Decky said, adding playfully, "but you can thank me again if you like."

Charlie stood and walked around the drum set to stand by Decky. She leaned up and kissed her on the cheek, saying, "Me, you, and the Jacuzzi have a date. Are you done reading for a bit? Are the new glasses helping?"

"To answer your questions, yes, the glasses are helping, and if you're going to get naked and get in the Jacuzzi, yes, I am done reading."

"I thought you might say that," Charlie said, and then asked, "What's in the packages?"

324

Decky sat the parcels on the pool table. "This big one is from your mom. The little one is from Crystal."

"Crystal sent you a package?"

Decky shrugged. "It has my name on it, but she probably just did that to make sure you got it. Open it."

Charlie opened the box, revealing a framed picture. She smiled and said, "No, I think this is for both of us."

Decky looked down at the frame. Crystal had caught Charlie and Decky laughing together, cowboy hats tipped back, the Oklahoma sunset in the background. It was a beautiful picture of them and Decky could not recall it being taken.

Charlie read the note accompanying the picture aloud.

> *Dear Charlie and Decky,*
> *In all my years of photographing weddings, I have never seen two people so in love, so absolutely suited for each other. Charlie, I do believe you found that thing we are all searching for, the one that makes us complete. I am so happy for you. Decky, it was a pleasure to meet you and I know that you will take care of my "home girl," as my teenaged daughter would say. I am making plans to come see you soon. Hope you like the picture. I think it captures the love and laughter you two share exquisitely. Stay in touch.*
> *Love you,*
> *Crystal*

"That was really sweet," Charlie said.

Decky picked up the picture, examining it. "Yes, that was very nice of her. We do look happy, don't we?"

Charlie smiled up at her. "Yes, we do, and we are." She reached for the larger package. "I wonder what Momma sent," she said, pulling the tab to open the end of the box.

Decky put Crystal's photo down on the table, watching as Charlie pulled two brown paper and bubble wrapped rectangles from the box. An envelope fell on the table. Decky picked it up and read what was written on the outside.

"Charlie, open this first."

It was too late. Just as she finished speaking, Decky heard the sound of paper rattling and Charlie gasp. She looked to see what had caused this reaction. On the table in front of her, Decky saw a framed painting and immediately understood the response.

She heard Charlie's drawn out and whispered, "Wow."

In the background of the scene depicted, a small campfire burned, emitting a glow in the center of the canvas, drawing the viewer's eye there first. Decky's eyes moved from the fire, down the canvas to a riverbank, where a buffalo robe lay crumpled in a pile beside buckskins, recently removed. Moonlight sparkled off the reeds, the trickling water, and the glistening wet bodies of two women lying in a shallow pool in the foreground. They were locked in a passionate kiss, arms and legs entwined. Grace and Merdy, the portrait of desire.

Decky finally spoke. "We are so hanging this in the bedroom."

"I can't believe my mother had this all these years," Charlie said, still a bit stunned.

Decky handed the envelope to Charlie and picked up the frame to look at the artist's signature. "It says T. E. L. Thora Ethridge Lynch." She nodded at the envelope. "Maybe you should open that now."

Charlie pulled a sheet of paper from the envelope and began to read the letter to Decky.

Dear Charlie,
I've always wanted you to have these paintings.
When you open the packages, you will know why. There

326

are more paintings of my grandmother's visions, depicting Grace and Merdy's life. They are yours when you want them. I chose to send these two for specific reasons. I don't know if you are aware that the Comanche did not tell stories in terms of this person was in love with that person, not in words anyway. If a young man fancied a girl in a story, the teller would have him portray it in his actions. He may dance for her, or sing her songs, bring her fresh game, perform acts of bravery, or some other act of love would be performed. In our culture, actions speak louder than words.

In the one painting, I see an act of love. I see it in its purest form. Two souls completely devoted to each other. There is nothing more beautiful than that. In the other painting, I found the confirmation I had been waiting for. My grandmother's vision of you was real and the path you would walk was laid out for you long ago. You have found your soul mate, Little One. That too is a very beautiful thing. As it was ordained, so shall it be.

May God continue to bless you both, for you have truly been blessed. Believe in love, it never ends.

Love,
Momma

Charlie placed the letter on the table and unwrapped the last painting. Silhouetted against a blazing red sunset, the two young blond girls from Thora's vision walked hand in hand toward the crest of a large sand dune. Decky pointed at the picture.

"Look, she even has us on the beach."

Charlie laughed. "That's the Beaver Dunes, not the Outer Banks."

327

Decky wrapped an arm around Charlie and kissed the top of her head. "Believe what you want, Little One, but either way, you and I were meant to have sand between our toes."

Charlie gazed down at the painting. "My mother must have freaked when she met you."

Decky grinned. "You kind of freaked too, if I remember correctly. You did say you didn't normally hop into bed with someone within twenty-four hours of meeting them."

Charlie turned and put her arms around Decky's neck. "How could I refuse after you told me I walked out of your dreams?"

Decky chuckled. "That was a good line, wasn't it?"

Charlie's tone dripped "come and get me," when she said, "Got anymore good lines, big girl?"

Decky's grin widened. She pulled away from Charlie and started for the door.

"Where are you going?" Charlie asked, confused.

Decky held the door open, indicating Charlie should follow her, saying, "Actions speak louder than words. You get the boots. I'll get the hats."

Recommended Reading List

Beaver County (Images of America Series) by V. Pauline Hodges Ph.D., Harold Kachel and Joe Lansden

Black Elk Speaks: Being the Life Story of a Holy Man of the Oglala Sioux, The Premier Edition by John G. Neihardt

The Boy Captives by Clinton L. Smith, Jeff D. Smith and J. Marvin Hunter

The Captured: A True Story of Abduction by Indians on the Texas Frontier by Scott Zesch

Chickasaw Lives: Explorations in Tribal History by Richard Green

Chickasaw Lives: Profiles and Oral Histories by Richard Green

Chickasaw: Unconquered and Unconquerable by David Fitzgerald, Jeannie Barbour, Amanda J Cobb and Linda Hogan

Comanche Dictionary and Grammar by James Armagost

Comanche Ethnography: Field Notes of E. Adamson Hoebel, Waldo R. Wedel, Gustav G. Carlson, and Robert H. Lowie

The Comanches: Lords of the South Plains (Civilization of the American Indian Series) by Ernest Wallace

Dynamic Chickasaw Women by Phillip Carroll Morgan and Judy Goforth Parker

Empire of the Summer Moon: Quanah Parker and the Rise and Fall of the Comanches, the Most Powerful Indian Tribe in American History by S. C. Gwynne

Historical Atlas of Oklahoma by John W. Morris, Charles Robert Goins and Edwin C. McReynolds

Horse, Follow Closely: Native American Horsemanship by GaWaNi Pony Boy

329

Out on the Panhandle

In the Bosom of the Comanches: A Thrilling Tale of Savage
    Indian Life, Massacre, and Captivity Truthfully Told
    by a Surviving Captive by T.A. Babb
Kidnapped and Sold By Indians -- True Story of a 7-Year-Old
    Settler Child by Matthew Brayton and Chet Dembeck
The King Ranch Quarter Horses: And Something of the Ranch
    and the Men That Bred Them by Robert Moorman
    Denhardt
Liberal and Seward County (Images of America) by Lidia
    Hook-Gray
Listening to Our Grandmothers' Stories: The Bloomfield
    Academy for Chickasaw Females, 1852-1949 by
    Amanda J. Cobb
Nine Years Among the Indians 1870-1879 by Herman
    Lehmann and J. Marvin Hunter
The Oklahoma Panhandle (Images of America) by Sara Jane
    Richter
The Worst Hard Time: The Untold Story of Those Who
    Survived the Great American Dust Bowl by Timothy
    Egan

Recommended Documentary – "Two Spirits"
Learn more about this powerful movie at www.twospirits.org

About the Author...

Lambda Literary Award Finalist, R. E. Bradshaw, a native of North Carolina and a proud Tar Heel, now makes her home in Oklahoma with her wife of 25 years. She is the proud mother of Jon, a very fine young man raised by lesbians. (Authors note: "Bite me, Family Research Council.") Holding a Master of Performing Arts degree, Bradshaw worked in professional theatre and taught University and High School classes, leaving both professions to write full-time in 2010. She continues to be one of the best selling lesbian fiction authors on Amazon.com.

Made in the USA
Lexington, KY
13 February 2013